An Outbreak of Peace

by Sarah Pirtle

Illustrated by Louise Godchaux,
Bethany Schneider, Amanda Cohen,
Heather Swenson, and Elena Kaulenas

with Tanya Demarais, Britt Dionne, Noah Fisk,
Fiona Kaul-Connolly, Sabine Kaul-Connolly,
and others

New
Society
Publishers

Philadelphia, PA   Santa Cruz, CA

All inquiries regarding requests to republish all or part of *An Outbreak of Peace* should be addressed to:

New Society Publishers
4527 Springfield Avenue
Philadelphia, PA 19143

ISBN 0-86571-105-4 Hardcover
ISBN 0-86571-106-2 Paperback

Cover by Tom Leamon

Permission granted by Sweet Honey in the Rock for use of lines from their song "Seven Principles," © 1978 by Bernice Johnson Reagon, from their album, *B'lieve I'll Run On..., See What the End's Gonna Be*, on Redwood Records, 1978.

New Society Publishers is a project of the New Society Educational Foundation, a nonprofit, tax-exempt, public foundation. Opinions expressed in this book do not necessarily represent positions of the New Society Educational Foundation.

To order directly from the publisher, add $1.50 to the price of the first copy, 50¢ each additional. Send check or money order to:

New Society Publishers
P.O. Box 582
Santa Cruz, CA 95061

For Bette, and a very special
group of artists;
For my sister Betsy
and in memory of
my sister Lucy

Contents

A multicultural glossary appears on page 367.

CHAPTER ONE

Cassie

There is no denying that Larkspur is scenic. It's in the foothills of the Berkshires, and the main road curls up around the mountains on the way to the lake. The tourists love it. They slow their cars down and take in the view. But when you're sweaty and hot and dying for a swim, all I can say is it's the pits to bike up that hill. That's what I did every afternoon last summer.

It takes me twice as long to pedal up to the lake as it does to coast back home, but it's worth it. The water at Larkspur Lake is really clear right down to the minnows nibbling at your legs. I mean, Larkspur Puddle. That's what Terry calls it. Like everything else in town, the lake is pretty tiny.

It was one of those July days that starts off cool and sneaks up on you slowly. Sweatshirt weather. I hadn't wanted to get out of bed.

I stayed listening to the shades at my windows flap in the wind and touched the patches of sunburn on my arms and legs. I didn't know exactly what time it was because my alarm clock had read the same thing for a month. The last day of seventh grade I'd pulled out the plug and left it out, but I guessed it was pretty early.

I lay there trying to reel in my dream. It was the first dream I'd ever had about my grandmother, and I was determined not to lose it.

I closed my eyes again and tried to remember it. A hill in Larkspur was turning into a steep mountain. I was climbing alone. A huge wall of gray rock appeared. I dug my fingers in and tried to hoist myself up. As I fell back down, the earth felt spongy like a trampoline. I began to yell, and the yell echoed over nothing but rock. There were no birds, no people, just my voice echoing.

Then my grandmother appeared. She was out on a ledge above me. "*Babcia*, wait!" I called to her.

Her warm scarf was blowing like a long rope I couldn't reach. She looked as tall and strong as ever. Her nose, her cheekbones, made her seem proud, even noble, like an eagle. She turned her head toward me, and her words came drifting like fog, "Keep climbing, *góralka*."

"I can't find the path," I told her.

A warm orange color covered her. I'd never seen colors in my dreams before. "Don't give up," she said. "I know you can make it." Then she disappeared, and the other traces of the dream dissolved.

I felt lonely. I sat up in bed and reached up to touch the paper cut-out design on my wall. I felt the edges of the paper and watched how the bright rooster feathers blended into flower petals. I could still see *Babcia*'s hands unwrapping it with me. When I'd opened it, I'd known I was her favorite. She'd had it mailed specially from Poland. That was a month ago, during her last visit before she died.

Sunlight was jumping out from the edges of the shades. As I rolled up the shade nearest my bed, I thought, how can the sun shine like normal if *Babcia*'s not alive?

Góralka means mountaineer. She had called me that when she saw me boosting myself up our stairs three at a time. She said we were all mountaineers to live in this hilly town of Larkspur and that it looked a little like the foothills of the Tatra Mountains in Poland, where she was born. I knew when she called me *góralka*, she was trying to say that she saw the wild stubbornness I kept hidden, and she liked me that way.

I reached for Sneakers at the foot of my bed. She purred as I lifted her up. As she let me hug her, I glanced at all the postcards from Terry taped around my dresser mirror. We wrote each other every day. I thought to myself, why is it I can't tell Terry what's really happening to me this summer? Why does the world suddenly feel like a crazy place to live in?

Sneakers began to dig her claws into my arm. I put her on the floor and gave her an old art eraser to bat around. I picked up the latest postcard from Terry.

"Hey, Cass!" it read. "I went with Johnnie's family last night to the Lobster Hut, and they let us eat at our own table like a date! (I guess he's not really mad at me after all.) Then we went to a dessert place where you dip strawberries into a plate of fudge. See the other side for what I look like now." It was a photo of a pig.

I re-read the P.S. she had squeezed onto the side of the card. "It sounds like Ned has a crush on you."

It bothered me that she said that. She knew I'd never want to be more than friends with him.

I'd known Ned since first grade, as long as I'd known Terry. Ned was always too neat. When we danced together at the square dance during the big Larkspur July Fourth celebration, his sweat smelled like gingerbread. I wished she'd just talk about Johnnie without trying to invent a boyfriend for me.

It was the first summer Terry and I had been apart for so long. The first death either of us had known. The first serious boyfriend either of us had had. And now there were only postcards to try to carry the news back and forth. Were there things that she didn't know how to write about, just like there were for me?

She sounded different. She seemed to be doing exactly

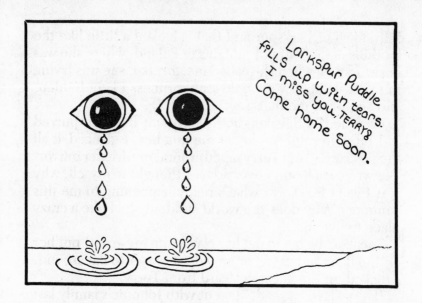

Larkspur Puddle fills up with tears.
I miss you, TERRY.
Come home soon.

what we'd said we'd never do, getting into stupid guessing games and schemes with boys. She was always worried Johnnie was secretly mad at her. I couldn't understand why she'd picked someone for a boyfriend she couldn't talk to better than that. I liked the guys in our class that I could joke around with and really talk to.

We were having the opposite kinds of summers. She wrote me about all the different restaurants her family went to and the different beaches they visited. It always sounded like she was having so much fun. My parents spent the summer talking about ways to save money and looking worried about how business was going at their new print shop. Terry never had to worry about money, and I didn't think she really understood what it was like to have someone close to you die. I felt like I was spending the summer alone, even when I went swimming at the Puddle.

I reached for a blank sheet of stiff paper the size of a postcard. My parents had given me a whole stack from their shop, and each morning I made a drawing for Terry on one side and then wrote a note on the other.

I stood in front of the mirror and picked up a brush. Everyone says I look a lot like my grandmother. Straight brown hair. Blue-gray eyes. High cheekbones. Square chin. I brushed my hair quickly and slipped a barrette into it.

I drew goblins on the postcards for Terry. That's what Terry called them, Cassie's goblins. The way I made their faces showed the kind of mood I was in each day: sleepy or goofy or angry.

I squinted my face in front of the mirror and tried to look fierce. When I got the expression I wanted, I began to copy it onto the paper with a black felt-tip marker. It was hard to keep my face frozen so tightly so I tried to draw quickly.

It was the worst summer to be apart from Terry. We had figured that the only way we were going to make it through until the middle of August was to write every day. In Larkspur, going into eighth grade means going into the same building with the high school kids. Terry seemed excited about it, but I wasn't. We were used to being with each other non-stop, and I was afraid we wouldn't end up in the same classes.

I was also afraid of being in the same building as my older brother Sam. He was going into tenth. I figured he might make fun of me in the halls or maybe say mean things about me to his friends. The only thing I was looking forward to was hopefully getting a better art teacher.

I added a snarl to the mouth I was drawing. How would I really describe the summer to Terry? I'd tell her why I was going to the meadow every morning, and why the new drawings I did there felt so special.

I liked to lean my back against a large willow tree and let it become a green room with the leaves hanging down all around me. I felt safe. The tree was like a boat in the middle of an unpredictable sea. I wanted the willow tree to tell me that *Babcia* wasn't really gone and that the world really did make sense.

I was furious that *Babcia* had died. I felt cheated. It happened right after school got out. One morning there I was at Terry's house waving goodbye as she and her family drove off for Cape Cod, and then I came back home and Dad was crying. *Babcia* was his mother. My older sister Jill was crying, too, but somehow tears wouldn't come for me.

I couldn't stand that *Babcia* died with strangers. There was no one around her who knew she was someone special. Dad wasn't there holding her hand, and I'd had no chance to say goodbye.

She was on an airplane. It would have been her first visit back to Poland in over thirty years. She died quickly, of a heart attack, with a half-written letter to us in her lap.

I'd been furious at my parents. Why didn't they tell me that her heart was weak? Why were they trying to protect me? I would have said something different to her when she was last here! I would have told her much more about how I love that paper cut-out of the rooster she gave me.

Mom and Dad kept trying to find the words that would change me back from the angry person I'd become to their daughter who could cry easily and let the tears wash away her pain.

Mom reassured me that the last thing you say before a person dies isn't what sticks. It's all the times together. She said that memories of a person are like drops of water in a river. Every drop matters.

Dad told me that it was highly unusual for anyone to die during a plane flight. Maybe he thought that if he didn't say that, I'd be afraid to ever walk onto an airplane.

The airline said there had been an unexpected amount of turbulence during the flight. There had been lots of air pockets which made the plane dip suddenly so it felt like it was going into a dive.

6

I knew *Babcia* had been afraid to travel because of all the talk in the papers about bomb scares, but she was determined to go. Her favorite sister in Poland was very ill, and she wanted to see her before she died.

The airline gave us her letter. It said she'd just gotten word that her sister had been moved into the intensive care unit in the hospital. She was in a coma. "It sounds like she was heartbroken that she wouldn't see her sister again," Mom said gently.

"Don't say that!" I had yelled. It sounded weird to me. I couldn't explain why I was so mad about everything. I'd never heard about people being angry when someone died, only sad. I didn't want to talk to Mom about it because I was afraid I'd seem selfish to her.

All my tears hardened inside me, stuck together in a hard ball with my anger and grief. I couldn't find a way to bring them out, until one day when I walked to the meadow near our house.

I headed down the path through the tall weeds until I was far away from the road. Then, facing the rows of cattails in a swampy section, I began to yell. "It isn't fair! If she had to die, it should have been after her trip and not before. I hate it!" I threw the angry words into the still water. "It's so stupid. How can the world be like this. I want *Babcia* back!"

At first it hurt when the tears began because I was afraid they would go on and on without an end and I'd be left exhausted like this for the rest of the summer. I cried for a long time as I walked farther into the meadow.

And then I was surprised by a patch of blue starflowers. They were like a blue cloud fallen to earth, little white-blue petals grouped into stars, denting into the tall grass. They broke into my hopelessness, and my tears began to ease. *Babcia* would have loved a drawing of those flowers.

I remembered how much I had loved it when *Babcia* watched me draw. She said I had a Polish flair for details. I had always wished my art teachers could be more like my grandmother.

Last year in seventh grade, my teacher would throw a quick compliment at me like, "You certainly have a lot of talent," and then she'd just walk away.

Babcia was different. She would notice things and sit and talk about my drawings. She'd say, "I like the way you used dark blue paint in back of that red chair. It sets the chair off just fine." Or, "That's a nice line you used to make your clouds. How did you know to echo the curve of the mountains?" She'd point out things I was only half aware of doing, and it made me remember them. It was like she climbed right onto the page with me, and we'd rest there together.

Suddenly there was an idea where nothing had been a moment before. As I stared at the starflowers that looked like dabs of blue paint in the grass, I decided I would work on a special art project while Terry was gone. I'd fill a whole art pad with pictures made just the way I wanted to make them—no art teacher, no assignments— just drawings that made sense to me.

That idea made the lonely summer something more than hanging around the house making excuses why I didn't want to help Sam with his carpentry project changing the attic into his bedroom. I had a project of my own. I was making a collection of drawings of all my secret thoughts.

Every morning, I biked to the meadow. I had always liked that old gnarled willow tree, and it became my favorite spot for drawing. I would lean my back against the tree trunk and let ideas just stroll up to me. I drew one picture of me riding on a lightning bug. Once I lay in the tall grass and drew how everything looked from down there. I drew another of walking on Mars in a spacesuit. Sometimes the drawings were about *Babcia*, but somehow everything I did was for her. I could imagine her lingering over each picture and encouraging me to do it my own way.

I heard the distant sound of water swishing in the sink. My parents were up. That would mean it must be around seven o'clock. I packed the postcard to Terry in the pocket of my backpack so I could add a message later. As I reached for my art pad on the shelf, I glimpsed the paper cut-out design again. I remembered that my grandmother had called me *góralka* and that she liked my stubbornness.

"Sneakers, come here you little spaghetti cat." She didn't move from where she was licking her front paw and using it like a washcloth to clean her face. I let her be and put a large box of crayons into my pack because my markers were getting too dried up. I was still saving up for fancy colored pencils. Then I added my bathing suit and a towel for later. I could already imagine the sun in full blaze by the time I'd bike to the Puddle.

I put on my backpack and hoisted Sneakers onto my shoulders. She rested there like a shawl. "You noodle cat," I said. "Promise me, no meowing."

I guessed from the quiet upstairs that my parents were already in the kitchen but nobody else was up. Maybe I could make it all the way out the door this morning without Sam and Jill waking up and bugging me to find out where I go every morning. Maybe I could have a peaceful breakfast alone with Mom and Dad.

I twirled Sneakers back into my arms, turned the doorknob very carefully, and began to tiptoe slowly down the hall. We made it past Sam's door without disturbing his snoring, then over the three creakiest floor boards in front of Jill's door without a sound. I could smell her Desert Song perfume. We continued all the way down the staircase without a hitch.

"Congratulations," I praised Sneakers, scratching her under the chin. "You set a new record for cat quiet."

When I looked down the hall into the kitchen, I saw Mom at the table, cupping her hands around her coffee mug and staring off into space. I stood looking through the doorway at her. Her hands remind me of tree roots in the pictures of a fairy tale. I knew up close there'd be ink stains in the creases of her knuckles. She never seemed to wash all the ink away from her work at the print shop.

The sun coming through the yellow kitchen curtains made Mom's face look more rosy than usual. I wanted to rush in the room and give her a hug, but she was deep in thought.

Daydreaming is one of the habits I've inherited from her, and the rest of my family always teases us both about it. Like if Sam notices me staring at nothing in particular, he'll yell, "Hey, Earth to Cassie." He thinks that's really funny. And Jill calls Mom and me the stargazers.

But Mom defends us. She says that daydreaming is a sign of great intelligence, that when you're daydreaming your brain is putting new thoughts together. I like that.

My art ability comes from my mother's side of the family, *Babcia* said. Mom can twist straw into beautiful baskets. And at Easter time, she holds an egg incredibly still and traces thin lines in wax with a special pen.

Mom looked up as I came in. I dropped Sneakers on the floor by her dish. It was already filled with cat food, and she began to munch eagerly. I got a bowl down from the cupboard for myself and a box of cold cereal. "Want something to eat?" I asked Mom.

"Oh, sweetie, no thanks." She shook her head as if brushing thoughts away and reached her arms out for me to come over for a hug. "Cassie, I haven't seen you up so early for weeks."

I was considering telling her about my new drawings and why I was so eager to be off in the morning, when I noticed her face shadowed by a cloud of worry. "What's happened?" I asked. Since *Babcia*'s death, it seemed anything unexpected could leap into our lives.

"Nothing new," she said. It's hard to read her expressions sometimes. Her mouth turns up more on one side than the other. She told me once that when she was my age people said she looked like an elf.

"Where's Dad?" I asked.

"On the phone right now. Looks like we're not working with our biggest customer any longer." She hesitated for a moment. "It's the Tolltorgan Company."

I just stared at her. That's the company where Terry's father is one of the vice presidents. "Maybe Mr. Cameron can do something about it. He'll be coming back to work soon for a few days each week." But Terry would be away four more weeks. I hated reminding myself of how long I'd have to wait to see her again.

"I don't think he can help." She took a slow careful sip of hot coffee. "I'll explain another time. I don't want you to get concerned, Cassie. We're not going to have to close the print shop or anything like that. We'll get new customers to take their place."

Dad came in and ruffled my hair. "How's my sweet patootie?"

I gave him a hug and pulled at his moustache like I usually do, but he didn't react. It felt like part of him was already at work. He's been like that most of the summer.

I remembered Mom saying to him "Don't worry, Walter, every new business takes a while to get off the ground. You can't expect to make money the first year."

"But we should at least be breaking even," Dad had answered. "I'd almost rather we had that long commute to Harris Press again instead of all this extra worry." They used to work together at a print shop in a city east of the university. It had been their dream to open a business together here in Larkspur, but none of us knew how long they could keep it going.

Sam says that Dad looks like a walrus now because he's put on a lot of weight, probably from a mixture of sadness and worry. He has a round head that's getting bald. Jill says he's working harder than usual to forget about *Babcia*'s death.

Suddenly the two of them acted like an invisible time clock had gone off. Mom got up quickly, and Dad grabbed some fruit out of a bowl.

"Two breakfasts on the run," said my mother. She

turned back to lean down and kiss me. "Now, Cassie, promise me you won't worry."

"I won't," I told her automatically. It seemed there was always something I was supposed to forget about.

I heard the putt-putt-putt of our old Volkswagen starting up faithfully, and then its sputter as it traveled down our long dirt driveway. I relaxed into my mother's chair. It felt good to have the kitchen all to myself.

Do thoughts just come to you or do you make them come? I thought about the old familiar box of crayons in my backpack. I was looking forward to using them again. I spread blackberry jam on a muffin all the way around the edges. And then I heard it.

Brrm Brrmmm—it was a strange low rumbling sound. Brrrm Brrrmm, like drums or thunder. What was it?

I'd never heard a sound like that before. My mind began racing wildly. All at once I thought I knew what the sound meant, and I prickled hot and cold all at once. The thing I've secretly dreaded was actually happening. A nuclear bomb was going off.

What should I do? Grab Sneakers? Yell for Sam and Jill? Should we all run for the basement? How could I reach Mom and Dad? Why did we have to be apart at a time like this!

I leaped toward the kitchen window, afraid I'd see the sickening sight of a gray and orange sky. Instead as I pushed back the curtains, I saw our oak tree, clouds, blue sky, a robin. We were safe. I sat down again. My heart was pounding. I held Sneakers close and rubbed my nose against her forehead. It was good to feel her warm fur.

Brrrm. There it was again. The noise seemed to be coming from our street. I opened up the front door and looked out.

A tar truck. That's what it was. Large and smelly, lumbering like an elephant, a tar truck rumbled slowly down the road. Why did I have such a weird thought? How could I mistake a tar truck for a bomb? I thought to myself, "If Terry was with me she'd say, 'That's Larkspur for you. The town is so quiet that even the sound of a truck will scare you out of your wits.' " The thought of Terry put me in a better mood.

I listened to the deep hum of the motor again. It didn't really sound like most trucks. I stood at the door for a moment and watched the road crew rake tar into the huge potholes in our road. It looked like hot work for July.

What if it had been a bomb? *Babcia* said that nearly all of Warsaw was destroyed in World War II. The Old Town, seven hundred years old, had been demolished, and they had rebuilt it carefully from old photographs and drawings. If Larkspur was bombed, who would rebuild it? What would happen to the mountains?

I tossed my head the way my mother does to shake the thoughts away and tried to go back to my usual routine. I put Sneakers outside while I threw together a quick lunch. But, as I look back, I think I know why I drew the kind of picture I did that day.

CHAPTER TWO

The Meadow

I couldn't wait to get to the meadow. As soon as I turned my bike in that direction, I felt better. The thick smell of tar followed me as I pedaled down the road, past Louisa's house—Jill's friend who first taught me about drawing—and past the cornfield. I pushed my bike through the tall grass at the hidden entrance and up a slope to my favorite spot by the willow. From up there you see nothing but woods and mountains stretching below.

Then for a second as I was looking across the hills, I imagined what a mushroom cloud would look like peeking over the horizon.

Stop this, I told myself. But how? I concentrated on how good it felt to be in the meadow and took a deep breath. With *Babcia* dying, it seemed like anything could happen anywhere.

But Larkspur is the safest place I can imagine, I reminded myself. We never lock our door at home. Our cousins in Boston can't believe it. My mother even leaves her keys in the car sometimes when she stops to pick up the mail at the post office.

I never feel nervous about being alone here in the meadow. There's something about the mountains all around the town that makes it feel really safe. It's also the people. They're really friendly. When I'm in my parents' print shop, lots of people say hello to me by name, and I love stopping to talk with people at the farm stands. One stand gives me free pumpkins in the fall.

We've lived in Larkspur about ten years, although Gus, who owns the general store, kids us that we're still newcomers. Some of the people in town say that their grandparents and even great-grandparents lived on farms here. But there are also a lot of newer people like us, especially artists and craftspeople who've moved here from the cities and like to work out of their homes.

There's a bunch of other new families since the busline started that goes into Crowningburg where the university is. Lots of teachers and students live here, including people from many countries. In fact, one reason I like Larkspur best of all the other hill towns in Western Massachusetts is that there's more people of all different races here, and people from different cultures like us being Polish.

I heard someone at the print shop say once that Larkspur was a melting pot. Mom answered that it's more like a patchwork quilt because each different part still stays special.

Every month there are multicultural gatherings at the town hall. I've eaten curries, sushi, spicy soups, and many kinds of chicken dishes. There are also special programs and displays. At the end of December, Vera Taylor leads a celebration of *Kwanzaa*, which is like an East African harvest festival, and in the spring there's a combination Passover and Easter gathering. Sometimes Mom teaches *pisanki*, Polish Easter egg dying.

I thought about the times that people in town have helped each other. Like when the Goldsteins' baby was sick, people took turns bringing dinner to their house until he was well enough to come home from the hospital

There was a sign-up sheet in Gus's general store. And signs are always appearing on the bulletin board there when anyone needs help finding or borrowing something.

I wanted to place a notice at Gus's saying, "Girl, thirteen, afraid of nuclear war. Please help." Or better yet, "Larkspur girl seeking guaranteed future. All adults in town please do something to make things safe again."

I reached into my backpack and found my card to Terry. It would help take my worries away. I wrote a message on the back of the goblin drawing. I didn't want to tell her about my fears of bombs. Just ordinary things. "Jill and her friends are invading our back yard tonight so I'll be hiding in the den. Or would you like me to spy on Eddie and report his latest stupid jokes and whether Jill's going to break up with him yet???! And guess what? I think my drawings are getting better!" I crossed out the word "better" and changed it to "more interesting" so it wouldn't sound like bragging.

I knew it wasn't just bragging, though. Something about drawing in the meadow and not in a classroom was making all the difference. I hoped I would have a whole art folder filled up by the start of school.

Then I noticed Sneakers popping out of the pricker bushes and coming through the grass. She follows a special path to reach the meadow directly from our backyard; it's a path that humans could never travel. I think she crawls underneath the thick brambles in back of our yard. She'll do anything to come and find me.

The day before, she'd fallen asleep right in the meadow, and I drew her lying on her back with her white stomach fur looking so adorable. But today was different. She didn't even want to let me hold her. She wriggled away and went off to do some stalking.

I turned back to my work, took out my sketch pad, and opened just past the drawing of Sneakers to a clean sheet of paper. I usually like the moment when I sit with my back against the willow and wait for an idea to come, but

my thoughts were jumbled. I drew jagged lines every which way and then turned the page for another sheet.

I looked out and watched the wind blow the purple clover, the Queen Anne's lace, and the pink and purple phlox. The sight of them made me feel better, and I began to fill the bottom of the page with wildflowers.

I worked first in pencil. Then I opened up my box of sixty-four crayons to color them in. All the best colors were worn down to a bunch of stubs, and all the reject colors like clay and sandalwood were the only ones long enough to use. I peeled down the edges of paper around a pink crayon that looked like the color of phlox. When I tried it on my paper, it looked terrible.

"How can I be a real artist when I don't have the stuff I need? I'm so sick of worrying about money." I knew if I told my parents how important it was to me, they would help me get the colored pencils I wanted, but stubbornly, I wanted to buy them for myself. I remembered the box of pastels Louisa has in her room. She arranges them carefully in rainbow rows. I wished I could have something like that.

I threw all the crayons on the grass in disgust and stood up. I wanted to move. I didn't want to think about bombs or war or old crayons or anything. I left my things there by the tree and raced down the slope at top speed. I just let my legs carry me like a deer.

I headed toward the woods. When I got close, I could smell the pines. I followed a path that leads deeper into the woods to a stream. It was so silent that it seemed like animals were holding their breath and watching. I headed toward the water where there are huge boulders covered with green moss. When I was little, I pretended that this moss was really emerald jewels.

I was walking rapidly. I brushed aside a low branch when I suddenly noticed a spider's web caught in the light that was coming through the pines. It was the largest web I'd ever seen. One more sweep of my arm and I would have broken it.

When I looked closer I could see the spider who made it. She was thick and brown, and she had only seven legs, not the usual eight. She moved herself along the web using each of her legs differently. Some held onto the threads, and others pulled her forward like the pinchers of a lobster. When she got right to the center of the web, I swear she looked at me.

I have to admit that I'm secretly convinced that Sneakers and I can understand each other and that's the way I felt about this spider. I felt that she was saying, "What kind of animal are you? Will you be careful of this web?"

So I tried to tell her I could be trusted. I sent the message to her in my mind the same way I've read that some people try to talk to dolphins, through their thoughts. I figured that the spider had probably already met other humans, and I explained that I wasn't usually the kind who just plows right into things without noticing.

I wanted her to know that her web was safe with me. I told her that I was an artist and looking at her web, I figured that she was an artist, too.

"And we have something else in common," I said in my mind. "We both love this meadow and want it to be safe always."

"How?" I imagined she asked.

"Can you make words in your web like the spider in the book *Charlotte's Web*? It would be neat if somebody was walking through the woods and found your web with a message in it like 'Make Peace.'"

The spider pulled herself up higher along one of the central strands and then paused again and looked back at me. I imagined that she was answering, "No, I can't do things like that."

"There's not much I can do either," I told her through my thoughts. "We humans have to wait until we've lived long enough for the earth to go around the sun twenty-one times and sometimes even longer before other people will listen to us." As these words came to me, they felt like an excuse.

A bird called, the spider shifted farther up to the top of her web and then walked away and disappeared. Somehow I felt I had just made a promise that I had no words for. I would find something I could do—although I didn't know what yet.

When I walked back along the path, I knew exactly how I was going to finish my drawing. The sun was hot on my back. I took off my sweatshirt and tied it around my waist the way Jill does.

When I got back to the willow tree, I grabbed my pencil and started to make bugs standing on all the wildflowers I had drawn. Then I drew other animals: birds, squirrels, raccoons, chipmunks, caterpillars. I sharpened my pencil and put tiny peace signs in their arms, and megaphones for them to yell through. I kept drawing more details. I had squirrels painting peace messages on acorns and birds holding signs in their beaks. When I had animals and insects covering the whole meadow, I drew the sun smiling down in approval.

The drawing made me laugh. It was different from anything I'd ever done before, and I felt a lot better.

Then I caught sight of the crayons I had tossed onto the grass. They were baking in the sun, and had melted into funny curling shapes. They looked like the old birthday candles you find underneath napkins and cake crumbs at the end of a party. They were so curved that it was hard to jam them back inside the crayon box.

My stomach was rumbling fiercely, so I opened up my bag of food and attacked. I wanted to polish off my lunch, then jump on my bike and head for a swim as fast as I could.

I took another look at my picture. I would never ever say this out loud to anyone, but I really like my drawings. I added the pad to the backpack, lifted it on my shoulders, and started riding.

I passed Louisa's house and our house again and then came to where our small street joins one of the main roads in Larkspur. There's a dead-end dirt road off to the left side at the intersection. I glanced down it. That's the part of Larkspur that has always interested me the most. The houses poking out of the woods aren't box-shaped. They look like they have high ceilings and lofts and unexpected windows.

Half-way down the road is where a famous potter lives. When Terry and I used to go out on Halloween night, we'd try to peek down her long walkway to see what the rest of her house looks like.

Right after it, there's a house completely surrounded by a thick row of pine trees where they say a hermit lives. We call that the goblin house. We never stop there on Halloween.

After you pass that side road, the main road really starts to climb, and the rest of the way to the lake is almost all uphill. The road is so steep that with each push of the pedal I would sweat and complain, so I'd made a game to see how far I could get without jumping off my bike and walking it. I used the two houses along that stretch of the road as markers to measure my progress. And I made bargains with myself. I'd say, "If I can make it to the Granger's mailbox, then Mom will let me buy a new bathing suit." Or, "If I can make it past the whole length of the old Hodge's place, then Sam won't tease me in front of his friends next year." Stuff like that.

I had made a rule that I had to invent a new challenge every day. I always took the first thing that popped into my head, and today my thoughts were on the meadow. I said, if I can pedal as far as the mailbox, then my family and all of Larkspur will always be safe. And if I can get past the old Hodge's place, then no bombs will ever fall anywhere.

As soon as I thought that, I wished I hadn't picked it. I know that it doesn't really make a difference how far I pedal, but when you start making bets with yourself, it's hard to take them back. And it's one thing to be up against losing the chance for a new bathing suit and another to risk everything that matters.

I pushed and strained and was determined I was going to make it. I got to the mailbox and felt like I wanted to dissolve in a puddle of sweat, but I kept going.

I put my head down and concentrated on each push. I was breathing really fast, and my face was so sweaty it felt on fire. My throat tasted like buttermilk. I knew I had made it around the bend because the road evens off a little, and I was picking up speed before the final hardest pull. Soon I knew I was getting close to the driveway at the old Hodge's place, but I didn't want to look up because then I would lose my stride.

Suddenly someone yelled, "Look out!" and I saw a U-Haul sticking out into the road. I braked quickly, but that wasn't enough. I put my foot out to grab for the ground.

It was the method I always kept in mind in case I needed to catch myself. I pushed my bike out of the way as I fell.

"Are you okay?" It was a boy's voice somewhere over my right shoulder.

Am I okay? I couldn't reply. My knees couldn't stop shaking. I was glad to be safely on the ground. It could have been a whole lot worse.

"We don't usually leave a U-Haul truck hanging out into the road. I'm sorry if you got hurt. I was just going to move it." I looked at him more closely. He was tall like Sam, but he looked older, and he had greenish eyes and black hair.

I still couldn't talk. I knew I was okay, just a little dazed. I didn't feel bruised or anything. But the words wouldn't come. I was still frozen.

"Can I help you up at least?" he asked holding out his hand.

I reached for it. I liked his friendliness. As he pulled me up, my pack fell off my shoulders and everything in my outer zip pocket came spilling out. Crusts of sandwich and melted crayons lay in a pile.

"That explains it. Crayons for lunch. They would make anyone dizzy. Better than wax beans, I guess."

I looked up at him, and without intending to, I began to laugh. Before he'd looked so serious, and now he was acting kind of goofy, maybe for my benefit, as if he wanted to rescue me from the wave of embarrassment I was feeling. I began to relax. I looked down at the crayons and crumbs. They looked like strange carrot and celery curls. "I think you should try some," I told him. "They're really delicious."

"I knew you grew corn in Western Massachusetts, but I didn't know you had a crayon season, too." His grin danced and lit up his eyes. Just as I was thinking how cute he was and beginning to get embarrassed again, he held up two crayons to either side of his mouth, keeping them in place with his upper lip. He looked like a walrus. "I'm Zack. I come from Antarctica. Who are you?"

I tried to think of something funny to say in response. I held a curved crayon up to my forehead. It reminded me of a rhinocerous butting, so I leaned down my head. "I'm Cassie. I'm from the jungle."

"I'd better get out of your way!"

"Your van better get out of my way, or I'll toss it over my head."

Zack smiled. "Well, Cassie, you're the first, what would you call it, Larkspurite, I've met."

I helped him pull up the back ramp of the U-Haul, and then he started the engine and moved it out of the street. "You got your license already?" I asked.

"Naw." He flipped the keys back into his pocket. "I've only driven this thing a few feet."

"My older sister has her license. You just have to be sixteen and a half here."

"Well, give me a couple of months, and I'll be driving."

So he was sixteen. Three years older than me. There I was, not only talking but joking with a high-school boy I'd never seen before. That's what Zack is like. He can make anyone feel at ease.

Next thing I knew, I was walking into Zack's backyard and meeting his mother and drinking lemonade. They were talking about the city they'd moved from, and I was telling them about Larkspur and really babbling, telling them lots of things, like about the raft at the lake, and how high the snow gets in the winter, and what things to buy at Gus's store and which are a rip off, and about Sam building a loft in the attic for a bedroom.

I told them that my parents had opened a print shop last fall, and how I had helped paint "Kaczenskis' Printing" on the sign. I even gave them one of our cards that I carry around to use as a ruler when I'm drawing. Mrs. Clemmons, Zack's mother, put it in her wallet.

Zack described the way I'd rescued myself from the near collision. "I thought I was watching a stunt artist. She lowered herself to the ground like she'd been practicing that move in her sleep."

I'm terrible at taking compliments but I managed to glance at the two of them smiling at me.

Afterward, Zack and I went back out front to look at my bike and see if it was hurt. I dreaded looking at it so I was glad he went with me. I picked it up off the side of the road. There was no way I could ride it. The front tire no longer pointed straight ahead.

"Kaput," said Zack in a fake accent. "Looks a little grim. We'll need to X-ray and check for broken bones. Careful, he...."

"He? It's a she. Her name is Maybelle," I said, thinking up something on the spot.

"Well, she could go into shock at any moment. We better transfer her to our clinic. She may need an extended stay. But don't worry. We have the most modern facilities here." We carried my bike back toward their garage because it couldn't be wheeled.

"Would she like a single or a double room?" Zack asked.

I didn't know if he was clowning around because I was younger than him, or whether he was always like this. I liked it, but I also wanted him to know that I could get serious. "Zack, I could take her home, and my sister or brother could probably figure out how to fix her."

"No, no. I insist. This was the scene of the crime. We bend it, we mend it. Just tell me how to get to your house, and I'll bring her back when she's all fixed up."

So I agreed to leave Maybelle with Zack, and Mrs. Clemmons gave me a ride home. As we drove down the steep road, I remembered the promise I'd made on my bike about getting all the way up the hill without stopping. After all, I'd bet that Larkspur would always be safe. I wondered if nearly crashing into Zack's U-Haul meant I'd kept the bargain or that I hadn't. I guessed it meant something entirely new was going to happen, but I had no idea what that could be.

"I think I'll head down to the store you were telling me about, Cassie," Mrs. Clemmons said as she dropped me off in front of my house. "It's just around the corner from the white church with the tall spire, right?"

"That's right," I told her, "But don't buy the strawberries. The farm stand farther down the road has much better ones."

"Well, I'll try the farm stand then. And Zack will bring your bike back soon. He used to work at a bike shop in Syracuse, so your bike is in good hands." We waved and then I strolled up the driveway, feeling happy.

Two days later, Zack came riding up on my bike. I was in the back pulling up weeds around our tomato plants.

"Cassie, I've got news for you. We had to do an organ transplant. But our patient has recovered quickly."

"She survived the operation?" I said in mock surprise. My bike had a shiny new wheel rim and a new tire. All the spokes were straight again. "Thanks. It really looks great."

I had a bunch of weeds in my hand. "What's that?" said Zack. "Her homecoming bouquet?"

I didn't know whether to laugh or groan, his jokes came so unexpectedly. He reminded me of my father. I threw the weeds at Zack like confetti.

"Did it cost a lot of money to fix her?" I asked.

"All I can say is it's lucky you have Blue Cross."

"No, really. How much do I owe you?"

Zack turned down his mouth. "Hey, it's a gift, Cassie."

CHAPTER THREE

Secrets

"Zack, I think you should come over right away," I said
on the phone a week later.

"What's up?"

"Ice cream emergency. My dad and I are about to put
Baked Alaska in the oven."

"Say no more." When he jumped off his bike at our
back door, Dad was just lifting the dessert out of the oven.
"So there really is such a thing as Baked Alaska." He
watched Dad cut into the toasted meringue. "I thought
it was just a rumor."

Dad served him a piece with fudge ripple ice cream
dripping. "Dig in, Zack. Go ahead. You don't have to wait
for anybody else."

I licked ice cream off my fingers and kept my eyes on
him while he ate his first bite. "We've hooked him, Dad,"
I said.

As Sam and Jill came in, I quickly grabbed the seat
next to Zack at the table in our breakfast nook. Sam rinsed
dirt and sawdust off his hands and with a quick motion
dried them on his shirt. Then he grabbed a stool from
the counter and brought it up to the table. I noticed that

Jill had changed into a sleeveless turquoise sweater since dinner, maybe because she knew Zack was coming.

Zack had been over at our house a lot in the past week, and it seemed really natural to have him around. I remembered what Mom had said earlier that evening— "Zack doesn't just make friends, he makes relatives." That's what it felt like. It was funny to think we'd only known him a short time.

Tonight Zack had brought over a small telescope. After Zack, Sam, and I had had seconds on Baked Alaska and everyone had clapped for Dad and me as the chefs, we went into the backyard and took turns looking at the sky. Zack even pointed out his own made-up constellations. He grouped together new combinations of stars and invented names for them. For instance, he said one zigzag of stars was called "The Larkspur Skyline" and another he named "The Pole Vaulter with the Hiccups."

Jill pointed to the Big Dipper. "In the Clemmons guidebook to the stars what would that be called?"

A thought came to me immediately so I answered first. "How about 'Cat With the Longest Tail in the World'?"

"Cassie, you hang out with Sneakers too much," Jill said. She dug her hands into her pockets and rocked back on her heels. "You're getting cats on the brain."

Zack sort of chuckled which I didn't like. Then Sam called him over. "Hey, Zack, I want to show you the lumber I got for free today. Some guys were tearing down an old house, and they said 'Take what you want.'"

Zack headed over. He always walks kind of slow and casual, and he likes to let his arms swing. He had on his usual blue jean jacket over a green T-shirt. I thought he seemed a lot older than my brother, even though, being a junior, he was just a grade ahead. He leaned on our fence as he talked to Sam and scratched his dark, curly hair.

In my mind, Sam looks almost the opposite. He's wiry, with red-brown hair like a fox. He moves quickly, and he holds his back really tight and straight, almost like there's

Zack

a board underneath his shirt. He always wears muscle shirts, those sleeveless kind, and I thought the reason was to show off how much bigger his muscles had gotten over the summer.

I knew Sam would start pressuring Zack to help him work on his room. Sure enough, in a few minutes I heard Zack saying, "Don't ask me. I'm just a city slicker who's all thumbs." But later, when Zack had gone home, Sam proudly announced that Zack would be coming over in the morning to help him.

"So you finally roped him in," said Dad.

"Are you kidding, Dad? He got interested in using our power saw, that's all. He said he practically flunked shop."

Sam was so happy it made me squirm. It was a big deal to him to work with Zack. He kept talking about how fast he would get the room done now and how he'd be able to move up to the attic before school started. But all I could think about was how he'd be hogging all Zack's time.

And that's just what happened for the next two weeks. All they'd talk about was that stupid room, and I hardly saw Zack at all. I kept hoping Zack would quit soon, the way Jill and I had.

Early on in the summer I'd worked with Sam for two whole days. Jill had lasted almost a week. Even though Jill and I really like to do hammering and sawing, we both thought Sam was too bossy to be around. Jill was relieved when her swim-team practice started up and she didn't have to keep making excuses when Sam bugged her for more help.

But day after day, Zack kept working along with Sam without any sign of quitting, and he seemed as proud of how the room was going as Sam was. I began to wonder if Zack had forgotten about me.

One morning, I heard them outside really early. The back door opened downstairs, and Sam yelled "Hey, Zack, let's break for some food." I heard the sound of our power saw shutting off and went downstairs so I could have breakfast while Zack was there.

I stopped in the den to look for some sheets of extra long paper in the desk drawer, and Zack came in looking for me.

"So, Cass, how ya doing."

"Waking up."

"We've been out on the roof already."

"Yeah, I know. I heard you."

"There's a great view up there. Have you climbed out?"

"Sure, I go up there a lot. But nobody else knows that."

I put the paper into my backpack and moved toward the hall, but Zack paused. "Well, want to do something today? Want to go swimming or something?"

I didn't say anything at first, I was so surprised and happy.

"Sam and I finished all the work we can do this morning, and he's heading for the store. I could wait here for you until you're ready. I know you're usually busy in the morning." I liked the way he added that. Now if Jill had said the same words, it would have sounded like she was prying. And Sam would have said it like he was mocking me. But I liked the way Zack just plain mentioned that I'm busy and he didn't want to interfere.

"Super!" I said. It was kind of a dumb expression, but it was the first thing that popped out of my mouth.

Sam yelled from the kitchen, "It would be even more super if you'd get your bathing suit and towel off the counter so I could work here." I took my time walking into the kitchen. Then I sighed really loudly as I stuffed my things into my pack so Sam could hear me. He didn't even look up. He likes to give me the "You're just a piece of furniture as far as I'm concerned" treatment.

Jill was sitting on a stool with a towel on her head from washing her hair. She was going to a party that night. Her best friends were getting ready to leave for college soon. She had her foot propped up on the counter and was painting red polish on her toes. She looked embarrassed to see Zack.

"You're here early," she said. "You must think you live here or something."

Zack scratched Sneakers on her itchiest spot underneath her chin. "Sneakers has invited me to come around anytime I want." He took a can of cat food out of the refrigerator and began to fill her empty bowl.

"You're a sucker for cats, Zack. She's already been fed," Jill said. She held up the bagel she was about to cut. "Want half of this?"

Zack opened his mouth in an exaggerated look of hunger.

Jill laughed and put the bagel in the toaster. She took the towel off her head and shook her wet curls. "I'm driving Sam over to the hardware store, and then I'm going to the lake. Do you want to come with me?"

I held my breath. I was sure he'd want to go with her instead. Jill was going to be a senior. Maybe I was wrong to think that I could be friends with someone three years older than me. Maybe now Zack was just Sam's and Jill's friend and not mine.

Before he could answer, Sam started out of the room and then turned around and yelled to me, "Hey Cass, do me a favor."

I was leaning my elbows on the dryer which is in a nook of the kitchen where he throws his tools. "What?" I'm not so invisible to him when he needs something.

"Toss me that cat's paw over there."

The cat's paw was right next to me. It's a long metal tool with a hook on the end for prying up nails. But for a joke, I lifted up Sneakers.

"Oh har de har har," said Sam as he looked at Sneakers in my arms.

Jill put her hand on her hip. "I've always said you have a very active imagination." She spoke in her most grown-up voice as if trying to widen the years between us.

"Yeah, more like an active volcano," said Sam. "Always erupting at the wrong times."

I took a sponge from off the counter, aimed it at the back of his head and let it fly. Sam ducked and it hit his arm. I flung the back door open and ran out. I wanted to get on my bike as fast as I could.

Everything in the garage was pretty messed up from Sam moving things around. Some fishing line was tangled up in the doorway worse than necklaces in a jewelry box. I had to pry some tomato stakes loose from the wheels of my bike to get it moving. I could feel myself getting angrier and angrier.

When I rode down the driveway, I thought I could hear them laughing inside the kitchen, and I figured they were probably laughing at me. I raced down the road.

When I got to the cornfield, I got off and began to gather stones in my hand. I threw them down the rows of corn and watched them roll over and over in the dirt. I could feel my tears growing hot and heavy like rain waiting to fall. "Why do they have to say that embarrassing stuff in front of Zack! And why do they have to hog him all the time. I met him first!"

Then it came to me—I'd left my backpack at home. I couldn't believe it. How could I be so dumb? I'd wanted to get out of the house so fast, I'd forgotten it, and now maybe Sam would find it and look inside like he's been wanting to do all summer. I closed my eyes and made some wishes. "Please be too busy to notice it, Sam. And Sneakers, I think it's on the dryer. Climb up and go to sleep on top of it."

I didn't want to go back with all of them there. Maybe later I'd go, in an hour when I could be sure they'd all be gone. For now, all I wanted to do was to sink into the meadow and just disappear.

I got back on my bike and headed out. When I rounded the corner and I could see the entrance to the meadow up ahead, I heard the sound of a bike behind me. I turned around. It was Zack. "Wait up," he called. I stopped my bike and he caught up to me.

I stared at him. "What are you doing here?"

"Looking for you."

"But how did you find me?"

"Find you? That was easy."

The question I really wanted to ask him was, "Why did you find me?" Then I noticed my blue pack on his back.

"Here, Cass. I've seen the way you guard this." He lifted my pack off and handed it to me.

I shifted it over my shoulder and mumbled, "Thanks."

"Not the easiest morning, huh," he said.

"I don't enjoy people laughing at me if that's what you mean."

"I wasn't laughing. Hey, you know about twin stars? I think you and I have twin imaginations. That kind of stuff happens to me sometimes."

"Oh, yeah?"

"So where are you going now? Want company?" he asked.

"No, it's really kind of secret." I paused. "Well, I don't know." Suddenly I felt the full weight of the loneliness of the summer hit me.

"So blindfold me. I'll promise on pain of death that I'll never reveal your location."

I gave him a look and thought a minute more.

"And anyway I can't tell the difference between a corn stalk and a pine tree. I'll never find my way back there even if I wanted to."

I smiled against my will. As usual it was his jokes that got to me, and I took the chance. "Okay, I'll show you," I said.

We got back on our bikes and headed down the road to the break in the weeds. He followed me along the path around tall, ugly, red stalks of sumac. We passed the swamp and the tall grass and then pushed our bikes uphill. As we got closer to my favorite spot, I realized I was feeling both excited and nervous.

When we reached the top of the hill and got to the clearing by the willow tree, Zack let out a whistle. The meadow looked more beautiful than usual. It had rained in the middle of the night, and the smell of wet dirt and wild flowers was in the air.

"You should see it in the spring," I told him. "Right here is totally covered with flowers. There are daffodils, crocuses, everything." I always thought it was weird to have flowers in the middle of nowhere. There was no abandoned house nearby or anything. It was one of the magical things about the meadow for me.

"Beats the city." He grabbed the lowest branch of the willow tree and pulled himself up. He zoomed up the branches as fast as a bee after honey, and I climbed after him.

"I didn't know city slickers could climb trees," I said.

"Yeah, it's a habit. Find a tree and I've got to climb it. Especially trees like this. We had a great tree in our backyard in Syracuse. Hey, I'll be climbing trees when I'm eighty."

"Do you miss your old home?"

"Sure. I miss my friends. And I miss my dad." Zack looked over at me. "You already knew that my parents have separated, right?"

"I guess so. But I figured they might be divorced."

"Naw. Just separated. They're going to try a year apart while Mom teaches at the university."

"So then maybe they'll get back together again," I said.

Zack stared out at the hills. "Yeah, but I don't know if I care. Who wants to have a bear for a father. He always seems angry about something." Then he reached his hands out to the lowest branch and swung back down to the ground. "Still, I miss him." I guessed the subject was closed. I felt glad to know something about him that maybe Sam and Jill didn't know. It was as if I'd only seen Zack on a black and white television and now the whole thing had switched to color.

I swung down, too. We walked along the ridge by the willow and I pointed down to the path in the woods below that leads to the stream. "That's my favorite place to walk," I told him.

34

"Is that what you usually do when you're here all morning? Go hiking and stuff? Because when I was carrying your pack it seemed like there were books in it, and I thought that you might come here to read." He caught my look. "Hey, don't answer if you don't want to."

Then I took a leap. It felt like the moment of sailing off the rope swing at Larkspur Puddle. You're just hanging in the air for a minute, hoping you'll hit the water and not the cliffs. I gulped, opened up my backpack, and took out my sketch pads. "I come here to draw," I said.

"Well, that figures. I should have guessed."

"What do you mean?"

"It figures that you're some kind of artist."

I opened up a small, red, beat-up pad, and we sat down. It was the oldest pad I owned. I'd been carrying it around that week because I was sorting out all my old pictures to pick out the ones I wanted to show to my new art teacher when school started.

I opened the cover, and Zack stared at a picture of a small girl with her arm in a cast sandwiched in between two large doctors. The cast and the doctors heads were huge. "This is the first drawing I ever did. It's okay to laugh. It looks pretty funny to me."

But Zack didn't laugh. "Hey, this is the way doctors look when you're young," Zack said. "How old were you when you drew this?"

"Eight, I think. I broke my arm at day camp." I remembered back to that summer. Even eating had been impossible. I couldn't cut my food or hold onto an ear of corn without help. I flipped another page. "These are kind of funny."

"Good funny. I'm impressed that you saved your notebooks, Cass. That means you're serious about it."

"Yeah. That's because of Louisa. You haven't met her yet. She lives in the house by the cornfield. She's an amazing artist." When Zack gets really quiet listening to me, I find I can just keep talking more and more. It was like that then. I told him how Louisa asked me to be her model that summer and how I'd stand still while she sketched me. "I didn't really mind posing," I explained, "because I couldn't go swimming with my cast on anyway."

"So Louisa taught you about drawing?"

"In a way. When she'd draw me, she'd tell me what she was thinking. Like what she had to do to make the picture turn out looking like me. And when my arm healed up, she gave me this sketch pad as a present."

"Can I see another drawing?"

I flipped ahead to the middle of the book. "Here's Sneakers when she was a kitten." She'd fallen asleep with an alarm clock in her bed.

"The clock is almost as big as she is."

Suddenly the memory of that drawing was so fresh it surprised me. I remembered hiding it from Sam, and I remembered the way he used to chase me and grab the sketch pad out of my hands and then turn the pages and say something mean about every drawing. I used to think I was a terrible artist. But that day when I found Sneakers asleep in her bed, I wanted to draw her so much that I didn't care what Sam or anyone said about my pictures. I knew there was nothing that could make me stop drawing.

"Can you show me something you did this summer?" he asked.

I pulled out a postcard. On one side was my most recent goblin drawing for Terry, and on the other side was a cartoon. "Hot off the press. I drew it this morning. I send Terry a drawing every day." I held the goblin face up to mine and made the same expression.

"You draw looking in the mirror?"

I pretended to look offended.

"Hey, I don't mean you look like that," he pointed to the goblin, "I just mean...."

"Yeah, that's the way I do it."

"So have you tried this one yet?" He squished his mouth over to one side.

"Something like it." I imitated his expression.

"What's this cartoon on the back?" He read the words "Reading Enrichment Class."

My cartoon showed me crashing into Terry's reading class and helping her escape on the back of my bike. I explained it to Zack. "Terry's father makes her go to reading classes every morning to get ready for eighth grade. It's silly because Terry's a really good reader. He just has this idea that the only way you learn things is in classes. He even makes her go to swim classes every afternoon, and their cottage is right by the ocean. Can you believe that?"

"Some vacation," said Zack.

"I know. So I wanted to pretend that I could free her. Did you recognize Maybelle?"

"Oh, yeah. You're a really great artist, Cass."

"I hope her parents don't see this." I laughed.

"Will you show me something else?" I paused for a moment. It was one thing to show him pictures I did five years ago or funny drawings that didn't have to look that good anyway and another thing to show him something more serious.

I opened up my latest sketch pad and turned back to the pages I'd done of Sneakers asleep, the ones I'd drawn right before I'd met Zack. "You'll recognize who this is," I told him. While he looked at Sneakers, I was surprised to find how hard it was to wait for his reaction. There was something inside me that began to shrink back like a hand pulling away from a hot stove. "This isn't Sam," I reminded myself.

When I'm waiting for an opinion, every second before the first words I hear is torture. I looked at the drawing again. Sneakers had her noodle cat look, lolling on the grass with her head turned to the side.

"I like her expression," said Zack. "She looks so comfortable."

Then I showed him another where Sneakers had her

paw over her eyes. It was one of her cutest ways of sleeping.

"It looks like she's practically breathing. This is really great. I had no idea you could do things like this." I let out a sigh. "And the way you drew her tail wrapping around her is really neat."

Good. Something specific. It meant he really liked it and wasn't just making it up.

He was in the middle of turning the page when I realized he was turning in the wrong direction without knowing it. He wasn't turning toward another drawing of Sneakers but toward the drawing I had done in the meadow the day I met him. It was too late. There it was in front of him. The flowers, the bugs, the peace signs. Silence. He looked up at me. He wasn't smiling. He had an expression I couldn't read.

More silence. He leaned on his hand like he was thinking and then nodded his head.

"You know Cass," he began, "This is really something special." I unclenched my fingers. I hadn't realized I was holding them so tight. "Wow, this is fantastic." He exploded like the bubbly Zack I'd come to expect. "I didn't know that you thought about things like this."

I looked at the picture again, and as I looked at it I remembered some of the creepy feelings about nuclear war that had leaked out that day. Here, right now, it felt safe to remember.

"Have you ever shown this to anyone before?" he asked. I shook my head. "Do you have more like this?"

More? There were lots more. There was the picture I'd drawn last week of the solid plastic dome that could fit over all of Larkspur and protect everybody in town. There was the picture I called "Noah's Ark" of a huge spaceship landing in the meadow. I was helping to get the animals on board so they could orbit the earth in safety.

The ones I showed him were of Zandi. She's a girl I invented who lives on a planet where there are no wars

or guns or violence of any kind. I'd made up lots of drawings about her. The first one I turned to was of Zandi holding a special globe which I'd decided was the way she sent messages to me through mental telepathy. Another drawing showed her looking through a telescope from her outpost on Planet Z.

I could tell Zack liked it a lot. "What's she looking at?"

"The Earth. She agrees that things are getting pretty weird down here."

"Cass, why don't you come over to my house now?"

"Right now?"

"Yeah. There's something I'd like to show you."

"What?"

"Something from Planet Z."

CHAPTER FOUR

Zack's Notebook

I couldn't wait. I biked all the way up the hill without even walking my bike. The bet I made with myself was that Zack and I would keep having fun together, and he wouldn't forget about me as soon as school started

When we arrived, we went inside to say hello to his mother who was typing in her study. Then Zack grabbed a pitcher of iced mint tea out of the refrigerator and poured it over ice cubes into two tall glasses. I carried them outside while he went to get whatever it was he wanted to show me.

My favorite place in their yard is a grassy spot in the back that's surrounded by huge snowball bushes. I put the tea down and lay on the grass to wait. I could smell honeysuckle in the air. I thought back to all that Zack had said to me this morning, like about having twin imaginations, and wondered what his surprise would be.

He returned with a faded blue three-ring notebook that was so worn many of the threads were coming apart from the blue cover.

"Are these drawings?" I asked.

"Well, you'll see. A little of everything. I don't really draw. I collect."

I read the cover. In block lettering he had written "EXPERIMENTS IN PEACE." It looked like it could have said "EXPERIMENTS IN CHEMISTRY." I liked the fact that it wasn't decorated with a lot of peace signs. It was plain, and that made it look more serious.

He put the notebook in my hands and let me open it. The first page inside had a dot in the center surrounded by seven circles, each larger than the next. That was all. I looked up at Zack for an explanation, but the expression on his face seemed to say, "You'll figure it out. Keep going." He looked pleased to be showing the notebook to me, as if I were unwrapping a present or figuring out a puzzle he had designed.

Beyond that page, there were section dividers. The first divider was labeled on the side, "The World." I skipped that for a moment and read the next: "America and Other Countries." The third one said: "Inside America." I opened it up.

There was a photo of a building that had to be the White House. Two girls were standing in front of it reading letters. "That's Hannah and Nessa Rubin," said Zack as if he was particularly glad I'd started there. "They're from Vermont, and they brought thousands of letters to the President. Can you imagine it, Cassie? They collected that many letters."

"Who from?" I asked.

"Kids. All over the country. I wrote them a letter, too. I was in junior high."

"About what? What do the letters say?"

"The kinds of things that your pictures say."

I felt tiny bubbles of excitement. Here were kids who would like my drawings, who would understand what they were about.

"Where are they now?"

"You mean, Hannah and Nessa? In college, I guess, or maybe graduated. A friend of a friend gave me the photo.

He was there at the White House, too. About a dozen kids were with them."

"And they read all the letters out loud?"

"Yup, they read them all. They were supposed to meet with a press secretary and give their letters to him, but he canceled their meeting. And the mail room wouldn't accept their delivery, so they refused to leave."

I couldn't imagine even writing the President's press secretary, let alone standing in front of the White House fence. I liked knowing there were kids like that somewhere.

I turned the page and found another photo. "What's this group doing?" I asked Zack.

"They're from S.T.O.P. Do you know what it is?"

"Yeah."

I'd heard of S.T.O.P. groups before from my mother. The first group began near here at the Northfield Mount Hermon School about the same time she was going to a lot of movies and talks about peace work. I knew that the letters stood for Student/Teacher Organization To Prevent Nuclear War.

"Well, those kids are planting a rose bush in their school courtyard. It's like a wish for peace, Cass. You know what I mean?"

I did. I thought about my drawing of the flowers from the meadow. That morning each of them had seemed like a wish for peace.

"Where did you get the photo?" I asked.

"My social studies teacher. Four of us did a project on kids who are peacemakers. The whole thing is in there." He looked at it with me.

I saw a newspaper article about a children's art exchange with kids in the Soviet Union, a flyer about a camp called the International Children's Summer Village, lots of drawings, and a couple of short reports.

I'd never heard of these kids before, except for Samantha Smith. I'd seen her picture in the newspaper when she went to the Soviet Union. These were regular kids—and there were so many of them! Each group was doing something different.

I saw a photo of teenagers at the Northfield Mount Hermon School acting out a play they'd written about their secret fears of nuclear war. It was called, "Changing the Silence." And there was a flyer about Jody Lester and Maya Gillingham who went on a tour to different high schools in 1984 to get others talking about their own hopes and fears. They sounded brave. Of course they'd never come to Frontier High in Larkspur. Our principal would never have let them in.

"Who drew this picture?"

"Carlos. That's a S.T.O.P. group getting on a boat in Japan. If we couldn't find a photo, we would make up what it probably looked like. I shouldn't say 'we,' Cass. I just wrote things and helped with the thinking. The others were the real artists. You'll see when you find the charts I drew." He made a face. "Except you could say," he added, "that this whole notebook is my drawing. I draw with my mind."

I don't like to hear people say they can't draw because I think everybody can, but I didn't know what to say about it then, so I just kept going. I turned the page. "Did Carlos draw this?"

"No, Cheryl did that as a going-away present. That's Carlos on the left, with Tony and Cheryl. I already miss them a lot. Well, that's the end of that section." He went inside to get some paper.

I read all the headings on the dividers now. They were, in order: "The World"; "America and Other Countries"; "Inside America"; "Our State"; "Our City" (which had been crossed out and now read, "Our Town," I guess for Larkspur); "Other People"; "My Family and Me." The last one was marked private so I didn't read that, but I crisscrossed through most of the others. Seven headings. That explained the seven circles in the front.

It was like a scrapbook. He had stapled in clippings

from newspapers and magazines and photocopies of articles. He had lists of books to read, and he'd checked off the ones he had finished. He had photos from magazines and photos he'd taken and a few more drawings by his old friends. Lots of the sections seemed to have ideas he'd thought up himself. There were charts and sketches for streets and buildings and machines. I knew Zack must have done them himself because the squiggle of the lines looked exactly like his handwriting. "You are an artist, Zack," I thought to myself.

I wanted to go back and see how his mind would draw the world so I turned to that first section. I could tell by the funny block shaped lettering that Zack had typed the words on a computer.

WORLD COMPUTER BANK

It's 2012. The top computer experts from every country have teamed up for peace. They work for the new world government now.

Computer One holds a list of every country, how many people live there, how much food they need to get from other countries, and what kind of food they can grow themselves. It helps make sure that the food in the world goes to people who need it, so no one needs to starve anymore.

Computer Two houses information about all the radioactive materials in the world and where they are stored. There's a phone hook-up to talk to the guards and some way to alert the computer if a leak starts in any of the storage places.

Computer Three does the same with poisons and chemical wastes. There's also a way to check up on any clean-up program going on in any place in the world. BLEEP! "Hello, India? How's your work going cleaning up the Ganges River?"

Computer Four monitors all nuclear weapons sites. It helps to verify that all peace treaties are working.

I paused. I liked reading about these things. Just seeing them on paper helped them begin to come true in my mind.

"Where did you get the computer to write on?" I asked when he came back. "I've never seen one at your house."

"It's my dad's. He knows a lot about computers." I wondered if he and his father looked anything like each other and reminded myself to ask Zack to show me a picture of him someday.

I glanced ahead in the section. Zack had made up fifteen different ideas for what computers could do to help the world government. Some were typed, some handwritten, some so scrawled I could hardly understand them.

"I keep working on the list, adding more when I get a new thought," Zack told me. A funny image popped into my head of Zack suddenly getting an inspiration while he's swimming out to the raft in Larkspur Lake. He's half way there, but he spins around and swims back to land, dries off his hands with a beach towel, and makes a new entry before he can lose his thought. Or he's playing outfield in a baseball game. An idea comes to him, and while the catcher is fumbling with a stray ball, he takes out a pen and writes it on his blue jeans. Yup, sounds like Zack.

I turned to the section called "Other People." This had lists like "Why People Fight With Each Other," "Experiments in Breaking Up Fights," (with dates and descriptions of what he tried to do and whether it worked), "Why I Get Mad at People," and "What is an Enemy?" I spent a lot of time looking at that.

Then there was a list called "Peacemakers." There were names of people I recognized right away, like Martin Luther King, and others I'd never heard of before. There was a page for each letter of the alphabet. For instance, under F it had Randy Forsberg.

"Who's Randy Forsberg?" I asked him. I was embarrassed not to know.

"She's the person who first thought of the Nuclear Weapons Freeze. We studied her in school."

"And who's this next person, Lionel Franklin?"

"Oh, Lionel. Great guy. He lived on our block in Syracuse. He gave out winter clothes to anybody who needed them. He kept a whole room of gloves and scarves and jackets and boots. People would give Lionel their old clothes." He sounded like a peacemaker all right, although it seemed unusual to put him right next to Randy Forsberg. Still, it made sense when I thought about it more.

I wanted to see what other ideas he had come up with. I turned to a new essay:

The High School I Wish I Went To

No more walking from class to class in a cinder block building that's just a cut above a jail. No more being judged by how you do on a multiple choice test instead of how you think and write and solve problems. No more sitting in rows. No more wondering how you're going to get through the next boring minutes, hours, weeks, months.

What would make it better? For one thing— Projects! Projects that you sign up for yourself, that could take you out of the building to work with anybody who can teach what you want to know.

I guess you couldn't do expensive projects like flying to India or living in China for a year. But if I had my way, I'd go to work on the *Clearwater*.

"What's the *Clearwater*?" I hesitated asking. Maybe everybody knew but me.

"It's a boat that sails up and down the Hudson River. It teaches people about water pollution, and it's helped get people to clean it up so now you can swim in it again. I've heard the river used to be as muddy as coffee, and now you can see clear to the bottom."

"Wow. That's a big change."

"My parents and I drive down there every summer for the *Clearwater*'s Hudson River Revival. It's a folk music festival, and it's so great, Cass. Thousands of people come to it now. I used to wish I could sneak on board the ship and just run away and never come home."

In Zack's description of the way he wanted things to be, every city and town that had a lake or river near it would have a small boat like the *Clearwater*. For science class, kids would help scientists test water samples to see how clean the water was each week. Then for English class, they'd put the results into an article for the town newspaper to print. In art class, you could make a comic strip for kids about pollution. For social studies class, you'd track down anybody who was polluting the water and go talk to them.

I'd love to go to a school like that. I'd want to do different projects, of course, than the ones he'd thought of. If I could get credit by working with a different artist in Larkspur every year, I'd stop dreading waking up Monday mornings. I thought of myself going off to school and not getting on the school bus. Instead, I'd walk around the corner to the potter's house. I'd be in heaven.

I turned the page, and Zack leaned over my shoulder to see where I was. The next section had a lot of cross-outs and things stapled and pasted on. "I'll just explain this next part." We were in the "Our State" section. "For starters, every single town in the state would have its own recycling center and its own safe energy department."

This section didn't sound as interesting to me. "Larkspur already has a recycling center," I said trying to hurry it along.

"Yeah, well, Larkspur is ahead of lots of the others. But I know it doesn't have a conflict resolution center."

"What would that do?"

"If people were having a fight, like if two neighbors were arguing about the dog that one of them owned or about anything and they couldn't work it out, they would go and get help settling it."

"They should call it the fight center."

"But it would do other things, too. Like if parents were getting a divorce and they were trying to figure out what was best for the kids, they would get help there. Or if teachers wanted to teach their class how to get along and settle problems better, someone from the conflict resolution center would come and help at the school."

"We could have used that last year in our class," I said. "By the end of the year, there were two big cliques and the kids hated each other. There were fights on the playground and lots of yelling in class. Miss Fielding, our teacher, looked happier when school let out than I did."

"You hungry yet?"

"Yeah." I hadn't packed any lunch before I'd hurried out that morning.

"I'll go in and make something. Do you like meat loaf sandwiches?"

"With lots of ketchup." When he went inside, I turned

back to an earlier section and read some more. I found a clipping from a magazine about a solar-powered city in Arizona called Arcosanti that would house five thousand people when it was finished. Right after that there was another clipping from a 1981 copy of *Soviet Life* about a solar-powered city in an area called Ashkabad.

I put the notebook down and lay back on the grass. I heard the loud buzz of a queen bee getting nearer and nearer. It brushed against my hair, but I didn't move. I think it liked the smell of shampoo. It swirled around as I held my breath and then luckily moved away. That was one thing Zack's world could never do away with—bees and bee stings. There were some things like bees and mosquitoes and hurricanes and tornadoes that would always be a problem, but the other bad things like people trying to blow each other up or hunger or pollution— those he was saying could actually change.

I liked the world he painted. It seemed to make sense, like it could really happen if enough people wanted it to. It was a world I'd always thought should exist but didn't know how to find before. I looked up at the cloud puffs in the sky. It wasn't the way I pictured Planet Z. There people could travel in helium balloons to the top of jeweled skyscrapers, and you could strap jets onto your shoes and fly. This wasn't a magical fantasy, but it felt safe, and I wanted to live there as much as I'd ever wanted to visit Zandi.

I heard the metal screen door bang, and Zack came back balancing sandwiches and a bag of chips. I didn't feel like talking and neither did he. I just ate and licked the ketchup spilling over the sides of my sandwich. I felt like I was hovering somewhere in the future, and I wasn't ready to crash back into the regular old present yet.

Zack suddenly put his sandwich down. He licked his fingers, ripped a piece of clean paper out of a pad he'd been doodling on, and began to write furiously. If I had tried to draw him at that moment, I would have shown smoke coming out of his ears, like in a cartoon.

He picked the notebook up off the grass and made an elaborate show of hiding it behind his back and not letting me see where he put the new entry.

"Now you guess."

"How can I? There must be three hundred sheets of paper. How am I going to find it?"

"All I can say is you'll know when you do." He gave a grin and hummed a little tune as if to needle me.

I picked up the notebook and held it up so I could see the edge of all the papers. I was looking for one that stood up a little more than the others, but there was no even line of paper to go by. The whole edge of them was pretty ragged. Many of the articles had been inserted with the holes punched every which way.

I grabbed a handful of corn chips and contemplated what Sherlock would do. But right now I didn't want to act like a logical detective. I felt more like being a seagull flying where the wind took me and eventually arriving at my destination.

When I was finished eating, I turned back to "Inside America."

I found a section that said, "Solar Club Houses" and began to read. It was an interview that Zack had written up with his next-door neighbor in Syracuse who was a solar architect, and it was dated six years ago.

> *Zack*: What are some things kids could do to learn more about solar energy?
> *Daria*: Easy. Build solar club houses. Think about that. If you built one here in Syracuse and then you took a picture of you and your friends sitting inside it in the winter time, you could send the picture to a magazine and pretty soon kids all over the country would start creating their own.

Underneath the interview Zack had written, "Untried idea. Still on the back burner."

I stopped reading and began to daydream. Solar club houses! What would they look like? I was itching to draw one. And Zack was in fifth grade when he'd written that interview. I was surprised to think he'd kept his notebook that long. What if he had gone ahead and built one?

I imagined what Zack must have looked like as a fifth grader and then pictured him getting all of his friends involved in looking for old windows they could use for their club house. Then I imagined them with hammers prying off the boards on the south wall of an abandoned shack and putting in the windows. In my mind I drew a picture of Zack and his friends sitting inside the finished club house in the winter time with their hats and gloves off, all smiling.

"Blueprints," I said out loud, "That's what's inside this notebook, blueprints for all the different ways things could be." Just the way Sam had made up a blueprint for the way the attic would look when he was finished, Zack was drawing up blueprints for the world. "I wish lots of people could read this, Zack." I wanted other people to enter this secret city. And I wanted them to be so excited about his ideas that they'd want to make them happen right now as much as I did.

I knew that the notebook wasn't really in the right shape to show to people yet. You couldn't just place it in the Larkspur Library and hope that people would react.

"Well, I wish there was another way to give people a picture of it all," I told him. Zack smiled mysteriously and didn't say a word.

So I turned back to my exploring. "Our Town." That was the section I'd been saving to read last. I flipped over the pages that were about his old home town of Syracuse and got right to Larkspur. I wondered if there would be anything there yet. One sheet of crisp new paper sat in that spot. New paper!

I had found the needle in the haystack

"Do you mean it?"

"Yup. Give me a day or two, and you'll see flyers about this all over Larkspur."

"Count me in. You got your first member," I told him.

"Member? How could we have the group without you, Cassie? It was your drawings and, I don't know, the way you read today that gave me the inspiration for it."

It's not like Zack to flatter people, but still I looked at him again to see if he was kidding me.

He read my mind. "It's true, Cass."

"I could help deliver the flyers," I said, "and my parents might even print them at their shop for free."

He was so excited that at that moment the whole art display seemed as good as done as far as he was concerned.

When I biked home, speeding down the steep hill, I felt I could fly. I wondered how things like Zack's idea actually happened. Who would come to the group? Could we actually do it? I couldn't think of anyone I knew who'd be interested in joining except Louisa. Not Jill. Certainly not Sam. "Maybe Terry," I thought. "Yeah, Terry's got to come! I'll beg her to join!"

The next morning Zack called and asked me to come over and make a drawing to put on the flyer. No one else in my family was home so I left a message in the usual place, our blackboard in the kitchen. We always put our messages in code.

I thought about how to make a code with Zack's name. Then I drew a box with stars all around it, and inside the box I wrote:

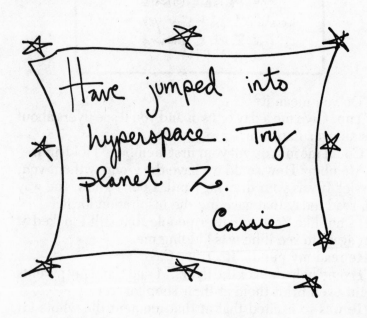

CHAPTER FIVE

The Camerons

The flyers were printed on bright goldenrod paper so they'd stand out. I'd drawn a picture of Sneakers in a peace T-shirt holding an artist's palette. We used up the first fifty flyers that my parents made for us in three days. Some we mailed, some we passed out, and some we posted at places like Gus's store.

I even mailed one to Terry in Cape Cod. It would just reach her before she returned at the end of the week. I was counting the days until Friday. After dinner Friday, every time the phone rang, I yelled that I'd pick it up. Finally around nine o'clock the call came that I'd been waiting for.

"Cassie! I just walked in the door THIS MINUTE! WE'RE HOME!"

"OH, TERRY! I CAN'T BELIEVE IT!" I pulled the phone cord as far as it would go and settled with my back on the living room rug and my feet propped up on the seat of a chair.

Sam passed by me and yelled into the kitchen, "Anyone who thought they were going to use the phone better give up hope."

55

I didn't even bother to give him a dirty look. Terry and I were talking as fast as we could, interrupting each other, laughing, letting our words tumble back and forth. We talked on the phone for over an hour and a half until Dad yelled, "Hey, aren't you going to see Terry tomorrow? Why don't you both get some sleep." Even then it took us ten more minutes to get off.

Terry and I spent the next day at the Puddle. She had a new bathing suit, and she'd gotten her hair cut.

"What do you think?" she asked as we stood in front of the mirror in the changing room. She carefully combed her bangs.

"It looks nice," I said. Her brown hair was cut short and stylish. It framed her face and made her brown eyes look even bigger. There was a line of green eye shadow right above the curve of her eyelashes. Last summer, she would never have worn it to the Puddle. I decided not to mention it.

As we chose a place to sit down on the beach, Terry said, "I can't believe what's on your beach towel. It's Mickey Mouse and Goofy, right?"

It was so faded that it was hard to see, but seven years ago when I had first picked it out at a store, you could tell they were throwing a beach ball to each other.

Terry spread out her towel and lay down. It was lime green with black zigzags.

"Yeah. Remember, I used to have a pair of sunglasses that came with it?" I wondered whether she was going to make fun of me for still using it.

Instead she said, "I know a store down at the Cape that would probably pay you ten dollars if you still had those glasses. It's full of nothing but comics and old things from cartoons. I got a keychain for Johnnie there with Daffy Duck on it."

"Did he like it?" I scratched a bunch of mosquito bites and then dug my nails in the sand to make myself stop.

"Yes and no. He said it looked dumb, but he liked it because I gave it to him." Terry propped her head up on her elbows. "I miss him so much! Wait until my pictures come back tomorrow and I can show you what he looks like." Then she suddenly looked around the beach. "Is Zack here?"

I didn't like the fact that talking about Johnnie had reminded her to ask about Zack. There was no comparison. "No, I don't think so," I said.

"Well, would he come right over and say hello to you if he showed up here? Or is he more the indirect type?" she asked.

"Of course he'd say hello." I felt angry. How could I explain to her that Zack wasn't like that. Besides, we were just good friends. It was entirely different.

A radio near us was playing "I Sold My Heart to the Junkman." When the song was over, the announcer said something in an annoying sing-song voice. I tried to block out the sound. I watched a girl standing by the water send a frisbee in a smooth arc and a boy further down the beach catch it with two hands.

I wished we were sitting somewhere quieter like in the meadow where all you hear is the sound of the wind sweeping the willow leaves. "Want to go to the meadow?" I asked.

"Not really. I'm exhausted. I just want to lie here."

We were silent for several minutes. For me at least, it wasn't the comfortable kind of silence. Finally, I admitted to myself that I wasn't saying enough of the things I was really thinking. "You know, this is the first weekday I haven't gone to the meadow."

Terry rolled over and looked at me. "That's right." Her expression changed, like she was coming out of a fog. "And you have all those new drawings to show me."

"Yeah. A whole art pad full." I was glad she remembered.

"You know, it's kind of weird to be home," Terry confided. "I can't get used to it yet. Let's go over to your house."

I was so happy she'd changed her mind. I jumped up

and shook the sand off Mickey and Goofy.

We whizzed down the hill, braking our bikes and then letting them out. When we got to the bottom, we coasted as far as we could go before pedaling again.

My house felt cool and dark after the ride. I grabbed two bananas from the top of the refrigerator, and we climbed the stairs. I didn't want to head up to the attic and show her Sam's new bedroom or stop to do anything else. I went straight to my art pad. But as I lifted it up, I felt nervous.

We sat down on my bed. I couldn't wait for Terry to ooh and aah over each drawing like she usually did. She started turning the pages too quickly.

"Which one do you like best so far?" I said to slow her down.

Terry flipped back a page. "This one." It was of me riding on a lightning bug.

"They're really different, aren't they? Don't you think they're better than what I've done before?"

She leaned back on my bed and began fiddling with a necklace I'd left there. "Oh yeah, Cassie, a lot better." Her voice was a monotone. They're probably the best you've ever done." She put her head down on my pillow.

I should have waited to show her the drawings when she was more awake. I closed up the art pad and began to feel exhausted myself, as if there were a weight on me.

We went over to her house for dinner. We had roast chicken and fresh corn dripping with butter. By the end of the evening I was too tired to bike home, which isn't like me. I called my Dad. He came and picked me up and attached my bike to the rack on the back.

"The dog days got you?" he asked when we were in the car.

"What's that?"

"They call the last weeks of August the dog days. I don't know why. It always reminded me of dogs lying in doorways with their tongues hanging out, just too worn out to move."

"Yeah, it's the dog days," I said. We rode home without saying anything else. What was it really? It was having things go differently than I'd wanted them to. I'd waited all summer for this day to arrive, the first day back with Terry, and I hadn't really had much fun.

And it had something to do with my grandmother, too. I'd gone for several weeks without missing her or thinking about her death. And now it was as if a bunch of tears were catching up to me. I almost wanted to be sitting in somebody's lap, but I felt too old.

The next morning, Terry called to say that her parents were yanking her away to some stupid family outing, so I spent the day helping Zack deliver our second batch of flyers. We biked to different parts of Larkspur and put the flyers in mailboxes. It was just what I needed, something simple.

We hadn't gotten anyone but Louisa to sign up. Zack decided he'd bring some flyers to Larkspur Lake and see if he could interest anybody there, but I didn't want to go with him. I pictured the older kids like Riley who hung out at the raft and figured they'd probably make fun of us. The last thing I wanted to do was explain the idea to somebody like Riley. But Zack was ready for anything.

If he was discouraged, it didn't show. Even when both Sam and Jill had turned down his invitation to be part of the group, he just shrugged his shoulders. Sam said he'd be too busy putting the final touches on his new room in the attic, and Jill said she had to go to swim-team practice. I knew they both could have found a way to come if they had really wanted to. It was more than okay with me if neither of them joined, but I wanted somebody to be there.

"Why is 'peace' such a dirty word?" I asked Mom at dinner.

"What do you mean?" said Sam. "It doesn't have four letters."

"I know what Cassie's saying," Jill added. She pulled at the corner of one eye to adjust her contact lens. "There's something about the word 'peace.' You start picturing something boring."

"Zzzzzz," said Sam, pretending to snore.

"It's not just that it's boring," I said. "Some people are really afraid of the word."

"Some people?" asked my father as he placed a platter of *gołąbki* in the middle of the table. I dished three of the stuffed cabbages onto my plate, and Dad ladled out some tomato sauce.

"Well, some people like Terry's father," I answered.

"You mean Bob Cameron doesn't want Terry to come to Zack's group?" asked my mother.

"Yeah. I mailed her a flyer. She said he looked at it and told her it didn't sound like the kind of group for her. It sounds like he's practically forbidden her to even bring up the subject. I don't get it."

"I bet you're hoping he'll change his mind once they've been home awhile," said Mom. "Maybe he will."

"Yeah." I was glad my mother was sympathetic, but she didn't sound too convinced, and there was another tone in her voice that I couldn't figure out.

"And if Terry doesn't go then I can't go," Sam mimicked in a high-pitched whine. I shot him my most dagger-like look. At the same moment, Zack's page on "Family Fights and How to Stop Them From Starting" flashed through my mind against my will, and I looked back at my food.

"What's Mr. Cameron got against the group?" Jill asked.

"I bet it has something to do with the fact that he's the big computer whiz at the Tolltorgan Company," said Sam.

"Oh, I get it," said Jill to him under her breath.

"What do you mean?" I asked, but Sam just gave me a smirk. "What do you two know that I don't?"

Mom turned to me. "We can talk about it later, honey, after dinner."

"No, I want to talk about it now."

"We've only just told Sam and Jill last night while you were at Terry's," she said.

"Told them what?"

Dad looked at my mother and then put his fork down and leaned toward me. "You have a right to know, Cass. It's just complicated."

Mom got up from the table. Her mouth was tight.

"Do you remember when we said in July that we had stopped taking printing jobs from Tolltorgan?" asked Dad.

"Yeah," I answered. "Only I thought they chose somebody else, and you lost the jobs."

"No, we tried to make it sound that way at the time. Actually, we were the ones who decided we didn't want to do work for them anymore."

"But why?" The last thing I needed was to have my parents and the Camerons in some sort of fight. Was that why Terry's father was against the group?

"We found out something about Tolltorgan," said Dad, "and we didn't think it was right to keep on doing printing for them."

Before I could ask what it was, Sam butted in. "I thought Mom was the only peacenik in the family. What's come over you, Dad? Did Mom talk you into it?"

I didn't like the word "peacenik." Sam said it like it meant "Martian." I thought our whole family was proud of Mom when she'd organized a petition drive in Larkspur a few years ago for the Nuclear Weapons Freeze. But what did peace have to do with Tolltorgan?

"Look, Sam, a lot of thought has gone into this," said Dad, looking tired.

"Tell Cassie," said Jill.

"Well," said Dad, "while I was printing up a few things for them, I figured out another type of work Tolltorgan is involved in. But I didn't do anything about it. Then June came, and I began to have second thoughts about working for them." I knew June meant *Babcia's* death. Dad leaned back in his chair. "How can I explain it?" I noticed the break in his voice. "It felt so meaningless to have my mother die like that, in some airplane without any of us around. It was horrible. It was like the regular world cracked open and I looked at things differently."

"Like what?" I asked.

Mom put her hand on the table close to mine. "Honey, Tolltorgan does work connected to nuclear weapons."

"YOU'RE KIDDING!" I must have shouted from the look Sam gave me. "That's impossible. It's a computer company."

"Yes," said Mom. "They make some of the computer guidance systems for rockets that carry nuclear weapons."

"You're wrong. I know you are. Their computers are for schools and places like that. I'm sure. Our elementary school had one."

"They make that kind of computer, too."

"Actually, that's probably why Frontier High has one of the best computer classes in Western Mass.," said Sam. "Tolltorgan donated the stuff."

"It makes them look like upstanding citizens that way," said Jill. "And all the while they're making things that can blow up the world."

"That's not really fair," said Dad. "They are upstanding. They probably feel they are defending our country. They're being patriotic in their own way. Your mother and I just felt that patriotism for us means not contributing to nuclear war."

"But what does it matter to have one little tiny print company say they aren't doing business with Tolltorgan? Do you actually think that's going to accomplish anything?" Sam blurted.

"No. But it feels right to my conscience. Maybe I can sleep better," said Dad.

"And wake up poorer, that's for sure. They were your biggest customer. What if your whole business folds because of this?" said Sam. "Why don't you go back to being apathetic like the rest of the world?"

"What are you thinking, Cassie?" asked Mom nervously. "You're awfully quiet."

"I think you're going to ruin my friendship with Terry," I said, and I ran out of the room.

It became silent in the kitchen. Then I heard Dad say, "Florence, I'll go talk to her."

"No. Let me."

My mother appeared in the doorway carrying the rest of my dinner. I just sat frozen on the couch. "I don't want it."

"I was waiting for the right time to tell you."

"Yeah. I just want to be alone."

"Maybe I made a mistake in not telling you along with Jill and Sam."

"That's not what bothers me."

Jill came into the room and sat with us, and I glared at both of them. "Look, this is really hard for Mom and Dad," she said. "They're really taking a risk."

"They're messing with my friendship," I said. I could speak easier now that Sam wasn't listening. But each word seemed to make the ache worse. I'd always wished my parents could be closer to Terry's and do things with them, invite them over for dinner and things like that. Now there was no chance of that ever happening.

"Hey, Mr. Cameron wouldn't have let Terry be in the group even if this hadn't happened. He doesn't like that kind of thing. You know that."

I did know that, but I wanted to say, "Don't you know the Camerons are my second family! I'm closer to them than to our aunts and uncles and cousins."

"Your father and I sent Bob Cameron a copy of the letter we sent to the President of Tolltorgan. It was very clear and cordial," said Mom.

"That makes it worse. Wasn't Mr. Cameron the one who got Tolltorgan to switch over to your shop? I think it stinks."

"Well, Bob wrote a nice note back to us. We haven't stopped speaking to each other."

"And think about it, Cass," said Jill. "Didn't Dad pick you up at the Camerons last night?"

I remembered that Dad had made a point of coming in the house and saying hello to Terry's father. Nothing had seemed unusual at the time.

"Hey, isn't this your big cause, you and Zack?" said Jill. "End the arms race. Down with nuclear weapons. You'd think you'd understand what they're going through."

"I do understand," I yelled as I stood up. I didn't look at either Mom or Jill as I went out the front door.

I went down the walk and began kicking a stone down the driveway. I knew where I was heading. I was making my way toward Terry's house. I wasn't going to tell her. I just wanted to be with her and make sure that nothing had changed between us.

I wondered if Terry knew about her father's job. She couldn't know. She would have said something. Maybe Mr. Cameron himself didn't know what they did with the computers he makes, I tried to tell myself. But he had been one of the people who started the company.

Suddenly it didn't seem so easy—our peace group and our art display and letting people know all the great ideas Zack and I and the other kids would have about the kind of world we wanted to grow up into.

I walked the whole mile, thinking about Terry. Then finally, there was their neat front yard, and the picture-perfect row of snapdragons. There was their picket fence with the yellow and gold lilies along the edge. It was comforting to see it all, although the house looked bigger than usual. I thought about the peeling paint on our front shutters.

Terry's younger sister, Pinky, was lounging in the front door. She stood with one hand on her hip and bright red nail polish on every finger and toe. She's the oldest fourth grader I know. She was wearing a T-shirt from the local rock station and a row of neon-colored bracelets on her wrist. There was a candy cigarette hanging out of her mouth.

Without changing her expression, she yelled over her shoulder, "Theresa, Cassandra is here."

Terry came running right away. She looked really glad

to see me—like her old self, not half asleep. "Come to my room! My *pictures* just came in!" she called excitedly, grabbing my hand and pulling me down the hall. Terry likes to emphasize words. It's her style, her whole family's style really, and I'm used to it. I like it, in fact. I even imitate it sometimes without knowing that it's happening.

"Okay! I'd *love* to see them," I answered.

We walked down their hallway, passing their photo gallery, about twenty framed pictures of their family at different ages. I saw picture after picture of the four of them smiling: at the beach, around a Christmas tree, in their back yard. I knew all the pictures with my eyes closed.

We entered her room. Everything was as usual: her shelves of china horses, the posters of unicorns on every wall. We sat on the flowered coverlet on her bed in our favorite positions, shoulders hunched, knees pulled up.

"Well, here they are," said Terry eagerly, holding up a stack. "Here's *Johnnie!*"

I looked at the top photo. A boy a little older than us was squinting into the sun. It was hard to get an idea of what he was like.

"That's not such a good one of him. Look at this. He's much cuter here." The photo showed him lifting two kittens into the air as if they were barbells. "Aren't they adorable? That's Vinnie and Minnie." She showed me every picture from three rolls of film.

I was surprised how bored I felt. Terry is really one of the most interesting people to listen to that I know, but I was more than a little relieved when Mrs. Cameron knocked on the door to say it was time for dinner.

"Oh, hi, Cassie. Now I know it's late and you've probably already eaten, but I *do hope* you'll stay and at least sit with us," she said smiling from the door. The Camerons always eat about two hours later than us. Mrs. Cameron was wearing a new necklace of seashells. She has a whole collection of beautiful necklaces.

65

I watched as the shells changed from pink to white in the light. "I probably could eat something," I said. My appetite was coming back.

"Good. That's the old Cassie we know," said Mrs. Cameron.

I followed her into their dining room and relaxed as I slid into my place at their table, right next to Terry. Mr. Cameron greeted me as usual, asking how my summer reading was going. It was Pinky who broke the spell.

"You know that Terry can't go to your *peace* group," she said matter of factly, as if she were asking for seconds of lamb roast.

I decided to play it calm and cool. It's the "no big deal approach" in Zack's notebook. (If I had a notebook I'd file it under "Dealing with Brats.") I just looked at Pinky, smiled, and said, "I know." Then I suavely picked up my fork and went on eating.

But Mrs. Cameron insisted on offering an explanation. "Yes, that's true. Terry's got to use that time getting ready for school. We *have* been away a long time, and there's *lots* to do." I wished she hadn't said anything. How long does it take to select narrow-lined notebook paper and sharpen a couple of pencils?

"That's right, you've got to be prepared when school starts," Mr. Cameron added. But then he brought the conversation around to a different topic. "So tell me Cassie, is the diving board fixed now at Larkspur Lake?" I was very grateful.

Yet when Mr. Cameron drove me home later that evening, I had trouble getting the usual cheery note into my voice as I waved goodbye and thanked him.

After he drove away, I discovered I'd left my bike propped up against our back porch. I wheeled it into the garage in case of rain and thought about the evening. Even if Mr. Cameron was feeling as uncomfortable as I was, he was making a special effort to be nice.

Maybe for him the whole rift with my parents was just a matter of business. Maybe it didn't gnaw at him the way it was gnawing at me. It seemed he could look at me and not be reminded of my parents' letter.

I wanted to talk about it with myself in a drawing on scratch paper and then throw it away and be done with it. From the way Terry was acting, I'd bet anything that Mr. Cameron hadn't told her. Probably she had no idea that there was a link between Tolltorgan computers and nuclear weapons.

I guessed that Mr. Cameron would expect that my parents hadn't told me either. I'd leave it that way. It would just be a secret, something to bury and not dig up again. We'd leave it as a bunch of business that had nothing to do with Terry or me.

On Monday morning, I went back to the familiar routine Terry and I had before she went on vacation. Instead of loading my backpack with art supplies, I threw in just a towel and bathing suit. I dashed through breakfast, washed the dishes, fed Sneakers, jumped on my bike, and rode straight to her house. It felt odd to whizz past the meadow without stopping.

Terry was fixing her hair when I arrived. I went upstairs and sat on the side of the bathtub while she used a blow-dryer and then added mousse to her hair. I loved the way the bathroom smelled of apricot soap.

There was a copy of *Teen Fashion* magazine, and I leafed through it while I waited for her. It was taking almost as long as it used to take her to french braid her hair. She kept changing her bangs around.

The "Makeovers" section in the magazine was interesting, although I liked the way two of the girls had looked before better than how they had turned out afterwards. There was also the typical kind of advice, things like if you're overweight wear stripes going up and down and if you think you're too skinny wear stripes going across. I never bought magazines like that. They always put me in a worse mood instead of a better one. I was surprised to see a label with Terry's name on the front that meant she had a subscription to it.

"Look at that guy!" Terry pointed. "Drool."

The couple in the ad were walking through a pile of leaves. "Well, he's cute, but I think they look too much like Barbie and Ken."

She laughed, and put her hand through my hair, "Cassie, why don't you get your hair styled while we're at the mall? Just like mine!"

"Not today," I said.

"Well, put on some of my eye shadow. It would look great on you."

"I'd look silly. Come on, let's go."

We went back to her room, and she held up a pink envelope. "To Johnnie," she said. She showed me the back where she had added S.W.A.K. I guessed I'd be hearing about Johnnie non-stop again today.

Mrs. Cameron drove us to the Littlefield Mall and dropped us off. "I'll meet you in front of the fountain at noon," she said.

Right away I pulled Terry into the art store. I'd bought a beautiful set of colored pencils there a week ago, the professional kind. I had to have them before the start of our group.

"It's next Monday," I said out loud to Terry.

"What is?"

"The group Zack's starting." Then I brought her over to the portfolios. "Which one do you think I should get?" I knew already the one I wanted. While she studied them, I thought about the group. Even if no one came but Louisa and Zack and me, it would be fun.

"This one," said Terry. She pointed to one that was heavy clay-red cardboard, not the expensive kind with zippers, but nice with a simple way to close it, and a handle.

"That's my favorite, too," I said happily. It was just the kind Louisa had. I wanted to sort out my favorite drawings from all my art pads, tear out the ones I wanted, trim the edges, and put them inside. I paid for it and had a few quarters left for a snack later.

We both tried on fall clothes for school. We went to three stores, and I wished over and over again that I hadn't worn my blue blouse with buttons down the back because it's so hard to change out of. Terry bought two skirts, and then we sat down at one of the little tables in the bakery.

She ordered a jelly donut and a coke. "Go ahead, get the same," she said. "You've got that guilty look on your face about eating junk food. Go ahead, it won't matter."

I laughed and ordered a glazed donut and a coke. I was in the mood for junk food. It usually happened when I went to the mall.

After we carried our food to the table and got settled, Terry took a long sip of coke and said, "Tell me more about Zack."

It seemed funny to talk about him at a shopping mall. I knew that they are one of his least favorite places.

"Is he your boyfriend or something?"

"*No!* Are you kidding? He's going into eleventh grade."

"Well, do you have a crush on him? You act like you do."

"Stop it. We're just good friends." I wished we were talking about him somewhere else. The mall is the kind of place where liking someone means it's got to be romantic.

"Well, is Jill going to go out with him after that nerd Eddie goes to college?"

"Eddie would throw a fit. No, Zack's a friend of our whole family."

"I don't really understand what he's like, Cassie."

So I started at the very beginning and tried to tell her more than I had covered in my letters. I told her all the details about nearly crashing into his U-Haul and about him fixing my bike. But I skipped the part about his notebook, "Experiments in Peace." I felt like it was Zack's secret even though he hadn't said I couldn't tell anyone about it. I was afraid I wouldn't describe it right, and it

69

would turn out sounding weird to Terry. Besides, there was something about the velvet-covered manikins and the hot pink neon signs flashing "Sweet Treats" that made the future described by Zack and the articles he collected feel very, very distant.

"So what was it you were doing with him on Saturday?"

"Delivering flyers about our group."

"Oh that."

"Terry, is there any way you can convince your Dad to change his mind?"

"I don't know." The flat tone of her voice made it seem like she wasn't very interested.

"Or what if you just came to the group anyway and didn't tell him." I had to find some way to have her be there.

"Cass, you know what he's like. He always has to hear about everything I do. And if he found out I'd been there, he'd go on and on about how disappointed he was in me."

"I guess so." I didn't want her to give up so easily.

"And I guess I don't really understand about the group," she said. "I mean, what's so fun about drawing pictures of peace?" She surprised me. It didn't sound like something I'd expect her to say, and I wasn't sure how to reply. Is a peace group just one of those things that either sounds great to you right from the beginning or leaves you cold so that not much is going to change your mind?

A drawing I saw in Zack's notebook came to mind at that moment. It showed a person in the United States playing music with someone in the Soviet Union. For me that's really exciting. When I saw that picture, I thought I'd love to meet a Russian girl or boy my age. But someone else could look at the same picture and think, "So what, who cares?" Or maybe, "That would never really happen."

I looked across the table at Terry. I was feeling so distant from her I might as well have been looking at her across the ocean. If she didn't want to join the peace group, would she also want to stop being my friend? I wanted to chase that thought away.

"I've got to tell you about Pinky. She is such a pain. I have to lock my door now because she tries to steal a look at my letters from Johnnie."

I guess you could say it was a relief to have Pinky as a common enemy. I warmed to the topic and drew a cartoon strip on my napkin of Pinky sneaking into Terry's room. At the door she gets stuck on the doorknob because Terry has placed wonder glue there to trap her. Terry laughed.

I wanted to say to Terry, "Don't you realize this will be the first time I've ever done anything without you?!" I wanted to say, "Don't you realize that starting next Monday for five whole days I won't be waiting for you while you finish fixing your hair? We won't be riding off together on our bikes. Or giggling over the things that happen in the group."

But instead, all I did was add fiendish details, boobytraps and trapdoors, to the picture of Pinky. And let the ice in my coke melt. And feel a little sick inside.

CHAPTER SIX

The Tigers

I was too excited to eat. It was like I was back in third grade, and it was the first day of school. Zack had told me there would be lots of other kids coming to the group, but when I arrived at the door of the Congregational Church, the minister and I were the only ones around. Reverend Ames explained that Zack was over at Gus's store picking up some supplies and led me inside the building.

"Here's your room," he said, opening a blue door on the second floor. There was an old piano against one wall with hymnals stacked on the top, Bible pictures, and shelves of beat-up toys. There was a heavy smell in the air that I liked. It reminded me of being deep in the woods in the fall. Zack had already arranged the room, putting aside the nursery size chairs and placing pillows around a large, braided rug.

As soon as Reverend Ames left, I went straight to the long windows across the front and looked out. There was a perfect view of Larkspur. The leaves were just beginning to turn red and yellow. Looking off to the left, I could see the hill where I live.

"Hey, Cass. First ones here, huh." It was Louisa. She

was wearing a headband, and her blondish-brown hair came to the middle of her back. I could tell she was as excited as I was.

Her arms were full. She had two gallons of cider and a bag of oranges. When she put them down onto a table with other food, it was like she couldn't just leave them there without making the whole thing more organized. She began grouping the cups and cider on one side and rearranging the crackers, chips, and fruit neatly on the other. "Zack said he brought enough food for the week, but he doesn't know these kids. They'll go through it in a day," she said.

"Are a lot of your friends coming?" I asked.

"Just three, but one of them is Riley, and we all call him the Bottomless Pit." I felt a little dread inside at Riley's name. He was Jill's age, but he used to be a friend of Sam's. Over five years ago, Riley had been at our house, and I remembered the way he and Sam had ganged up and teased me. I hoped, as my mother would say, that he'd grown up a lot.

Louisa turned back the pages of her sketch pad. I watched her long fingers. Her hands look like the hands of someone who plays the violin, they're so delicate. "I've been carrying something around for you." She held up a drawing she'd done of me back in June.

"I remember that day. I kept slapping mosquitoes and you kept yelling at me not to move so much."

"That's why I could only draw one of your arms." I looked closely at the sketch. In it, I seemed both young and old at the same time. That's how I often feel. But today I felt mostly young. I wondered if I'd be the youngest in the group.

Suddenly, we heard loud voices coming from the hall and footsteps, including a heavy clump, clump, clump, like someone was going up the stairs three at a time. "I hope this isn't going to be too peaceful, or I might fall asleep," said a girl's voice. Someone laughed. She continued, "I stayed up a bii-iit late last night."

"Don't worry, April. As long as Treena and I are here, you can be sure it won't be peaceful." The boy turned into the open doorway and ducked his head out of habit. He was very tall and thin with reddish-brown hair sticking up in spikes.

Louisa jumped up to greet them. "Howdy, guys."

"Hey, the Awesome Threesome have arrived," crowed Riley. I looked up to see three high-school kids standing in the doorway. One of the girls had long, dark hair and was dressed mostly in black with high boots. She was yawning. The other girl had on blue jeans with a long, oversized white shirt. I knew her; it was Treena. Her parents have a maple sugar farm in town. She was tall and thin and strong. I'd watched her lifting sap buckets. This summer I'd seen her driving a tractor.

When Treena saw the high front windows, she bounded over. Even looking out the window she couldn't stand still. She tossed her head, and her pony tail bounced "Look! You can see all of Larkspur. There's my house. There's your house, Riley."

"I didn't think Riley lived in a house," drawled April. "I thought he lived in a tree."

"Hey, I live in a cave," said Riley, beating his chest.

April raised her eyebrows. Her features reminded me of someone in *Teen Fashion* magazine. She had a small nose that came to a point. But unlike Treena who was freckled and sunburnt, April looked like she'd stayed indoors all summer. Her skin was pale, pale white—even bluish white—like a snowdrift. I thought of her as the queen of winter in a fairy tale.

She went over to sit down next to Louisa. She propped her feet up on a chair, and I could see the thick heel of her boots. I wondered how it must feel to walk in them. "Tell me, how boring is this going to be today? I didn't really want to come, but they dragged me," April said.

"I don't know. It should be good. I mean, I'm not really sure what's going to happen," answered Louisa.

"We're just going to try it for a day," said Riley. "Treena met the guy who started this thing over at the lake, and

74

he convinced her to come." Riley looked like a lightning bolt because of his red hair sticking straight up and his long, tall skinniness. As he turned his head to survey the room, I ducked and pretended I was invisible. I was terrified that one of them would start asking me questions and terrified also that no one else would show up.

Then I heard more footsteps on the old oak staircase. Four more kids came in the room, all my age or younger.

"Oh good. Baby-time," muttered April, and she slunk over to join Treena at the window.

"Hi, Cassie," said Ned. He smiled at me a little too broadly. My first thought was that maybe he'd joined only because he'd heard I was going to be there. "This is Rodney, my little brother."

Rodney mumbled a greeting. He had short, sandy hair and looked like a smaller version of Ned, but without any of the neatness. He was carrying a jumbo pack of magic markers and a box of Legos. He went over to the rug and dumped them out.

"My mother made me bring him," explained Ned.

"I didn't know you were coming," I said

"Yeah, Zack told me all about it."

"Zack? How do you know him?"

"I met him at the lake. He taught me his special Syracuse jack-knife one day when we were out on the raft. Do you know him, too?"

"Sure. I bumped into him the first day he moved here." I wanted to make sure Ned knew I met him first. I was feeling a little possessive about Zack. Every time someone mentioned they knew him, I pulled back inside. Had I imagined being one of his closest friends?

"Is that you, Cassie?" said a voice behind me.

I turned around. "Hi, Kisha!" Even though she was two years younger than me, I knew her from school. She was on the Class Council. Something was different about her appearance. "You got your hair cut!"

"Yeah, for the summer," Kisha said. It was in a short Afro.

"Oh, keep it short. It looks really nice."

"A lot of people have told me they like it." Kisha looked a lot older than she had before.

Her younger sister Shari's hair was more the way Kisha's used to be. She had high pigtails braided on either side of her head and blue checked ribbons that matched her checked blouse. Hers were the kind of braids you wanted to undo and play with. She ran over to join Ned's brother Rodney with the Legos.

Then Maritza arrived, and I ran across the room to greet her. We're in the same grade, and I was so relieved to see her. Last year her family moved here from Puerto Rico because her parents got jobs teaching at the university. We had just started to get to know each other, but we laughed at the same things in class. I liked her sense of humor.

"What have you been doing all summer? I haven't seen you," I said.

"Dancing! I took a class every day over at the mall." Maritza did a motion on her toes that was both graceful and funny, like she was mimicking one of the dancers on T.V. "What have you been doing, Cassie?"

I was about to answer, when we were interrupted by a loud bang on the piano. Treena and Riley were giving their own rendition of *Chopsticks*. They began with the low notes and moved up to the high, gaining in speed like a record put on 78 rpm. Only the sight of more food stopped them. Zack was coming in the door with another bag. Two more new kids were with him, and they helped him add food to one table and then set up paper and art supplies on another.

Riley immediately strolled over. He glanced over the spread of food. "Gus's finest, huh," he scoffed.

"So you don't like year-old Twinkies," Zack replied with a grin. Riley ripped open a bag of chips, munched a handful, and made a face.

"Ancient?" asked Zack.

"Prehistoric," said Riley. "Are you the guy in charge here?"

"In charge? Not exactly."

I looked around as Zack spoke. How could anyone even attempt to be in charge of this group?

Treena had found a large lump sticking out of one wall. It was covered with a sheet. She pulled the sheet off and revealed a fake tiger's head mounted on the wall.

"Boy Scouts of America, Troop 83, 1954," recited Treena from the plaque. "Get a load of this!"

Riley turned his gaze in her direction. "A velcro tiger!" he proclaimed.

"That's called felt, Riley," corrected April from across the room.

"And he's beautiful," squeeled Treena. She flung her arms around the tiger. "This is my pet. His name is Arnold. Say hello to him, April."

"Oh brother. It's my policy never to talk to stuffed animals." She groaned. "Especially when they're mounted on the wall."

When Zack asked us all to sit together on the rug, I already guessed it would be a lost cause. Sure enough, April stood off to the side, crossed her arms, leaned against the piano, and let her long black hair fall over her eyes. Riley sat in a nursery school chair with his knees against his chin, and Treena created a cozy perch on top of a book case leaning her head against Arnold the Tiger. The Awesome Threesome.

I counted the kids in the room. There were now thirteen of us, a pretty large turnout for Larkspur, but it was a totally different type of group from what I had expected. I pictured that everyone would feel like Louisa and me, really eager to get started, but instead Zack could hardly be heard for all the interruptions.

First, Rodney had to get an apple. Then, some other kids wanted something to eat, too, and when they went over to the food table, they managed to get into a fight about who would eat what. Next, Riley began fiddling with Rodney's magic markers, and Rodney threw a fit.

Zack couldn't finish his description of the art display and what he hoped the group could do for peace. He began again, and this time a loud clatter stopped him. It

was Treena. She had been kicking her feet, and she'd accidentally knocked a pile of books off the shelf.

If my Dad or one of the teachers was in charge instead of Zack, they would have yelled at her to get down off the bookcase. It seemed important to Zack to let her do what she wanted to, but I wasn't convinced his method was going to work. He tried to stay calm, but he was beginning to look flustered.

"How about this?" he said finally. "Why doesn't everyone take a piece of paper and draw your own idea of what peace is."

"Ah, peace. The sages' quest down through the ages," quipped Riley.

"I think I'll draw a cow," said Treena.

"I think I'll go to sleep," said April, and she pulled her long hair over her face.

They were funny, but they were beginning to drive me crazy, too. I headed straight for the lone table in the corner, hoping for some quiet. Ned and Louisa joined me there, and Maritza, too. We hunched over our papers and tried to begin. I waited for a thought to come to me, but I felt stuck.

Just then Treena challenged Riley to a push-up contest right in front of the supplies table, and we had to contend with their groans and laughter and with the complaints of other people stepping around them.

"Where's the pencil sharpener?" Shari asked.

"Right over here," yelled Riley.

"Where?" said Shari twirling her braids a little nervously.

Riley rolled over on his back, opened his mouth and gnashed his teeth. He pointed to his mouth. "Just put your pencil in here and I'll grind it up for you." With his orange, spikey hair he looked like a lion.

Then Treena took notice of her. "Oh, braids! I used to have braids." She descended on Shari who stood frozen in wonder as Treena insisted, "Hold still. Let me show April how I used to look." Treena had the gentle parental air of someone with a lot of younger sisters and brothers, but Shari looked not only curious but scared.

Treena coaxed Shari to stand beside her and place her braid as if it were her own. "You see what I looked like, April?" Shari stood still, afraid of what might happen next.

"Let's see what Riley would look like in braids," yelled April.

Riley caught the fear in Shari's eyes. "Not me. I'm busy," he responded. Shari escaped and joined us at the table. For several minutes, she just sat there drumming her fingers. I hadn't drawn a line.

"Who invited them?" grumbled Ned in a low voice.

"I did," said Louisa. "They were in my art class last year, and they care about peace. They're all fantastic artists."

"If they'll ever do anything," added Maritza. April was curled up in a stuffed chair trying to sleep.

It was a wasted morning. It had been so hard to draw that Maritza and I finally gave up figuring out a picture about peace. We started drawing goofy pictures for each other to see if we could make the other laugh.

"Sorry Zack," I said as he came around to get an idea of how our pictures were coming and saw my sketch of a worm with glasses. "It's just too hard to work here."

Maritza held up one of her cartoons. It showed two monkeys grinning. She can draw any kind of animal. "Peace is like a barrel of monkeys," she joked.

"Only in this group, it's more like a zoo," I added.

At the lunch break, some of the kids went to eat outside, including the trio. The room felt calmer to me the moment they left.

I sat down next to Maritza and opened up my bag lunch. I asked her if she wanted to swap anything for half of a peanut butter and jam sandwich. She gave me half of a turkey salad which I thought was a good deal. They also didn't taste bad together if I took a bite of one and then the other.

I looked at Maritza's long thin eyelashes and thought

it would be more interesting to try to draw a picture of her. Maritza's got that kind of alert face where even her eyelashes look intelligent.

Zack sat down with us. So did Louisa. "Well, nice try, Zack," she said. "Sorry the group's turning out to be such a failure."

"It'll get better," he said, but his voice couldn't hide his discouragement.

"How many people finished a drawing today?" Louisa asked him.

"You and Ned. And then there's the worm and the monkeys." Maritza and I laughed. "I guess the group today is different than I expected."

"Zack, I've got to say, it's kind of hard to draw about peace anyway," Maritza said. "It's not just that it's noisy here. It's hard to know where to start. It's not like drawing a horse."

I agreed. When Zack went to get something out of his coat pocket, I whispered to him so nobody could hear, "Why don't you show everyone your notebook? That might help give the group an idea of what peace could be like."

"Thanks, Cass. I didn't bring it. I want to let people think up their own ideas first." I could see the discouragement on his face.

"Well, I brought a present for you." I took a crumpled

newspaper clipping out of my backpack. It showed an art teacher in Vermont holding up a package of paintings she was mailing to a class in the Soviet Union.

Zack opened up the folded piece of paper and studied the article. "This is neat, Cass."

"My Dad found it in the newspaper, and he clipped it out for me."

I thought I could see the wheels beginning to turn in Zack's head. "Louisa," he asked, "how do things go in your art class?"

"What exactly?" Louisa replied.

"How does the teacher get you started?" Zack continued.

Louisa thought a moment. "I guess she presents some kind of a problem. She makes up a question, like—'Can you do a still-life if you only use straight lines?' Something like that."

"She gives you a question, and you try to answer it. That might work."

"Nothing will work with these kids. They're hopeless," said Maritza.

"Nobody's hopeless," said Zack.

"What about Riley?" I asked. "How could you ever get him to do anything but joke around."

"Riley? I bet he's a great actor," said Zack.

Maritza put on the expression of a conceited actor, and we both cracked up laughing.

"No, really," Zack added. "Riley's a real leader. I can tell."

"And what about the others?"

"April's brilliant. She just needs enough sleep. And Treena is full of energy," Zack was back to his old self. He seemed really excited.

Heavy footsteps signaled someone was returning. The door pushed open, and it was Treena riding piggyback on Riley.

"Where's April?" asked Louisa.

"Out having a smoke."

"Well, can Zack and I talk to the two of you?"

"Oh, oh. Here it comes. What are you going to do? Kick us out?" asked Treena.

"No, just the opposite," said Zack. "We need your help in making the group more interesting." Treena shrugged her shoulders and climbed down. The four of them gathered in a huddle over in a corner of the room. First, I watched Zack's hands moving with animation as he talked. Then I could hear a lot of laughter. They stayed talking together until everyone else drifted up the stairs.

When the room was full again, Riley stepped forward. "Welcome to our three-ring circus," he said. "I'm your master of ceremonies this afternoon." Treena clapped loudly. So did Zack.

"Oh brother," said April.

"And in the center ring, all the way from that great little town of Larkspur, we have the fabulous, the tremendous—Treena."

"Okay everyone," said Treena. "On your feet."

"What's going on here?" asked April.

"I'm going to teach you a song I learned at camp this summer."

"Your camp! I'm going back downstairs."

"No you're not. We're going to have some fun here. Everyone, stand up." We stood.

"Now, I want you to wave your hands in the air like this." We imitated her. "Now, as you wave your hands, I want you to shout, 'Peanut, peanut butter.'" For some reason, we followed along. "Then you bend down and repeat, 'And jelly, and jelly.'" We bent low like in a vaudeville routine, all thirteen of us, and we looked really funny.

"Now that's just the chorus. Now we've got to make the sandwich. 'First you take the peanuts and you grind them, you grind them.'" We stomped our feet. Riley was hysterical the way he did it. He wiggled his whole body and looked like he was about to fall. Then he pretended he'd fallen into a vat of peanut butter and insisted we had to help pull him out.

Next, we moved onto mushing up the peanuts and

83

stomping the grapes. From there Riley really got carried away. He kept creating more verses. He insisted we become one huge assembly line squirting the jam out into jars. He had Kisha stand stiff like a robot and hold up the jars. Rodney was the spigot where the jam comes out, and Ned was the inspector of the plant. We loved it. We picked and stomped and assembled and finally spread the jam and peanut butter on the bread, all with great gusto.

As we sat down again, I was a little breathless from laughing so hard. I had kept my eye on Maritza through the whole thing, and we kept laughing together. She came up with the funniest motions.

"This is the way to begin the afternoon," said Riley. "Making fools of ourselves." I caught Maritza's eye and made a weird expression to see her laugh again.

"Onward! Onward!" called Riley. "No time to rest. Everyone grab a piece of paper and a pencil." He flung pieces of paper left and right. We grabbed them and got books off the shelf to back up our papers. I settled back and waited expectantly.

"For our next act in this really big show, we have the one and only Zack Clemmons. Take it away, Zack."

"And do I have a question for you!" said Zack, exaggerating his voice up and down. "Sit back. You will have… How much time will they have, Riley?"

"Exactly 19 minutes and 60 seconds, no more, no less."

"You'll have that much time to answer this question in any kind of drawing of your choice. The question of the day is," and then his voice slowed down and became more focused, "What is one of the biggest changes you ever made in your life?"

It took me by surprise. Ned, too. "Zack, what does that question have to do with the peace display?" he asked.

"Well," and Zack squished his face with his hand the way he does when he's thinking, "It's an intuition. It seems to me that our display will be asking people in town to make some changes, maybe some hard ones. So I wanted us to get a chance to remember changes we've made."

"So we'll be more understanding of them," Treena added.

"And we'll tell them, if you don't listen to us, we'll make some changes you may not like, like rearranging your kneecaps," said Riley. He caught April's look of disgust. "Just kidding," he added.

"Actually, Zack, I think that's a very good question," said April.

"Thank you."

"Would you repeat the question again, Zack," asked Ned.

"Yeah. What's one of the biggest changes you ever made?"

"That's easy," said April. "It was when I moved here from New York. I walked through the center of Larkspur, counted the number of stores I saw on the fingers of one hand, and said, 'You've got to be kidding!'"

"When I moved here from Puerto Rico, I couldn't get used to the cold," added Maritza.

"Excellent, excellent. I can see we're off to a grrr-eat start," said Riley. "Now for the whole time we're going to have absolute silence."

"Oh no," said Treena. "What if there's a fire or the roof caves in?"

"Not even then. Absolute silence."

"Except if someone needs some help," Louisa broke in. "Then just ask me."

"That's true. That's the only exception."

"But Riley," said Ned. "You were one of the biggest offenders before. What are you talking about, we have to be quiet!"

"I'll admit it. But I've seen the error of my ways. I shall not make even the tiniest little mooing sound."

"This I've got to see," said April.

"No, I'm serious. Isn't Zack saying that people can change? All right then, this will be the biggest change I've ever made, keeping quiet for twenty whole minutes."

And he did. The silence was delicious. I heard the leaves rustling outside and smelled a breeze coming in through the screens. April and Shari whispered off in a corner with Louisa. People crumpled paper, leaned back in their chairs, scratched mosquito bites, but no one else talked.

I bent over my drawing pad. My mother had bought me a new one for the start of our group. I think it was partly because she knew how sad I was that Terry wouldn't be there. Not being with Terry seemed the biggest change at the moment, but I didn't want to draw that. I thought about the time I had the cast on in third grade, but that didn't interest me so much. Then I remembered something that happened to me when I was even younger, and I drew that.

When the twenty minutes were up, Treena and Riley pretended they were alarm clocks and let out a "Brrrrrrng." It was a short time, but it was probably as much silence as the group could take. I took out one of my new colored pencils and shaded in a few areas. Then I looked up.

"Now for the third ring of our fantabulous show—Larkspur's own Rembrandt, the incredible Louisa."

Louisa stepped forward.

"What we're going to do next is have a chance to share our drawings. But only if we want to. It's fine to keep your drawings private."

"No matter how much we beg and scream," said Riley.

"That's right." Louisa pushed her hair behind her ears. "And we won't go around the circle and take turns because then if you want to say 'I pass,' sometimes it feels stupid."

"Not to mention, 'I pass out,'" added Riley.

"Riley, what are you trying to do? Make up for your glorious moment of quiet?" asked April.

Riley nodded. Then he pretended to zipper his mouth.

"Whoever wants to will go first, and we'll go on from there." Louisa looked around the circle. "So, who's first?" She spoke with encouragement, as if she was opening a door and inviting us inside.

Kisha raised her hand. "I'll get it over with." She looked at Shari, then back at her picture and held it up halfway.

"I can't see," said Rodney.

"What's it about?" asked Ned.

Kisha held the picture up higher. "This is me when I was a lot younger." She pointed to one of the figures in the drawing. "It's the day I found out that my little sister was deaf."

"Shari is deaf?" Rodney asked.

Kisha and her younger sister Shari shook their heads. "No, it's our baby sister." She pointed to the smallest figure. "Now we've been learning sign language."

"That's a great drawing," said Louisa.

"Yeah," echoed Maritza. She was next to Kisha. "I like the way you showed you were surprised." Maritza opened her mouth and made her eyes wide in imitation.

Kisha smiled. I thought she was brave to go first.

"I want to go next," said Rodney. He held up his picture. "After Thanksgiving, my grandfather and I both decided to go on a diet together. Here's Grampy."

"Great details on that exercycle," said Riley. Rodney smiled to hear him say that.

"I guess I might as well get it over with," said April. I was surprised to hear her voice. It was quieter than usual. I could barely hear her. "I couldn't figure out how to show this in a drawing, but Louisa thought of a way."

"It's a really good drawing, April. Go ahead. They'll love it."

"Well, my parents got divorced last year, and my father married this woman. How would you describe her, Treena?"

"Not your type."

"Yeah, so she comes into the house and suddenly everything has to be changed. I can't put my clothes where they were, I can't even sit at the same place at the table because *she* has to sit across from my father. It's weird." She held up her drawing. It showed two views of her dinner table, one before the divorce and one after her stepmother had moved in.

It was clear that April loved to draw. She'd added in the pattern of the wallpaper in the room and the food on the table. I was surprised, though, that she'd shown us something so personal.

"That's an amazing drawing," said Zack.

"That's our April, she's amazing," said Treena. April looked pleased. She heaved a big sigh.

I guess this is what peace is like, I thought to myself. It's safer. Somehow I felt that I was supposed to go next. "Supposed to" is maybe a funny way to put it, but suddenly I knew that I wanted to speak. I wanted to feel everybody looking at me in that same interested way.

"I'll be next."

"Yea, Cassie," said Zack. I could see he was rooting for me. Maybe he knew what a big step this was.

"I remembered when I was very little and my father told me it was time to give up my blanket," I began.

Several kids chuckled. It was a good chuckle, though. They were laughing with me and enjoying what I said. "So I threw my blanket away in the wastebasket one morning. And then I heard the garbage truck coming, and I ran back to get it."

Maritza laughed as I held the picture up.

"That really happened?" asked Ned.

"Yeah."

"That's funny," said April. They really liked it! The rest of the afternoon, I floated.

Lots of kids showed their drawings. It wasn't like a class where some people's were praised more than others or you felt like you were getting a grade. It was something new. No one got put down. It felt great.

"Before we leave today, I have a burning question I've got to ask," said Riley. "How can I come back tomorrow to a peace group that has a tiger for a mascot. Now really." He directed our gaze at Arnold.

Treena chimed in, "Of course he's our mascot. We ferociously want peace, don't we?" Maritza and I groaned.

"Or we could think of it this way. Bringing peace might take the strength of a tiger," said Louisa.

"Yeah. So why don't we call ourselves the Tiger's Group?" said Maritza.

"But I thought we were Zack's group," added Ned.

"We can't call it that," Zack jumped in. "It's already more and more *our* group and less and less *my* group. I just thought it up."

"Well, then how about 'The Peace Group'?" asked Shari.

"Not enough pizzazz," said Kisha. "I'd rather call it Arnold's Group than that."

"So let's make it the Tiger's Group," Maritza repeated. And it stuck.

CHAPTER SEVEN

Surprise

How could I tell Terry what the Tigers were like? It was like describing a carnival. I tried to explain about the Awesome Threesome. I tried to explain about showing my picture. I tried singing the peanut butter song. But all together, it didn't add up to the same as being there.

I wanted her to know everything we did so it would be as if she'd been there, too. She listened politely, kind of like the way I listened to her stories about Johnnie. I could see she wasn't as eager to find out about it as I was to tell it, and that made me even sadder.

The next day when Kisha leaned around the corner of the door and said, "Psst, Zack, I've got some new kids here who want to join," I caught myself hoping Terry was hiding there as a surprise. But they were neighbors of Kisha and Shari waiting out in the hallway to see if it was okay to come in.

"Can they be Tigers, too?" asked Shari.

"I don't know. What do you think?" Zack turned around to the rest of us to make it clear that it wasn't for him to decide. It was up to all of us.

"Why not?" said Maritza. She was wearing a flowered

blouse with a lacy collar, and it made her curly black hair circling her face look like loops of fine lace.

"Sure. The more the merrier," said Louisa. Zack looked around the whole circle. Everyone seemed to agree.

"Come on in," he said. Twin boys, skinny and shy, walked in with their older sister who was probably Kisha's age, in sixth grade or so. Later, Rodney brought his best friend with him.

The room was filling up fast, but there was a noticeable gap. Rodney put his finger on it first. "Where are the awful threesome?" he asked.

"You mean the Awesome Threesome," said Louisa. "I don't know. I thought they'd be here by now."

I remembered Sam's comments last night at the dinner table. "It sounds like you have mostly elementary kids in your group," he'd said.

"A little more than half, so what?"

"You need high-school kids to really do anything."

"That's not true," I told him. "Plus we also have older kids like April and Treena and Riley."

"Riley! He's there?" I nodded. "I can't believe it. I bet he won't last long."

"Why?"

"Well, Riley and his friends are, I don't know, sophisticated."

"Are you kidding? Riley, sophisticated?" I could still see him in my mind rolling around on the floor as a pencil sharpener.

"You know what I mean. They like to be part of something that's actually going to happen. The whole idea of an art display about peace just doesn't fit here in Larkspur. Zack could do something like that in Syracuse, maybe, but not here."

At the time, I told Sam he had no idea what he was talking about, but the trouble with Sam was his words could still hang around in my head and get to me.

It was odd to be meeting again without those three. No one was jumping up to reach Arnold the Tiger or playing *Chopsticks* on the piano or crowding the food table.

I wondered if it bothered Zack as much as it bothered me that they hadn't come back. "Well, let's start," he said. "Welcome to the Tiger's Group, day two." It made me feel better to see him grinning that wild grin of his. People answered him with growls coming from all over the room. "How about somebody doing a song or game to start us off," said Zack. But no one wanted to.

"It's too sad trying to sing without Treena leading us," said Shari. "I don't want to sing any old song like 'Old McDonald Had A Farm.' " She made a face.

Zack waited to see if there would be a volunteer, but we just looked back at him. "Then, let's go ahead with the question of the day."

Ned had moved closer to Zack. His shirt that had been so neatly tucked in when he arrived, and was always that way at school, was now pulled out. "Can I ask the question today?" he said.

"I suppose so," said Zack. As Ned was about to begin, the Awesome Threesome burst into the door with a flourish.

"Never fear, we're here!" shouted Treena.

"Old McClemmons had an Aardvark, yuk yuk yuk yuk yuk," sang Riley. All three of them were carrying boxes full of something. April was wearing a fishnet top over a leotard and the same pair of boots.

"Here's my question," said Ned. "Where have you guys been?"

"Actually we had some very important work," said Treena. "This!" She plunked her box down. "This is a whole bunch of things we can use. April's father gave them to us. Some of it's from his trip to Japan."

"There's a lot here," said April. "You've got to see these books about Hiroshima and Nagasaki where America dropped the first nuclear bombs."

I knew about the bombs, but I also didn't know. I hadn't thought about them much. In school last year when we studied World War II, my teacher had said that America used nuclear bombs in 1945 to end the war and that they actually saved many lives. At the time I wondered about that, but I didn't raise my hand to question what she said. If someone like Zack had been in the class, though, he probably would have mentioned that we could have ended the war some other way.

"And that's not the only stuff here," said April. She pulled at a long strand of hair. "There's magazines and pamphlets from different peace groups. My Dad saves every little thing. I'll pass 'em around so you can take a look." She lifted up a stack from the boxes.

"So you are loyal Tigers after all," said Louisa. "I thought you'd given up on us and you weren't going to come back."

"Give up? Hey, we just started," said Riley. "Now, no goofing off. I want to get right to work. I'm all ears to hear Ned." He flung his legs over one of the nursery school chairs, pulled his big ears out, and grinned.

"Riley, even when you're being good, you're impossible," said April.

"I know." He noticed that all eyes were on him. "Well, far be it for us to interrupt things. Carry on!"

We did. All of the new kids introduced themselves, Louisa explained the way we worked like it had already become a tradition, and Treena led another song.

When the stack of books and papers from the boxes came around, I chose a book with a red cover called *Hiroshima No Pika*. It had paintings, and I hoped they would be less scary to look at than photographs. I turned to a page in the middle of the book. It showed a mother holding her daughter while flames licked above their heads. The fire was a pinky peach swirl like a spirit out of control. Thick charcoal brush strokes showed fallen timbers the color of ashes or wet earth.

Before I had time to look at another page, Ned called out to get our attention. "Here's the question I want us to use for our drawings today," he said. He looked at Riley to make sure he was listening. "Why did you want to join a peace group?"

"Not a bad question," said Louisa.

"So I could carry heavy boxes upstairs," said Riley.

"Absolute silence," Ned said in mock seriousness. "Try it."

I arranged some pillows against a shelf in a corner of the room. I liked the faint smell of old books. It reminded me of the basement in the town library. Along with my drawing pad, I took the book and stared at it some more, forgetting the room around me.

The book told the story of the girl and her mother and father after the bombing. It followed them as they fled to the river to ease their burns. The pictures were so vivid that I could feel the flames and hear the people around them as they cried out to each other. I saw a swallow with singed wings and a dead cat floating in the river.

I had expected that paintings of the first atomic bomb blast would scream at me in horror, but these actually drew me in and let me look. I could feel the gentleness of the artist even as she showed us a nightmare. It was as if underneath these scenes of what was terrible in life, I felt the artist herself reminding me also of all that is good. I stopped at a picture of a mother holding her baby who had died.

Ned's question came back to me. Why had I joined? Because I worried that Larkspur could look like these paintings of Hiroshima someday, with flames and charred bodies. But I didn't want to draw that. And I'd joined because of *Babcia* dying. Suddenly, she'd disappeared from my life. A nuclear war would mean we'd all disappear. *Babcia's* death made it more real to me.

I looked at the back flap of *Hiroshima No Pika* hoping there would be a description of the artist, Toshi Maruki. I was in luck. There was a picture of her. She had soft cheeks and her mouth was half open like she was about to speak. I learned that she was over seventy when she'd

94

made the book, close in age to my grandmother. I had joined this group because of the people like the two of them who cared.

And because of the pages in Zack's notebook. I remembered all the drawings I'd done alone in the meadow back when I thought I was the only one in the world who worried about these things. His notebook told me that there were other kids out there, kids I hadn't met yet, like me. They wouldn't think we were stupid or weird to try to do something for peace. They thought it was important.

I turned to the back of the book. The last painting showed children writing names on paper lanterns. They floated these on the river of Hiroshima at the anniversary of the bombing in memory of those who had died. A girl in a deep blue kimono held a lantern close to her heart, and it burned bright orange.

A hazy picture started to form in my mind. That's the way my ideas come. There's nothing definite, but if I can even start drawing a few lines, the rest gets clearer and clearer.

I drew rocks and stones. It became a cutaway drawing of the ground. You could look beneath the earth and see the roots of trees and the passageways of animals. I drew a girl pushing from underground through the rocks. I wanted to make it seem like a candle was inside her and outside her at the same time. I didn't know exactly who the girl looked like. She wasn't me. She was a person who could push through rocks like a flower in the spring. I had joined the group to feel more hopeful. She was a lantern of hope.

I kept erasing and trying new lines. I was just beginning to get the candle flames the way I wanted them when the room got noisy. Louisa was calling everyone together to make a circle. I drew a little more and then closed up my pad so no one could see it.

I let others volunteer to show their drawings. Mine was nowhere near done. Riley's was funny of course

Well, funny and scary at the same time. He showed a nuclear war happening because of a ridiculous accident. One of the new boys, Ben, drew war like a dinosaur on the attack.

Treena drew herself playing basketball with her sister when the court suddenly turns into a target for a bomb.

"What's ground zero?" Ned asked. That was the label she'd put on the basketball court.

"That's the name they give to the place where the nuclear bomb hits," Treena explained. I started to get that creepy feeling in my stomach.

Then Kisha spoke up. I could see she was having trouble deciding whether or not to show her drawing. She held it face down. Then she turned it over.

"I sometimes have bad dreams about war," she said. It was a picture of herself sitting up in bed with a bomb breaking through the window of her bedroom.

I watched Zack's face as she said that. He turned toward her and spoke in a softer voice than I'd heard him use before. Rodney stopped kicking his chair to listen. "That must be pretty scary," he said. She nodded. "What are your dreams like?"

"Once I dreamt that a bomb was above our roof waiting to fall." Kisha looked at our faces and then away. "And then I ran and ran to try and reach my parents but I couldn't find them. That's the part of the dream I hated the most."

"Sounds pretty terrifying," said Zack.

She nodded again and looked down. Her sister Shari seemed surprised to hear about her nightmares. I guess Kisha had never mentioned them to her before.

"How many others of us have had dreams about nuclear war?" Zack asked. I looked around the circle. Zack and Louisa were raising their hands. So were at least half the group. I'd never had a nightmare like that.

"What did you do after you woke up from that nightmare? Did you tell anybody about it?" Zack asked Kisha.

"Well, I told my mother, and I sat in her lap. She said anytime I have one of those dreams again I can come and get her."

"You're lucky," Louisa said. "When I told my mother,

she said I was being silly." Louisa imitated her mother's voice. "Let's talk about something more pleasant."

"My father said I shouldn't mention things that could never happen." Ben drew little figures along the edge of his paper as he spoke.

"Doesn't he know about all the bombs there are?" asked Ned.

"I don't know," said Ben.

"Sure he knows," said April. "He just doesn't want to scare you."

We were all silent, waiting for somebody else to talk. There was a feeling in the room like thick dust clogging the air.

Shari and her friend began playing a kicking game with their feet. Rodney and Ben shifted in their seats like they wanted to stand up.

Zack looked over at the rest of us who were quiet but brimming with words that wouldn't come out yet. Then he turned to the restless ones in the group. "Some of you want to go outside for a while with me?"

More than half the group went with him. I stayed upstairs and so did Maritza. I could hear them playing Freeze Tag outside on the church lawn. Shari giggled really loudly, and somebody shrieked "Gotcha." I wondered if Zack had ever been a camp counselor.

Treena climbed onto the top of the bookcase and sat next to Arnold the Tiger. She rubbed her nose against his.

Louisa gathered up some crackers and a bowl of grapes and brought them to one of the small blue tables. "Want to come over here and keep talking?" she asked. We moved over to sit around the table.

"I hate all this," said Treena, jumping down to sit with us.

"What do you hate?" asked April.

"I hate that we have to be afraid. The whole thing is so gross. Kids having nightmares." She shook her head.

"I know what you mean," I said.

"And on top of everything, we can't talk about it anywhere. What are we supposed to do? Just shut up about it?" Treena yelled.

"Yeah, a friend of mine said to me yesterday, 'Why are you joining a peace group? We're not in a war!' Can you believe that?" said April.

"We might as well say we're in a war," said Treena. "We're sending arms all over the world, and we have so many nuclear weapons, we're ready to fight any second."

"Well, what can we do?" Maritza asked.

"My grandmother works for peace," Kisha said. "She took a train to the Pentagon and helped tie a ribbon all the way around it. And she made a quilt that had pictures of me and Shari and our sister on it. One of April's magazines has a picture of the Ribbon Project on the front." Kisha held it up, and I leaned over to take a look.

"A bunch of these magazines show things people are doing for peace," said April. She spread them out on a table, and we began thumbing through them. "But they're mostly demonstrations, and frankly, I can't see us parading in front of Gus's store demanding an end to nuclear war. What would that prove? We've got to do something that makes sense."

"Yeah, we can't go to the Pentagon," said Treena. "And I want to do something right here. I still like Zack's idea of putting our pictures into an art display for the town. That seems about the right speed for Larkspur."

"Yeah, I like it, too," said Louisa. "The pictures we did today would really fit."

"We could make it part of the fall foliage craft fair," said Ned. "My mother sells handmade children's toys there every year."

"With Mrs. Fairchild in charge of it? She'd never let us enter," said Treena.

"Plus I want to have something all our own," I added.

"We could copy pictures from these magazines," said Kisha, "and show people what they could do to stop a nuclear war from happening."

"We could come up with our own ideas, too," said Louisa.

"I'd like to try drawing what a world at peace would look like," said Treena.

"What Larkspur could be like," added Maritza.

We heard the creaky front door open and the kids come running back upstairs. Ben ran in first and went right for the food table and began gulping cider.

"Hey, don't drink it all," said Rodney.

Shari and another girl her age were grabbing at Zack's jacket and racing around trying to tickle him.

"Come on, Clemmons, get yourself together," said Riley.

"We've got something to tell you," Maritza said.

People stood around, passing cider and mostly listening while we explained.

"We want to go for it," said April. "We want to do the display."

"So let's make it official," said Riley. He emptied out one of the cartons he'd helped to carry upstairs and grabbed a thick black magic marker. He held the carton up to Arnold and made an exaggerated show of drawing his face on the box. "There. Everything for the display goes in here. Protected by Arnold."

That was the day we really got moving. We were like a toboggan pushed off the top of a hill. For the rest of the week we kept picking up speed.

Each night at dinner, I was beaming. I didn't say much, though. I wanted to keep it kind of secret. I know what it feels like to go on and on about how great something's going to be and then have the whole thing fall flat.

"How's Planet Z?" my father liked to ask.

"Out of this world," was all I would answer.

As soon as the phone was free after dinner, I faithfully called Terry, but each night we felt more distant. By the end of the week, the amount of things we hadn't shared together was like a mountain between us.

At the same time, more and more new people were joining the group. Kids kept bringing their friends, and I wished I could bring Terry.

At the meetings, Zack took it as his job to help the new kids who arrived feel part of the Tigers. He'd show them where things were kept and give them a folder to store unfinished sketches or things they weren't sure they wanted to submit for the display.

Reverend Ames said he didn't mind it if we left things in the room overnight. We set up the box with Arnold the Tiger's picture on it and the books and other things from April's father on the side of the room near Arnold. Reverend Ames started calling the room the Tigers' Den until April complained that he made it sound too much like the Cub Scouts.

Friday was our last day before school started. That morning before our meeting began, I stopped by Gus's store to get something to drink for lunch. I was looking over the juice bottles, trying to find my favorite combination—apple and peach—when I heard a voice behind me call out, "What do you say, Tiger?"

It sounded like Riley. As I responded with the growl that had become traditional in our group that week, I heard two more growls from other aisles in the same small store. I stalked over to the bread and pastry area and found Louisa and April.

"Two chocolate layer cakes," I exclaimed.

"It's a surprise."

"Because it's our last day."

We piled our items on the counter by Gus. He stood for a moment smoking his pipe and looking at us. Then he took the pipe out of his mouth. "Just what is this tiger stuff I've been hearing all week?" he asked.

Riley joined us, and the four of us gave Gus our best growls.

"Some kind of sports team?" Gus pursued.

"Something like that," answered Riley.

"And we need lots of chocolate," said Louisa as Gus

rang up the cakes. "But don't tell Zack we got them if he comes in here. He'll think we're breaking our training."

When we reached the room, Riley and I walked in front of Louisa to block the view of her package. She slipped it behind the stack of hymnals.

Treena was throwing a mock tantrum. "Whaa! I don't want school to start and the group to be over!"

"You know that Zack said we'd get together over Columbus Day weekend," Ned told her.

Kisha gave Ned a look that said, "Can't you take a joke?" and pulled out his shirt tail that was still tucked in.

"Whaa! October's too far away," cried Treena, flinging herself down on the floor while April laughed.

"Up. Up. I'm leading the game today," Riley called out. Treena rolled onto her side and propped her head up. Riley reached out his hands and pulled her to her feet. She came flying.

"You know this game, Treena," he told her. "It's called 'Knots.'" He stretched his hands out to gather us into a circle.

"All I can say is, why knot!"

"Okay," said Riley. "Everyone put your right hand in the center. Now grab onto someone's hand." We looked like the weaving of a potholder as we reached out into the circle.

"Now with your left hand reach out in another direction and grab hold of the hand of someone different. You don't have to know whose hands you have."

"That's good. I'm not even sure which are my hands anymore," mumbled April. We were now one big mass all linked together, one giant knot.

"And now we untie ourselves," called Riley. "But without letting go." We stayed frozen for a moment and just laughed. It seemed impossible.

Then Treena saw a way she could duck under a pair of hands and loosen up the circle a bit. Several others tried the same move. Sometimes, it worked. Sometimes, it just made the knot tighter.

Maritza stepped over another pair of hands, and that helped, too.

At this point, I was twisted around backwards looking outward from the circle with my hands crossed in front of me. I felt pinned. Every time the loop of hands moved, I was more trapped instead of less. It was beginning to feel uncomfortable. Another wave of movements boxed me in even tighter.

My crossed hands felt like a straight jacket. Finally, I let out one word, "Help!"

I could see heads craning around to look at me and heard some speculation about what to do.

Treena knew the fine points of the game. "What you do in a case like this is call for Magic Scissors," she said. She let go and stepped out of her position for a moment. She pretended to hold a giant pair of shears. With them, she snipped above both my hands so that I was allowed to release them. I wheeled around and faced into the circle and grabbed hands again.

"Cassie, you're free," said Maritza.

"What a mishmash," I said.

From there it was easy, even simple. Treena returned to her location. We had a few more twists and turns to undo, and then, there we were, standing back again in one loop.

"Thanks," I said to Treena as we sat down together.

"Anytime," she answered.

As we all assembled together, sprawled on pillows and all over the rug, I counted heads. There were twenty-two of us today. We'd almost doubled in size since Monday.

I got out my manila folder and flipped through it trying to decide what I wanted to work on first. Louisa had brought in a set of rapidograph pens so we could ink over pencil lines in black. The rapidographs had a different weight in my hand than a regular pen, so I had to get used to them. But I liked the skinny lines they made. Rodney was even sharing his jumbo marker supply.

"We've got to have a meeting before we draw," Treena

yelled. "I want us to decide where we're going to have this display!" She erased a section of the blackboard and tossed a piece of chalk in her hands. "Okay. What are your nominations for where you want to hold it?"

"This church."

"No, too small."

"The school."

"Can't we please have it someplace different!"

"The town hall."

"Yeah. There's lots of bulletin boards there."

"And we can carry more over from the elementary school."

"So who do we ask?" asked Zack while Shari and Rodney drew all over the blackboard.

"Gus," said Riley. "I bet Gus would know."

"Okay, I'll ask Gus during lunch break," volunteered Zack. Louisa shot me a glance, and I knew what she meant. While he was out, we could set up the surprise party. I winked back at her.

"What's that wink for, Cassie?" Zack asked. Zack doesn't miss anything.

"I was just thinking of Gus," I fumbled. "He's under the impression we're some kind of sports group."

"Well, Zack, tell him it's for a pep rally," Treena laughed.

"I've got it! I've got it! I've got a wonderful idea," April exploded.

"Out with it already," Riley called.

"Why don't we have our art display on January first? It will be like a new beginning that way."

"Brilliant. Haven't I always said she's brilliant?" said Treena.

"Sort of a pep rally for the New Year," said Riley.

"Oh, brother. 'Fight, team, fight' is not exactly my idea for our slogan," April answered back.

"But that's so far away," said Ben.

"Yeah, it's only August. You want us to wait until January?"

"That's no good," said Ned. "There'd be snow on the ground. No one would come out."

"But think of the symbolism," said April. "The New Year!"

"And if we have it too soon, we won't have enough drawings ready," said Louisa. "I want to fill the whole town hall."

"Take it from me," Riley said to Ned. "I'm an old timer. I've been around. These things take time."

So the Awesome Threesome talked us into it. I didn't know what I thought. I had lots of drawings ready right now, but I guessed I could stand to wait. Besides, I hadn't even tried to finish my favorite drawing, the one that tried to show the feeling of hope.

April and Zack and some others kept on discussing the plans while the rest of us did what we felt like doing. I finished inking over the pencil lines of two sketches using one of Louisa's rapidograph pens. Then it was time to break for lunch.

Louisa and Treena and I kept our eyes on each other and on Zack. The minute he finished his sandwich and left to visit Gus, we jumped into action. I started making paper chains. Shari and Kisha and Ben helped me. We decorated the windows, the top of the piano, even Arnold. Riley put his cap on top of Arnold's head.

Treena drew a heart on the blackboard that said, "We love you Zack," while Louisa passed around a card for everyone to sign.

Just as Ned and Rodney were arguing about whose turn it was to take out the trash from lunch and had knocked over the wastebasket someone had left in the middle of the room, Kisha spied Zack coming out of Gus's store. "He's coming," she yelled.

They scrambled to pick up the trash as we heard the old oak door of the church opening. We ran to hide. Silence. We could hear him whistling on the stairs. Step. Step. Step.

"SURPRISE!" Treena and Kisha threw confetti. Louisa

and April came forward, each with a chocolate cake with candles.

"Who's birthday?"

"Yours."

"Ours."

"It's a 'Thank-you Zack' party."

Out came the card. Riley had cartooned people surfboarding on the ocean. When Zack opened up the card, it read, "Thank you for launching this peace wave," with all of our names.

Zack looked from the card to the heart to the cakes. He was speechless, even a little bashful. "What can I say! You all are the ones who've been doing everything."

"Hey, if you hadn't been around, what would we be doing now?" said Riley. "Hanging around on the Larkspur raft. Come on. Take credit."

"Do you have a surprise for us?" Kisha asked him. "Did we get the town hall for January 1?"

"Yup. It's ours," answered Zack, still a little happily dazed.

"What did Gus say?" Treena continued.

"Well, it turns out that you were right, Riley. Gus is the one in charge of signing up groups to use the town hall, since it's just down the road from his store. Then he has to report to the town council, and it's up to them to give the final okay. But he thought it would be no problem."

"Is there any chance the selectmen might object?" asked Ned.

"It depends on whether you tell them it's for a peace display or a pep rally," said Riley.

"I didn't really tell Gus much about it. The store was crowded so we had to talk while he was ringing up orders. He just got out his calendar for the town hall, saw the date was clear, and gave it to us."

"I guess he figures he knows us," I added. "We've been his best customers this week."

"So I asked him to write down the Tigers' Peace Display

for January 1, and he did," said Zack.

"I'll drink to that," said Riley. He poured cider for everyone, a special, sparkling cider like fake champagne.

Louisa raised her glass in a toast. "It may be the last day before school starts, but it's not the end. We're just beginning."

We replied in true Tiger form, "Grrrr-eat!"

CHAPTER EIGHT

Amphibians

I could see the bath house at Larkspur Lake from the bus window. It looked forlorn without a collection of bikes around it, and even the reds and oranges of the maple trees couldn't cheer up the drab cinder block. The bus lurched ahead toward its next stop.

It had been a hard first two weeks back at school. I hardly ever saw anyone else from the Tigers, and there was a new distance between Terry and me that I didn't understand. As I rode the bus, I tried to imagine each person in the Tigers somewhere in town and wondered if they were missing the group also. I felt so cut off from the others.

The bus came to a stop and a handful of kids got off. One of them was Maritza. She turned around to wave at me. We'd invented a new kind of hand signal, a wave that looked more like a mouth opening. It was a silent Tiger growl.

I watched as she headed down the road. Then the bus went into gear, and we started around the curves and bends that led to my stop. Already, after two weeks of riding, I felt I knew every whine, every jiggle, every sputter the bus made along the route.

"Cassie, I've got to tell you, that signal you make with Maritza really looks kind of dumb," Terry whispered to me. "People will wonder what you're doing."

The bus might as well have rolled over, I was so shocked to hear her say that. "Well, I don't think so," I mustered. Then I turned back in my seat and folded my arms.

"Besides, it's like her parents come from another country."

"Puerto Rico isn't exactly another country," I said.

"You know what I mean. She looks different. I don't know, so foreign, so...."

I didn't let her finish. I could feel my whole body churning. "Maritza's wonderful," I shot back at her. I was so angry that I couldn't get out all the words I wanted to say: Foreign? That's not a put-down! Maritza looks beautiful. Who says everyone has to look alike!

"Well, I'm Polish," I said. "Do I look different to you? Do you not want to talk to me?"

It took tremendous willpower not to start screaming at her right there on the bus. I stood up and eased past her to the aisle. My stop was coming soon.

"Hey back there, sit down. Wait until the bus stops," said the bus driver. Terry shoved over into the window seat, and I sat down again, hugging the aisle arm rest and creating as much distance from her as I could.

"I didn't know you'd get so upset," Terry said in a voice that I imagined meant, "Why are you getting upset over such a little thing?" Then she continued, "I mean, everyone knows Maritza has an accent."

"Big deal." My blood was boiling. Whoever invented that phrase knew just what I felt at that moment.

I shot out of my seat just as the brakes ground to a stop. I was the first person out the door. I slung my backpack on my shoulders and jogged up the road until I got to our driveway. Then I let the tears come.

"Terry! How can you be like that!" I exploded angrily.

I wished she was right there to hear exactly what I thought. I went into the house, paced back and forth, and collapsed in a chair. Sneakers jumped onto my lap but I pushed her back down again. I felt the impulse to call somebody, but the person I always call at times like that is Terry.

In a few minutes, Jill came in the door. She'd been on the same bus. "What's up, kitten?" she said. It was a name she used to call me when I was much younger.

I took one look at her face bending over me, and I felt my tears ready to fall again. She put out her arms and gave me a hug—and the tears spilled out.

"I hate everything. Everything!" I cried.

"Did something happen with Terry?" Jill asked. "I thought I noticed something on the bus." I tried to talk but hard sobs welled up in my throat. She just held me until I was able to speak.

"She's so changed…ever since this summer. I don't know. I just feel like I don't have a best friend anymore…. And she said mean things about Maritza. I couldn't stand it."

"Maybe she's jealous because Maritza's your closest friend in the Tigers."

"That's no excuse for what she said."

"Or maybe she's mad because her father wouldn't let her join," Jill offered.

"I don't think so. It's almost the opposite of that. It feels like she doesn't care about anything. Or at least not the things that matter to me. All she cares about is this one girl Sharon liking her. Sharon's one of those real popular girls, and when I hear them giggling together, I want to throw up." I made a face. "And I hate school!" I got up to get a kleenex and blow my nose.

Jill opened up the refrigerator and poured two tall glasses of cider for us. "Welcome to the club," she said.

I took some sips of cider. "School is blech. I hate being the youngest kids in the building. I only like one of my teachers, and I didn't get the art teacher I wanted. Miss

Leamon only takes one of the eighth grade classes, and it's not mine. I've got a new teacher who is really into cartooning. I don't think he likes my style at all."

I thought about the portfolio I'd bought and all the time I'd spent picking out the drawings to go into it. I hadn't even showed it to him yet because I was afraid of what he might say. When he gave comments on kids' art work, he always seemed to have his mind on something else, as if he thought it was an insult for someone like him to be teaching a bunch of eighth graders. Art class was nothing like the Tigers.

"And I miss our group. We're mostly in different grades, so I never get to see anybody anymore." I let out a long sigh. "After the Tigers, who wants to go back to school?!"

Jill laughed. "Are you hungry?" she asked. I nodded. "Well, I'll go foraging in our cupboards." She opened up a cupboard door. Nothing here." She opened up another one. "And a great big nothing here—oh, correction, one thin granola bar. Want to split it?"

I opened my mouth wide, and she gave me half. As I looked at Jill, I thought, some good things have happened since the group. I don't remember ever being able to talk this way with her before.

She sat down next to me at the table. Usually when we're talking together, she seems to be concentrating more about how her hair looks or who's going to call on the phone, but today she was looking right at me and seemed to be listening to every word I said.

"Want to hear more?"

"Sure. Tell me your hundred reasons for hating Frontier High. I'll give you a hundred more."

"This isn't about school, it's about Terry. You know on the bus, when you saw Terry and me arguing?" She nodded. "It was because Terry started putting Maritza down, and it made me sick. She acted like everybody is supposed to be white like her, and if you're not, you don't count." I felt my anger returning at full boil. "I can't believe how snotty she was. I hated hearing her talk like that! I really wanted to hit her." I looked over at Jill to see her reaction. "Right there on the bus, me, who's so into peace, wanted to hit her. Weird, huh?"

"Well, you've slugged Sam lots of times."

"Yeah, but this is Terry, and I wasn't in a peace group then. I felt on fire. I felt like there was a bomb inside me and I was going to let it explode."

"Cassie, it's okay you were angry. You didn't actually hit her."

"But I wanted to."

"Well, I think you did great. I don't blame you for being furious."

I heaved another sigh.

"And I like the way you spoke up. Hey, Cass, maybe you could do a drawing about it."

"What do you mean?" I don't like it when people give me suggestions about what to draw.

"You could draw how the world will be when people stop doing racist things."

"You sound like Mom."

"Well?"

I thought it would make a good drawing, but I knew tonight I wasn't ready to draw or do much of anything. "Maybe I'll try it sometime." I just wanted to be up in my room, hugging Sneakers and staring at the ceiling. I took my half-finished glass of cider and started upstairs. Part way down the hall I turned around. "Jill?"

She looked up.

I felt a little shy as I called to her, "Thanks."

"Sure, kitten." Upstairs, I tracked Sneakers down, and we spent a long time cuddling. I kept hoping I'd get a phone call from Terry.

After dinner the phone rang, and it was for me, but it wasn't Terry. "Hi, Cassie." It was wonderful to hear Treena's voice. "I don't know about you, but I'm going cold turkey without the Tigers. I can't wait until October to meet again."

"I agree."

"So the Awesome Threesome has gone into action. We got Reverend Ames to let us use the church every Thursday afternoon. And we're going to try to get the Tigers declared an official club at school. Want to come this Thursday and do some drawing?"

"Do I ever." I put down the phone and spun around. I dashed down the hall to the kitchen where Dad and Jill were finishing the dishes.

"Our group is meeting again! Soon!" I told them.

"So Planet Z is back," said my father. Once he has a joke with me, he repeats it over and over. He dried his hands and gave me a hug.

"Want to come, Jill?" I asked. As the words tumbled out, I suddenly had second thoughts. It was my group now. I didn't want to be treated like someone's younger sister.

"Maybe. But I don't really like to draw that much."

"There's probably other things you could do," said Dad. "Right, Cassie?"

"Yeah," I said hesitantly.

"Like what?" asked Jill.

"They'll need to make posters, plan out how to put the display together, I don't know. Deal with unruly members?" Dad handed Jill a stack of dinner plates, and she lifted them onto the shelf.

I grabbed a handful of silverware and started to sort it. I wasn't sure I wanted her there, but it didn't make sense to be so exclusive about a peace group.

"I guess Zack would be glad if I showed up," said Jill as she fingered the beads in her coral bracelet. "Last thing I heard, your group was pretty small."

"Not that small. But why don't you come along? At least for one meeting. It'll be fun."

"I'll give it a try."

When the bus stopped in the middle of town Thursday, Jill and I and a dozen others got out. Treena had spread the word to lots of different kids. I couldn't help hoping that by some miracle Terry would be joining us, but she had gotten off at her usual stop. We didn't even wave to each other.

Our bus had been the last one to leave the school. I expected to find other people inside the church building when we got there. I didn't expect to count over thirty.

There was a place to sit next to April, but I looked for Maritza. She saw me and moved over on the rug to make space. There was no way I was going to tell her what Terry had said about her. It would only make everything worse.

"Can you spend the night at my house Saturday?" I said, "I mean, *Puedes quedarte en casa el sábado por la noche*?" I wanted her to see my progress in Spanish class.

"*Si, le preguntare a mami.* I'll ask my mother."

"*Bien*," I answered.

Maritza smiled at me. "*No puedo esperar.*"

"*¿Qué?*"

"I said, 'I can't wait.'"

Zack was waving his hands to try and get people's attention. He had all of us go around the room and say what we were interested in doing for the display. Jill wasn't the only new person who wanted to do other things besides drawing. Zack scribbled down what everyone said on a sheet of paper.

He looked around the room. Kisha and two of her friends from sixth grade were sitting on the piano bench. Treena was next to Arnold the Tiger. A dozen of us were in the chairs, and a dozen more were sprawled all over the rug. "Now how are we going to do this? I guess we should get into smaller groups."

"I've got the answer to what we need here," said Riley. "It begins with c, has two m's and two t's, and almost rhymes with Riley."

"Oh brother," said April. "It must be some kind of food." She flung back her long black hair.

"Nope."

"I've got it now. Committee. Right?" said April.

"That's right. And your prize is you get to head the first one."

"Ick. No thanks."

"Come on April," said Treena. "How about publicity? I'll do it with you. I have an idea for the poster."

Riley drew himself up taller and gave them a look of approval just the way Mr. Greenwald, our principal, would do it. He pinched his face in, smiled, and pretended to hold his lapels. Maritza and I laughed.

"Okay, okay, no one can escape me." Riley pointed his finger and scanned the room as if it was a search light. He looked like a detective. When he pointed to Ned, he said, "You! Where were you the night of the twenty-fifth?"

"Okay, Riley, what do you want me to do?" said Ned.

"I don't know. What else do we need, Zack?"

"We've got to get tables and bulletin boards to put the exhibit together," he said. "Actually, I wouldn't mind doing that."

"Off the hook this time, Ned," said Riley. "Who'll be on Zack's committee?"

It was no surprise to me that Jill was one of the kids who raised her hand.

"I'll work on labels for the drawings," said Kisha. "We might want to put words with some of them, you know, for an explanation." She pointed to her two friends. "We could work together and interview other kids to see what they wanted us to write."

"Very cunning and clever," said Riley. "We'll call yours the Wordsworth Committee." He was getting into the spirit even more.

Kisha's friends giggled, and I heard one whisper, "Is he always like this?"

"Now we need a Paramount Pictures committee to put the drawings into a brilliant thematic design."

"That's got to be Louisa's. It sounds like her specialty," said Zack.

"I think it's unanimous. Louisa, you're our nominee,"

said Riley switching into a radio announcer's voice.

"Okay, I accept," said Louisa reluctantly.

"What about the 'I hate committees' committee," asked Ned, "for those of us who just want to draw and do nothing else."

"Ingenious," Riley responded. "There's got to be a committee to suit every need. So be it. Let the 'I hate committees' committee be written into the records."

That was the committee I joined. It seemed a safe one, but before I knew it, Zack was dividing it in half. He asked me to take the youngest new kids and explain about the project.

We had to spread out into the smaller Sunday School rooms to work. I went with six of the new kids to a room just big enough to fit a table, some chairs, and a shelf. There were two little windows near the ceiling. As I turned on the lights and invited the group to sit down, I tried not to think about how much it looked like a dungeon cell.

"Look at this! A sword," said one young boy, and he grabbed a cardboard tube and started swinging it at his brother, Derek.

Luckily, Derek took the tube away from him and told him to sit down. Derek is someone I've known since kindergarten. Last year, Terry had a crush on him. It was funny to see him talking to his brother. I could remember when he used to run around our classroom with toy guns.

As his younger brother Stevie got settled in his chair, Derek flashed me a look that I interpreted to mean, "I have no idea what Stevie will do next, but I'll do my best to stop him when he does it."

I tried to remember what Zack did when he started our group, and I asked everyone to say their name and what grade they were in. That went okay, and then I tried to describe the art exhibit we were making.

"We draw pictures of what a peaceful world would be like," I began. I looked around the room to see if I was being clear and was met by blank faces. "Like we imagine what we'd like to have happen in Larkspur by the time we're adults." Still nothing more than glazed-over looks. "Here's an idea. You could draw the kind of school you'd like to go to—"

"No schools!" yelled Stevie, Derek's brother.

"I suppose you could draw that." Somehow it wasn't turning out the way I wanted it to. "How about for today if you all draw whatever you like drawing best," I finished. "Okay?"

Heads nodded. I handed out paper and pencils, explained where we kept the art supplies, and they began to work.

I knew right away what Derek would draw—rocket ships. He's been drawing the same types of things as long as I've known him. Rockets, planes dropping bombs, machine guns, people chasing each other, all carefully drawn with a lot of detail. In fact, one of my memories from first grade is of sitting across from him in the lunchroom. He and one of his friends were pretending their milk cartons were battleships. With their straws, they bombed each other's milk cartons until there were puddles of milk all over their trays. I remember thinking, "Why do they enjoy doing this?"

Now here I was watching both Derek and Stevie cover their papers with rockets and guns. Derek added a sign to his drawing that said, "No more bombs," but the whole thing seemed just an excuse to draw bombs going off.

I opened up my folder and fiddled with an unfinished drawing, but it was hard to concentrate. Then out of the blue, I took a new sheet of paper and drew one of the polliwogs down at the stream. I drew it climbing out of the water for the first time. It looked confused, as if it couldn't get used to being on the land after living only in the stream.

That's how I feel, I thought. I'm a puny polliwog. I don't know how to describe what peace is, or help people imagine it. How can we imagine something we haven't seen? I'm an amphibian. All I've known is the water, and now I've got to climb out and breathe air for the first time. I have no idea what happens from here.

Stevie finished quickly and began folding blank paper into paper airplanes.

Why did he come? I wondered. Does he really want things to change as much as I do? I thought a moment. He must. I guess he's just stumbling around the same as I am.

I asked Stevie to come with me. While he was fooling around in the hallway, I stopped at the bookshelf by Arnold the Tiger and picked up an envelope marked "Snacks" that was filled with change. I wrote my name, the date, and took out $1.50 and wrote it down. Then Stevie and I walked across the street to Gus's and bought a pack of molasses cookies for our small group. I figured I could justify the money because we needed it, or at least I did.

When we came back, Stevie passed the cookies around the table, and we all sat munching together. Their faces no longer looked new and strange to me. Maybe we were all like a bunch of polliwogs trying to figure out how to become frogs, how to leap and jump.

"Can I come back next week?" Stevie asked.

"Sure. You're an official member of the group now," I told him.

When we finished up and I walked into the corridor, I saw Jill talking with Zack. They came over to me.

"Cass, how did your group for those new kids go?" Jill asked.

"I don't know. Okay, I guess." I couldn't think about it. I was thinking about the way they were standing together. If I didn't have a crush on Zack, why did it bother me so much? I wished I could call up Terry and talk to her about it.

"I bet you did great," Zack added. "Like I said before, we couldn't have the Tigers without you."

I sort of smiled and took my time walking down the church stairs trying to act casual like everything was okay. But I couldn't wait to talk to Jill.

Later that evening when Sam was already up in his room, I knocked on her door. "So how did you like the Tigers?" I asked.

"Okay," she said as she finished doing sit-ups on her fuzzy white rug.

"You don't mind not doing art work?"

"Naw. It's okay with me." She moved into doing side stretches.

I decided to just leap and ask her. "Think you'll be going out with Zack now?" I wanted to make her promise she wouldn't. After all, he was like part of our family.

Jill paused and looked at me. "Just because we're in the same group? You know I'm going out with Eddie."

"But he's in college. So I thought you might want to go out with Zack."

"No way," she said, almost too strongly. "Anyway," she started into her toe touches, "Zack's too young for me."

I didn't argue and say, "What does one year younger matter?" I had the answer I wanted. "So I'll see you there next week," I said.

"Yeah, sure. I'll be going next week." Maybe she'd like the group. I knew she hated high school now with all her friends gone. Maybe the Tigers could be a haven for her, too.

CHAPTER NINE

The Wall

There had been a wall between Terry and me for over a week. We weren't talking to each other at school, and I was afraid to call her.

"The phone's free. You can reach Terry now," my mother called. She'd just finished a long phone conversation after dinner.

"That's okay," I said, and stayed in my room. My mother didn't think anything of it. I suppose she thought I'd been over at Terry's house that afternoon. It took several days before my family figured out that Terry and I were actively avoiding each other.

At school, I knew where Terry was every moment—which classroom she was in, whether I was about to pass her in the hall, who she was talking to at lunch—but now, instead of looking for her, I made sure to turn the other way. I felt worse and worse, but I didn't know how to stop it. Each time I avoided saying "hi," each time I took a late bus home, each time I didn't pick up the receiver and dial her number made it easier to keep things the way they were. It was turning into a cold war between us.

When I saw Terry talking to Sharon at lunch, I imagined

she was saying bad things about me, and I began gathering words, like stones, to throw back at her. I was so caught up in figuring out the possible mean things I might hear, and the meaner things I would say in response, that my head was always filled with terrible thoughts.

I spent a lot of time at home in my room with the door closed. I'd think things like, "I'm sure Terry likes Sharon better than me. She probably doesn't even like me anymore. Who cares anyway? All she ever talks about is Johnnie." Words like that kept repeating inside my head, and I couldn't chase them away. The more I said them to myself, the more I believed them.

I convinced myself that she probably thought the Tigers were stupid and then got mad at her about that. It sort of made me feel safe to have things ready to say back at her, but it mostly made me feel weighed down with all those stones ready to throw.

That next Thursday before our group, I couldn't wait for the last class of the day to be over. It was math, and it was the only class that Terry and I were in together. Sharon was in it, too. If I looked at the teacher, Mr. Barker, writing on the board, both of them were directly in my line of vision, so I mostly looked out of the window and watched squirrels chasing each other in the oak trees.

Suddenly I remembered a section in Zack's notebook called, "What Is an Enemy?" One of the things he'd said was when someone becomes your enemy, you begin to look at him or her differently. It was true. I looked at the back of Terry's head. I could see the wave of her curls, and I told myself her hair looked too neat. Before, I would have thought only good things about her. Now, only criticisms came into my head. Instead of thinking, "That blouse looks new," I thought, "Terry acts so conceited about her new clothes." I had to admit that I was turning my best friend into my enemy.

How could I stop it? I wasn't sure, but now that I'd figured out what I was doing, I felt pretty awful about it. So I promised myself that I would do something that day to try to reverse things between us and help take down the wall.

Out of the corner of my eye, I saw Mr. Barker striding angrily up the aisle. "Okay, Miss Cameron, pass that note over to me." He reached out his hand. Terry quickly gave him the note Sharon had just thrown to her. Then she ducked low in her seat.

Mr. Barker opened it and held it up for the rest of the class to see, the way he does with every note he catches.

It was a drawing. Sharon had made a picture of a tiger's face with a purposely ugly expression. A caption read, "The Tigers have bombs on the brain. Keep out!"

Some kids snickered, but no one really laughed hard. If anything, it was a stupid thing for Sharon to do. With all the new kids who had just joined, it seemed to me it was going to become a really popular club at school.

I was furious. All my good intentions of a minute ago suddenly flew right out the window. Terry and Sharon blurred into one in my mind. Here was proof that Terry really did hate the Tigers after all. Why else would Sharon think she would laugh at the note? This time when the bell rang, I wanted them to notice me when I walked past. I clenched my teeth so they'd know I was really angry.

When I got to the church, I was relieved when Ned hit me with a handful of leaves. I wanted to be in a fight. I ran after him and got him back. Ned and Derek picked up armfuls of leaves and backed me up against the church. Red, yellow, and brown leaves tumbled over me like a rainshower.

Then Kisha, Shari, and Maritza came running and helped me chase the two who had just showered me. We followed them to the pine grove where Ned and Derek each ran a different way. Kisha and I followed after Ned. He ran completely around the building and then ducked into the church. Kisha and I stood on either side of the door with our arms full of leaves. We stood there waiting, trying to hold in our laughter. He didn't come. We laughed harder. We'd get the best of him.

As the large, wrought-iron doorknob turned, Kisha and I got ready. We were hidden behind shrubs so Ned couldn't see us if he just peeked out.

We were so quiet, we could hear the footsteps. By the time I saw the pair of fancy black shoes, it was too late. We had already covered Mrs. Fairchild with leaves. I recognized her immediately. She's one of the deaconesses of the church. She brings the church bulletin to be printed every week, and she complains if there's even one tiny smudge on any of the pages.

Ned came out of the door looking a little sheepish. "I guess those were supposed to be for me," he explained.

"Well," sputtered Mrs. Fairchild. "You certainly surprised me." She looked at me and then over at Kisha. She tried to be a good sport about it and began brushing leaves off her clothes and out of her hair. But her sweater was one of those kind that hangs onto things, and little leaf pieces stuck all over it.

"We're so sorry," said Kisha.

"Can we help?" I asked.

"No, no. I'll do it." Mrs. Fairchild began to pick off the pieces, but the leaves were so dry and brittle that the job was harder than it looked.

I racked my brain for what to do. "We could come over tonight and help clean your sweater." I wondered if she would mention this to my parents.

"Thank you, no," she said stiffly. "I'm late right now to pick up my husband. We have a party to go to." With that, she hurried off.

The six of us sat on the steps and tried to figure out what to do next. Would she report us to the church and have the whole group kicked out of the building? Would she just forget about it? Maybe she'd remember being our age and having leaf fights herself.

We slowly climbed the steps and told the rest of our

group what had happened. I guess it was good we talked about it. Just shrugging our shoulders and putting it out of our minds was tempting. But we couldn't. It felt like now we were in the peace group, everything we did had to matter.

It was Treena who came up with a great suggestion. She said we should make Mrs. Fairchild a bouquet of bright leaves and fall flowers, if we could find any, and write her a note. So Ned and Kisha and I spent the rest of the afternoon gathering the most brilliant maple leaves we could find. Maritza helped, too, and she found some late-blooming daisies. We went over to Gus's store and got a small piece of wire from him to wrap the stems. Then we wrote the note and apologized and said we hoped that the leaves came off her sweater okay. It was actually fun doing all of that. But the fun stopped when we tried to decide who would bring it to her house.

"You live closest to her, Cassie," Ned said.

"I know, but why don't we just leave it for her at the church."

"What if she doesn't come back here until Sunday and it looks all wilted?" Maritza pointed out. We kind of chuckled at the thought of her finding it like that and getting even madder at us.

"Okay, I'll take it there on my bike," I gave in, "but I won't ring the doorbell. I'll just leave it in the mailbox."

Everyone was relieved to have it settled, and as soon as I got home, I started off on my bike before dinner so I could leave the bouquet at her house before she returned from the party. As I pedaled closer, a lump grew in my throat. I had to pass Terry's house on the way. I resolved to hunch my shoulders and put my head down and pedal as fast as I could.

I passed Louisa's house and the meadow. Then, when Terry's house appeared around the bend, I looked down at the road, biked hard, and pretended it wasn't even there. When I got to the Fairchild's, sure enough, their car was gone. I placed the bouquet so that it peeked out of the mailbox and would be easy to spot. Then I swung my leg around and got back on my bike. It had been easier than I had expected. I felt like whistling. This peacemaking stuff wasn't so difficult after all. She'd just see the note, and everything would be patched up.

I turned my bike around and started for home, but up ahead I saw a surprise. There was Terry raking leaves in her front yard. There was no way I could avoid her.

I stopped. My heart was pounding. This whole fight is her fault, I told myself, but I knew it wasn't true. Remember what happened in math class! I imagined myself going up to Terry and yelling at her. That thought felt so mean, it scared me. I tried to rope in my anger like a bucking steer at a rodeo.

I pedaled slowly, getting closer.

I'll just go past her. Probably she won't notice me, I lied to myself. Then for a moment, I was in Terry's shoes. How would she feel to see me ride by? Maybe she wants to stop this war, too.

The full craziness of the situation hit me. Here I was drawing pictures of peace every chance I got, and meanwhile I was keeping my own war going. If I wanted the Americans and Russians to make peace, didn't I have to learn how to do it, too? How could I expect countries to solve problems if I couldn't settle this argument with Terry?

"Hi," I called out. Terry turned in my direction. She didn't seem startled to hear my voice. Maybe she'd noticed me coming and had fought with herself not to run inside.

"Hi," she responded. It was a relief to finally hear her voice. There were no sharp edges to it.

I half looked at her and half looked at the ground. "What are you doing?" I asked. It was a dumb thing to say.

"Nothing much." It was then I noticed her eyes were red from crying. I had to know what was wrong.

"Want to talk?" I asked, hoping she'd say yes.

"I guess so, but not inside."

"What about the shed?" It was one of our special places. It's way in the back of her yard and looks out on her fir trees.

We didn't speak as we walked together. Our feet made a crunching sound through the leaves. I noticed it was getting darker and the sky had a pinkish color from the setting sun. You could feel Halloween around the corner.

As soon as we sat down on the bench outside the shed, Terry spoke out. "Cassie! You rode right by my house without even stopping," she protested. There was a gulp in her voice.

"I did stop."

"I mean ten minutes ago. I saw you out of the window."

"I was going to the Fairchild's place."

"Why?" Then it dawned on me what had happened. It must have taken a lot of courage for Terry to stand outside waiting to see if I'd come by again. I explained to her about my errand.

"I understand that, but why don't you come over here or call me up anymore?"

I could feel myself wanting to counter with, "Well, why don't you...." and held myself back. I didn't want to make things worse. It was like trying to use a muscle that didn't get used much, to hold back my anger and hurt long enough to be able to find out what else I wanted to say.

"Terry," I began. I tried to search for the right words; I was near tears, too. "I miss you." My tears started to tumble. "I'm sorry I avoided you."

"You are?"

"Yes."

"You don't hate me?" she asked. "I was so afraid after what happened with the note today. I had to wait outside just now to tell you. I never say bad things about the Tigers. That's just Sharon, not me. I think it's a *great* group, Cassie." She was crying now, too.

I liked hearing that familiar rise in her voice. "Of course I don't hate you, Terry. I was really mad, but that's changed."

126

I took out a crumpled kleenex from my pocket and blew my nose. She wiped her eyes. I wanted to just forget everything I was going to say. I knew I didn't want to yell the way I had sometimes imagined doing in my mind. But I had to say more.

I looked up. "Can I tell you some of the things that have bothered me?"

She looked away. "I've really dreaded this," she said.

"I know. Me, too."

"I guess we could take turns. Okay, I'm ready. Tell me." Terry stiffened up and looked scared.

I hated to see that frightened look on her face. "Terry, the whole time I'm talking, will you remember that you're my best friend?"

"I will."

I took a deep breath. "Do you remember when you said Maritza is different?"

She nodded. Her eyes were wide. At least she wasn't going to act like it didn't happen.

"Well, I was really furious. The idea that you would put anybody down, but especially Maritza, because she's not exactly like you—as if you're the 'normal' one—it's just not right. I hate that! And I didn't expect that you would do that kind of thing!" I was saying it really strongly but not so strongly that she wouldn't listen to me. My arms and shoulders were tight. "Do you know what I mean?"

"Yeah," said Terry. One arm was crossed and she was hiding her face in her other hand. "It was a crummy thing for me to say. I don't know why I did it."

"You thought about it?" I was so relieved that she wasn't trying to defend herself or make excuses.

"Yeah, of course I thought about it. That was the day we stopped talking to each other."

I took in a long breath and let it out. "Maritza's really my friend now. And I don't want you to even think things like that ever again."

"I'm trying to tell you I feel bad about it. Of course it's

not going to happen again. It was a mistake."

That was such a big step, I almost wanted to stop right there. "There's other things I've got to say," I told her reluctantly. I had to bring it all up now, or it would just be stuck inside me. "Maybe this part is silly, but I really got tired of hearing stories about Johnnie. You never noticed how I was feeling, like I didn't matter to you. It seemed like all you wanted to do was talk about him."

I paused. I was talking pretty fast because I was afraid. I looked at Terry's eyes. She was still listening really closely.

"And the hardest thing right now," I continued, "is that you can't be in the Tigers. I can tell you're not even interested, and that makes it even worse. And now you spend all your time with Sharon." The memories of the week prickled inside me. "It feels like you like her better than you do me."

"Well I don't."

We both paused. I was glad she said that, but I could hear the anger mixed in with it.

Terry put her hands on her hips. "You know, I feel left out when you're off with Maritza or somebody else from the Tigers. It used to be we only had jokes with each other. And it seems like you put the Tigers ahead of our friendship. I mean, you know I can't join. Why is it more important for you to be there than with me?"

Suddenly my anger was rising again. I felt the knot between us grow tighter. I wanted Treena to rush in with the magic scissors and free us.

"Magic scissors," I said.

"*What?*"

"I'm getting mad again, and I don't know what to do."

"Well, I'm mad, too, Cassie, and you've got to give me a longer time to talk." I knew she was right, but I hated to hear it. I realized I felt scared to sit there and really listen—just like Terry had been afraid to listen to me.

"It's hard to see you go off with the Tigers all the time. And even if my father let me join, you know I can't draw.

You're the artist and I'm not. How *could* I join the group?"

I'd never thought about it like that before.

"And if I did join," Terry continued, "you'd probably rather be with the other kids than with me, and then I'd feel even worse. I hardly know anybody in it."

I wanted to leap in and interrupt her, but I held myself back. Terry needed to talk without being stopped, just like I had.

"There's one more thing," said Terry, "I broke up with Johnnie. We had a really stupid fight on the phone, and he hung up on me. So then I wrote him an angry letter, and I told him he better call me right back, but he didn't. What a jerk he turned out to be."

"Oh, Terry! I wish I could have been there to talk with you. That must have been terrible." As much as I didn't like Johnnie, it still mattered to me what happened to her.

"It wasn't as bad as I expected. I mean, I only knew him four weeks. I've known you eight years, Cassie. I was more upset about you."

"You were?"

"Of course."

"I should have brought you that bouquet with the apology note. Should I go back to the Fairchild's and take it from their mailbox?"

She grinned, and I stood up. It had become completely dark outside. The house in the distance looked like a jack o'lantern. We walked back along the path. I was walking so fast I was practically skipping. We'd done what seemed impossible. We'd made it through our very worst fight ever.

"Next time we're angry, do you want to tell each other sooner?" she asked me.

"Yeah, it's so scary, but I'll try."

When we went inside the Cameron's house, there was an extra place setting already there for me at the dinner table.

"I took care of it," Pinky said.

"What do you mean?" Terry asked her.

She pursed her lips and answered with a serious air, "I put two and two together."

"Meaning what?"

"Meaning that I saw Cassie's bike. And when her parents called, I told them she was here and I figured she'd be staying for dinner."

"Good work," Terry said. She hadn't said words like that to Pinky in a long time.

Everyone seemed especially nice to us that night. Mrs. Cameron kept offering me seconds, and Mr. Cameron didn't ask me any questions about school.

"See you tomorrow," I called to Terry at the door. "Save me a seat next to you on the bus."

"Okay," she answered. Terry stood outside watching me, and we waved at each other until I rounded the curve out of sight. I switched on my bicycle light and it shone a little funnel of brightness over the road. The tall grass looked brown and frosty.

I passed by the meadow and thought of the animals living there who were huddling in the cold. I sent hellos winging out to them. I wondered if the spider was still alive. If she could have followed me around today, she would have been proud of me.

As I biked past Louisa's house and turned into our driveway, the world felt friendlier and safer than I'd ever known it before.

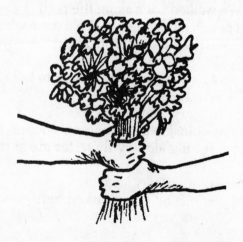

CHAPTER TEN

Origami Cranes

It was a cold, rainy Sunday, just after Halloween. The sky was pearly gray. I put on my poncho and rain boots and hiked to the meadow. The willow tree still had its leaves, but they were yellow. The spots where I knew flowers had once grown were now dry stalks of brown.

I liked tramping around. I went into the pine forest, past the clearing where I'd seen the spider and on to the stream. Everything looked silver: the rocks, the water, the bare trees, the sky. In the distance across the stream, I could see more silver gray: a stone wall I forget about when the leaves are on the trees.

I crossed the stream, climbed up the embankment, and hiked to the wall. It turned out to be farther away than I had expected. When I got there, I was huffing and puffing. I sat down where two edges of the wall made a corner. Here, two yards met. The wall enclosed one, and there was an open path in the other. I took it and followed it deeper into the property until I saw the roof of a building through the trees. It was the house where the potter lived, the house that Terry and I had always wanted to visit. I saw a balcony along one side and bubble-shaped sky lights on the roof.

I was tempted to go farther, but I turned back, walking alongside the wall to return to the stream. As I looked over the wall I suddenly realized that that yard belonged to the hermit, the man who hardly ever left his house. I began to walk faster. It seemed silly to be so scared of meeting him, but I've always been afraid of his place. I hurried along back to the stream.

As I came out of the pine forest and into the open meadow, the rain changed from a drizzle to a downpour. I snapped the sides of my poncho for more protection from the rain and walked home.

"You got a phone call while you were out," said Sam.

"From who?" It couldn't have been Terry. She was visiting her relatives. Maybe Maritza? I'd stayed over at her house on Friday night.

"It was Langston." I noticed Sam's expression. He was trying to keep his usual bored look on his face, but he seemed surprised that his friend was calling me. "He said there was a Tigers' meeting at his house this afternoon."

"When?"

"Soon. In a half an hour. You guys even get together on weekends?"

"Why not?"

"I don't know. I'd rather do other things. Since when was he part of the Tigers?"

"Since school started, I think."

"Well, he invited all three of us," he added quickly. "But I told him Jill's at work, and that I wasn't interested."

"Did you tell him I'd be there?"

"Are you kidding? Of course. I know how addicted you are. I don't think you've missed a meeting yet."

After a plate of hot chili, I put my poncho on again and got ready to walk. It was too slippery for biking, and Langston lives less than a mile away. He lives right next door to the potter's house, down the back road before you head up toward Zack's place. I wanted to ask him what it looks like inside. Dad says I should consider being an architect because I'm so interested in houses. I remembered that Langston's house looked pretty special from the outside, too, with a circular window on the front door.

It was so misty that it seemed the sky had closed over like a bowl. I trudged over the wooden walkway that goes up to Langston's front door and leaned over to watch the water rush along in the stream underneath. As I stood up again, there she was, Mrs. Yutsumi, the potter, walking along in a tan raincoat.

To my surprise, she also turned in from the road and came up the walkway. "Are you coming here for the peace group, too?" she asked me.

"Yes." I was a little shocked to be standing right there talking to her. She's one of the most famous artists from Larkspur. My parents said that people came from all over the country to buy her pottery and that her pieces are in museums. She looked about my mother's age.

When we came in the door, Shari and Kisha and about eight others were there, but not Zack. He was away for the weekend in Syracuse. And only two-thirds of the Awesome Threesome had made it. Treena was home helping her family sell squash and bags of onions at their roadside stand.

"I'll take your poncho," said Langston. He hung it up on a peg in the hallway. "So Sam couldn't leave his palace in the attic to come over?" Langston smiled an easy smile.

"Naw. Not for the Tigers."

As I walked into the room, I felt I was entering a place of excitement. From the large picture window in Langston's living room, the world outside was a flat, misty gray, but inside the warm brown patterns in the fabrics on the walls seemed to set the room in motion. There were instruments on the top of the book shelves: drums of metal and of wood, hollow gourds strung with shells, strings of bells, and large metal gongs. And each wall had several framed photographs. One photo showed Langston with Mrs. Yutsumi and her two sons. They were laughing as waves crashed around them.

Langston watched me take it all in. "My mother likes to travel," he said. "Sometimes Yukiko's family comes with us."

"What does your mother teach at the university?" I asked.

"Afro-Am. Afro-American Studies. And she does some theater, too."

"Where's Vera?" asked Mrs. Yutsumi. "Where she usually is? Working in the darkroom, right?"

"Yeah. She's developing some photos for a deadline, but I'm sure she'd want to see you."

"I'll just go back and say hello before we start," she said.

The doorbell rang, and Langston opened the door. He looked out and then pretended to shut the door again. I heard laughter as whoever was on the other side pushed it open. "Langston!" Two older girls who were new to the Tigers came in. I thought they looked familiar, but I couldn't place them at first, except that I knew they were both seniors.

"Well, hey there, Coreena. Hey, Pam. You actually made it."

"Langston, of course we did," said the taller girl. "Your idea of giving directions is to describe every single tree, and, I swear, practically every leaf you're going to pass." She took off her jacket, and it caught on a carved medallion around her neck. She took the necklace off over her cornrowed hair and walked into the room.

When she stood near Riley, I realized she was only a few inches shorter than he. Now I remembered why I knew her. She was Coreena Robinson. Last winter, *The West County Daily* sports page ran a picture of her practically every week. She played center for the basketball team. I'd heard Sam say she had a good chance of getting a sports scholarship to go to college next year. Her playing drew a big crowd.

"How's it going on the old court?" said Riley.

"I'm off the court now," said Coreena. I guess she was sick of talking about basketball. "Langston said this would be fun."

"Fun? If you came here for fun, you're in the wrong place," Riley grinned.

Pam grabbed Riley's arm and tried to twist it around his back. "Stop it! Tell her to behave herself, Coreena. You know I'm just a weakling."

"You got to go easy with Riley," said Coreena, and she pretended she was going to put him into a hammer lock.

I'd heard that Pam also played basketball really well, but she wasn't as famous for it as Coreena. Pam was a few inches shorter, and she stood a little stiffly, while Coreena seemed more relaxed, even proud of her height.

After Riley escaped, Pam noticed me standing there. "Aren't you Jill's sister?" she asked. Her short hair was a silvery color.

"Yeah. Jill would probably have come, too, if she didn't have to work." I was getting used to talking to older kids without feeling as embarrassed as I would have last year.

"At least she didn't say Jill's baby sister," said Coreena coming over. "You're Cassie, aren't you? I was at a party over at your house this summer, but I don't think you were home."

"I think I was hiding in the house," I said.

Langston called for everybody to come into the dining room. The table there was covered with squares of bright art paper: green, turquoise blue, midnight purple, pink, gold. He asked us each to take a piece of paper. Then we sat together on his living room rug, and Langston explained why he had invited us.

"Here's a riddle," he said. "What's flat but can fly?"

"Riley's car," said April.

"I don't have a car."

"Then Riley's feet," said Coreena.

"Very funny."

"Something about this sheet of paper?" Kisha asked.

"Yeah, it's origami paper. You can fold it into paper

peace cranes," said Langston. "I'm just learning to make them myself, but the person who taught me is my mother's best friend, Mrs. Yutsumi. She's over here today to show us how to do it."

"Is she from Japan?" asked Kisha.

"Her grandparents came from Japan," said Langston. "She's third-generation Japanese American."

Just then, the two women came out of the hall, laughing, in the midst of conversation. I liked seeing two grownups who were best friends. Langston's mother had on a long, denim apron to cover her clothes as she worked in the darkroom printing photographs. She had a flame-red scarf over her hair. It looked pretty next to her black curls and chestnut brown skin.

"Here are the Tigers," said Langston proudly, "and this is my mother, Vera Taylor, and our friend, Yukiko Yutsumi." I liked looking back and forth from one to the other. They both seemed happy to be with each other, and so smart and bright.

"Yukiko, I'm going to go back to work. Nice to meet everybody," Mrs. Taylor smiled.

Mrs. Yutsumi sat on a low sofa with the gray, rainy day behind her. Her hair was twisted up and held with a butterfly-shaped barrette made of wood and pearl. "Now to start with, I want you to call me Yukiko, not Mrs. Yutsumi. It's too formal. When Langston told me about your peace display, I thought you might be interested in the origami paper cranes. It's an art my grandmother taught me."

She took a golden sheet of origami paper and began to fold. Her hands coaxed the paper this way and that, molding it like clay. At the very end, the folded triangles suddenly became wings. I gasped.

She smiled at me. "It's beautiful, isn't it? I'll show you all how to do it." And she led us, step by step.

Folding was easy in the beginning. First, boxes. Then, rectangles and triangles. Crisp lines. Next, you folded toward each corner like the shape of a kite. Suddenly, it became three-dimensional. Then, you had to bend the paper in your hands and make a four-pointed star. And after that you gathered up the points of the star together like petals joined into a bud.

I couldn't fold the paper just right on this step. It kept slipping in my hands. Yukiko folded it for me and got me past this point. From here, we creased the petals of the bud shape and they reopened into a form that looked just like a fox. I loved the way the paper continually shifted its shape.

It wasn't a fox for long. Four times you folded it inwards toward the fox's nose. That was when it began to look like a bird. As you made an easy fold upwards, you got ready to make the wings. Inside out it went, and the wings really took form. All that was left was to crease the wings downward and pinch the paper head to form a beak. Beautiful! Like magic, the flat paper had become a paper crane.

I took a piece of silver paper and started on a second crane. It wasn't enough to fold just one.

As I was making the kite-shaped folds, Mrs. Taylor came back in the room. "Yukiko, I'd like to get your opinion on these photos. Could you take a look?"

"We'll let her go for a minute," Langston joked. He pointed to the growing pile of completed cranes in the center of the table. "How do you like them, Mom?"

"Nice. Looks like you got everybody hooked on making these. Maybe you'll be able to get a thousand by January first like you hoped."

When they were out of the room and Langston was helping us with the most difficult parts of folding, Shari asked, "What did your mother mean about making a thousand?"

"Have you heard the story of Sadako of Hiroshima and the thousand paper cranes?" asked April. She unlaced her boots and got more comfortable on the floor.

Hiroshima, Japan. Yukiko's grandparents came from Japan, the country we dropped nuclear bombs on.

"I've heard her tell the story," said Langston.

"Was she in Japan then?" asked Shari.

Kisha gave her a look. "No, she's an American."

Langston seemed uncomfortable. "Look, during World War II, Yukiko's whole family was put in an internment camp."

"What?" said April. "What in the world is that? It sounds terrible."

"You never heard?" said Langston. "All the Japanese Americans were forced into internment camps in the 1940s. Yukiko said one hundred fifteen thousand people were in those camps. She was born in one."

"But why did they have to go there?"

"They were arrested just for being Japanese American. The government was afraid. But they didn't put Italian or German Americans in camps, even though we were at war with those countries, too. The whole thing really gets me." Langston took a photo down from the wall. "Yukiko's family had to live in a horse stall on a race track for a while before they were sent to the camp. This is how big it was. Her whole family had to fit into that small space. Yukiko went back there this summer with my mother to take pictures of it."

I looked at the photo and felt sick. How did such a horrible thing ever happen? Why hadn't I heard of this?

Yukiko returned and saw us looking at the photograph. We were all silent for a moment.

But Shari wanted to speak. "Langston said you had to live there," she said.

"I hope it's okay I got this out," said Langston. "We started talking about the cranes and the war, and I don't know, I just thought of it."

Yukiko nodded. "No, I'm glad you're looking at it." I could tell how much she liked Langston. "That's Santa Anita in that photo. My family had to live there for a few months, but I wasn't born yet. It was when my mother was pregnant with me." She reached for another photo of a low building in the desert. "I was born in this camp.

Manzanar. It was there that my grandmother did a lot of paper crane folding."

"Didn't she have trouble getting paper?" asked April. "It looks like it was in the middle of nowhere."

"She saved any scraps of paper she could find. Gum wrappers. Old newspapers used to wrap food. Others helped her, although it made some people uneasy. Some even told her to stop because the officials didn't want to see anything that had to do with Japan. But she kept on."

I saw images of people sitting on cots, turning gum wrappers into paper cranes. The glittery silver paper in my hands reminded me of the silver foil inside the wrappers. I was in shock.

Kisha filled the silence. "I never knew about the camps."

"They sound gross, like concentration camps," said April.

"I don't have any memories about them. I was three when we left. My family never talked about it when I was growing up, and I wanted to understand more. That's why Langston's mother and I went back to take the photos."

Langston put the pictures back on the wall.

"My grandmother said that the cranes were a sign of hope. In Japan they symbolize long life, and for her, folding the cranes was a reminder that we'd get out of the camps safely some day. When I was about ten, she started to show me all about origami."

Langston said, "I was thinking that we could try to fold a thousand of these cranes."

"That would be perfect for your peace display," said Yukiko. "In art school I got very interested in the story of Sadako. I once did a series of decorations on my pottery all about Sadako and the paper cranes. If she were still alive, we'd be about the same age."

"Will you tell them the story, Yukiko?" he asked.

Yukiko sat forward in her chair with the air of a storyteller, her hands poised. "Sadako was a girl who lived in Hiroshima, Japan. She was just two years old at the time of the nuclear bomb. Sadako and her family survived the bombing, but later they discovered that Sadako had the dreaded disease leukemia." Yukiko used her hands for emphasis as she spoke. "The radiation from the bomb had hurt her bones."

"How old was she then?" Shari asked.

"She was older than you. She was more her age." She pointed to me, and I shuddered.

"One day, her best friend Chizuko came to visit her in the hospital." I thought of Terry and me.

"Chizuko brought a piece of gold origami paper," Yukiko continued, "and she taught Sadako how to fold the paper cranes. 'There is an old story of our people,' Chizuko said. 'If you want something very much and you work very hard and fold one thousand paper cranes, the gods will grant your wish.'"

"Did they fold a thousand cranes?" Shari asked.

"Wait," said Langston.

"Sadako and Chizuko worked very hard. Their families and their friends helped them. Every day after school, children would come to Sadako's bed in the hospital and fold paper cranes. Then they would string them together and hang them above her bed to cheer her up." Yukiko's fingers opened and closed as she described the crane folding.

"Did she get well?" asked Ned.

"No. She was determined not to die, but she had leukemia very bad. So she wished not only for her own life but for all children everywhere to be safe always from nuclear bombs. With each paper crane, she made a wish for peace in the world."

"Is this a true story?" interrupted Shari.

"Yes. It really happened. And she folded six hundred and forty-four paper cranes before she died."

"Oh no," I said suddenly.

"But her friends finished her work so she could be buried with a thousand cranes. And then they made a book of her letters and sent it to people all over Japan. When young people heard her story, they raised money to make a statue of Sadako in the square in Hiroshima."

April sat up and pushed her long hair behind her ears. "My father saw her statue. He said that people from all over the world come there on the anniversary of the bombing. It's on August sixth, isn't it?" Yukiko nodded. "He brought me back a paper crane, but I never knew how to fold one before. My father saw thousands and thousands of cranes hanging from Sadako's statue."

I was glad to hear that. An idea came to me. "Can I take some paper home?" I asked Yukiko.

"Certainly. As much as you want." I picked out ten sheets of paper in different colors and stuck them in a book so they wouldn't get wet or wrinkled.

"So did she get her wish or not?" asked Shari.

"That depends on how you look at it," said Langston. "So far, there hasn't been a nuclear war."

"But we don't exactly have peace." Ned didn't look up from his square of blue paper.

"So why don't we fold a thousand cranes for the art display," said Louisa. "The whole display is a wish for peace."

"Maybe we can have a thousand cranes by next Thursday and surprise Zack," said Shari.

Langston laughed. "We'll be lucky to have a hundred. They take a long time. Anybody else want to take some paper home?"

As we thanked Yukiko, I kept looking at her face. I could feel such strength inside her. I wanted her to meet my mother. Mrs. Taylor came out to say goodbye to us. I thought she and Yukiko and Mom would all like each other.

A car honked. "My mother's here. Want a ride home, Cassie?" Ned asked.

"Can I have one, too?" asked Louisa. We waited while he laced up his boots.

I heard Yukiko speaking to Langston's mother. "Vera,

I just completed my third set of dinner plates, and I've decided that after all of these holiday orders are out of the way, I'm going back to doing pottery for myself. I've done too many plates and bowls that all have to look alike."

"What about the sculptures you talked about doing this summer?"

"The ones about my dreams! That's exactly where I want to start."

"And then we could put them on display with my photos."

Ned was ready. I snapped up my poncho, said goodbye, and ran out to the car with him. I sat in the back seat next to Louisa, carefully cupping a folded crane in my hands. It was green, Terry's favorite color.

After dinner the rain had stopped. I held the crane in one hand and rested it on the handlebars as I biked to Terry's house.

"Hi, Cass. How's the Tigers?"

"Great. We even met today," I said. "And, I have something for you." I brought the crane out from behind my back.

Terry held it in her hand. "Wow, that's excellent!"

"Can I show you how to make it?"

"You know how?" she asked. "Yes. You *have* to."

We sat down on her bed, and I took her through each step, the boxes, the rectangles. Yukiko had given us a diagram in case we forgot the steps. Terry saw the patterns right away. Her long nails creased the paper neatly. She was faster and more accurate at it than me. I'd expected she would be, and I felt happy to see her picking it up so quickly.

When we got to the four-pointed star, the hardest step, she thought a moment, and added an extra backwards fold that made the whole step easier.

"How did you think of that?" I asked her.

"I don't know. It just seemed logical." She zipped through three more cranes in the time it took me to finish two. "I love this," she said.

"Just what I suspected, you're a natural," I told her. She smiled. "Guess who taught me?"

"I don't know."

"Mrs. Yutsumi!"

"You got to meet her? What is she like?"

I shrugged my shoulders. How could I explain? I no longer thought of her as a famous person who turned out bowls like magic. I remembered the musical sound of her voice as she helped us through the hardest parts of the paper folding and the look in her eyes when she found us looking at the photo of the internment camps. "I don't know. I really like her. She said we could call her Yukiko, and she told us that in Japan they take a needle and thread and gather the cranes together on a string. Want to try?"

Terry ran into the kitchen to get her mother's sewing basket. It wasn't as easy as it sounded to string them up. Terry saved out the green crane I'd given her and took the other seven and laced them together with a pink thread. They looked like flowers.

It was the best time to ask my question, but still I hesitated. I was so nervous that I asked instead, "Do you want to hear the story of Sadako that Yukiko told us?"

She did, so I repeated it for her. As I spoke, I felt I could see Sadako's face in her hospital bed, encouraging me, wanting her story told.

"You see, Terry, I've got to work with the Tigers. I've got to do something." Then my real question burst out of me. I had carried it with me for so many weeks now. "I haven't asked you this in a long time, but will you join the group now? We're trying to fold a thousand cranes in time for the peace display, and you could really help."

"Oh, Cass."

"You wouldn't have to do any pictures. You could spend your whole time folding paper cranes."

"I don't know."

"And I'll help you meet the rest of the kids. Plus Derek's in the group now."

144

She laughed at that. "All I can say is I'll think about it. I really will."

We left her room and walked down the hallway together.

"What's that in your hand, Theresa?" asked Pinky. She startled us, she'd appeared so quietly.

Terry held up the green peace crane.

Pinky examined it. "Oh, a bird," she said.

"A bird in the house?" Mrs. Cameron called from the kitchen in alarm. She rushed in and saw the crane. "Why, that's lovely. Where did you get this?"

"Cassie made it for me," Terry told her. "And she taught me how to do it, too."

"Well, girls, why don't you show us?"

We sat down on the Cameron's couch with two pieces of origami paper and went through the steps. Pinky and Mrs. Cameron studied every move. "How is that ever going to become a bird?" Pinky asked at one point. I knew what she meant. I had been surprised, too, the first time I watched Yukiko bring this flat piece of paper to life.

As I left to go home, I looked over my shoulder to discover Mrs. Cameron rearranging the decorations on the mantlepiece to make room for our paper cranes.

CHAPTER ELEVEN

Cassandra

"Daddy, you can't draw. That doesn't look like a horse. That looks like a kite with legs," said Pinky from the den.

"Then you give it a try, Penelope. Push the control button and then letter K and the screen will erase." I heard the faint hum of their computer.

"Daddy's teaching Pinky about computer graphics," said Terry. We were in the Camerons' kitchen trying to create a milkshake that would taste like a banana split. The Camerons have all different kinds of syrups in the door of their refrigerator. We mixed chocolate and strawberry syrup with ice cream and chopped bananas in their blender.

"Cassie, can you come here?" Pinky yelled.

"We're in the middle of something, wait a minute," Terry yelled back. She let the blender whirr and then poured the foaming drink into two tall glasses.

"I think we should add pineapple, too," I said, giving it a taste.

"Cassie, we need you," Pinky howled. I went into the den where she was huddled over the computer terminal with her father. "Daddy's trying to draw, but he doesn't know what he's doing."

"Cassie, have you ever seen a computer do anything like this before?" asked Mr. Cameron. He typed a series of letters to start one of the programs, and a graphic of Snoopy appeared.

"Oh, yeah. Sam used to have one of those on his door."

"Really?" Mr. Cameron typed different letters for another program, and a cartoon figure of the Avenger appeared.

"No, I haven't seen that one before," I said.

"I have a disc here that allows you to create your own pictures. Would you like to give it a try?"

It was fun at first but also frustrating. You could make just one line at a time. Pinky insisted I draw a horse, but she said it didn't look much better than the one her father did.

Mr. Cameron came to my defense. "This isn't Cassie's fault. This program has some built-in limitations. You can't draw curved lines with straight ones anymore than you can put a square peg into a round hole. Right, Cassie?" I nodded in appreciation. "Let me show you an even more interesting program." He typed the words "Design Star" onto the screen, added a few more commands, and then asked me to create a simple pattern.

I made a pattern like leaves. He pushed two buttons, and it turned over on its side. He pushed another combination, and four other leaf shapes appeared on the screen. He pushed a third series, and the whole design doubled in size.

"This is really great," I said. Mr. Cameron looked pleased. He showed me a page in a booklet that listed which buttons to push for which result and let me play with it. I made up a whole new shape like a feather. I blew it up large and then added a bug shape inside of it. At first Pinky couldn't keep her eyes off the screen, but after a few minutes, she lost interest and turned on the television.

"Daddy, I've been meaning to ask you something,"

Terry said after Pinky had moved to the other side of the den.

"What is it, pumpkin pie?"

"Cassie's been wondering if I could join her club."

I winced and stopped working on the computer. I wanted to say to her, "Did you have to put it that way?" I wished I could leave the room, but I guessed it gave her courage to have me right there. I tried to look like I was concentrating on the pattern I was making so I would just blend into the background. I was hanging on every word they said.

"Now which club is this?"

"The Tigers Club."

It seemed to me that Terry's approach might work, but then Pinky chimed in, "You know, Daddy, the *peace* group."

"Oh," he said. "Is that still going?"

"Yes, it's become one of the biggest clubs at school, and I'd really like to go to it."

"Well, Terry, I feel as I did before. What does a group like this have to offer you?"

"But they do all kinds of art work."

"Honey, you know you're not an artist. You have other interests."

"But I really want to be there." Terry's voice was close to tears.

Mr. Cameron paused for a moment and looked at her more closely. Then he went over to his pipe rack and began filling one of his pipes with tobacco. "I'm thinking about what's best for you. Groups like this can get kids all riled up. I wouldn't want the group to give you nightmares."

"But I'll just make paper cranes. I can do that. You know, the cranes. They're the the ones you thought were pretty on our mantlepiece."

Mr. Cameron puffed on his pipe. "You might start with something like paper cranes, but then they'll bring you into something else. You'll get in deeper, and you'll end up all upset. You know how upset you were when we saw that movie at the aquarium this summer about whales. I don't like to see you so worried."

I knew that Terry had started to cry, but I didn't think Mr. Cameron had noticed it yet. "But I want to go," she said. "Tell him, Cassie."

I wanted to run out of the room. Instead, I thought fast. "It's really different, Mr. Cameron. We have lots of jokes. It's not depressing. It's fun. And we draw good ideas for Larkspur. And—I don't know what else to say."

"Let me ask you this. Who's the adult in charge of the group?"

The adult in charge. "We don't have one. We do it ourselves." I imagined Riley posing as our supervisor and shaking Mr. Cameron's hand. What a thought!

"Well, I'm sorry then, honey. I really am. The club as you describe it, Cassie, doesn't sound like a bad one, but there really needs to be an adult supervising."

"But, Daddy, I'm in eighth grade."

"Well, I guess I have to go now," I said. I started for the door.

"I'll come say goodbye," said Terry. Mr. Cameron leaned over the computer and switched it off.

"Can you believe it, Cassie?" Terry said when we got to the hall. "He treats me like a baby."

"Well, I won't give up. We'll find some way for you to be part of the Tigers. You're a tiger at heart. I was proud of the things you said."

"I couldn't have said them if you weren't in the room."

"Here's some more sheets of origami paper I brought you."

"Thanks."

I waved goodbye to the paper cranes on the mantle. "Guard the house," I told them, and Terry laughed.

A week later, on Friday, I passed Terry in the hall after second period, and we both threw notes into each other's hands as usual. I couldn't wait for her to read what I had written. My note said:

> You are invited to an adult-supervised activity this
> afternoon during study hall. Miss Leamon's leading
> a Tigers' class. You've got to come!!!

Miss Leamon was our official club advisor now, just on
paper. We wouldn't let her come to any of our real
meetings at the church. But as far as the school rules went
for clubs, the Awesome Threesome had talked her into
signing as the advisor for the Tigers. She'd taught art at
Frontier for over twenty years.

I wished she was my teacher, but she mostly taught
the oldest grades. I hoped I could get to know her better
and then be able to bring in my whole portfolio to show
her. Louisa had asked her to let us come and work in the
art room during last period, and Miss Leamon had said
she had a special art activity she wanted to try.

I came into the room late. I had come from gym. I'd had
trouble with my locker, and then it had taken me a long
time to get changed. Terry was there sitting on a stool off
to one side looking very uncomfortable.

"Finally," she said when I came into the door. "I don't
know any of these kids." Riley was juggling art erasers.
Treena was laughing over April's vivid description of how
she'd gotten busted for smoking in the girls' room.

"You've just met the Awesome Threesome," I told her.

"Well, what are we going to do, anyway?" she asked.

"First, you get the official greeting." I made a face and
growled. "And then you learn the official handshake." I
made my hands into claws.

"Stop it. You don't have stuff like that."

"I don't know what we're going to do. I guess Miss
Leamon's going to lead something. Now remember, this
is not your typical Tigers' meeting."

Miss Leamon had set up strips of gauze and dishes of
water and plaster of Paris. She had us put vaseline over
our faces and then cover them with soaked gauze to make
face masks. Terry did my face first, and then I did hers.
It felt really wet and gloppy. Terry was careful when she

did around my eyes. I was glad, because I heard Riley moaning when Treena put the paper strips too close in and blocked his eyesight.

Miss Leamon said that once the masks had dried, we could paint them any way we wanted. We could make them into faces of war or faces of peace, or angry faces or ancient faces. I came up with the idea of making my mask into an old, old woman who had seen many wars and was trying to speak out for peace.

"Sounds like Cassandra," Miss Leamon said when I told her my plan.

"Right. That's my name."

"I mean Cassandra in the old Greek myths," she explained.

"I know the story, but I don't like it. Nobody listened to her."

"Well, it's a different age now. Maybe now we will. Make a Cassandra who's heard this time."

"I'll try." Miss Leamon moved on to talk to April about the colors of paint she would need for her mask, and I thought about the myth. Cassandra in the legends was known for saying what was true even when it was unpopular. I thought about the secret I'd been keeping about Terry's father and Tolltorgan. I knew we had promised to tell each other everything, but I didn't know how to even begin to talk to her about it, or even if I should.

If my dad was doing something creepy, wouldn't I want Terry to tell me? I said to myself. But I wasn't sure. Maybe I wouldn't want to know. Plus I couldn't imagine my dad ever doing anything terrible.

I thought about Mr. Cameron smoking his pipe and the look he had on his face when he saw Terry's eyes filling with tears. He looked really hurt. I could see how much he loves her. It was so confusing. I couldn't believe this was the same person designing computers for nuclear bombs. He must think that he's helping, I decided. He must think that he's keeping her safe by doing that. I

decided I'd talk to Zack sometime and tell him my secret and see what he thought I should do.

I went into the storage room to look for pipe cleaners to use for the hair on my mask. When I came back, I saw Terry laying a gauze strip along the edge of Riley's cheekbones.

"Riley, how come you get two masks?" I asked.

"Easy. For my two heads. You know I have two heads, Cassie. And how come you think you're the only one who can have an expert make your mask?"

Terry blushed. Treena and April came over to watch her work. "You're a pro," said Treena. "I got paste all over myself. Look how neat you're doing it."

The bell rang for the end of school. Terry and I stayed late while she finished Riley's mask. We missed our bus and Louisa drove us home. When she got out at her house, I said to her, "What are you going to say when your mother asks why you missed the bus?"

"I'm going to tell her I had to stay after for an adult-supervised activity."

CHAPTER TWELVE

The Second Revolution

There were just a few flakes when we were waiting for the bus to come. It was so early in the morning that the sky still had streaks of pink, but clouds were gathering for a really big blizzard. I tried to catch the snowflakes on my tongue and hoped that when the bus arrived it would be empty, and the driver would tell us to go back home because school had been called off. Sometimes people get panicky during the first snowfall and cancel school.

Louisa's younger brother was bragging that he'd talked for five hours on the phone to Sharon last night. I knew which Sharon he meant. "And her father couldn't call home, and he had to get the operator to cut in on the line."

"Are you taking her to the Thanksgiving Dance?" asked Sam.

"I don't know. But Louisa is going." Louisa tried to quiet him. "With Zack." Both Jill and I stiffened.

"I thought Zack didn't like dances," Jill said.

"He doesn't. I don't either. That's why we're going together. It doesn't mean anything."

"What do you care?" asked Sam. "You're going to the dance with Eddie."

Jill got red. "I was just asking."

The bus was late, but it came. Most of the kids were wearing parkas and mittens they hadn't put on for a year. I got on the bus first. When I saw the empty seat next to Zack, I went straight for it. I've noticed that when people start to go out with someone new, sometimes they leave their old friends behind. I had to see if anything was different between us.

Zack smiled at me. "Hey, Cass, I hear you've got some news?"

"I don't know. Nothing really."

"Well, Treena told me that Terry came along to some sort of Tigers' meeting with Miss Leamon."

"Yeah!" I was glad he realized how important that was.

"And Treena said you made this outrageous Greek mask and that she wants to put it on the wall next to Arnold the Tiger."

"Really? I didn't know that."

"Sure. So he won't be lonely."

"I hope Arnold doesn't eat it," I laughed. Nothing was different. I figured if Zack had decided he was going to that dumb dance, I was glad he was at least going with Louisa and not someone I didn't even know.

Zack opened up a spiral notebook and showed me two pages of writing with a lot of cross-outs. "I'm trying to write my dad a letter. He wants me to write him every week, but it usually turns out to be every month. Sometimes I'm just too angry at him to feel like writing." He ripped the pages out and stuffed them in his pocket.

I noticed that Zack had his jean jacket on. "Zack, you're going to freeze," I said.

"Hey, don't tell me this is going to be some serious snow. It's not even Thanksgiving yet."

"You'll see," I told him.

By lunchtime, the snow had drifted so high in the parking lot that the town snowplow was outside clearing the driveway. Just as I was deciding which looked worse, the tuna salad plate or the chili, a crackling sound broke into the noise in the cafeteria, and we heard Mr. Greenwald, the principal, calling off school for the rest of the day.

Someone tossed a bag lunch up in the air. People yelled and whistled, and the whole windowsill filled up with kids leaning over to see just how bad it looked outside.

"I know what I'm going to do," said a girl. "I'm going to get out my skis."

"It's Thursday. I'm going to the Tigers," said a boy I didn't recognize. It was funny to overhear him talking about our group.

"The Tigers? What in the world is that?" asked the girl. "Is that like going to the dogs?" I didn't appreciate her humor. The boy said something in reply I couldn't catch because the crowd of kids behind me began to push and one of the teachers yelled for everyone to get away from the window.

As I sat down, I was surprised to find myself feeling a little disappointed. You mean everybody in school didn't know about the Tigers? Not that I thought the club had become a household word in Larkspur or anything, but I thought at least in school it was pretty well known.

At the church that afternoon, the group that gathered was pretty tiny compared to the size it had gotten to early in the fall. Most of the younger kids had stopped coming, like Ned's brother Rodney and Ben who'd drawn the picture of the dinosaur. Kisha was the most loyal member from South Street Elementary School, and she wasn't there. Neither were Riley or Maritza or even Zack. There were just seven of us, and I could feel some panic in the air. The snow made the date of the art display feel a lot closer.

"We don't have enough art work yet!" Louisa moaned. "I want to see our stuff plastered all over the whole town hall. What is this?"

"Hey, you think that's bad," said Jill. "All we have is three bulletin boards. We might as well hold the display in Gus's store."

"And we're not doing so hot in the paper crane department either," said Langston. "Three hundred and twelve. Kind of pitiful."

"We've got to get more kids to join," said Jill.

"That's no solution," said April. "They just come once and stand around, and then they never come back again. No offense," she said to Claude, the new boy I'd seen in the cafeteria, who was sitting with us.

"Well, you've got to tell me what I can do," said Claude. He crossed his arms and relaxed back in his chair.

"Fold paper cranes," said Langston.

"Make drawings," said Louisa.

"I'm not so hot at drawing," Claude replied.

"How are you at twisting Mr. Greenwald's arm?" asked Jill.

"For what?"

"Bulletin boards," she answered. "I asked him a month ago if we could borrow some of those kind on the rolling casters, and all he said was 'I've got to think about it a little longer.'"

"Yeah, I know what that means," said Claude. He talked kind of slow and cool. "I'm on the Student Council. That means you'll wait forever."

Jill looked at him more closely. "Student Council, huh. You got an 'in' with Mr. Greenwald?"

"He knows my face, and that's about it."

"He knows my face, too," said April, smirking.

"You mean, he knows where he can catch you smoking," said Treena.

"That should be your New Year's resolution, April," said Louisa. "Giving up the old cigs."

"What's it matter? The world's going to blow up before I get lung cancer."

"Don't say that," said Louisa.

"What are you, superstitious? You know and I know it

will probably happen. I'm just saying it out loud, that's all."

"No, it's not!" I said. The words came out stronger than I expected. I felt like it wasn't me talking but that mask I made of Cassandra that was now on the wall.

"Whatever," said Treena. "Nothing's going to happen if we don't deal with Mr. Greenwald. I tried to put up a poster in school to tell people about our group and he told me I had to take it down."

"He did? Why?"

"He didn't like the picture of a mushroom cloud on it. He said that shouldn't be in the halls." Treena pulled her knees up into a ball and then pulled her bulky turtleneck sweater down over her legs.

Mr. Greenwald was hard to figure out. You couldn't always predict what he would and wouldn't like. He'd been principal of a huge high school in Ohio for a while and coming here to Larkspur, my Dad said, was a kind of an early retirement for him. He said that Mr. Greenwald was slow to make up his mind because he was still trying to figure out where the school committee and people in town stood on different issues, and when he wasn't sure what to do, he usually got stern.

"Listen to what happened to Cassie and me," Jill said. "We got permission from Miss Leamon to be in the art room during lunch to work on drawings. We said our parents would donate paper from their print shop, too."

"Because Miss Leamon said it would be better if we weren't using school supplies," I added, not wanting Jill to tell the whole story. "And it wasn't so easy to talk Dad into letting us have much paper."

"So anyway, we finally get everything set, and Mr. Greenwald blocks the whole thing. How do you like that!" Jill pulled her hair back, feathering it, as if her fingers were combs.

"Yeah," said April. "And this is the same guy who begins the school year with his famous 'our school is the home of democracy' speech. Some democracy. He acts more like King George."

"Well, I think we should go talk to him," said Treena.

"You can. I don't want to waste my time."

"You know what he'll say. That it's not up to him. And then he'll just wait for you to forget about it," said Claude.

"Except that we won't forget about it. Not us." Treena ceremoniously placed her hand on Arnold the Tiger's nose. "I vow on Arnold's nose to fight ferociously to make the Tigers the best-known club in the school, and I won't give in until there's a mailbox with Arnold's face on it in the front office."

"Impossible," said Claude.

"Watch me give it a try."

Just then, we heard the oak door bang open and voices on the stairs. "You mean, the second bus is just getting here?" said Louisa.

"You should have seen what we've been through," said Ned, the first in the door, his cheeks bright red. "We had to get out and help push the bus out of the snowbank."

"And Riley got the whole bus to give the Tigers' cheer as we pushed. What a riot."

"In fact, we got three new recruits as a result. Meet Mickey and Kyle and Stan," said Zack.

"Hi, Kyle," said Jill. "So Riley twisted your arm, huh."

Kyle smiled at Riley like maybe she wanted to be around him more than she wanted to be in the Tigers. Her long, straight, black hair was held with three silver hair clips that matched the row of silver bracelets on her arm. I knew from Jill that Kyle had been born in Korea and been adopted by American parents when she was a baby.

"Welcome. You can help with our secret plot," said Langston.

"Secret plot?" asked Kyle.

"What are you plotting?" asked Stan. He had longish black hair and wore a faded army jacket. He played guitar in the school stage band. His jacket had all kinds of buttons on it, like "If wearer depressed, administer chocolate immediately."

"We're plotting the overthrow of Mr. Greenwald," said April.

"What?"

"It's the second revolution. The Tigers stand firm against injustice."

"Huh?"

Langston got everybody to sit down and helped us draw up a list of our requests. "We've got to give this thing style," he said. He turned to the back of his social studies book and began reading, "'When in the course of human events it becomes necessary for one people to dissolve the political bonds which have connected them with one another....' That's the way we've got to sound. Only we've got to change some of the words. How about, 'We dissolve the political divisions that have kept us apart'?"

"What's he reading from? The Gettysburg Address?"

"No, that's the Declaration of Independence," said Ned.

"Only we've got to call it the Declaration of Interdependence," Langston added.

"Yeah, keep going."

"'A decent respect for the opinions of mankind...'"

"Humankind," said Zack and Louisa.

"'Humankind requires that they should declare the causes which impel them to the separation.' No, we've got to say 'unity.' We declare the causes which impel us to unity."

Langston put that all together and made a first paragraph. Then he wrote up all the demands we thought of for Mr. Greenwald

> We hold these truths to be self-evident, that all students should know as much about peace and the means of peacemaking as they do about violence and war. To these ends, we petition for:

The right to place posters on the walls of the school asking for contributions for our peace display.

The right to meet with teachers at a staff meeting in early December to tell them about the display.

The right to put a notice in every English teacher's mailbox describing class assignments they could make about peace and asking them to submit any suitable compositions.

Permission to use twenty bulletin boards for January first. (We promise we'll have them all back in place by the time school starts on Monday.)

The right to place a collection box in the school office so students can submit artwork and writing for the display.

The right to fold paper cranes in study hall.

The right to spend lunch hour in the art room to work on the display since it's part of a recognized school club.

"What do you think?" asked Langston.

"Amazing," said Kyle. She smiled at Langston.

"I don't think that's enough," said Louisa. "I think we should add something about what we study.".

"No, that takes too long to change," said Claude.

"We can at least mention it," Louisa argued.

"Zack, can you put in something about conflict solving, you know, that stuff you showed me?" I didn't want to mention his notebook in front of everybody.

"How about the right to make the study of conflict resolution mandatory like health or gym class?" said Zack.

We added that and two more points to our petition:

The right to study about nuclear weapons and the arms race in social studies classes.

The right to study ways of peacemaking and famous peacemakers; the right to celebrate the birthday of Martin Luther King, Jr. with a special school assembly each January.

"I've got another idea," said Zack. "I want to add something about all the recruiters that come here. When

I went into the guidance counselor's office today, I saw all this military stuff on the bulletin board. It looked like recruiter month. Next Wednesday, there's going to be an assembly with the Marines in the gym. And that's just for starters."

"They came last year," said April. "Two guys do karate moves while another Marine acts like a stand-up comedian so all the kids will like them, but he makes a bunch of tasteless jokes. Or at least last year he did, remember Treena?"

"Oh yeah. Most of his jokes were really sexist. It bugged me so much, Louisa and I walked out," said Treena.

"Treena dragged me. It was kind of embarrassing to just walk out in the middle with all the kids looking at you," said Louisa.

"Well, you were the one who kept groaning about how much you hated it," said Treena.

"I know," said Louisa.

Treena added, "I just wanted us to stop sitting there talking about how creepy they were and do something."

"Well," said Zack. "There's two events this month."

"What?"

"The day before Thanksgiving, the Air Force comes, and one of their helicopters lands on the ballfield after lunch."

"They're doing that again? Last year, they took Mr. Greenwald for a ride in it. No wonder he let them come back."

"We should add something in our declaration about that," said Louisa.

"Like what?"

"Like equal time to do an assembly of our own," said Zack. "And pamphlets to give to the kids who go see the recruiters that tell them more of the whole story. We had those in my old school." So Langston added those to the declaration.

"Now, who's going to be the one to bring this to Mr. Greenwald?"

"I will," said Riley. "He and I are real buddy, buddy."

"Yeah, you probably spend the most time in the office of any of us," said April.

"Listen, I can wear a wig. I'll disguise myself as Patrick Henry so he won't recognize my face," he said.

"I think you should go, Louisa. You're the A student."

"Yeah, you go with Claude. The two of you are our best bet," said Zack. "Not me. He doesn't know me—yet."

Claude and Louisa made an appointment with Mr. Greenwald for the same day as the Marine's assembly. When the day came, I bumped into Louisa after third period as we filed into the gym.

"Are you nervous about Mr. Greenwald?" I asked her.

"Yeah, I want to die."

It was about to start so we sat together in the bleachers. The whole school had to come. In the center of the gym, mats had been set up for the karate demonstration. Three Marines came in. Two of them talked really loud and looked straight ahead as they talked. The other was the comedian. The whole thing went pretty much like April had described it, only Louisa said the jokes were new. It was weird to see everybody laughing while two guys fought. It made you feel like you were in a Roman amphitheater watching two gladiators.

Suddenly, the Awesome Threesome stood up and slipped out the side door. Fifteen minutes later, they were back. Just as the Marine acting as the comedian was saying, "Now, this next karate move is for the young ladies in the audience," and Louisa whispered to me to expect something sexist, the three of them stood up with signs.

"THIS ASSEMBLY IS UNSUITABLE FOR IMPRESSIONABLE YOUNG MINDS," said Treena's sign.

"I THOUGHT THIS STUFF WENT OUT WITH THE STONE AGE. USE YOUR SMARTS NOT YOUR FISTS," said April's.

"THE DINOSAURS WERE BETTER. THEY ONLY KILLED FOR MEAT," said Riley's.

The Marines tried to ignore them at first. The comedian tried to think of a put-down to say back at them that would get the kids laughing and on his side. "I thought long hair and peace signs were part of the Stone Age," he said. I could see that April didn't like that comment very much.

Mr. Armstrong, the basketball coach, went over to the Awesome Threesome and escorted them out. As they left the gym, I could hear Riley yell, "But what about freedom of speech?"

At the end of the assembly, Claude came rushing up to Louisa. "Did you know those guys were going to do that?" he asked.

"Are you kidding? You never know what they're going to do. They probably just thought of it on the spot."

"Well, it's going to make it a lot harder to talk to Mr. Greenwald now," said Claude. "I think we should tell him that they're not part of our group."

"Hey, I thought it was funny," said Louisa. "Besides, he'll know they're in the Tigers. Maybe it will help."

Two full tables of Tigers assembled in the lunchroom to hear the results of the meeting. Terry was sitting next to me. We didn't usually eat with the older kids, but today was special. I was staring at the oily marks on the cafeteria ceiling. Kids had a tradition of throwing butter pats up there.

It was Terry who saw Louisa and Claude come into the lunchroom first. "I don't think it worked," Terry said to me.

"What?"

"Turn around, Cass. They're back." I looked around and saw them. They even walked with a droop.

"Did he give you the 'got to think about it' treatment?" asked Treena.

"I wish he had," said Louisa.

"We're too 'political,'" said Claude.

"And don't forget 'unpatriotic.' That's the one I really liked."

"Unpatriotic!" said Stan, one of the new members. "The

164

most patriotic thing you can do is prevent this creeping nuclear crud from taking over our country."

"What about the Marines?" I asked.

"Their assembly got him all revved up. I think our plan to meet with him after the assembly backfired," said Louisa.

"Yeah," said Claude. "I did what you suggested, Zack. I told him there are a lot of kids who don't like those military assemblies, and we should have equal time, but he didn't agree."

"Are you mad at us?" said Treena. "Do you think he wouldn't give you a chance because of us?"

"Now that you mention it," said Claude.

"I don't think so," said Louisa. "He said the same old stuff he always says. He just doesn't think peace is patriotic. And he didn't say 'no' to everything. We can put notices in the teachers' boxes and posters in the halls."

"But we can't have time to talk to the teachers at their staff meeting," said Claude. "He said if he gave time to one group, he'd have to give it to all the groups."

"Did he take you seriously or did he act like we're just a bunch of kooks?"

"I don't think he took us seriously at all," said Claude, "And actually Treena, I am kind of pissed at what you three did. I think it was a really dumb thing to do before our appointment."

"Yeah, well, April's still at it," said Stan.

"What do you mean?"

"She told me she was going over to the guidance office to picket."

"I want to see this," said Ned.

"I don't," said Terry. We made plans to meet each other before sixth period, and I went off with a couple of kids to find out what was up.

When we got to the hall by the guidance office, April was there holding up the sign she'd had at the assembly. A young Marine was standing by a table with recruiting information. His face looked like Sam's from a distance.

He had the same kind of tough look, only Sam looks more bored than tough.

I don't know what he said, but suddenly April began yelling at him, "That's not true. What you really do is turn boys into killers!"

The Marine looked surprised for a second. He didn't seem much older than April. A pale, almost scared look crossed over his face. Then he locked his jaw and switched back to his stare.

"I don't want you sending any guys I know to some crappy training center trying to make them all tough and macho." She picked up a flyer that said something about job training. "And I happen to know that some of these promises can turn out to be a pack of lies."

He turned away and gave her a look of disdain. It made her madder and she screamed at him, "Get out of our school!"

"I don't think she should yell like that," I said to Zack.

"April, come back and have lunch with us," he said.

"No, he's turning guys into baby killers, and I want him to admit it."

"I don't think that's the way Martin Luther King would have done it."

"Zack, keep out of it."

"Hey, I'm in it, too." He put his arm on her shoulder and she shook it off.

A guidance counselor came out of the office and stared at us. "What's going on here?"

"Nothing," said Zack.

"I hope not. I thought I heard someone yelling." He motioned to the Marine that he had someone waiting to talk to him, and they both went inside the office.

April slumped against the wall and pulled her long hair across her face. She put on a vacant look that was like a wall coming down. It scared me a little to see her disappear into a private world with all of us standing there with her.

"We're with you, April. It just doesn't seem like a good

idea to do it that way," said Zack, sitting next to her.

"I don't want to talk," she said. "If I talk, I'll start screaming again."

"Yeah, why attack that guy," said Treena. "That's like fighting violence with violence."

"I'm not violent, I'm just angry."

"But it's not going to work," said Claude. "It's not going to change his mind or Mr. Greenwald's mind."

The door of the guidance office opened, and I wondered if it would be the counselor again with a detention pad. Instead, it was Miss Leamon. She came over to the eight of us lounging in the hallway. "What is this? A Tigers' convention?" Then she noticed April huddled over. "Was that you I heard giving that recruiter what for?"

"Yeah, I'd like to kick the guy out. If it wasn't for people like him my uncle wouldn't be sitting in a Veterans Administration hospital staring into space for the rest of his life."

"Oh, I see." Miss Leamon changed her lighthearted tone to one of concern. "Listen, someone's going to come along and send you all back to the cafeteria or give you a detention. Why don't you come with me to the art room?" She slipped the strap of her shoulder bag over her silver gray hair and searched for her keys.

Stan and Ned decided to go back to the cafeteria, but the rest of us followed her up to the second floor. April sat on a stool and folded her head down onto an art table as if she just wanted to go to sleep and let the world go away and not bother her anymore.

Miss Leamon interrupted her. "Here's paper and a pen. I want you to put whatever is going on inside you onto this paper. Right out there, all your feelings."

April lifted her head without saying a word and took the pen in her hand. She covered her paper with her arm so none of us could see and began to draw.

"So I guess that you folks liked the Marines' assembly about as much as I did," Miss Leamon said. She tied a smock on over her clothes. It was completely covered with paint splatters.

"Look at that smock," teased Langston.

"I know. When I retire this spring, they're going to give me a gold plated smock instead of a gold watch."

Treena was doodling with a magic marker on a piece of colored paper from the scrap pile. "Listen, guys," she broke in. "I think we've got to do some kind of skit when the Air Force comes. We have to do something, whether or not we have Mr. Greenwald's blessing."

"You think so?" said Claude. "Like what? You're not going to shout 'baby killer' or something like that, I hope."

April didn't hear him. She was engrossed in her drawing.

"I don't know what we'll do, but I think we've got to do something," said Treena. She crunched up the paper into a ball and threw it at the ceiling. "We don't have to just stand by and let this helicopter land on the lawn. We've got to have some skit going on instead."

"We can't pull something like that off," said Claude.

"My mother is good at getting ideas for skits," said Langston. "And she can sometimes borrow costumes from the theater department."

"Well, I'll be your chaperone," said Miss Leamon. "What do I have to lose? They can't fire me before I retire. Come back to my room this afternoon. We'll talk more about it."

"We'll call it 'The Second Revolution,'" said Langston. "If Mr. Greenwald wants patriotism, we'll give him patriotism."

The bell rang for next period. As I left the art room, I caught a glimpse of April's drawing. It showed a young soldier whose face looked as scared as that Marine had looked when he let his guard down for a second.

Miss Leamon pulled up a chair and sat down next to April. "Let me write you a pass so you can stay here another period and work on this longer."

I went out into the hall and the motion of people racing

to lockers swallowed me up. I wanted to find Terry or Maritza. Walking down the stairs this time of day was like walking through a flood. I found Maritza at her locker. "*Hola*, Maritza," I said.

She looked in a big hurry. "Cassie, I want to tell you. I can't stay overnight this Friday because I have to babysit my sisters. But you could come to our house. Besides it's your turn."

"Yeah, I bet I could do that. And did you get an invitation in the mail from our family?"

Maritza was balancing her books in one hand and bending to close her locker with the other. "No. What invitation?" Her notebook fell from the top of the stack of books and papers scattered on the floor. "*Ay!*"

I helped her pick them up. "You'll see," I said as I handed her a stack of math papers.

"Oh, tell me! *Pero dime*. Tell me!"

"Got to go," I teased and ran down the hall.

CHAPTER THIRTEEN

Disturbing the Peace

My mother put two bags of groceries down on the kitchen counter. "You know who I saw at Food Mart? That boy with the red hair."

"Riley?"

"Is that the one...?" Mom made a gesture of hair sticking up.

"Yeah. That's Riley. Don't you remember he used to come over to the house a long time ago and hang out with Sam?"

"No, I didn't recognize him. But he recognized me. He said to tell you that he was buying up all the tomatoes so no one would throw any tomorrow, but I didn't get the joke. He said you'd understand."

I laughed. "Some of the Tigers are putting on a skit for the school." I looked inside the bags to see if there was anything interesting. A carton of eggs was on top of one, but a bag of honey hermit cookies sat on top of the other. I tore the package open and gave one a try.

"Cassie, help me unload these groceries first before you start eating everything. It's my turn to make dinner, and I want to get started."

"Sure," I said with my mouth full of cookie. I reached in a bag and lifted out a tiny box of poppy seeds. I walked slowly over to the spice shelf and put the box inside. I felt sort of in a daze. Every teacher wanted to get in a test or a quiz before the Thanksgiving holidays. I was ready for a vacation.

"At that rate, the frozen food will melt before you get to it."

"What?" Then I caught on. So I went into a speedy Charlie Chaplin routine rapidly gathering up cans of soup and juice and placing them in the pantry like a wind-up toy. "Better?"

"Not much. Look, Cass, I'm tired."

I eased up. "So the Silvas are still planning to come for Thanksgiving, right?" I opened up a new package of paper towels and slipped it into the rack.

"Oh, yeah. Carmen said her family was looking forward to it. I saw her at the print shop today. We finished running off her booklet of poems. Did you know Maritza's mother was a poet?"

"Really? Can I see one of the booklets?"

"You'll have to ask her for one when they come over. Maritza has a lovely drawing on the cover."

"And was Maritza with her mother when she came to the shop?" I asked.

"No, but her younger sisters were. Do you think you can help find the furniture for your old doll house so they have something to play with when they come?"

"Yeah," I said absent-mindedly. I was trying to think where Maritza might be. Did she have a dance lesson on Tuesdays? Then I remembered that Maritza would be over at Langston's house this afternoon. She was one of the brave volunteers, along with Coreena and Stan, who were working with his mother to prepare for the skit.

The rest of us in the group were plugging away at the drawings, trying to get somewhere with the display. I hadn't been very inspired lately. Nobody had. And fewer and fewer kids were coming to the meetings. Someone had made a comment to me that being in the Tigers didn't sound like very much fun. I tried to explain to her how great it was. We put up posters in the halls that said, "Bored? Join the Tigers," but we were definitely in a slump.

The only good thing was that even though Terry wasn't coming to any of the meetings at the church, she did keep asking me how things were going. And she seemed concerned when I told her they weren't too great.

"Would you hand me that bag of rice?" my mom asked.

I gave it to her. Then I lifted up a jar of stewed prunes and made a face. "What are these for?"

"For the *pierogi*. I'd like you to help me stuff them when you get home from school tomorrow. That way, we won't have to leave all the cooking for Thursday morning."

"I might not be home right away," I said. I was thinking of the skit and what might happen as a result of it. It made me nervous.

"Well, whenever you get here." She added butter and maple syrup to hollowed out halves of acorn squash and put them on a cookie sheet in the oven. "Now Mrs. Silva and I hope none of you children will be disappointed if we don't serve turkey on Thanksgiving."

I hated it when Mom referred to us as "the children." She only said it when she was overwhelmed with details. I looked at her. "No turkey?"

"No. Carmen described the roast pork she likes to make. Lots of garlic and delicious crackling on top. It's something the Silvas often have on holidays, so we thought we'd have it instead."

"But Maritza said we'd have turkey stuffed with plantains. She told me how the plantains get all fried and mashed up with garlic. It sounded really good."

My mother heaved a big sigh, and I decided not to push it. "I thought everybody was trusting Carmen, your father, Hector, and I to think through this dinner and figure out what will go well with what."

"Yeah, I know." I folded up the paper bags that were

now empty. I liked following the creases and making them flat again, like reverse origami. I was in a bad mood. Maybe because I kept thinking of all the things that could go wrong tomorrow.

Mom turned a pot of boiling rice down to a simmer and put a thawed casserole in the oven along with the squash. Then she sat down on a stool at the counter. "Come over here," she said. She took my barrette out of my hair, twisted a section of it into a short braid, and put the barrette back.

I still liked it when she played with my hair.

"So the skit tomorrow is something special?"

"I hope so."

"And are you acting in it?"

"No way. I'm on the support crew."

"*Duża rośnij*," she said. "Do you remember what that means?"

"Oh sure. *Babcia* used to say it to us when we were little. Grow big."

"You're going to grow so big for being so good. *Duża rośnij*. I don't know everything you're doing with the Tigers, but I'm really proud of you the way you've stuck with it."

"I'm stubborn. You've said it before."

"Did I used to call you stubborn? I don't remember. You're just right." And she kissed me.

The Air Force helicopter was scheduled to land on the school baseball diamond after lunch. On Wednesday morning, the announcements said that everybody should bring their coats to lunch and wait there until they heard over the loudspeaker that it was time to go outside.

You could tell who was in the Tigers when you came in the cafeteria. We were the ones who didn't have our coats with us. I stood at the window talking to Terry who was holding her parka in her hand. When we saw Mr. Greenwald walking heartily toward the baseball diamond with an Air Force officer to meet the helicopter, we both began to scratch our heads.

Riley saw the signal and went over to the teacher in charge of the lunchroom. He produced the pass that he'd faked, and the teacher let him by. He'd agreed to do the dirty work, and it had taken him a lot of plotting to figure out how he was going to accomplish it. Riley said he'd been in trouble so many times that one more time wouldn't matter.

The sound of the helicopter above the school was unmistakeable, but another sound broke in. It was the loudspeaker system and Riley, in a disguised voice, was talking fast into it.

"Please stay in your seats. There will be a fifteen-minute delay, but we have some entertainment provided for you." The sound system cut off sharply. Someone must have grabbed Riley.

"I hope it's not the Air Force band," said a girl when the sound of a snare drum began.

It was Maritza on the drum. She had borrowed it from her older brother, and he'd taught her how to play a simple rat-a-tat-tat. With her was Ned playing the fife and Stan carrying an electric guitar. They were all dressed up in colonial costumes that Langston's mother had borrowed. They looked like the *Spirit of '76*.

The three of them walked up to the front of the cafeteria. Stan smoothly plugged in his guitar, while Maritza slipped off a cloth covering the amplifier. By the time someone from the office got back on the loudspeaker, Stan was wailing on his guitar so loud you couldn't hear what they were saying. And I don't think anyone cared. Zack and others went along the tables asking kids to stay seated so the teachers would have less of an excuse to break it up. Meanwhile, Miss Leamon talked to the teachers on duty in the lunch room and explained that she was in charge of the skit and would take responsibility for whatever happened.

Then Coreena stepped up to the mike and began to sing. She didn't hold back at all but let her voice out full and strong, swinging her head to the music. It was a bluesy melody.

Well, my name is Deborah Gannett,
Aaaand I fought for this country,
Oh, yes, well, I fought for this country,
And now it is your turn my friends
To work for liberty.

"What's she singing about?" asked someone.

"I don't know, but she's great."

Then Stan strummed some low notes on his guitar. I looked around and saw Mrs. Taylor, Langston's mother, in the back of the cafeteria with her camera. I was glad somebody was getting pictures of all of this. Coreena switched from song to story now.

"I'm Deborah Gannett," she said. "I fought with the Fourth Regiment right in this very state of Massachusetts. I told them my name was Robert Shurtliff." She laughed. "Were they surprised when I came to collect my pension and they found out I was a woman. Black people fought in nearly every battle of the Revolution. I've come back across these two hundred years and more," and here Stan made more low notes on the guitar for emphasis, "to say that we've all got to band together, now or never, to fight today for freedom. Only this time it isn't the British we're fighting, or the Russians, or any one nation for that matter. We're fighting for independence from nuclear weapons and for the right to work for peace."

Then Treena stood up and talked about what the Tigers were doing and how other kids could join. A bunch of us passed out petitions for kids to sign. The petition repeated the things we'd asked for from Mr. Greenwald. Stan kept strumming his guitar, and after Treena finished, he went right back into the rock melody he'd been playing.

Coreena stood up and began the second verse of the song. I'd heard her say before that Mrs. Taylor had written it. Coreena tipped back her head and sang right into the mike just like a pro.

> A country ruled by weapons
> Is ruled by tyranny.
> Oh, yes, it's ruled by tyranny.
> Now we must band together for peace and harmony.

Meanwhile, members of the Tigers had blocked the three exits. Louisa, Zack, and Claude worked with Miss Leamon to talk to the other teachers and persuade them to let the show continue. More teachers kept rushing down the hall to the cafeteria to find out what was going on.

Coreena never got to start the next verse. Ned had given his signal on the fife that Mr. Greenwald was in sight. We gathered up the petitions as quickly as we could and gave them to Treena. It wouldn't be long now.

As Mr. Greenwald strode down the hall toward the cafeteria, Zack went right up to meet him. Zack had told me he was going to introduce himself and say he wanted to explain what was going on. If Mr. Greenwald didn't want to stop and listen, he had some jokes ready like, "Hey, I can get you front-row seats for this concert."

Mr. Greenwald looked impatient and angry as he halted. His eyebrows were narrowed and his mouth was set. Through the glass walls of the cafeteria, I watched Zack standing there speaking to him calmly. Mr. Greenwald's face relaxed for a moment. He said something back to Zack, and then he pushed on ahead.

Coreena timed it perfectly. Just as Mr. Greenwald walked through the door, she had the whole cafeteria singing "America the Beautiful" with Stan accompanying on the electric guitar. They got as far as "God shed His Grace on thee," when somebody pulled the plug.

Treena waved her arms for quiet. We'd practiced this part. If Mr. Greenwald thought we were mocking him, it would ruin the whole thing.

I didn't envy Maritza and Ned. They had to get back

in formation as the *Spirit of '76*. They walked alongside Treena as she held the petitions out toward Mr. Greenwald. Maritza did a drumroll that I thought sounded really great, and then Treena boomed out as loudly as she could, "General Washington," and she saluted him, "your troops are ready to go and fight bravely for our democracy. You need only say the word."

Mr. Greenwald tried hard not to crack a smile. "What in the world is going on here?" His confusion turned to anger. "Is this somebody's idea of a joke?"

Treena reddened but stayed firm. "No. We're serious. It's the second part of the American revolution."

"I'd call it disturbing the peace," he said. "You're keeping members of the United States Air Force waiting outside with this monkey business."

I was afraid that April might yell out "good," but we were well-disciplined. We knew if we could keep him on the other side of anger, we'd have a chance. Mr. Greenwald had a certain expression where his face hardened up tight and stony, and I didn't see it yet. Once he got furious, there was no turning back.

"General Washington, I'll speak for these troops here." It was Miss Leamon. I didn't think this part was planned. "It was this same great state of Massachusetts," she said, imitating Treena's official tone, "that held the famous Boston Tea Party."

"So this is the Larkspur Lunchparty," said Treena.

Mr. Greenwald had to try hard to keep a straight face when he looked at Miss Leamon. "I'll take these petitions back to my...headquarters and look at them." Then he folded his arms and turned toward Treena. "But some of these troops are going to have to spend time in the guard house." He drew himself up sternly and began to yell, "I want all of you Tigers—that's who's behind this thing, right?—to stay here with Coach Armstrong. Everybody else, get your coats on and MOVE! I want to see you outside in one minute, lined up by homerooms on that baseball diamond the way we line up for fire drills. Now, GO!"

His yelling made me shiver. I'd never had a detention at Frontier High. I could have pretended I wasn't in on it, since nobody knew that I'd tipped off Riley, but I wanted to stay with the group. Terry waved to me as she filed out with two girls in her homeroom, while I stayed behind in a seat.

Kids left the cafeteria in silence under Mr. Greenwald's gaze. I saw Vera Taylor signal to Coreena that she thought she'd done great. Then she slipped out with her camera.

Coach Armstrong didn't have much of a lecture to give us. And when I looked around the room, I noticed that a few kids who'd never even been to a meeting before had stayed behind with us rather than go out and greet the helicopter.

We never got to put a mailbox in the school office with Arnold's picture on it. That really bothered Treena. She wanted to be the one to stroll into the office and set it up. Riley got in the most trouble for sneaking onto the loudspeaker, but Mr. Greenwald was easier on the rest of us than we expected. I know it was because of Miss Leamon. She went into the office after school to confess her role in the whole thing and had a pretty good talk with Mr. Greenwald about our group. She said he has a better sense of humor than he usually shows in public.

I was a little nervous about the story of the skit getting around town, but Mr. Greenwald did promise that we could borrow some bulletin boards, and I had a feeling we were going to have more new members after that than we knew what to do with.

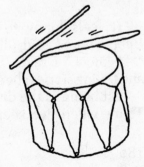

CHAPTER FOURTEEN

Día Del Pavo

Our house was filled with delicious smells, and we were waiting for the Silvas to arrive.

"Cassie," said my dad. From the look on his face, I knew it was going to be a joke. "Why don't you call up Maritza and have her bring that drum along so the two of you can re-enact your skit for us?"

"Don't give her ideas," said Sam. "We've talked about it enough already. I'm starving. When are we going to eat?"

"Around four. Give me a hand putting in the leaves of the table," said Mom.

Sam, Jill, and I helped her pull out our dining room table and drop in two more sections so there'd be room enough for the five of us and the six Silvas to all fit around it.

"It feels funny to be having Thanksgiving without *Babcia* here," said Jill.

"I know," I said. "She'd be helping to fix the *pierogi* and telling stories about when she was a girl in Poland."

Just being in the dining room reminded me of *Babcia*. That's where we keep the eggs she decorated and her photos. I used to sit with her at the table alone, and she'd take things down from the middle shelf on the hutch, which I thought of as her shelf, and talk to me about them. It was the first holiday without her. That's why I wanted Maritza's family here with us. If it were just us alone, we'd probably sit around missing her and feeling sadder and sadder. With the Silvas here, too, the meal could still be special.

"Carmen said in Puerto Rico they call this day *Día Del Pavo*," my mother said as we pushed the sides of the table to snap the leaves into place. "Turkey Day."

"Only this year, no turkey," said Jill. "It's okay. At Eddie's house tomorrow, I'll have plenty of that."

I'd tried to eat just a small breakfast and only soup for lunch so I'd have room for an early dinner. We were having our most favorite dishes. Mrs. Silva was bringing *pernil*—roast pork—fixed with mashed garlic and spices and *arroz con gandules*—rice with pigeon peas—that Maritza said was delicious. For dessert, there would be rice pudding, *arroz con dulce*—made with coconut milk and raisins—and a poppy-seed cake Jill had baked the night before. To begin the meal, we'd made *barszcz*—beet soup—plenty of *pierogi* with different fillings, and cucumber salad. Plus there'd be the little extras like Mom's homemade pickles.

When the Silvas arrived at our house, Jill showed Maritza's two younger sisters the old doll house she'd set up for them in our living room, and Mr. and Mrs. Silva joined my parents in the kitchen.

Maritza's older brother, Roberto, and Sam wanted to head right away for the basketball hoop in our back yard. The sky looked stiff and gray with waiting snow. It was so cold, I couldn't believe they'd want to play basketball out there without gloves. My mother said they had to help Maritza and me set the table first, so the four of us walked reluctantly into the dining room.

Sam and Roberto began lifting the dinner plates down from the hutch. They were trying to get the work over quickly. Sam gripped one of the plates like it was a frisbee and pretended he was going to throw it across the room to Roberto. It was good to see them joking around. I wanted our families to like each other.

I opened up a drawer and took out blue linen placemats and matching blue napkins. Maritza put her hands up for me to throw her some. One napkin landed on her head. She flung it off, and we began fixing the place settings around the table.

Roberto was taller than Sam and had bright brown eyes like Maritza's. Sam knew him already from intramural basketball at school. We discovered they had something else in common. They both thought it was ridiculous for their sisters to be part of the Tigers.

"Cassie, you're in the Tigers, too?" asked Roberto. He said the word Tigers as if it were something creepy.

"What's wrong with that?" I answered. I felt proud of our group after yesterday.

"Oh, nothing. Just that you Tigers act like a nuclear bomb is going to drop on your head any minute," said Roberto.

Sam laughed hysterically.

"Well, Lourdes and Alicia like the Tigers now," said Maritza. She crossed her arms and looked straight at Roberto.

"Oh, I know them," said Sam.

"They're our second cousins," said Maritza.

"Oh, really. Well, I always thought they had more sense than to join a hopeless cause," said Sam.

Roberto thought that was funny and clacked two spoons together by Maritza's ear as if to say "so there."

"Just ignore them," I told Maritza.

Maritza did. "They told me they want to join our group because they liked our skit so much." She casually walked around the table adding folded napkins to the placemats I set down.

"And they aren't the only ones," I added. "Lots of kids said they liked it. Remember the girls who came up to you yesterday on the bus and said they liked the way you played the drum?" They were older girls who'd never spoken to either of us before.

"That's right," said Maritza.

"Skit?" said Sam. "I wouldn't call that a skit. That was more like a bad joke." He was putting forks and spoons on the table like he was throwing grain to chickens.

"Yeah," said Roberto. "If I'd known what you were going to do, I wouldn't have loaned you my drum."

I looked at the scattered silverware and grabbed the rest of the forks out of Sam's hand. "Why don't you just leave this to somebody who knows what they're doing?" I said.

"Gladly." They went hooting out of the room.

"Jealous!" Maritza called after Roberto, but they were already running out the back door. "Nobody's ever told him he plays the drum well," she said to me, "because he doesn't. He just bangs it."

"You were great yesterday," I told her. "Especially when you had to stand up there after Mr. Greenwald came in. How did you have the guts?"

Maritza shrugged and looked pleased. We circled around the table straightening each setting of silverware.

I liked having the dining room all to ourselves. The fading light of the day came in through the curtains, bouncing back into the room through two mirrors on the wall. There was lots of dark wood in the room, but it wasn't depressing the way the church sanctuary furniture was where we had *Babcia*'s funeral. This wood had more of the feeling of a forest.

It was Mom's hobby to rescue old furniture from ugly coats of paint, and she had collected most of the things in the room at barn sales in Larkspur. The frames around the antique mirrors, the table, and the funny curlicue-backed chairs were all things she had scraped and sanded and varnished. She said it was like recovering the forgotten lives of people in the town.

"Look at this," I said when we got the table looking

neat again. I handed Maritza an egg from our *pisanki* collection on the hutch.

She turned it around in her hand. It was covered with red, black, and orange geometric designs. "It's so light and shiny. I thought it was made of wood."

"No, it's a real egg. Mom shellacs them when she's done. That's how come it looks that way. And you can see where she made tiny holes in the ends to blow out the yolk." One at a time, I carried six more eggs on their wooden stands over to the table. "My grandmother made these. You see how the color is deeper? Some of them are older than I am. Feel this one." I handed her my favorite. "It still has the yolk inside. That's the way *Babcia* always did it. She wouldn't hollow it out. She'd just let the yolk dry up."

Maritza turned the egg around in her hand. It had a rooster on either side against a black background. Then, ringing around the roosters were orange and white and red zigzags like the rays of the sun. Each line was perfectly even, perfectly spaced, yet they didn't look stamped by some machine. That's what I loved about them. You could tell a person had held the egg and thought about the decorations they wanted to make next.

Maritza shifted the egg back and forth from side to side. "The front and the back match exactly," she said. "These must be really hard to make."

"They are." While she looked at all the eggs, I gazed up at the ceiling at nothing in particular. I liked to look at the loops in the chandelier and just enjoy the cool blue feeling in the room. The old beams reminded me of the inside of a barn, but more elegant. We don't use the dining room much. Usually, we're in too much of a hurry. When we do eat here, it means we'll be taking our time. It means food served in blue china bowls, not just scooped out of a pan on the stove and whisked over to plates in the breakfast nook.

I liked being around Maritza. I'd never had a friend before who enjoyed the quiet in a room the way I did.

Sometimes when I sat in there alone, I thought about the families before us who lived in this farmhouse, back when there were still cows outside in the barn instead of all the things we store there now. I imagined the smell of freshly mown grass and the people resting at the end of the day.

"Who did this egg?" asked Maritza, picking one with a simple design of triangles.

"Me." From her smile I knew she had already guessed it. "This is the only one of mine I've ever saved. *Babcia* marked it out for me, so I could keep the lines even. It's hard to hold the stylus still enough for the wax lines to come out right."

"It's nice, Cassie."

I wanted to think of something to make her laugh. "You wouldn't believe what I did once. I was holding one of the kind where the yolk is still inside."

"And you dropped it?"

"Uh huh. It just slipped out of my hand, and did it ever stink up this room."

Maritza's laugh was like bells. "I'd like to take one for Roberto's pillow. Just kidding." She picked up an egg with a pine tree in the decoration and ran her fingers over the lines. "Do the different pictures mean something?"

"They do, but I can't remember much about it, even though *Babcia* explained it to me enough times." I felt bad about that. I didn't want the special things *Babcia* had told me to die with her.

Eating Polish foods and having special family expressions had always been private for me. It was one thing to go to the St. Stanislaus Church where everyone was Polish, but it was *Babcia's* church, and my parents didn't go regularly. At school, my being Polish was mostly invisible.

Sometimes I had to endure Polish jokes, and I always wondered if the joke teller knew I was Polish and had said it anyway. I was confused about what to do. I usually gave a weak smile so I wouldn't stand out and get picked on. Besides, there were so many jokes and jabs and mocks about being too tall, too short, and whatever, it seemed like everyone was supposed to be a good sport.

You were supposed to just take it all in, the way I did, or dish it out twice as hard. That's what Sam did. I wondered if he ever felt hurt at all the mockery that flew fast and furious between him and his friends. It didn't seem to bother him. But it must. I knew that I got hurt sometimes, especially when I heard Polish jokes. I wanted to scream, "You don't know who you're talking about." But I never said, "Stop," the way I wanted to.

I wanted to share with Maritza a little more of my world. I pointed to a picture made out of cut paper that showed a woman seated at a party table. Above her head were swirls of leaves and flowers. It was a little larger than the paper cutting of the rooster in my bedroom. "See how even her eyebrows are made of paper," I said. "This is called *wycinanka*. It means a paper cutting."

"Vee chee …," Maritza began.

I repeated the word again.

"Vih tsih NAHN ka," said Maritza in perfect imitation. And then she added in Spanish, "*Que lindo.*"

Before she explained to me that she'd said it was beautiful, I answered, "*Gracias. Si, es bonito,*" so she'd know I understood.

"*Muy bien!*" said Maritza. She smiled.

"*Gość w domu, Bóg w domu.*" I looked at her face to see how she would react. Then I translated in a slow voice like my grandmother's, "A guest in the house is God in the house." It was the first time I'd really talked in Polish to one of my friends. Not that I knew a lot of phrases, but some *Babcia* had said to me so much, they kept ringing in my mind.

Then Mom pushed the swinging door open, and Maritza's mother came in carrying the *pernil*. Close behind her was my father with a sharp knife and a serving plate to hold the pieces of pork roast.

Maritza's sisters came in holding dolls from the old doll

house. It was awkward standing around until my mother pointed out where everybody should sit.

Hector Silva agreed to say a short blessing. "Thanks for this delicious food and for this wonderful company."

"*Buen provecho*," said Roberto.

For a minute, I didn't want my father to respond in Polish, in case people thought he was being corny, but he did. "*Smacznego.*" Mrs. Silva smiled at him, and I felt better. Maybe it was safe to be ourselves here.

I put something from every dish on my plate and then took turns tasting a little of this and a little of that. I ate a serving of *arroz con gandules*, which had onions, green peppers, and garlic mixed in with the rice and peas. Then I followed it with the cool sour cream and cucumber salad.

"*Mami*, can I have some *cuerito*?" the littlest girl asked.

Mrs. Silva handed her a piece of the rind.

I asked for some, too. It was rich and crackling. I had two more pieces, four *pierogi*, and seconds on *pernil*. By the end of the meal, I felt completely and happily full.

I watched both of our fathers enjoying each other's jokes. Laughter ringed the table, and even after dinner when the Silvas said it was time to put the girls in bed, they lingered talking with my parents. I figured that even though Jill probably wished there was somebody in the Silvas family close to her age and Sam might be unhappy that Roberto had sunk more baskets then he had, we'd probably be having more family visits together.

"Cassie, do you know about the party tomorrow?" asked Maritza when we finally had a chance to speak alone again.

"The party at Langston's house to thank his mother for her work on the skit?"

"*Si*. Want to come with me?"

"I do, but isn't it just for the cast? I mean, it's not for all the Tigers, right?"

"True, but I'm sure you could come, too."

"Won't mostly older kids be there? Like Coreena and Stan? I don't really know them," I said.

"I don't either. But Langston will be there, of course. I mean, it's his house."

"Yeah, he's a lot of fun."

"*Mami*," Maritza called. "Could you pick up Cassie and take her to the party tomorrow?"

"Take Cassie? Certainly." Mrs. Silva carried two paper bags with empty serving dishes and plastic containers of leftovers.

Dad flicked on the outside light, and it lit up the flagstones of our front walk. "See you tomorrow," I said to Maritza. She climbed into the back seat of their car. Mr. Silva carried the youngest girl who was already very sleepy and put her in Maritza's lap. I stood on the front step and kept waving to them until their car was all the way down the driveway and out of sight.

CHAPTER FIFTEEN

Peace Like the Ocean

The next evening when Mrs. Silva picked me up, I was wearing a sweater vest that Jill had given me for Christmas a year ago. It was royal blue with a V-neck. I hadn't worn it much before, but it was the first thing I thought of for the party. The Taylor's house was less than a mile away, just straight down our road and then around the corner, so before I could start to get really nervous, we were there.

As we walked up to the front door, I told Maritza, "I want to live in a house like this when I grow up, with a bridge in the front yard." We stopped to look down at the frozen water in the stream.

"I like the house all right. But I don't want to live practically in a forest," she said. "Dancers have to live in cities."

I didn't think that was true for all dancers, but I figured she knew more about it than I did.

Mrs. Taylor answered the door and showed us in. She remembered my name and that made me happy.

When I come into a house, I like to poke around and see where the rooms are and what special things people have put on their shelves. I'd only seen the two front rooms before when I'd been there to learn paper crane folding. Now I noticed that there were plants everywhere, as if the forest had been brought inside. A huge fern hung in the dining room, and all the windowsills were filled with greenery. Mrs. Taylor watched me taking it all in and asked if I wanted to see her darkroom where she does photography.

"This is my favorite part of the house," Maritza whispered as we followed her down the hall. Maritza had been there several times to work on the skit.

I looked at the framed photographs on the walls. One was of Langston sleeping on a couch with the sun coming in through the window, and another showed Yukiko throwing a pot on the wheel. I stopped by a picture of Langston standing by a huge waterfall with spray rising around him.

"Where's that?" I asked.

"In Zimbabwe. And that falls is even larger than it looks. It's one of the seven wonders of the world. I love the name. It's called The Smoke That Thunders."

While she went into her darkroom, Maritza pulled me over to another photo. "This is Judith Jamison. She's really famous." Then she looked closer. "*Mira!* Vera's got her autograph." I looked at a tall Black dancer in costume holding a frilly umbrella. "I saw her perform at the university this year," said Maritza. "I'd give anything to dance like her."

"Here's a picture of you, Maritza." Vera Taylor held up a photo fresh from the darkroom with Maritza balancing on one foot and playing the drum. She had other photos of Coreena singing and of Stan and Ned and Maritza as the *Spirit of '76*.

"Oh, Vera, I can't believe you got this one," said Coreena. Everyone in the cast was calling her Vera now. "I thought nobody saw me scowling like that."

"You mean, when Mr. Greenwald was speaking? No, I didn't miss that. And I got some good candid shots of him, too," laughed Vera "Zack, you're in some of these," she called as he walked into the room.

"Zack, Mr. Greenwald is looking at you like you're a Martian," said Maritza.

I looked at the photo. Zack was blocking Mr. Greenwald from getting past him, but he looked so relaxed and natural that he seemed totally unaware that Mr. Greenwald was in a hurry to get into the cafeteria. Mr. Greenwald looked more surprised than furious.

"What were you saying to him?" I asked.

"Welcome to Planet Z."

"No, really."

Zack took me aside and whispered, "Will you come back to the kitchen for a minute?"

While Maritza and the others looked at the rest of the photographs, I followed Zack into the kitchen where we found Langston cutting up a paper bag. I had a guess what they were doing. "Baked Alaska?"

"Yeah, an attempt," said Zack. "I brought the recipe over."

"And we've got the pound cake and the ice cream," said Langston, "but what in the world is this paper bag for?"

"You cut it to fit on a cookie sheet so the Baked Alaska won't stick to the pan," I explained.

"Hey," said Langston, "somebody has walked into this kitchen who actually knows what they're doing."

"I know what I'm doing," said Zack.

"You do?" said Langston. "Cassie, get us out of this mess before Zack turns this into scrambled eggs and ice cream."

I looked at the pan where Zack was beating the eggs.

"How does it look?" Zack asked. "How come nothing's happening?" He was sloshing the eggs around with a fork.

"Well, you separated out the egg whites fine. That part's right. But it will go quicker if you use an egg beater or an electric mixer."

"We don't want to use a mixer or Vera will hear,"

explained Zack. "This is a surprise."

Langston got a hand-held egg beater out of a drawer and while Zack worked on whipping the eggs into meringue, I cut the cake in half, and Langston and I began to pile on the ice cream.

Just then we heard Vera's laugh in the hall. Langston went to steer her into the living room. I tested the meringue, and it finally came to a peak.

"Is the oven hot?" I asked.

"Yeah, the light's on."

I spooned globs of meringue on the ice cream, and Zack and I quickly spread it down along the sides so that it covered over every inch.

Langston stepped back in. "Won't it melt?" he asked.

"It never has before."

"You missed a spot," he said, and Zack took an extra dab of meringue from the bowl and smoothed it over. Then we popped it into the hot oven.

We went into the den to hang out a bit and make it appear to Vera that we weren't doing anything special. Zack got caught up in talking with Louisa, and I saw him suddenly race back into the kitchen.

Langston got everyone's attention, and Zack walked in with the Baked Alaska. It was on a greasy cookie sheet. A small trickle of pink ice cream ringed the bottom, and the top of it was slightly burned like an over-toasted marshmallow at a campfire. But Vera was really excited. Zack and Langston scooped out a serving for her first, and she pronounced it delicious.

"Are you glad you came?" Maritza asked me as we were mixing fruit juice and club soda into our cups and waiting for servings of Baked Alaska.

"*I'm* glad she came," said Langston, overhearing us.

It was a small gathering: seven of us from the Tigers and Langston's mother. A lot of the kids who might have been there, like Ned and the Awesome Threesome, were away for the holidays. Coreena and Stan were talking about their physics class, and Stan was envious because

Coreena had just gotten an A on a test he'd nearly flunked. Only Maritza and I were younger than tenth grade.

I started to whisper to her, "I can't believe I'm at a high school party!" but I stopped. I didn't want to chance anyone overhearing me.

I heard Zack and Louisa laughing on the other side of the room. The next night was the dance. I wondered if by Monday they'd be as totally wrapped up in each other as Jill and Eddie were. I hoped not. Before Eddie went away to college, their private jokes and glances drove me up the wall. I couldn't stand the thought of Zack getting all moony-eyed like them.

The den had more of Vera's collection of instruments. Langston picked up a large gourd strung with tiny shells to show to Maritza and me. He shook it with both hands. "Sounds like a rattler, doesn't it? Watch this." He tossed it from one hand to another in rhythm. Then he threw it up and caught it on the beat.

"What's that called?" Maritza asked.

"A *shekere*."

"Will you show me how to play it?"

While Langston pointed out to Maritza the soft part on the bottom that you had to be careful not to hit, I noticed Coreena walking quickly over to where Vera was sitting. Vera had been in a conversation that had just ended, and I could tell Coreena wanted to be the next person to talk to her. I was curious to know what she was so eager to say, so I moved closer to them.

"I heard the University offered you a basketball scholarship, Coreena," Vera called out before Coreena could speak. "They must be pretty interested to make promises like that in November. Congratulations."

"Thanks," said Coreena in a voice that didn't sound that excited. She placed a bowl of pretzels in between them and sat down next to Vera on the floor.

"I hope you'll be in some of my classes," Vera added.

"If I go there, I will, but I haven't decided yet which school I want. Actually, I'm sick of the whole thing. The

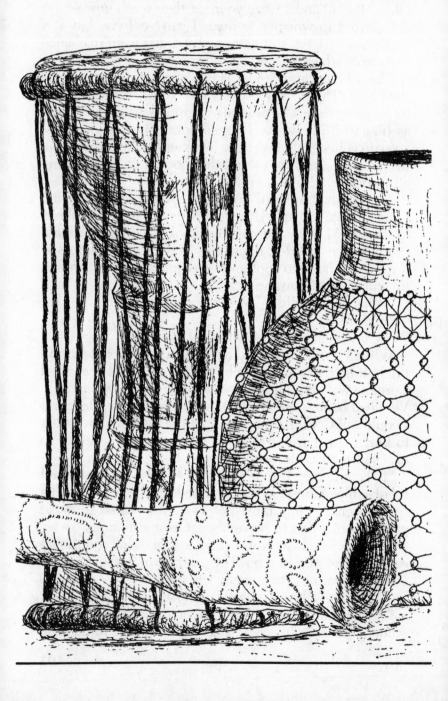

best part about playing Deborah Gannett was that people stopped talking to me just about basketball. Sometimes I feel like some kind of basketball robot."

"Hey, you blew people away with your singing," said Vera. "Even the first time you tried the song, you were great."

"That's what I wanted to ask you about," said Coreena. "Where did you hear about Deborah Gannett? She's real, isn't she? How did you write that song?"

"She's real, all right. Langston told me that all of you wanted the skit to be about the Revolutionary War, so I got a book about the history of Black people in colonial America." She pointed to a book on the coffee table. "I didn't want it to be just a white history lesson. As soon as I read about Deborah, especially that she was from Massachusetts, the song just came out." Vera was on the floor with her back against the couch. Her long tan and black dress was pulled around her. She reached for a drink of water. "But I'll tell you really truthfully, I'm not so happy with the way the words turned out. I think I wrote it too quickly."

Others moved pillows closer to them. We could tell that they were having the most interesting discussion in the room.

"Why do you say you're not happy with it?" asked Stan.

"Oh, no. You really want me to tell you?" She had a spirited look in her eyes.

"Yup," said Zack.

Vera took off her shoes and her shell earrings and got more comfortable. "Well, there I was in the back of the cafeteria watching the whole thing, and this fine young woman—you, Coreena—steps up there just the way we rehearsed it and starts telling everybody they've got to work for peace. Suddenly I thought to myself, 'Will the kids really understand what your group is about? Will they hear the words *weapons* and *peace* and only think of nuclear war?' That's why I was angry with myself. The song didn't say enough."

"But nuclear war is what we're against," said Louisa. "Everyone's got to get together and stop the bombs or we won't have a world to live in. That's got to come first."

"That's not what I think," said Stan. "That's not why I joined the Tigers."

Langston passed the rest of the Baked Alaska around the room, and Zack and Coreena dove for a piece.

"Why did you join, Stan?" asked Vera.

"Well, it's hard to explain. My drawings kind of say it. You see, I'm half Russian. I don't tell many kids that. My dad's family lived in Leningrad. And we're Jews. Being Russian and being Jewish aren't the most popular things."

"Tell him what you say about invisible bombs, Mom," said Langston.

Vera leaned forward toward Stan. "Invisible bombs are what I call prejudice and hatred. When I imagine a world of peace, I see racism and anti-semitism gone and all the other invisible bombs dismantled. I'm glad to hear you're putting your drawings in the display. I'd like to see them."

"Actually, I haven't put them in yet," said Stan.

"Yeah, I didn't think I'd seen them in the box," said Louisa.

"I wasn't sure they belonged."

"Sounds to me like they really do," said Vera. "It's the invisible bombs like mistrust and greed that start us building weapons and barriers between us. I think we've got to work against what leads to nuclear weapons, not just the weapons themselves."

"I bet they'd like to hear about that newspaper thing you do in your classes," said Langston.

"Yeah, what is it?" asked Coreena.

Vera plumped up the pillow behind her. "Well, I like to do this thing I call 'A Movie in Your Mind.' I say, 'Pretend you're opening up a newspaper in the future on the day that America and the Soviet Union are celebrating years of lasting peace. What other things would you find in the news? Would there be poverty? Would it be unsafe for women to walk in the streets at night?" And then people write their own headlines. You see what I mean?"

"That's neat. Why don't we try it now," said Zack.

"Aw, this is supposed to be a party," said Vera, smiling.

"No, let's do it," said Zack. "How do you begin?"

Vera looked at the rest of us. "Do you all want to try this?" We nodded.

Vera shifted her feet underneath her. "Well, to start off, everyone get comfortable and close your eyes so you can see things in your imagination."

"Wake me up if I fall asleep," joked Langston.

I sat cross-legged and closed my eyes.

"Now picture yourself in one of the rooms in your house. You can pick any room you want. Imagine that you're living in a time when there's no longer any danger of nuclear war. You feel very, very safe. Let your shoulders relax and really believe that it's true. Imagine that everyone you know is working to help make a peaceful and just world."

I saw myself in our kitchen, holding Sneakers.

"Okay, now there's a table near you with a newspaper on it. Pick it up and look at the front page. You see a photo there of Soviet and American leaders shaking hands and genuinely smiling at each other. They've just signed another treaty. Then open up the newspaper and see what else you find."

The room was silent. I could imagine that I was holding the crinkly sheets of a newspaper, and I could see the smile of the leaders. I pretended to open up the paper. A picture of a beautiful spot in the woods flashed to my mind.

"Okay," said Vera. "Some of you might have seen words or pictures, while for some of you it might have been less specific, more of a feeling. Whatever way your impression came to you, see if you can translate it into an article or event in the newspaper."

I saw the woods again, and the leaves seemed to be a

gleaming emerald green, but I didn't know what that meant. It didn't seem like news.

"When you're ready, tell us what came to your mind."

I opened my eyes. I felt I'd been miles away. It was a surprise at first to arrive back in the room.

Zack pantomimed that he had a newspaper in his hands. "There's a report here about hunger. It says everyone in the world has at least two meals a day now."

"And everyone has warm houses to live in," added Louisa.

"And look at this," said Stan. "No child abuse has been reported for a whole year."

"No teenage suicides," said Langston. "And teenagers have been interviewed all over America, and ninety-nine percent say they're feeling hopeful about their future."

"Battered women's shelters are closing," said Coreena, "because they're not needed anymore."

We were silent, and then Louisa thought of something else. "Medical schools and law schools are graduating equal numbers of women and men."

"Schools in science too, every kind of graduate school," said Coreena. She and Louisa laughed together.

"Soup kitchens aren't needed," said Maritza.

"Neighborhoods get together and fix a free meal once a day," said Zack.

"The Ku Klux Klan and the Nazi Party are forgotten because nobody wants to join," said Stan.

"Apartheid is long gone in South Africa," said Zack. "The liberation movement has won."

"And America has a Black woman for president," said Coreena.

"You'd be president," said Langston.

"I don't want to be. You'd make a better president," said Coreena back to him.

"Then what do you want to be?" said Langston.

"I don't know," she said.

"Maritza will be making her debut as lead soloist in a

dance company," said Zack. He was quick at thinking of things.

"We'll be on a world tour," said Maritza.

"But you'll still come back to perform each year at the university stage in Crowningburg," said Langston.

I hadn't said anything, and I hoped nobody had noticed. I couldn't think clearly. I wanted the world like that now, but it felt impossible. I felt very sad.

"What about you, Cassie?" said Vera. "What did you see?"

"It didn't really make much sense."

"What was it?"

"Just a picture of the woods."

"Yeah. That's an interesting thing to come to mind. There's lots of things that could mean."

"Like more parks," said Louisa.

"Or the forests being protected and less trees cut down," said Maritza.

I liked those ideas, but it meant something different to me. I wanted to feel as safe in the whole world as I felt when I was in the woods or the meadow. I wasn't ready to say that out loud, and from the look Vera gave me, it seemed she understood because she didn't ask me any more questions.

"All I know, Vera," said Zack, "is that when I'm around you, I feel like my brain cells are going to pop."

Vera laughed. "Now, how do you mean that?"

"I'm thinking a million things at once."

"So, tell me one of them," said Vera.

"Well, take our art display. We say it's about peace, but what kind of peace are we talking about in it? I want to stretch that word peace and make it take in all the things we just said. We want to do more than stop a nuclear war from happening, but I don't think it comes across."

"No, it doesn't when you look at your poster in the art room," said Coreena. "All you see is that great big mushroom cloud."

I remembered pages from Zack's notebook. One talked about his neighbor in Syracuse who gave away warm gloves in the winter. In another section, there were clippings about South Africa. Other pages were about people in Witness for Peace standing on the border of Nicaragua or about the *Clearwater* fighting water pollution. But the way we were going about things in the Tigers, nuclear war was what we mentioned most.

"The display could use a lot more in it," said Langston. "Maybe we could have a section called 'Stories about Forgotten People.'"

"Stories?" said Louisa. "I thought it was just going to be art."

"It doesn't have to be only art. We could have newspaper clippings or write things. I mean, I know a family I'd like to write about." He turned to Vera. "I'm thinking of the Carters. Things were so hard for them you could say bombs had already dropped in their lives."

"Yeah, the Carters. They were neighbors of ours in D.C. They had an unbelievable amount of health problems and not much money. We lived in a neighborhood where people would invite them over to supper and come by and visit them, but it was like they had one thing after another. She was too sick to work, then he injured his back at work and had to lie in bed in a brace. And when their son graduated from high school, he couldn't find a job for the longest time. Lots of Black teenagers have a really hard time getting jobs now. The one he got just paid him peanuts, and then he was laid off."

I thought of the MacLeod family in Larkspur. Their dairy farm had been bought out, and the kids looked skinnier every year. I often saw Mr. MacLeod sitting in a chair at Gus's store. His eyes looked empty, and his breath smelled like he'd been drinking.

I thought about Maritza when she first moved here. She'd said it wasn't easy for her even though her second cousins already lived in town. Now I remembered back to her first weeks in our class. Kids picked her last to be on their team at recess. I'd forgotten about that, but I bet she hadn't. I hadn't realized before now all the things that needed changing right here in our town.

My thoughts began to come together. "Why don't we rename our display?"

"Take out the word *peace*?" asked Stan.

"No. How about 'The Arts Display for Justice and Peace.' "

"Yeah, that's it!" said Langston. "That's a lot better."

Vera got up and went to the kitchen. She was smiling to herself. She brought back a pitcher of ice water.

"Pour it on Zack's head," said Coreena, "for his poor scrambled brain."

"The future's in good hands with us," said Stan. He put his hands on Zack's and Langston's shoulders, and they stuck out their tongues and make weird faces.

"Get serious," said Langston. He stood on his head and came crashing down with his feet on the couch.

When I looked over at Zack, he was staring at nothing in particular. Stan waved his hands in front of Zack's eyes to get him to blink. "What are you thinking?"

"I like Langston's idea of having stories of forgotten people. And I was thinking, 'What about us?' Maybe we could have a special heritage section in the display where each of us talks about our backgrounds and what they mean to us."

"Where's your family from?" asked Stan.

"I'm a mutt," said Zack. "I'm part German, Irish, Italian, French, and Finnish. I don't know much about any of them."

"Do you go to the synagogue in Crowningburg?" Louisa asked Stan.

"Yeah, my father is the cantor there."

"Oh, you must get your musical ability from him," said Vera.

"My father doesn't count my guitar playing as music, but he's the one who got me going with music lessons.

He just puts up with my guitar."

"How many different religions and nationalities and cultures do you think there are in Larkspur?" Zack asked.

"I don't know. You could ask a friend of mine, Byron Lewis," said Vera. "He teaches multicultural education. Or even better, talk to the Goldsteins about it. Ed and Betty were the ones who started the monthly multicultural gatherings down at the town hall. You come to those, don't you Cassie?"

"Yeah, usually." I was surprised that Vera had remembered back to last December when Mom and I went to the Kwanzaa celebration she had led. Mom went to the gatherings every month, and she often brought me along. In October, we'd met Cambodian families from Crowningburg.

"Well, I know Vicky Goldstein. I'll talk to them," said Stan.

"And I'll start thinking about how to set up a heritage display," said Zack.

"Maybe we should put our captions for all the drawings in both English and Spanish," I added.

"Nice idea," said Vera.

"I can think of people my parents would like to invite who might not come if it was just in English," said Maritza. "I'll talk to my Spanish teacher."

"But, Vera, you've got to tell me, you did like our skit, didn't you?" said Coreena.

"Oh, yeah! I was so proud of you. You kids have a spirit about you that really comes through."

"What do you mean?" said Maritza. We all wanted to hear more about what she liked.

Vera laughed. "You remember the photo of Treena where she's handing the petitions to your principal and she's standing there looking so tall and proud? Well, that's the kind of spirit I'm talking about. The words are important, but there's something underneath your words that really comes out."

As Maritza and I got our coats on to go home, she told

me she wanted to bring some of her books from Puerto Rico to a Tigers meeting, especially her favorite book of poems. She said children's reading books in Puerto Rican schools have lots of poetry in them.

"Maybe you and I could draw pictures to go with those poems," I said.

"Cassie, why don't you have something in there that's Polish? Like you could make some Polish Easter eggs with peace symbols on them?"

The eggs would be too hard to make, but I thought I could try a paper cutting that would show the things I love about the meadow. I could bring the spirit of my grandmother and of Poland into our display.

Vera gave me a ride home. I waved to her and then stood outside in the dark before going into the house. I looked up at the stars and tried to find the constellations Zack had invented. I chose one bright star to be Planet Z. And as I looked into the night sky, I thought, That's where peace lives, in the dark, waiting to be born.

CHAPTER SIXTEEN

Rembrandt
Speaks

"Do you have a crush on somebody?" Terry asked as we walked through the halls. "You're in a pretty good mood today."

I let my math book swing. "If I were still sending you postcards, I'd probably draw a grin."

"So? Do you?"

"I think a couple of guys are nice, but that's not why I'm smiling. I'm just happy today," I said as we got near the math room door. "I don't really have a crush."

"Who? Who?"

I stepped inside the room so I wouldn't have to answer.

Mr. Barker was handing out our quizzes from before Thanksgiving. "My parents will kill me if I get another C," Terry said as we waited for him to get to our papers. She looked at the sheet Mr. Barker held out to her and slumped into her chair. "I can't believe it; I got a D."

I looked at mine. "I got a C."

"You? You never get C's."

"Before anybody jumps out of the window over this quiz," said Mr. Barker, "I want to tell you I'm giving it over again. Those scores were disgraceful. So take out a clean sheet of paper."

It was an easier quiz than the first one. I handed my paper in early and found a leftover note in the back of my desk. I unrolled it carefully. Somebody from the period before had written it. It wasn't that interesting. It said the music had been lousy at Saturday's dance. Jill had already told me that. She didn't have much fun. Eddie wasn't into hanging around the high school and insisted they leave early. She didn't mention whether she saw Zack and Louisa there.

Nothing could dampen my spirits today. Mom had told me at breakfast that the posters for the display would be ready this afternoon. This was the day that the Tigers were going public.

For the rest of math class, my thoughts went back and forth between the geometry on the blackboard and the pictures in my mind of what would happen once everyone in town saw our poster. I was imagining people talking about it while they stood in line at the post office when I heard Mr. Barker call somebody's name sharply. I looked up, thinking that it must be me. But he was calling on a girl in the front row named Laurie. He put his hand out for the note he thought she was hiding.

"But it's not a note," Laurie protested.

"Really? You can't tell me you're doing geometry."

Laurie looked over at Terry, and they both began to laugh. "Yes, I guess it is geometry, well, sort of." She took a red piece of paper from behind the math book she'd propped up as a screen. It was folded into a paper crane.

Mr. Barker held it up for the class. I could see Terry hiding another crane underneath her desk. She must have taught Laurie. "I would hardly call this today's geometry lesson," said Mr. Barker.

"Well, could we do it tomorrow?" asked Laurie. "Could Terry and I teach the class how to make them?" She saw

Terry shake her head with embarrassment, but she kept speaking. "If we get all our work done, please?" Laurie was one of those kids who acted real sweet with teachers and could talk them into things I would never attempt.

"Friday, maybe," said Mr. Barker. He was weakening. Knowing Laurie, she'd bring in stacks of origami paper, and it would be a sure thing.

I told Langston about it that afternoon at the church. It wasn't an official Tiger's meeting. Just four of us were hanging out while Jill and Zack picked up the posters.

Treena held an armful of cranes. "Fly over to Langston," she joked.

"You got a thousand yet?" I asked him.

He led me over to a large cardboard box half filled with paper cranes. On the side of the box were crossed-out numbers and a total of 577. "We're over half way there."

"My math class might be making some," I told him. I could tell he wasn't worried about the number. He was different from Ned in that way. To Ned, everything was a big crisis, but Langston took things in stride.

"Cass, do you want to help me count these?" he asked pointing to Treena's cranes. "The new kids this weekend made them." Reverend Ames had let Louisa and Treena come in over the weekend and hold two meetings for new members. He was also letting us use the church every weekday until the art display.

Langston and I both began counting piles out loud, and after a few minutes, he started to lose track of where he was. "Thirty-five, forty-six, forty-what? A thousand and two, a thousand and three."

"Langston, you're cheating," I laughed.

"It's your fault. You're throwing me off." He turned the shoebox over and dumped the rest out on my head. As we were picking them up, Ned came in.

Ned pulled out his shirt, rolled up his sleeves, and as usual headed over to talk to me. "Guess what I saw in study hall today."

"Coach Armstrong break-dancing," said Langston.

"About as likely," said Ned. "This kid next to me was doing a picture about peace. He's not the kind of kid you'd expect. I asked him about it, and he said it was an assignment for his art class."

"He must have Miss Leamon," I said.

"Why?"

"She's been giving nothing but peace assignments. When I'm there at lunch, she shows them to me."

"What kind of things?" asked Ned.

"One of her classes is drawing cartoons that show how to solve a conflict."

"Like what to do when someone tries to smother you with paper cranes," added Langston.

"Get them back!" I said, running at him with the wastebasket.

"Truce," said Langston.

"Okay, truce." I sat down on a low table. "Well, I saw a long scroll one class is making with scenes from the life of Gandhi, and another class is doing the life of Harriet Tubman. Oh yeah, and I think the eighth graders are drawing 'what peace means to me.' "

"Hmm," said Ned. "That must be the class he's in. He was drawing a jigsaw puzzle that said, 'Peace is everyone putting in a piece of the puzzle.' "

"Hey, sign that kid up," said Louisa. She was seated by the windows in what I'd come to think of as her favorite spot. She had on a pair of new enamel earrings, and she looked especially pretty. Ever since third grade when she showed me how to draw, I've looked up to her.

I'm not jealous, I told myself. So what if Zack and Louisa go out with each other. Shouldn't I be glad for my two friends?

"Seriously, Ned," said Treena, "Ask him to join We need him!"

"Why? Didn't enough kids come this weekend?"

"Yeah, but look in the box," said Louisa.

Ned went over to the box with Arnold's face on it and

lifted up one finished drawing. "This is nothing. How could all those kids only come up with one?"

Treena flipped back her ponytail. "Most of the new kids tell me they don't want to draw. All I hear these days is 'I'd like to help but I'm not an artist.' "

"I'm fed up to here with that," said Louisa, putting her hand underneath her chin. "No, here," and she moved her hand up to her forehead.

"It's not the kids' fault," I said.

"I know it's not their fault. I'm still sick of hearing it," said Louisa. She pulled her brown hair back, put a rubber band around it, and bent over a drawing. She has an amazing ability to concentrate. I'd seen her go to work while Riley was giving April an airplane spin.

Treena traced over the pencil lines of a drawing with one of Louisa's rapidograph pens. "Here's some good news," she said, stretching out the words in a funny drone. "One of the English teachers told me she'd give us some writing from her class. Ms. Ochs is her name, I think.

She liked the skit. If we don't have enough artwork, we could fill up the display with compositions."

Louisa looked over at her. "You're using that pen all wrong," she said suddenly. She seemed to be in a crabby mood, and I didn't know why. "Don't press so hard."

"Okay. Okay. So talk to me about something else. You never told me much about the dance. All you said was it was fun."

"It was different than I expected."

"How?"

"When we got to the gym and the first song was playing, Zack looked at me and said, 'Do you like dances?' and I said 'No.' Then I asked him if he liked dances, and he said 'No.' So we walked around outside and went to the waterfall."

"That explains why I didn't see you there. Do you think you'll be going out together some more?"

"I wish. He's interested in somebody else, probably a girl in Syracuse. We'll still do stuff together, but it's not like what I had hoped."

I daydreamed that Zack's secret crush was on me and he was just waiting for me to get older. He'd never spoken about a girlfriend in Syracuse. It must be someone in Larkspur that he liked.

Riley came in the door with a handful of snow and began to throw little pieces of it into the air.

"Stop it, you're going to get splotches on this," said Louisa. "What do you think you're doing?"

"In the absence of confetti, I'm celebrating," said Riley.

I stood up and went to the door. "You mean they're here?"

Jill and Zack came up the stairs with four cardboard boxes. They were taped shut, but one copy of the poster was stuck to the top of each box. That's the way my mother always packages the orders at the shop. Treena ripped the poster off one of the boxes.

"It's gorgeous, it's gorgeous," she danced. We all took

a look. Louisa had made the picture, and Treena had hand-lettered the words:

> ARTS DISPLAY for PEACE & JUSTICE
> January 1   Noon – 6 P.M.
> LARKSPUR TOWN HALL
> Find out what local young people are thinking!

"You're a genius!" Zack said to Louisa.

"Oh, Louisa, you make me sick your drawings are so perfect," said Treena.

"Blech," said Louisa, ducking her head. "I'm so sick of hearing that." She sounded disgusted. Then in a sing-song voice she said, "Am I going to have to make my speech now?"

"Speech?" asked Treena.

Ned and I were arguing about who would get to hang up the posters in town.

"Quiet," said Riley. "Rembrandt speaks."

"Rembrandt Schmembrandt," said Louisa. "If anyone says one more thing about my drawing, I'm going to run out of the room."

"I don't get it," said Treena.

"I feel like people are putting me on a pedestal, and I don't like it."

"Hey, you should be proud of it," said Zack. "Some of us can't even draw a straight line." He meant it as a joke, but it seemed to me like the wrong thing to say. It was one of those phrases I was also sick of hearing.

Louisa wasn't in the mood for it. "That is just not the point. Straight lines, crooked lines, who cares. And Zack, you're one of the people I'm talking about. You're always saying you're not an artist."

Kids were usually too in awe of Zack to get really mad at him about anything. I was glad Louisa was telling him what was on her mind. I remembered the way he had put down his drawings when he first showed me his notebook. It had made me feel uncomfortable.

Ned heard the beginnings of an argument and came over. "You two can't fight," he said. "You're the Ma and Pa of the Tigers."

"And we're your little Tig-lettes," said Riley. "Goo."

"I'm not the Ma!" said Louisa.

I'd never seen Louisa angry before. Ned backed away like he wasn't sure he was supposed to be listening. Riley and Langston hung around the edges of the conversation trying to look interested in other things. I stayed close enough to hear.

Treena closed her work up in her folder and came over to sit right next to Louisa. "We think your drawings are great. I don't get it. What's wrong with that?" When Louisa didn't answer, she added, "Come on, tell me."

"What's wrong with it?" Louisa sighed. "Plenty. Plus I'm sick of people expecting me to be an expert. Those meetings for new kids weren't much fun this weekend. I had to explain everything over and over." Her voice trailed off like she was swallowing her anger. She slumped over with her head propped up on her arm.

"Hey you, with the new earrings, don't go to sleep on me!" said Treena.

"You want me yelling and screaming and jumping around the room?"

"Why not? Riley does it all the time."

Louisa looked at Treena like she was deciding whether to spill it all out. I wondered if she wanted to say more about Zack but couldn't. I knew what it felt like to be angry about several things at once and have it all mush together.

"You heard the way the kids talked this weekend, Treena," she said. "'Tell me what I should draw.' 'My work isn't good enough for the display.' And the one I hate the most, 'Oh, Louisa, I wish I could draw like you.' I feel like I make everyone feel miserable. They say they love my drawings, and the next minute they say they hate theirs. Well, I'm tired of it! This whole display is no fun for me anymore. I used to love drawing, and now I just want to hide what I do. I don't want people comparing themselves to me!"

I knew what she meant. When I made a drawing I really enjoyed, I'd go off to a corner of the room and work by myself. If someone walked by, I would cover the drawing with my hand. I wasn't worried so much anymore about people not liking what I did. I was more worried that they'd be jealous. I had been labeled one of the "good" artists in the group.

Louisa pulled strands of loose hair back behind her ears. "Zack, I'm not saying it's your fault. Just the opposite." She sounded less angry and distant.

Zack sighed. "Look, I stopped being an artist in second grade."

"Why?" Treena asked.

"Oh, it was stupid," said Zack trying to brush it away.

"What happened?" I said. I wondered if it were something like when I was afraid of Sam.

"Well," said Zack, propping his feet on the table, "I had this teacher in second grade who always made everyone in the class draw pictures of the same thing at the same time. So one day she said we were supposed to draw the nighttime. It was simple. You just make black sky with some stars. Only I loved stars so much that I got out crayons and made purple circles and orange stripes and streaks of red and green." He gestured with his hands. "That's what stars were like to me. And I thought it was the best thing I'd ever done."

Louisa pressed her lips together sympathetically as if anticipating what would happen.

"My teacher came along the rows and stopped at my desk. She picked up my drawing to show to the class, and I couldn't wait. I figured she'd like it as much as I did. Only when she held it up she said, 'This is not the way we draw night.' In front of the whole class."

"That's gross," said Jill.

"I never did anything else unusual after that. It pretty much ended my art career."

"Something like that happened to me," said Louisa. "I have this aunt who's a painter." She made a face. "She can be really bad news. When she found out I was learning painting, she decided to help me. Some help. I didn't even ask her. She thought I'd learn how to paint better if she'd point out every little thing that was wrong with my work. I hated it, and it didn't help my painting one bit. See that's what I'm trying to say. I don't want other kids to feel bad because of me."

"I know what my mother would say," said Ned. "She'd say that it's kind of lonely up there on a pedestal."

Louisa laughed. It was just like Ned to try to help her feel better.

"It's not something you're doing," said Zack. "I do it to myself."

"What about me?" said Jill. "I haven't done a single drawing for this whole thing."

"But you do other things," said Zack. "Like you told us we couldn't leave the bulletin boards that ugly, drab color. Even when I said it would be too much work, you insisted we get material to cover them over."

"That isn't anything," said Jill.

"Well, it is," said Louisa. "Everyone doesn't have to do artwork."

Riley stood up on one foot and held out his hands like a statue. "We all have our own fountain of creativity flowing like champagne." He opened his mouth like a statue in a bird bath.

"I don't know about you, Riley," said Treena.

"Quiet. Wouldst thou stifle my muse?"

"Well, I have a confession to make," said Zack.

"Oh, good, a juicy confession," said Riley.

"I don't know how juicy it is, but you've probably noticed that over all these weeks, I've only put one drawing into that box. And I've been feeling really bad about it. I don't think the rest of my drawings are good enough for the whole town to see They'd make the display look bad."

Riley shook his finger. "Uh, uh, uh. You've been holding out on us. Now do you have a change of heart?"

"Well, no. I don't think my drawings really fit. But I do have something else I could use. In a way, it's a piece of artwork. I've been working on it for six years now, but I haven't shown it to anybody here except Cassie."

"Hmm. I didn't know that," said Louisa.

"Bring it in," said Ned.

"Unless it's three stories tall and made of marble," said Riley.

"Naw, it fits under my arm." He started to have second thoughts. "It's kind of falling apart."

"Nope. You can't back out now," said Langston.

CHAPTER SEVENTEEN

The Snowball Effect

The next day, Zack waited until no one was looking and casually placed his notebook on a side table. Then he huddled over by the window and pretended to be interested in something outside.

Treena noticed the notebook first. "When did this show up?"

"Zack brought it in just now," said Kisha. "What is it? His scrapbook?"

"His masterpiece," Treena whispered to Kisha. "I think he's nervous about showing it."

Kisha opened it up at random. The pages fell open to an old newspaper clipping, and she began to read. "Thirty thousand snowcones! A peace group glued all of those onto cardboard. What do you think of this, Treena?"

"Let me see," said Treena. "Oh, I get it: snowcones, nosecones. They were supposed to represent all the nuclear warheads America has. I guess they wanted the people in their town to really see how large the number is."

Derek overheard them. "It seems like a waste of time and snowcones just to make a point."

"Are you sure we really have that many?" Kisha asked Treena. "I thought thirty thousand was the number of nuclear weapons in the whole world."

"No, America has thirty thousand nuclear bombs. It really is that many, and they're each way bigger than the Hiroshima bomb."

Kisha shuddered. "Then I don't think it's a waste, Derek, for them to glue all those snowcones. People should know about these things."

"It's the money spent on the bombs that's a waste," Treena added. "This says we spend four million dollars an hour on nuclear weapons, and thirty million dollars an hour on all of our defense. That's disgusting."

"Yeah, it is," said Derek, "when you think of everything that money could be doing." He was on his way to the snack table. "But don't anybody get ideas here about us gluing that many snowcones for the display."

I brought my chair over to join Kisha and Treena. "Let me show you some other parts of the notebook." Kisha looked depressed, and I wanted them to see the hopeful things that were there as well. I turned to the section that showed the kids who delivered the letters to the White House.

"That's neat," said Kisha. "Does Zack have clippings about the Ribbon Project, too? The one my grandmother helped with?"

Before I could look with her in the section called, "Inside America," Treena grabbed it from me. "Ooooh, I know!" she said. "We could put some of these pages in the display! Louisa, you have to come over here."

"Wait. I've got to finish this first," Louisa answered. She was drawing in her favorite corner.

"You're really going to like this stuff, Louisa," Treena called. "You could give some of these pages to kids who say they don't know what to draw. Do you want me to bring some of the pages over to you?"

As Treena clicked the ring binder, Zack appeared at her side. "Don't move anything," he said.

"Don't worry. We'll put it all back together again," said Treena.

Zack looked uncomfortable. "Hey, I just brought it for one day."

"Oh, leave it longer," said Louisa coming over. "I won't have a chance to look at it much this afternoon."

Zack was flustered. "Look, I've been collecting these things for six years. This is an antique. It's fragile. I don't want it in pieces flying around the group. Something could happen to it."

"What about if Louisa and I promise to guard it? We could have kids sign out pages like library books," said Treena.

"Or you could photocopy the pages kids want," I suggested.

Louisa got engrossed in looking through the notebook.

"And we promise we won't let anything get lost. We'll keep it organized the way you have it now," added Treena. "Zack, you've got to leave it here. We could pick out the best parts and have a whole section with them in the display. We really need that right now. It will make our display a lot larger."

"And more believable," said Louisa, pointing to the page she was looking at. "You've got facts here. I mean, these are real things: food banks and international computer hook-ups. It's so interesting."

"We'll take it apart, and then we'll put it back together just as it was," said Treena.

"Take it apart!" He took the notebook from Louisa and held on. "This is an old friend."

"I know. We'll take care of it. Please leave it here, Zack. We really need it," said Treena with so much enthusiasm that I knew eventually she'd convince him.

"Trust us," said Louisa. She gave him a special look. Whatever had or hadn't happened between them, he did seem to trust her a lot.

"Okay, but I can't watch," said Zack.

The rest of the afternoon, pages of his notebook

circulated around the group. I signed out the pages I remembered about the solar clubhouses and brought them to Kisha. "Want to help me draw this?" I asked.

"Sure." She pulled another chair over so I could sit next to her.

Ned was all excited. "You know what?" he said to Derek. "There's an article here that says we can safely dismantle nuclear weapons. This scientist says technologically it's no problem. You take the trigger out of the warhead, and it can't go off."

"What about radioactivity?" asked Derek. These sort of detailed problems were the kind that interested him. "And getting countries to trust each other enough to do it?"

"You could have inspection teams of scientists from all the different countries involved, and some neutral countries, too," said Claude, joining the two of them.

The next day, Wednesday, Ned came in with a picture of a missile being carefully taken apart. More kids were there than had come for a while, including some of the younger members. Derek's brother Stevie got interested in what Ned had done, and he tried to draw something like it. He worked on that as enthusiastically as he had once worked on drawing rockets.

A group of them got all wrapped up in the specific details: where the radioactive waste would go, how the metal parts could be melted down to make tools, and how the whole thing would be watched over by the inspection teams.

Louisa collected all of their drawings in a folder marked, "How We Could Dismantle the Bombs Someday." Ned crossed out the word *could* and changed it to read, "How We Will Dismantle the Bombs Someday." But Derek scoffed and said it was unrealistic.

Maritza brought in a whole stack of compositions from her English class with Ms. Ochs. They were all titled, "Larkspur in the 21st Century," but they were all different. Some were fantastical predictions. One talked about jeweled monorails carrying people high in the air. Some were depressing, like saying there would be a nuclear war and we'd all return to the Stone Age.

One person described farms in Larkspur with windmills and solar powered tractors. Another who had visited a Buddhist monastery in our county said if the nuclear power plant north of us were shut down for good, the monks could guard it. Jill thought those would make great drawings, and she looked for volunteers to illustrate them. She decided to display all the drawings and compositions about Larkspur along with a map of the town.

The whole art display was getting more interesting. We decided we wanted it to be like a fair with different booths set up around the display. Langston asked Yukiko if she would do an origami demonstration. Ned tried to get the high school band to play at five, an hour before the display closed, because that would help draw a crowd.

At first Yukiko hesitated about accepting the invitation. She told Langston, "I love to do origami, but people already tend to look at me as a foreign person from Japan. I'm third-generation American. I'm sansei. You know what I'd really like to do? Could Vera and I display her photos and my sculptures about the World War II internment camps for Japanese Americans? Then I would feel comfortable about showing the origami." Langston said we'd make a space for it and that he particularly hoped she would talk about the paper cranes and tell the story of Sadako.

Here it was the last day of November. The posters had been up only three days, but we were starting to get some responses. We'd put them all over the town: at the two gas stations, all over the post office, in the windows of all the stores, on the front of the town hall, at the schools. No place had escaped us. We had also put them up in places outside of Larkspur: at the mall, at the ice cream stores, and in different university buildings.

Treena's family offered to help decorate the hall. Stan's family borrowed from their synagogue a set of posters showing Jewish resistance to the Nazi concentration camps. The Silvas said they would invite people from the Latino communities in the area, and some of the university students who took classes with Maritza's mother agreed to translate captions into Spanish.

April's father said he'd help us set up a table explaining how the national and state legislative process worked. He wanted to provide the names and addresses of legislators and government offices as well as the dates certain votes were anticipated in the coming year. Derek decided to work with him. He didn't want it to come across as if we were pushing one point of view on the issues.

And we got a note from Vera: "I'm bringing my camera to this exhibit, and I want to photograph the whole thing. I can tell that this is going to be an historic occasion."

When Louisa counted up how many bulletin boards we would need for all the things we wanted to display, it came to thirty. Derek and Stevie's family volunteered to use their truck to haul the extra bulletin boards from the high school and elementary school to the town hall. It was all fitting into place.

"You've got to hear this letter we just received," shouted Zack that day. "It's from someone named Dr. Rudolph Aurelia. Does anyone know him?"

"He's that guy you never see."

"The one who lives near Langston?"

"Yeah, I can't believe he wrote us."

"His letter says:"

> My dear friends,
>
> I was so heartened to see your poster today. To know that right here in my own town of Larkspur, there are people working for peace is cause for great joy. I am looking forward to your exhibit. Let me know if I can be of any assistance. I am
>
> Yours truly,
>
> *Rudolph Aurelia*
>
> Rudolph Aurelia

"Can you believe it? He doesn't sound at all like the way I pictured him," said Zack.

"This means we'll actually get to see what he looks like."

"Be of any assistance. I can't think what he could do, can you?" said Treena.

"We don't really know what he's good at."

"We'll really get to meet the mystery man," said Riley. "You see? We're having an affect on Larkspur already. We're like a snowball that can't be stopped."

We were so very happy and excited that the superstitious part of me wondered if it could possibly last.

I called Terry that night to tell her about Dr. Aurelia. "Doesn't he have a neat name? I wonder what he'll look like." She was silent. "Terry, what are you thinking about?" I asked her. "Tell me. We promised we'd let each other know what's on our mind."

"Here goes," she said. "I can't come."

"To the display?"

"Yes. We're going to be at my aunt's for Christmas, and we won't be coming back until the next day."

"You've got to be there!" I practically yelled. I felt like someone was choking me. "There's got to be a way!"

Terry whispered into the phone, "Maybe I should run away from my aunt's house."

"Yeah, why can't you come back sooner?"

"I don't know. It's really stupid." In a low voice she added, "I don't think my dad had a very good reaction to the posters around town. Oh, Cassie, I've got to go. Mom's calling us for dinner."

"Terry, you're my friend, no matter what."

"I know, Cass."

When we got off the phone, I looked at the doodles I'd been making on the message pad—jagged angry lines so deep they creased through several layers of paper. Well, I'm not giving up, I thought.

Mr. Cameron and the secret work at Tolltorgan came back into my mind. Maybe there was no connection between that and Mr. Cameron's reactions to the display, but I realized I had to tell Terry soon. I couldn't keep protecting her. I dreaded it so much, I had been postponing it over and over again. Next week, I'll talk to her, I promised myself. I'll invite her for dinner a week from Friday.

At the Tigers' meeting the next day, Treena and April ran up the stairs and in the door at top speed. "Okay, guys, make sure you're sitting down," said Treena catching her breath. "You break it to them, April."

April pushed back a strand of her long hair. "We went into Gus's store to ask him if we could leave some extra posters there. Gus took one look at the poster and did a double-take." She imitated him. "He put on his glasses and opened up his calendar for the town hall."

"Yeah, yeah, then what," said Ned.

"Gus says to us, 'Didn't the selectmen talk to you yet?'"

"So I said, 'No. What's wrong?' and he asks us what kind of things we're going to put on display. I told him art mostly, and a few stories. Treena had a folder of art work and she took out the top drawing and showed it to him. It was one of yours, Kisha. The one that says, 'Throw food, not bombs.'"

"He should like that," said Riley. "More business for his store."

"Well he looked right at us," said April, "and asked, 'Are you trying to set up a protest in the Larkspur town hall?' and we just stared at him."

"Finally I said, 'Well, yes and no.' I mean, it is kind of like a protest."

"He turned to us and said, 'There's been some talk about what happened over at the high school when the Air Force helicopter came.'"

"I told him Miss Leamon thought it was okay," said Treena, "but he said that wasn't good enough for some people."

"He gave us his advice. He said, 'It seems to me that you or Zack or whoever should come talk to the selectmen's meeting next Wednesday. They're not sure if what you have in mind is appropriate for the town hall.'"

"And then he told us that one of the selectmen had asked him to erase our display from his calendar until he got back to him. Can you believe it?"

"Erase our display!" said Louisa.

"I don't know about the rest of you," said Treena, "but I'm pushing the panic button." She climbed up and pushed Arnold the Tiger's nose.

"Who are the selectmen?" asked Zack.

"And why aren't there any selectwomen?" added Kisha.

"Well, selectpeople, then," said Treena. "There's Mr. Sweeney, Mr. Goldstein, and Mr. Fairchild." Kisha and I shot each other a look. Mr. Fairchild! Did our leaf throwing escapade have anything to do with this?

"It will probably work out okay," said Zack. "It might even be a good thing to meet them and have them find out more about what we're doing. And Mr. Goldstein helped to start those multicultural gatherings. He'll understand what we're trying to do."

"But Gus makes it sound like we're doing something wrong," said Shari, twisting her braids.

"Naw," said Langston. "The Third Amendment of the Bill of Rights guarantees the right to peaceable assembly."

"But the hall is controlled by the town," said Louisa. "They could stop us."

"What we're doing is a public service," said Zack. "We're not just lodging a complaint. We've got proposals. They've got to let us have the display. I'll call up one of the selectpeople tonight and see what's going on."

"My mother is the town treasurer," offered Ned.

"Oh good. We'll make a deal," laughed Riley. "No town hall for the Tigers means no money for the selectmen."

"Oh brother, I can just see the headlines, 'Peace Group Bribes Town Officials,'" said April.

"We could have bribes," said Riley.

"What are you talking about?" asked Treena.

"Seriously," Riley insisted. "Although maybe it's better if we call it friendly persuasion."

"What?"

"We'll bribe the whole town. With door prizes. And free food. And radio announcements. We've got to make sure that everyone comes."

His enthusiasm caught on. People were eager to think about something other than the possibility of losing the town hall for the display. He went with a group across the street to start calling radio stations on the pay phone at the gas station.

I stayed behind. I felt discouraged. One discouraging thought began to lead to others. It was as if all my hopes were suddenly crashing down.

"Zack? Louisa?" I called over to them where they sat talking on the windowseat with Treena. "I want to ask you something."

"Yeah, Cass?" said Zack. He motioned me over to join them, and Treena moved over to give me a seat.

"I'm worried about something. What if people do come to our display, even lots of people, but all they do is look at it and walk away? What if they never actually do anything about it?"

"I've been worrying about that, too," said Louisa.

"Yeah! I want to sound the alarm," said Treena. "We could have a nuclear war in our lifetime, and I don't see anyone in Larkspur doing anything to stop it."

That night when I got into bed around the usual time, I didn't feel like sleeping. I kept thinking about the town hall. If it were such a big deal to the selectmen to have us even talk about peace, how could we ever hope they would actually work for peace in the ways the drawings illustrate? Maybe this whole art display wouldn't amount to anything anyway.

"I want to make a difference," I kept thinking as I fell asleep.

It was the middle of the night. I was looking for an air raid shelter. The siren I'd been dreading was screaming through the streets. I half knew it was a dream and half was afraid it wasn't. My arms and legs were numb. I was helpless. I couldn't run. Suddenly, Terry appeared. I

224

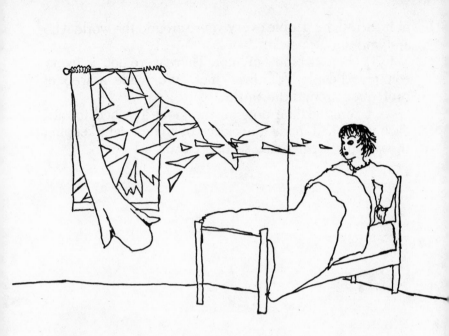

asked her if she would help me along, and she grabbed hold of my arm and pulled me with her.

We came to a place with lots of concrete that must have been the mall. We tried to hide, but there were too many people already in that shelter, and they told us we had to leave.

Then Terry and I got separated, and I was all alone. I kept calling her name, but she didn't hear me. I was totally terrified.

I woke up. I was sure it was a dream now, but the feelings stayed with me like a terrible taste. My left arm was numb. I shook it with my other arm to bring the blood back. I felt stuck to my bed. I couldn't make myself get up and find my parents. Something held me.

I closed my eyes, afraid the dream would return. I usually count sheep at times like this, but this time I knew it wouldn't work.

Instead, I began counting people. I thought of the people in Zack's notebook, and I imagined all the people in it and all the people everywhere around the world who are working for peace.

I saw them like dots of light. There were dots in every country. People I'd never met. We made a web of protection around the world.

As I counted, the dots on the globe reached toward each other and made a necklace of golden light keeping the world safe. In a few seconds, I was asleep.

CHAPTER EIGHTEEN

Upsetting the Apple Cart

I knew what I should do. I was home from school sick, and Mom was home, too. I should tell her about my nightmare. Zack always said that if you have a nightmare about nuclear war, you should be sure to talk to your parents about it. But I just wanted to forget it.

My breakfast dishes were still on the tray on my nightstand. I pulled up my blankets and rolled over. I could hear my mother slowly turning the doorknob to check on me. I lay still and kept my eyes closed so I would look asleep. I breathed slowly and loudly. It worked. I could hear her going back downstairs.

I still felt that heavy feeling that last night's dream had left me with. Mom thought I might be getting the flu. Earlier this morning, she had put a thermometer in my mouth. It had come out normal, but she'd let me stay home anyway.

Now that she was gone, I opened my eyes and looked around the room. On one wall was a poster of a rushing waterfall. On another, there was a picture of the Earth seen from the moon. It said, "Home." Zack had given it to me.

I opened up my social studies book to where I'd left off doing my homework last night. There were still several pages left in the chapter. I began reading on the top of page ninety-two, "The Kaiser's troops were readied at the border. The outbreak of war was impending." War! Too much talk about war!

I reached to the shelf above me and got down a ragged beanbag doll with button eyes. She'd been my comfort toy since I was very young. I hadn't held her for a long time. "Hi, Bluie," I said to her. "You look funny. All your hair's worn off." When Mom was a little girl, her mother had made Bluie. She always said that I would give Bluie to my own child someday.

I leapt out of bed. A prickly feeling was inside me. It reminded me of how I felt when I first realized there was such a thing as death. I had to move. I bolted out of my room and down the hall.

"Cassie! What is it? Do you have to throw up?" Mom was there on the stairs. I rushed into her arms, still holding Bluie.

"Mom, Mom, what if I never get to have a child to give Bluie to?" I was gulping hard.

"Honey, what do you mean?"

"We'll probably have a war, and I'll never get to grow up and have a family."

There it was. I'd told her. And now what would she say? I remembered what the other kids said their parents told them, things like "Don't be silly," or "That peace group must be putting bad ideas in your head." I dreaded hearing words like that. I'd talked a lot about peace before but never really about my fears.

She led me back to my room and we sat down on the bed. She smelled of rose soap as she drew me onto her lap. I settled into her arms, and she began to stroke my hair the way she had when I was little. "Pretty frightening, isn't it?" she said gently.

I nodded, my head against her shoulder.

"I knew you were upset this morning, and I wondered what it was about. I'm glad you're telling me." She said the words slowly to let me know how much she meant them. "It's really scary, huh?"

"Yes." It came out like a cry of pain.

She held me even tighter. "Tell me more, honey."

With her safely beside me, I walked back inside the dream. I told her about it, step by step. Then I got to the part where I was all alone. A bomb was about to explode any moment, and there was no place to run. That dull feeling began to pour back into me, seeping inside. I could feel myself beginning to shrink.

"Oh, Mama, catch me. Don't let it get me." I clung to her and began to sob so hard my whole back heaved up and down. I didn't care about anything but shaking that creepy feeling out of me.

"Cassie, I'm with you."

I was inside a whirlpool. All around me was a flood that had no sign of ending. A wave of tears hit me, and I clung to her.

"Honey, I won't leave you." Her voice wrapped around me, trying to stop the waves from swallowing me up.

I rested and waited, but I could feel more fear inside me like another wave coming.

"It seems like everything we're doing, all of our work," I broke off into sobs, "just doesn't seem to matter. And," the sobs were choking me now, "I don't think it's going to do any good at all." My body was a knot, squeezing out each word. These were the words I felt I'd been hiding from. I saw faces of people in town and at school—Mr. Cameron's face and Gus's and Sam's—and they were all scoffing at us. The worst thing was that I was starting to believe them.

"But it's got to matter, mama. It's so important. I just can't stand it." She gave me her hands and let me squeeze them tight, but it felt like the biggest wave was right above me, about to crash.

I shook my head. "No," I cried.

"That's right. Yell it if you want to."

"No! No! It can't happen!" My mother was encouraging me, but as I sat up I saw the tear stains on her face. For a second, I got scared again. "Are you afraid, too?" I asked.

She paused. "Yes, sometimes."

"You are?"

"It's hard. I don't talk about it with you kids."

"No, tell me."

"Well, I've wanted to protect you. But I used to wake up every morning and think, 'Thank you, God. The world's still here.' Cassie, what you're doing is making a difference. Believe me." And then she began to cry.

We held each other. It reminded me of when *Babcia* died, only then I couldn't cry, and now I was relieved we could cry together. That whirlpool feeling was gone. Instead, I felt like there was a river underneath us that could carry all the tears we had and hold us up.

"Mom, it would have been okay for you to tell me," I said.

"I'm not so sure. It would have been a burden for you to carry around."

"But when you were working on those petitions, I could tell you were really upset, and I wanted to know what was going on. It seemed like you were mad at me or something."

"No, I wasn't mad at you. I'm sorry you thought that."

"Mom, do you still get that scared? Do you imagine what our street would look like blown up and things like that?"

"I get afraid sometimes, but I don't feel so hopeless."

"Why?" I had to know. I hoped she wasn't just saying it to make me feel better.

"Remember when you were watching a movie one night about people living in caves after a nuclear war?"

"That was such a dumb movie. Yeah, I asked you to turn the T.V. off for me because I hated it but I couldn't move."

"And remember I said instead of those predictions of nuclear war, we should have more movies about what a world at peace would look like?"

"Yeah, I think of that sometimes when I'm drawing."

Mom looked far away and then back at me. "I've decided that we all have two voices inside us right now, and the problem is we're just listening to one of them. The strongest voice says there'll be a nuclear war, and we'll be the last generation. But there's a place inside of us that knows a nuclear war does not have to happen. It's a quieter voice. I hear it sometimes when I'm outside working in the garden. It says we're going to change so there won't be that kind of destruction."

I thought of the green quiet of the willow tree in the summer wind. I thought of the deep blue feeling in the dining room at Thanksgiving with Maritza. I let my breath go in and out easily. "We're not going to let these bombs take over," I said.

"That's right. We're not. It's our world, too," said my mother. That elf look was in her eyes.

"We're going to live." As I said it, I felt the words were true.

I thought about my mask of Cassandra. Miss Leamon

had said Cassandra's warnings would be believed this time.

Now I could hear sounds, the ordinary friendly sounds of our house: the tick of the old clock in the hall, the bubble of the fishtank in Jill's room. I rested for a while, just listening. Then I stood up and stretched my arms. My back cracked. I gave a huge yawn.

A new thought came to me. "Now I remember another part of my dream. There was a huge golden web or necklace around the whole world. It was made of all the people who are working or even wishing for peace. At first we were all alone, but then we reached out our hands and found each other. Together we made this golden light protecting the world."

"That's beautiful, Cassie."

"Mom, are you going to cry again?"

"I might. It's a really beautiful image. I feel like I see it, too. And you and Jill and Zack and all the rest of the kids in your group are right in there. And you're inviting the rest of us in town to join you. What you're doing is important, Cassie, no matter how it turns out."

"I guess so." I looked over at her. "You know what? You're the best."

She drew her mouth into a fish face, an old trick of ours, and she kissed me.

We walked downstairs together to fix lunch. I sat on a stool and chopped carrots and celery while she cooked noodles for soup. I felt warm inside, as if I were still bouncing along on that river.

When lunch was over, instead of going back upstairs to my room, I brought my social studies book down to the kitchen. I wanted to be near her. She was cutting up apples for applesauce. Soon the smell of nutmeg and warm apples would be filling the room.

"The outbreak of war was impending," I read out loud. "I don't want to read this stuff," I told her.

"Boring?"

"Deadly boring." I turned the pages ahead. "I want to get to where the war stops."

"First you'll have to wade through the usual long descriptions of the battles," said my mother.

"I get so sick of reading about them. 'The outbreak of war!'" I repeated in a low dramatic voice like a radio announcer. "What I'm interested in is the outbreak of peace." I caught my breath in a short gasp. "That's what we should do! Have an outbreak of peace!"

"Sign a peace treaty?" asked my mother.

"Sort of like that. Maybe everyone could get together in Larkspur and declare that we're beginning peace here."

"That's terrific! What would it be like?"

"A holiday. A beautiful, sunny day with balloons."

"And what would people do?" my mother asked.

"They'd all agree to do something for peace. Everyone. It would be a promise we would make together. But there wouldn't be rules. You could do it in your own way."

When Zack sat down to meet with the town selectmen, I was with him and so was my Mom. In fact, the small committee room was full to bursting.

We listened while they covered other items on their agenda—something about the town snowplows and something else about the fire hydrants. Then they got to us.

"Next item." Mr. Sweeney, the moderator, squinted at the sheet. "The Tigers' Club? Gus, can you explain what this is about?"

"This is that group that wants to put on a display about peace and nuclear war." I watched Mr. Fairchild blink. "Come on up, Zack."

"There's a group of us kids in town…"

"How many?" interrupted Mr. Goldstein.

Louisa handed Zack a sheet of names. "Well, seventy-two."

"Seventy-two? Let me look at that sheet." Zack passed it to Mr. Fairchild.

"We've never had seventy-two at once," Zack explained.

"The checks by the names show how many times they've come," Louisa added. Mr. Goldstein reached over to see the sheet.

"I see that my daughter Vicky has attended three times. I wasn't aware of that."

"Vicky's your daughter?" Treena blurted out from the front row. "She makes beautiful paper cranes."

"Quiet, quiet," said Mr. Sweeney. "I want to focus on one person at a time. Now, Zack, you've already answered one of our concerns. We want to make sure that the town hall is used for events that a majority of townspeople would support."

"Wait a minute," called Mr. Fairchild. "I agree. We hadn't dreamed there were so many involved, but these are children, underage, not voters. We can't conclude that they speak for the majority."

"How do you answer that, Zack?" asked Mr. Sweeney.

"Mr. Goldstein's daughter Vicky, Treena who's over there, Riley in the back row—all of us are speaking about our future. We don't expect that everyone in Larkspur will agree with what we say. And that's okay. That's not the reason we're doing it."

"Hey, we don't always agree with each other," Riley yelled out, and he got a laugh.

"But we are sure," Zack continued, "that this town wants to hear from us whenever there's something on our minds so big and so important to us that it could keep us working together on it week after week."

Mr. Goldstein nodded. "That's true. You've got me curious. What do you say, Frank?"

Mr. Fairchild took a deep breath. "Don't get me wrong, I'm all for listening to young people. And my wife and I appreciate their, er, peacemaking efforts that we've already seen." I was relieved to hear that. "But frankly, we've never had anything like this at the town hall before. I'm concerned where this might lead."

234

"I don't quite follow you, Frank," said Mr. Goldstein. "Where could it lead?"

"That's my point. Larkspur is one of the finest towns that anyone could live in here in America. Why upset the apple cart?"

"The apple cart?"

"Why change the way things are? Why rock the boat? I'm proud to live in Larkspur just as it is."

"I'm still not clear about what you're saying, Frank."

Mr. Fairchild flashed him a look that I thought meant he didn't want to spell it out in front of us kids. "You remember what happened at the university. It may be still going on now in other areas. Outsiders come in; generations get divided."

"But that's why these young people are coming to us," said Mr. Goldstein, "so we won't be divided. And besides, some of what you're referring to happened in the sixties."

"Don't fool yourself. It could happen again. We've got to think this thing through."

"Well, let's put it to a vote," said Mr. Sweeney. "How many are in favor of allowing the Tigers' group to have their peace display at town hall on January first?" He and Mr. Goldstein raised their hands. "And how many opposed?" Mr. Fairchild raised his hand while he looked at the ceiling. "Passed. Next item." He read from his sheet of paper. "Mrs. Kaczenski."

My mother walked forward. "Hello, Florence," Mr. Sweeney smiled, "What can we do for you tonight?"

"I understand there's a special town meeting scheduled for January fifteenth," she began.

"That's right."

"I'd like to add an item to be voted on at that meeting. I've got a petition here signed by over ten percent of the voters in Larkspur as required by town law." She and Vera had been busy for the last five days going around to people in town to get them to sign. She handed the signatures to Mr. Sweeney, and he thumbed through the pages.

"Everything seems to be in order," he said. "It looks like you have well over the number of signatures required. We'll check them, of course, but you've done what's needed. We'll put it on the docket for you."

"George, why don't you ask Mrs. Kaczenski what the petition says?" said Mr. Fairchild.

"Right, right. What will the town be voting on, Florence?"

"Actually, we've recommended that all residents of any age who are able to read be allowed to vote on this particular question. Cassie, why don't you come up and read it."

I stepped to the front, my new shoes squeaking. I'd practiced it so many times, I could practically say it from memory. "Resolved: that the town of Larkspur will declare an outbreak of peace, as defined in paragraphs two and three below, on this coming July Fourth."

CHAPTER NINETEEN

Violets in the Snow

"Hello, Mrs. Cameron." I pinched my fingernails into the heel of my hand and tried to take a deep breath.

"Hello, Cassie. Your voice sounds a little odd."

"I'm out of breath, I guess. Terry and I have been running around a lot."

"Isn't it a bit late to be calling, dear?"

"I know it's after nine, but Terry and I just noticed that it's snowing really hard, so we wondered if she could stay here overnight. Would that be okay? She could use some of my pajamas."

"I think so. It's not a school night. That should be fine. Would you put Terry on?"

"She can't come to the phone right now. She's, um, stirring fudge on the stove. Can I give her a message?"

"Well, all right dear. Just say we'd like to see her bright and early tomorrow morning for her Saturday chores. Now don't eat too much fudge."

"No, we won't, Mrs. Cameron. Goodnight."

I hung up the receiver and turned to Jill. "Oh, my God, that worked. What's next?"

"Next we pray that Mom and Dad get home soon with

the car," Jill said. I scrambled through the phone book to find Langston's number and dialed it as rapidly as I could.

"Langston! Is that you? I really need your help. This is Cassie."

"Sure. What's up? You sound kind of panicked." It was a relief to hear his steady voice.

"You know my friend Terry?"

"Yeah."

"Well, she's run away sort of."

"Her? Run away?"

"I don't mean run away from home, exactly. She's pretty upset, and she just ran out of my house. She might be heading over in your direction. I'm kind of scared for her. It's like a blizzard out."

"Doesn't she know to come in out of a storm?"

"Well, it's hard to explain. But would you go outside with a flashlight and look for her? Would you look all around your house and your road? I think she'll be coming that way. And would you call Yukiko, too, and ask her to watch out?"

"Sure, we'll help you. I'll call back later."

As soon as I got off the phone, Jill was ready with another idea. "Now call Zack," she said, "in case she does go up the main road."

When I reached Zack, he said he would borrow his mother's car and come pick me up so we could look for Terry together.

"Be on the lookout for her on the way here," I said. I threw on my parka and boots and grabbed my flashlight. Jill stayed behind to answer the phone if it rang. Sam helped us, too. He tried calling the university to see if he could figure out which program Mom and Dad were attending.

I walked down our driveway while the snow swirled thick and fast. I could feel it falling underneath my scarf and down my cold neck. Zack was there to meet me. As

I jumped in the car, he said he hadn't seen any sign of her. "Did she run away because you told her about her father and Tolltorgan?"

I only nodded. I didn't want to talk now—even to Zack. He turned the car around, and I felt the wheels sticking in the thick snow.

It was my fault that Terry was out in this blizzard. She ran because I had kept that secret too long. She ran because now she didn't even feel safe enough with me.

We'd talked up in my bedroom, and I'd taken my time building up to the whole thing. I told her how much I liked her father and how nothing could change that. But when I finally got to the part about Tolltorgan, she just kept shaking her head and saying she couldn't believe it. Then she said she was going down to the kitchen to get a soda.

Usually, even without words, we understood what the other was feeling, but it hadn't worked tonight. I should have gone downstairs sooner to check on her. I'd thought she wanted to be by herself. I figured if I went downstairs too soon, I'd be crowding her. But I was wrong, I guess.

And she didn't understand my message either. I wanted her to know that she could take her time, that all my waiting to tell her about her father and all my waiting now was because I did care, not because I didn't.

"Tell me more about what's going on," Zack urged. "She's running away from this news about her father?"

"I think she just feels like getting away from everything and everybody," I said. But with each step, I bet she was waiting for someone to find her. And our not coming drove her to take another step, and then another. I felt like a hand was gripping my throat. I had let her down. I hadn't come after her soon enough. And now she was outside in the gathering snow.

When we got to the crossroads, I pointed left. Zack said maybe we should get out to look for her footprints to make sure which direction she took, but I was sure which way she'd go. When she'd gotten here, I knew she'd go away from the busy main road and turn down the dead end street.

Zack got out of the car and looked around. He found the prints of her boots in the snow. He showed me with his flashlight. "You were right," he said.

A picture came into my mind of my one-year-old cousin when she was learning to walk. She'd leave one pair of hands and toddle forward in search of the next, lurching on one foot and then the other. But where were the hands to catch Terry? If we didn't find her soon, if she came to the end of the road, would she head for the woods and the fields that were so thick with snow?

A half-mile down, we saw someone waving. It was Langston. "She's here!" He motioned to the house next to his. "Yukiko found her." So someone had been there to catch her. I took my first deep breath since I'd found her coat missing from our kitchen.

Zack pulled his car into the driveway. Snow hung over the edges of the "Yutsumi Pottery" sign and low on the trees, making them like lanterns lining the walk. I couldn't believe I was walking into the house Terry and I had wondered about for so long.

We entered a tiled hallway and took off our boots. I practically ripped the laces, I was in such a hurry. There was a short walkway to the main section. Langston led us inside.

"Terry!" She was huddled in a blanket on a peach-colored couch. I raced over and squeezed her hard. "You're safe! Oh, I'm so glad." I took a good look at her. "Your cheeks are so red. Are you okay?"

Terry seemed to stare right through me.

"She's chilled to the bone but nothing more serious than that," said Vera, who had come over, too. She took off Terry's socks and eased her feet into the basin of warm water she'd just brought in.

"I wanted to find you so bad," I said, burrowing my head in her shoulder.

Yukiko came in with a tray and greeted me. She had a teapot with tiny cups that fit in your hand. I guessed she had made them herself. "This tea will warm you up." She handed a cup of tea to each of us.

Terry took a sip. "Yukiko found me," she said.

I held my fingers above the cup to warm them in the hot steam. "I asked her and Langston to look for you." I put down my tea and wrapped an arm around her. "I was so worried."

Terry let herself sink back on the couch to lean against me. The distant expression on her face was starting to thaw away. "I'm *so glad* you're here, Cassie." She settled in and huddled against me.

For the first time, I took a good look around the room. Strips of dark wood framed the white walls. There was a photograph of driftwood and a painting of gulls flying above a lobster pot. The table next to us held a paperweight of handblown glass that looked like captured bubbles and a large sea-green pot.

"Well, does everyone here already know?" said Terry suddenly. "Do they know about what you said?"

"No," said Vera. "We don't know why you ran away, and we don't have to know. Drink that tea. We're just glad you're fine."

Terry stiffened. "But they will! That's what you told me, Cassie. You said that somebody might write about Tolltorgan in the newspaper, and then everybody in town will hear." She seemed to be talking half to me and half to herself, but the others heard her.

"Should we go away, perhaps?" Yukiko asked Zack.

"Let's stay a little longer. We might be able to help."

"My dad is not a bad person," Terry cried.

I held her and whispered, "That's right. He's a wonderful person."

"And I don't want to have you accusing him of anything!" Terry pointed directly at Zack.

Zack blinked in surprise. "No, I would never do that."

"You better promise!" she yelled.

"I promise," Zack said, coming over to the couch. "Terry, the Tigers are not going to print anything in the newspapers about this. That's the last thing I'd want us to do. I think Cassie was just guessing that somebody else in town might bring it up in the newspaper."

"And if that happens," said Yukiko, "no matter what is said about Tolltorgan, we will make sure that the people involved, like your father, are treated with complete respect. That's certainly what they deserve."

"They better be. I don't want to have anyone attacking my father."

"Would it help if some of us talked to him?" asked Vera.

"What do you mean?" Terry asked.

"If I were your father and people in town were concerned about something I was doing, I'd want them to come to me directly and talk about it rather than criticize my work in the newspaper or behind my back." I watched Vera closely. I noticed the silver gray in her tight curls like a frosting of snow. She's so brave, I thought to myself.

"It might help," Terry said. "I have to think about it."

I heard a car drive up and hoped it was my parents. Yukiko went down the walkway and returned with my whole family, Sam included.

"Is she okay?" my mother asked. She spotted Terry on the couch. "Oh, honey, come here for a hug," she called.

"I can't get up without dripping water."

My mother looked at the basin and came over to her and stroked her hair. "You don't have frostbite, do you? Your cheeks are so pink!"

"No, I'm okay. Yukiko found me outside."

Terry whispered to me as people were introducing themselves to each other, and I passed it on to Vera: "No more explanations."

Vera nodded to me and then turned to the group. "Let's make this a proper celebration," she said. "I've got some cookies I can bring over from next door."

The ten of us feasted on tea, some sandwiches Yukiko made, and the cookies. I was exhausted.

"So you finally got to see the inside of your dream house," Mom said as she offered me the plate of sandwiches. "I've persuaded Yukiko to give us a little tour. You'll come along, won't you?"

But I couldn't move. I just stayed there on the couch and let all the commotion happen around me. Sam and Langston were talking loudly about something. Jill went on the tour with Mom. Zack and my father kept bringing Terry and me food.

My head began to nod. The noises blurred as I grew sleepier and sleepier.

I heard my mother say she had arranged for Yukiko to give Terry and me a pottery lesson tomorrow, but it sounded like it came from a dream.

As I rested my head, I could watch the snow falling in the light from the front porch. When I shifted my focus, I saw inside the house a pot of violets on Yukiko's windowsill. The flowers seemed to rise up on their stems in defiance of the cold.

The last thing I remember before Terry and I fell asleep there on the couch, huddled together like puppies, was the sight of those brilliant purple violets rising out of their small black vase in front of the snow-filled window.

CHAPTER TWENTY

Wobbly Bowls

The next morning, the sky was a cloudless blue. From our kitchen window we could see puffs of snow on the fir trees. Terry and I got the royal treatment at breakfast: Jill made us pancakes with walnuts and blueberry syrup.

Terry called home to ask if she could stay a little longer. She said my mother would drive her home by noon. She didn't say what had happened the night before, and she didn't say where we were going. As I laced up my boots, I saw her give me an okay sign from the phone.

It was about a fifteen-minute walk. It must have been a little strange for Terry to be going back over the same way she had walked the night before, but we kept busy trying to push each other into the snow. Whoever was on the street side nudged the other off the road and into the snowy bushes and fields.

The wind was blowing, and I could hear wind chimes when we arrived at the door. Yukiko called, "Come around the back," just as we were searching for a doorbell or knocker. She showed us to her pottery studio. We passed a garden with three stone statues now draped with snow. Little wood carvings peeked out from the branches of trees. In a clearing, there was a mound of carefully stacked bricks that Terry guessed was a kiln.

We entered a small cabin and stood by her wood stove for warmth. She offered us two wicker chairs where we could sit in front of her potter's wheel. She seated herself on the bench of the wheel, pushed her feet on the treadle and got it moving fast. Then she dipped her hands in some water and held them above the wedge of clay spinning in the center. For a moment, she closed her eyes as if offering a prayer.

Then her thumbs dove down into the center of the wedge and slowly opened it up. She held her hands firmly against the sides to even the walls, and then placed one hand inside and one outside the wall of the bowl. Her hands moved like wings, drawing the clay upward, thinning and raising the wall. They looked like dancing birds.

Yukiko handed us each a wedge of clay and showed us how to pound and knead it against a hard wood slab. "Beginning with a bowl on a wheel would be like beginning piano lessons with a concerto. We'll start with pinch pots to give you the feel of the clay." We rolled our clay into a ball and then with our thumbs did the same opening and strengthening and thinning movements she had done on the wheel. The clay felt cool at first but got warmer as we worked it. I liked squeezing it, but it was hard to pinch just right to make it thinner without breaking it.

"This is how you learn to listen to the clay, by working with it over and over." Yukiko smiled. She had the pearl barrette that was shaped like a butterfly in her hair. One strand of hair slipped down into her eyes, and she brushed it behind her ears with the side of her hand. Her face had a few splotches of gray clay on it.

I made one hard squeeze too many and the wall of my tiny pot broke open. Yukiko saw my face as the clay broke. "With clay it is so easy," she told me. "You just roll and start again."

As I rolled my clay back into a ball, she added, "But I always take a moment to pause and thank each pot for what it has taught me, especially when it is wobbly or broken." She encouraged me to hold the clay for a moment before I opened it up to begin again.

"Terry, this is what happened for you last night, when you ran out in the snow. I think you were feeling wobbly and broken like this. Am I right?"

Terry closed her lips tightly and nodded.

"And it looks now like you wish I would just forget the the whole thing and never mention it. Yes?"

Terry laughed a little.

"But it's from these very times of feeling broken that we learn so much. There you were running, and you turned around and let me find you. It's not a moment to be ashamed of but a moment to be proud of."

She led us over to the wheel to look again at the bowl we had watched her make. She ran her fingers along the walls as if listening. "I feel a large air bubble here, too large to repair. This bowl won't be strong. It would break in the firing." To my horror, she lifted the bowl off the wheel and it collapsed. She held it quietly for a moment and then rolled it back into a ball. Where there had been a bowl, now there was a lump of clay.

"You look so alarmed," she teased, "but you can always start over again. Look at the beautiful pot you are making now, Cassie, with the same clay that a minute ago was in pieces."

We placed our finished pots to dry. She led us into the main house, and we had a snack of cheddar cheese on sesame crackers. We took from our pockets the cut snowflakes we had made for her that morning as we sat in my bed, and she pasted them onto her living room window right above the shelf of violets.

I was disappointed when I saw my mother drive up to pick us up. "Next time we come," I told Yukiko, hoping very much there would be a next time, "I want Terry to show you how she folds paper cranes. She's really good at it."

"That's easy to believe. You do such careful work with your hands, Terry."

I waved hello to my mother from the door.

"Can we come back?" Terry asked Yukiko.

"Oh, yes. You must come back. We're just beginning. How about next Saturday? Is that too soon?"

"We'll be here," said Terry.

I took a look around the room again. I wanted to memorize the pictures on each wall. I liked best a watercolor of misty mountains. Maybe it was of mountains on the west coast, like in California, or maybe in Japan, but it reminded me of Larkspur in the fall. We walked along her tiled hallway to the door and waved goodbye.

Mom was reading a newspaper when we got into the car. She passed it over to us as we both squeezed into the front seat. "Have you seen today's paper yet? We're in it, Cassie!"

It was the first time I'd ever been in the newspaper. A reporter who'd been at Wednesday night's meeting had come to our house to interview us about our proposal for an outbreak of peace. There we were, Mom and me, on the second page of *The West County Daily*. Terry and I looked it over. It wasn't a bad photo. Mom and I were smiling at each other instead of at the camera, and it made it seem like we were sharing a secret.

"You know what this article means, though," Terry whispered to me as we pulled up at her house. "Things will be more and more out in the open."

"But remember, we all promised to help when that happens," I reassured her. "Not just me, but Yukiko, too, and Vera." I got out of the car to walk with her to the door. I couldn't find the words I wanted to say to her. She hadn't seen her family since I'd told her about Tolltorgan. "I hope your afternoon goes okay." I didn't want to be leaving her now, all alone with nobody to talk to. "Call me," I yelled as I got in the car.

My father was holding a stack of newspapers when Mom and I arrived home. "Here come the movie stars," he said. "I've already bought Gus's last five copies."

"I don't see why you had to invite the whole town over to our house," Sam complained as he leaned over the article that accompanied our picture.

"It does sound like that," said Dad. "'Any resident,'" he read, "'who wants to help create the definition of an outbreak of peace may attend a meeting at the Kaczenski household Sunday afternoon.' But tomorrow's my football day. That's the one day I glue myself to the tube. How can we have a thousand people coming into our house, Florence?"

"Half of Larkspur? I don't think so."

"Don't worry, Dad. Everybody will be too busy watching the game. They won't show."

"Everybody but me."

"You can move the T.V. up to the attic."

"But I won't be able to lie around in my slippers and old T-shirt. What will I do?!"

"Those are the risks and sacrifices of peace," my mother smiled.

"Seriously," asked Jill, "what if a lot of people do show up?"

"It's not the kind of event people flock to. I think we'll have the space. I wanted to make it an open invitation because you never can tell who might want to come."

The next day there were more people than we had chairs, but not so many that we couldn't fit the rest on pillows. Some people I'd expected: Zack, Louisa, Claude, Riley, Langston, Vera. There were also new people I wouldn't have guessed: a friend of Vera's named Byron Lewis who taught Multicultural Education, Reverend Ames, Ms. Ochs who had submitted compositions from her English class for the display, April's father, both of Treena's parents, and Gus's wife Dottie.

We worked for over three hours and went through four

large pizzas. There were lots of jokes, like Riley's pitch for special committees, and some minor disagreements.

"I think we've really got a problem here," said Byron Lewis about an hour into the meeting. I'd liked him right away. He was very direct.

"What is it?" asked Zack.

Mr. Lewis took off his glasses and rubbed the bridge of his nose. "I don't think that it's realistic to try to get one hundred percent participation from Larkspur."

Several other adults agreed.

"But we've got to try for everybody," said Treena.

"It will be safer that way," echoed Claude. "People will do it because they know that everyone else in town is going to. That's what will make it work."

"That approach could backfire," said Vera.

"Could we do it another way?" asked Reverend Ames. He brushed the pizza crumbs off his hands. I saw him exchange knowing smiles with Dottie. "From my experience, trying to get one hundred percent of any group is a little..." He searched for the word he wanted.

Treena supplied it. "Idealistic?"

"Well," said Reverend Ames.

"But it's okay to be idealistic about this," Treena continued. "There's nothing wrong with believing the best can happen."

I really admired Treena's ability to speak up like that. I agreed with her, but I couldn't imagine standing up to a bunch of adults that way. I hated speaking in groups.

"What do the rest of you young people think?" asked Ms. Ochs.

"I'm with Treena," said Louisa. "After all, it was our idea. I mean, Cassie's."

Ms. Ochs scanned the circle of faces to search for agreement. "Shall we try for one hundred percent and see what happens?"

"I know my congregation. I don't think it's going to work," said Reverend Ames.

"But we can give it a try," said Mr. Lewis.

By the end of the evening, we had a description we were proud of. Mom drove it to the office of *The West County Daily* early the next morning, and it was printed in the Monday edition in the "Good Neighbors" column:

What Will it Mean if Larkspur Declares an Outbreak of Peace?

Daily Staff Writer

Every person can contribute to peace. You can build peace in your family or neighborhood, or you can act for peace in your school, your business, or our town. Or your work for peace might start with America or with reaching out to other countries. You have the opportunity to define what peace means to you.

Each resident of Larkspur, not only those over eighteen, but every person who can read, will be asked to choose their own action for peace. Their action can take place at any point during the coming calendar year. On July 4th, a list will be published of every resident and their chosen peace activity. On this birthday of our country, we will celebrate our historic declaration of an outbreak of peace.

Not sure what to offer? Like to work with others? Residents will be proposing town peace events and town peace committees open to all. Possible events include an interfaith Hiroshima commemoration.

The resolution to declare an outbreak of peace will be voted on at the town meeting. If this resolution is passed, a committee will be elected to oversee the process, and members will visit every home in Larkspur during the spring to help residents define or select their participation.

World peace is a local issue. Peace starts inside our hearts.

By Wednesday, the first letter about the outbreak of peace appeared in the paper. A woman on the west side of town had written, "What about shut-ins who can't get down to the town hall to vote? Will we be left out?" Louisa and April swung into action. They decided they wanted to come up with an answer to all the questions posed to us in the paper. They arranged for rides for anyone who wanted to attend the art display or the special town meeting and called up the editor to let people know about it.

The next day, there were two letters in the *Daily*. One asked us, "Why don't you sponsor a contest for a town song about peace?" The other said:

> If you want to do something for peace in our town, I think you should do something about the Larkspur Lake Recreation Center because the amount of litter there is appalling. How any town that says it cares for its young people could provide such poor playground equipment and such unattractive facilities is beyond me. Why don't you find a way to address this problem? I think it would be an ideal way of building peace in Larkspur.

I agreed with the writer, but I didn't understand why she thought we should handle it.

"I wish people would stop writing 'why don't you...' because there is no 'you,' it's only 'us.'" said Louisa as she and April discussed how to respond.

"I know," said April. "The whole point is for each person to help make these things happen, not for us to do everything." But we didn't know how to make it easier for people to get involved.

On Friday, the first letter that spoke out strongly against our proposal was printed in the *Daily*.

> Dear Editor,
> I read about this outbreak of peace vote with some confusion and a great deal of consternation. Who is this group that purports to speak for our town? And why are they trying to undermine the very

cornerstone of our strength against the Russians?

I hope we will be allowed to participate in a thorough debate when it comes up at Town Meeting on January 15.

Erika Shipley
(Mrs. Edgar T.)

Next to it was the kind of letter I'd been dreading even more.

Dear Editor,

I'm a graduate student in economics and have been a resident of Larkspur for six years. I know that our small town can't singlehandedly call a halt to the whole arms race, but I believe we can call into question a piece of it. By this I mean the work of the Tolltorgan Company. This local industry is a hidden contributor to the manufacture of nuclear weapons. It has been a concern of mine for some time, and I am grateful that the outbreak of peace proposal provides a way for our town to address this. Anyone wishing more information on the Tolltorgan Company or on the process of economic conversion to peaceful goods and services may contact me through the university.

Lee Ames

"Yup, I read it, too," said Zack when I called him that night. "The cat's out of the bag. I guess it's time to follow up on Vera's suggestion."

"That someone should talk to Mr. Cameron in person?"

"And Lee Ames, too. I don't want to see a shouting match begin in the newspaper."

Vera and Yukiko had the same thought. Saturday morning, instead of having another pottery lesson, Terry and I went to Yukiko's home for a meeting with her and

Zack and Vera and Langston to figure out the best way to respond. My parents were too busy to be there, although they were interested.

Terry didn't want to go, but I talked her into it. We sat on the couch together. "I hope this is over soon, so we can just be with Yukiko," she said when everybody else was out in the kitchen.

"Did your dad say anything about the letter?" I asked.

"A little. Actually, I'm kind of relieved it was there because then I could finally ask him about that stuff without saying that you told me. But the whole thing is so hard, Cassie! I'm really confused. I mean, he's got his reasons."

"What does he say about the Tigers these days?"

"Nothing good. It's still a secret from him that I have anything to do with the group. I'm not really in the Tigers, if you know what I mean. The kids in the group say 'hi' to me at school, and everybody knows I'm your friend, but I've never gone to a meeting at the church. I'm not really part of things."

"Derek asked me if you were going to start coming to meetings."

That didn't bring a smile. She was still thinking. "Daddy always says he knows me so well. He tells me I'm not an artist and that I wouldn't like the things he doesn't like. How do I know if that's true? He says he does everything for my own good, but I'm old enough to figure out what's good for me."

"That's hard. You must feel kind of torn in half."

"Yeah. But I'm going to have to choose pretty soon. I refuse to miss the art display."

"So what did he say about the letter in the paper from Lee Ames?"

"Daddy just closed the paper up, like it didn't bother him because he's so sure he's right. But I wonder sometimes if he *is* so sure."

When the others came in and sat down, Terry grabbed a magazine off the coffee table and began to read. That way, she could be half in our discussion and half not. It was really brave of her even to be in the room, so far as I was concerned.

"It is the same problem as with the wobbling bowl," Yukiko said. "How can we change the clay with love and respect." She passed around glasses of juice and cups of jasmine tea.

"But I don't think that company wants to change," said Langston.

Yukiko settled on the couch and took a sip of tea. "I mean that we sitting here see that wobble." She put the tea down to use her hands as she talked. "We see that the work they are doing is not done for the whole, and they don't. They can't. They're too close to it."

"They probably feel that if their computer company doesn't get the weapons contract, their competitor will," Zack added.

"It's like the thinking of Tolltorgan is this wide," Vera held her hands about six inches apart, "and we're trying to help it be this wide." She stretched the span of her hands. "We're trying to find a way to tell them that when they contribute to nuclear weapons, they affect all of us, but we want to do that without making it sound like we see them as our enemies." Vera was sitting in the chair in front of the windows. The curtains were open, and the sunlight sparkled on the snow.

"I'm very interested in this work of Lee Ames over at the university. Do you know him, Vera? What does economic conversion involve?" Yukiko had that same eagerness I saw when she reached for a fresh slab of clay.

"Some of the Tigers called him," said Zack. "He told us that economic conversion means a company stops doing any work that relates to building nuclear weapons, but instead of closing down their whole operation and laying off the people who have been working there, they convert. They do the same type of thing that they are good at, but they make something else that has nothing

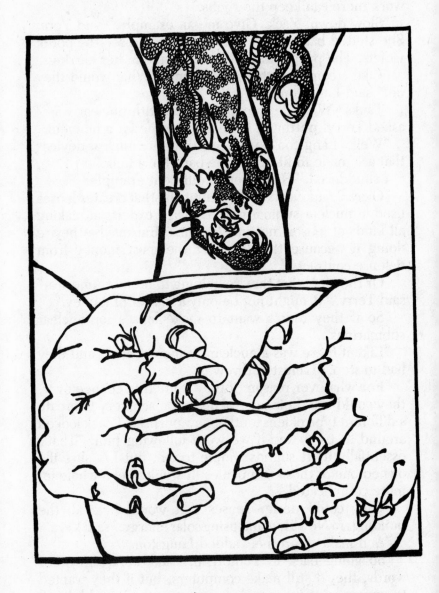

The Dragon of Creativity

to do with nuclear weapons. That way, the people who work there can keep their jobs."

"Slow down, Zack. Give me an example," said Vera. She shifted back in her chair, and I could see the pot of violets. The purple matched the purple in her earrings.

"Like a company that makes tanks. What would they do?" said Langston.

"Tanks? What do they have to do with nuclear war?" asked Terry, putting aside her magazine for a moment.

"Well," Langston explained, "there are nuclear devices that are made to fit inside the barrel of a tank."

I shuddered. "How about a different example?"

"Okay," said Zack. "Take a company that creates lenses used in nuclear submarines. They are experts at making all kinds of lenses, not just for subs But maybe they're doing it because they can get the most money from defense contracts."

"Or they feel that they're helping to protect America," said Terry. "It might not be only a matter of money."

"So if they didn't want to make lenses for nuclear submarines..."

"Like if there was a nuclear weapons freeze, and they had to stop," Langston threw in.

"For whatever reason, if they wanted to change over, they could use their same skills and machinery to create a different type of lens for that new purpose." Zack looked around at us to see if we were following him. "That's essentially it. It sounds simple to me, but I'm sure if I owned one of those companies, it would feel a whole lot more complicated."

"They could design lenses that would heat all the buildings in New England using solar energy," said Vera.

"And make a fortune," added Langston.

"So going back to Tolltorgan," said Vera, "in other words, they'd still make computers, but if they wanted to convert away from nuclear weapons, they wouldn't sell them to defense companies anymore."

"That's right."

"Maybe the same specialized computers could guide other kinds of planes," said Yukiko.

"Yeah. Why not?" I said. Several ideas for drawings were coming into my mind.

"But how will my father feel if all you do is tell him ways he should be different?" said Terry. The magazine was in her lap, and she was hanging on every word.

"Maybe we could invite him to speak at the special town meeting before the vote so that every side can be heard," I suggested.

"Hey, Cass. Not a bad idea," said Langston. "And we could show him the stuff the Awesome Threesome are collecting." He turned to Vera and Yukiko. "They're talking to Lee Ames to get examples of other American companies that have already converted away from war products."

"Well, I've got to say, all of you are really hot stuff!" said Vera. "I hope this peace vote passes so we can band together on some more projects. I like the way you operate."

"Zack, since you know so much about this, why don't you be the one who goes to talk to Mr. Cameron," said Langston.

"Uh, uh. Not me."

"Why not?" asked Vera. "I saw the way you talked to Mr. Greenwald. You'd be great."

"I'm not so hot with fathers."

"What do you think, Terry?" I asked.

"I don't know." She looked at Zack. "I think you'd need a haircut."

Zack laughed. "If it's anything like trying to talk to my dad, count me out. I don't want to fail you guys. You'd have to give me a crash course in being diplomatic."

Yukiko thought for a moment. "It's not what you say to him, Zack, it's how you say it. The words themselves are not so important. What matters is that before you go in to talk with him, you think to yourself, 'He is a person with the spark of God in him.'" She looked over at Vera,

"Am I being too religious?"

"No, I think you're right. You can say to yourself, I'm going to treat him as a friend." Vera paused for a moment. "I don't know, would it help to practice with a photo of your father? Think about it, Zack. You'll come up with a way."

By the time we left that day, we had talked him into it. And we had figured out a way to bring Terry more into our group.

That Monday, the Cameron's got a letter on beautiful rice-paper stationary. The card showed two wild geese flying across a setting sun. It read:

> I would be most honored to have the presence of your daughter Terry at the origami presentation January 1 to be held as part of the art display on peace.
>
> Terry has exhibited skill in the traditional art of paper folding, and I would like to have her there as my assistant.
>
> If there are three afternoons or evenings before the Christmas holidays which are convenient for your family, I would be most pleased to have an opportunity to train her further.
>
> I am yours most sincerely,
>
> *Yukiko Yutsumi*
> Yukiko Yutsumi

And that same day, the receptionist in Mr. Cameron's office made a notation on Mr. Cameron's calendar:

> 4:30 PM Friday
> meeting with Mr. Clemmons
> from Frontier High School.

CHAPTER TWENTY-ONE

Umoja

When the Holiday Craft Fair moved out of the town hall, we moved in. Vera, Zack, Langston, and I were the first to enter the building. Vera opened the side door with a key, and our footsteps echoed as we walked inside.

"This is way too large," said Langston. "We'll never fill this place."

The heat was turned off, and we didn't know how to turn it on. The room was cold and musty-smelling. It reminded me of rainy days at day camp and modeling clay.

I remembered coming to square dances in this room when I was still young enough to be clutching my mother's red-checked skirt. It had a crinkly petticoat underneath that made it stick out. I'd watched the couples spinning in patterns around this same floor.

Langston and I explored the hall. We climbed up to the balcony and opened closets. One was filled with tan folding chairs. The other had pieces of old cardboard. I thought of the rooms at home that my parents kept saying they'd clean out someday.

The lights began flickering on and off in different

combinations. "You got the stage that time," Vera yelled to Zack. "Now we've got to figure out which one works the spotlights."

"I'll mark the switches with masking tape," Zack yelled back.

Langston and I went down to the stage and he pushed a podium out from against the wall. "This is where the selectmen deliver their speeches at town meetings, right?" He leaned his elbows on the podium and put on a serious expression. "I've come to talk to you today about a matter that's been troubling the young people of our fine town of Larkspur. I'm sorry to have to mention it, but some things can be shoved aside for just so long. I'm talking, of course, about an outbreak," he paused, "of zits."

I laughed so hard I pounded my hand on the floor. "That's Mr. Fairchild. And then Gus would come up next and talk about all the anti-pimple weapons he has on his shelves. All the heavy artillery."

We joked around a while longer, and then we took out the pile of drawings we were supposed to mount across the back of the stage for the heritage section of the display.

"I've already tried to staple them together," I said as we studied how to get them up there. "But the paper's too heavy. They keep coming apart."

Langston climbed on a chair with a roll of tape on his arm. He reached up high and taped the first drawing. "How's this? Is this the right height?"

I measured out room for more rows of drawings beneath it. "Too low actually." The thirty-six square drawings were supposed to fit in six neat rows.

He taped it up higher and got down from the chair to look. The tape let go and the paper drifted down like a leaf.

"Maybe we should pin them to a sheet," I said.

"Maybe we should fold them into paper airplanes and forget the whole thing," said Langston.

I laughed. Being with Langston was so much fun. I could totally relax and be myself.

Vera carried a box in from her car and set it on the stage next to two long tables.

The heavy front door opened, and someone ran up behind me and put her hands over my eyes. "Guess who?" said a familiar voice.

"It can't be the famous Judith Jamison," I teased.

"Hi, Cass," said Maritza. She jumped up on the stage and began a series of spins. Then she ran back to where I was trying to pull broken staples out of the back of a stapler. "Which are you more excited about—Christmas or the art display?"

The real answer for me right then was that I was most excited about Zack meeting with Mr. Cameron at the end of the week. But I'd promised Terry that that was a secret. "No comparison. The display," I said.

Vera lifted out a red, black, and green cloth, and Maritza helped her to spread it evenly on the table. They added a woven straw mat and then put bananas, coconuts, and pineapples in two baskets. It was all for Kwanzaa, an Afro-American celebration based on an East African harvest festival. Mom and I had gone last year.

Red, black, and green. They were the same colors I'd seen on a poster Mom had hung in the shop about the liberation movement in South Africa. She told me green stood for the land, black for the beauty of the people, and red for their blood and their struggle.

The table would stay decorated for the seven days of Kwanzaa. The first night, December twenty-sixth, Vera was leading a program for the multicultural gatherings. Anyone in town could come. The last day of Kwanzaa was January first, and then this table would be joined by others and the whole stage would be filled with tables and bulletin boards making up the heritage section of the art display.

"Today's the first day of winter," said Maritza, "and we've already had enough snow to suit me."

"Why don't we hold a vote in town to move all of Larkspur somewhere warmer?" suggested Langston.

"Puerto Rico!" said Maritza. "I miss it so much. It's so beautiful. We have sun practically every day of the year."

"Every day? Take me with you!" I said. I was rubbing my hands and thinking of putting my gloves back on when Vera came in with another box and handed Langston and me a full pin cushion and an African print fabric with brown and black designs. We arranged the first six drawings in a row and began pinning them to the cloth. After only a few were pinned, I could tell it was going to be the perfect way to show them.

"It looks like a quilt," I said. Each drawing represented the heritage of one of us in the group. We had put onto our squares whatever we wanted others to know about us and our families.

I'd drawn pictures of famous Poles around the border of my square: Lech Walesa who won the Nobel Prize in 1983, Dr. Elżbieta Zakrzewska, one of the first women to be a doctor in America, and Tadeusz Kościuszko, someone who had fought against slavery after the Revolutionary War. I'd written the words, "Everytime I learn more about Polish people, I get prouder and prouder of being Polish" and glued pictures of each of my four grandparents onto the center of the square.

Kyle's drawing said, "My real Korean name is Hae-sook. It means 'Ocean of Virtue.' " She drew the outline of Korea with doves flying over the ocean. "I want everyone to know that some anthropologists think that Native Americans may have travelled from Korea to America. Koreans could be the ancestors of the first Americans."

A friend of Stan's had read Kyle's square and made one for herself. We pinned it up next. "My name is Cynthia. My father's family believes that we came from the earth and have been here always. We are not Americans. We are of the Mohawk nation. We don't recognize national boundaries that we didn't create." Around her words, Cynthia had drawn trees, and at the bottom, a range of mountains with a rainbow arching over the hills.

"Where's Coreena's?" asked Langston. "She asked me to read hers."

I sifted through the pile of drawings we hadn't yet pinned up, but I couldn't find it.

The front door of the town hall groaned open again, and Kisha and Ned burst in the door. They'd taken the school bus to the church and were carrying piles of drawings for the display.

"Where is everybody? Didn't they hear the announcement that we need help all this week?" said Ned.

Kisha unzipped her parka. "We waited around the church for others to show up, but nobody else came."

"Everyone's pooping out just when we need them," Ned complained.

"I heard some kids say they have too many reports and tests this week," said Maritza. She lay sideways on the floor with her head propped up on her elbow.

"Hey, I've got a composition due tomorrow I haven't even started," said Ned. That didn't sound like him. He was usually too worried about getting in trouble to risk handing in a paper late. "The Tigers come first," he said.

"Mine's done," said Maritza. "I turned it in yesterday." Maritza got her work done much faster than me. She liked to get it out of the way so she could concentrate on her dance classes. She began to do leg lifts like she was at home on a rug instead of this dusty wooden floor.

Zack carried a ladder to the stage. He set it up beneath some of the spotlights and twisted them around so they'd point more at the table.

Vera looked around at the five of us: Ned folding an intricate airplane out of a piece of scrap paper, me angrily shaking the stapler that had jammed, Langston doodling absentmindedly on the side of one of the cardboard boxes, Kisha and Maritza lounging on the floor with their coats and scarves still on. "You all look pretty wiped out," she said.

"I hate winter," said Kisha.

"I'm really bummed out because four times this many kids were supposed to be here," said Ned.

"I hate staple-eating staplers," I added. Could we really get this display ready? Setting it up looked like a much bigger job now than any of us had really counted on. If we couldn't even attach thirty-six little drawings to the wall in less than an hour, how were we going to put up everything else we had ready?

"This reminds me of being in the theater before opening night," said Vera. "You've got to expect to be exhausted, terrified, and convinced it's going to be a failure."

"It could be a real bomb," said Ned. Maritza groaned and threw her gloves at him.

"But that's no indication of how it's going to turn out," said Vera. "I always feel if you're not nervous before a show, it won't go well anyway."

"I don't feel nervous. I feel totally overwhelmed," said Ned. "Where are we supposed to begin? Wasn't Louisa supposed to make up a map of where everything goes?"

"I've got it here," said Zack. "There's some bulletin boards in the corner over there that Jill decorated. The map shows where to move them."

"I'll do that," said Langston.

"And there's a stack of drawings here that are ready to be thumbtacked to the first bulletin board."

Kisha reached for them. Ned threw his airplane from the stage. We watched it fly halfway across the room and then crash. He joined Kisha.

"The next essential thing is music," said Vera. She brought out a tape recorder.

"What tapes do you have?" I asked.

"Here. Put this on," said Maritza, looking through her collection. "We're using this music in my dance class."

"Sweet Honey in the Rock," said Vera. "My favorite!" She slipped the tape into the machine.

"Cassie, you know there's a *shekere* played on some of these songs," said Maritza.

"Did you know the first song on this side is about Kwanzaa?" asked Vera. "It's about each of the seven principles." She started the tape.

"*Umoja*," sang two strong women's voices in unison.

"Unity that brings us together," answered the harmonies.

Then the voices reversed. "*Kuujichagalia*," sang the higher voices like gold and green threads.

"We will determine who we are," the first voices wove back.

The song filled the hollow space and made me feel more at home. We would eventually change this dingy room into something great, the music seemed to say.

Vera took seven thin, white candles out of a box and set them in wooden candleholders. These were the candles for Kwanzaa, and she arranged them slowly. You could tell she loved doing it. She turned to Maritza and me. "We celebrate one of the principles of the African community each of the seven nights. *Umoja* is first."

Then she began to work on the second table. She spread a white cloth with gold Hebrew letters on half and took out a gold, decorated candle holder and nine candles. It was a menorah.

"Isn't that for Chanukah?" I asked.

"Yes, but it will be here for the first night of Kwanzaa when we celebrate unity. Chanukah and Kwanzaa both get eclipsed by Christmas, so this year I wanted to have a second table with holiday symbols from all different cultures. The Goldsteins lent me this menorah. I won't

leave it up now. I just wanted to see how it would look. A loan like this, you can't take for granted."

"But isn't Chanukah still going on?" I asked. "Don't they need it for their house?"

"No, the last night was, let me think, a week ago Sunday. You see, the Goldsteins and I have a tradition. They come to my house for one of the nights of Kwanzaa, and I go to their house for one of the nights of Chanukah. When I was there this year, I was so struck by something Ed said, I wrote it on a card to put with the menorah."

She looked inside the box. "Here it is. 'Chanukah reminds us that faith is stronger than brute force.' That really expresses the spirit of this art display, doesn't it? It reminds me of *Umani*. That's the seventh Kwanzaa principle. Faith."

I nodded. I was thinking more about her. Vera was great. She was so different from most of the adults I knew. She really took us seriously. I liked it when she talked so openly and you could see the way she thought about things.

And she was a spark of energy. Anything was possible to her. Her strength reminded me of the sycamore tree in the town square with its solid branches bending in each direction like open arms.

I blocked out the other sounds in the room to be just with her.

"Cassie, is there anything special you'd like to put on the table to represent Christmas in Poland?"

I didn't answer at first. Then, it came to me. "Homemade ornaments. We have some ornaments that are made out of egg shells. They're in the shapes of doves and roosters, but they're pretty fragile."

"You could bring them for the first night and then take them home again. I'm not leaving the menorah up during the art display. It's too special. Instead, I'll use a dradle to represent Chanukah. A dradle is a four-sided top with the Hebrew letters that stand for, 'A great miracle occurred here.' Is there anything else you'd like to bring?"

266

"*Pierniki.*" I said the Polish word, not the English, and just saying it opened windows. I saw the honey cakes baked in different shapes—animals, the wise men in the Christmas scene, a manger—and I thought of *oplatek.* That would never be brought for display. It was a wafer the priest blessed that had a Christmas scene stamped on it. I wondered whether we would have it this year without *Babcia* to bring it from the church.

"*Duża rośnij,*" I said so only Vera could hear.

"What's that?" she asked softly, with interest.

"It means grow big. It's an expression my grandmother used. She'd say it to us when she thought we were doing something especially good."

"So you like the idea for this display?"

"Yes," I answered.

Vera repeated the words after me. "*Duża rośnij.*"

The front door creaked again, and Coreena came in, still wearing her sweat pants from basketball practice. She nodded at Zack and then headed straight for Vera. It was easy to guess from the look on her face that she wanted to speak to Vera alone.

I moved back to the other side of the stage to help Maritza pin the rest of the heritage squares onto the fabric.

Vera and Coreena went to the back of the stage where they could talk privately. They turned two folding chairs away from the group, but Coreena's voice was loud, and I could hear her words pouring out. "Vera, I want to tell you before I go in there and tell Zack. I want out of this group and out of this display. It has nothing to do with me."

I was waiting for Vera to speak.

"I'm just ripping mad," said Coreena.

"Tell me. Keep talking," said Vera.

"I want to read you what I wrote on my 'heritage square.'" She used the phrase mockingly. "This is what's getting to me. How can I do this thing?! I don't know my heritage. I don't want to just say I'm from Africa. I want to point to my country, but I can't. My heritage has been stolen away, and I don't think these kids here understand that."

"Will you read me what you wrote?" asked Vera. She brought her chair closer to Coreena.

"Here's how it starts. 'I wish every Black person could live in an all-Black world at least a year, in a town with a Black mayor, going to schools with only Black teachers and books that talk about us. I wish I could dance, breathe, eat, sing only my Blackness.'"

Vera shifted forward to reach her arms toward Coreena but Coreena moved back, wary of anything that might cut off her anger.

Before Vera could speak, Coreena said with disgust, "Why do you bother setting up this Kwanzaa display for this town? These people are all racist. Look at them. They don't try to protect me from the racist things I hear on the basketball court when we play at those white high schools. They don't deserve to hear anything about our culture. They should go find out for themselves. Heritage display! If I wrote up half of what I think and posted it for the town, they couldn't stand it."

"Coreena, I'm with you."

"Then what are you doing living here in Larkspur?" she asked.

"You sound like my friends. They thought I was out of my gourd when I moved here. I lived in Washington, D.C. for more than ten years. That was a life as Black as I could make it, and that was essential to me. And then I got offered this job in the Afro-American department. They even said they would pay me to spend every August in Africa, in any country I chose. So I thought about it. I mean, it was a well-thought-out move, an experiment."

"Did it backfire?"

"Well, it doesn't always work for me. But people like Yukiko, the Goldsteins, who first talked me into sharing one night of Kwanzaa, and you kids in this group help make me glad I'm here. If you'd known me five years ago, you would never have thought I'd be in Larkspur right now."

Coreena laughed. "Hey Vera, I thought you were perfect."

"Perfect? No, I haven't stayed the same, if that's what you mean by perfect. I'm always changing. You don't get strong by accident, you know. It's work. Coreena, don't be looking at my life to figure out your own. You can't measure like that."

"My life! Basketball is all I do these days. I mean, I love the game—it's fun and it's fast, you've got to think quickly—but I keep thinking that there's a lot more to me than just this basketball."

"Well, one thing about you is you sure have got a lot of things to pick from. You're not just good at one thing. You're smart, and that means you can start something new and go right into it. Aren't you getting A's and B's in physics? And remember how you sang. You've got lots of possibilities ahead."

"I guess."

"But you've got to do it yourself. Don't let anybody, including me, tamper with that."

"I know. Let me read you the rest of what I wrote." Coreena turned back to the heritage square she had created. "'People keep asking me where I'm going to school, and I see these dollar signs in their eyes as if the only consideration to them is money. But I don't care how much money I get from any school in New England. I'm going to Howard University. I want to be with my people on my own terms and find out who I am to myself.'"

In the silence, I could just imagine Vera's face looking at Coreena with pride. She stood up and hugged Coreena. Langston called to her from the front of the hall.

"Langston, what did you say?" Vera looked out from the stage.

"Let's go home now, Mom. I'm starving."

Vera looked at Coreena. "I'm in the middle of something. How about another fifteen minutes?"

"Naw. We've already finished all that we can do."

"Mrs. Taylor, can you give us a ride?" asked Ned.

Vera didn't answer right away. "How about this, everybody come over to this table, and let's talk together before we stop for the day."

"Why?" asked Langston.

"You'll find out. Come on over."

Zack fixed the lights so the spotlight was off and only the softer lights came from the sides. Maritza and I and the others sat on the floor near the Kwanzaa display, with Coreena close to Vera.

Vera looked at each of us before she spoke. "The first night of Kwanzaa is about unity. *Umoja*. We can't have unity until we know each other's stories and struggles. I've been thinking about that while I've watched what Yukiko's been going through finishing her sculptures about the internment camps. You all know how important that is to her, I hope."

"Yeah," said Zack.

"I'm really struck by how much she'll be sharing at the display. She'll be telling about the camps, but she'll also be talking about Sadako and origami, and that takes her right back to her Japanese ancestry. She'll be reclaiming so much from her past."

"I don't know if it would be okay with Yukiko for me to tell you this," said Langston, "but Hiroshima is the city in Japan where her grandmother came from."

"Hiroshima!" I said.

"Yes," said Vera. "In the 1940s, most of the Japanese American families came from Hiroshima or Nagasaki. It was a cruel part of the bombing."

"I can't stand this!" said Kisha. "It's terrible!"

"I know. I feel like I keep hearing one horrible thing after another," I said.

"It's getting kind of unbearable," said Ned. The muscles

around his face showed the strain. "I don't want to believe that our country did these things."

"Other countries do gross things," said Langston. "Japan did terrible things, too, in the war."

"I don't care who did what," said Kisha. "I just want all of this to stop."

I nodded. That's what I wanted. A truce in the whole world instead of war upon war.

"It does feel unbearable," said Vera, "and that's the thing. We can't bear it alone. It's too much."

She opened up a cloth bag and pulled out a carved wooden spoon. "This was placed in my hand by a friend in Nigeria." She passed it around for each of us to hold. "It's the most special thing I have, and I put it here next to this menorah. Your ornaments, Cassie, will be here on the table, too. They'll stand side by side and represent our wish for peace between all people. We don't want to be divided from or invisible to each other."

I thought of how the table would look. I won't bring only the ornaments, I told myself. I want something more personal for people to see. The *pisanki*. I'll bring one of the eggs *Babcia* made.

"Sometimes when I see African spoons and masks and sculptures in museums, I get an uneasy feeling because they were once used with such reverence in ceremonies. They weren't supposed to be ripped away and made into art for other people to collect. So I want to bring these things together with full respect, in the hopes that one day there will be new ceremonies of unity that we will make together."

"But, Vera," said Coreena. "You can't force people into being unified. There's just too many years of oppression. It seems sort of fake to me."

"You're right, we can't pretend unity. I'm looking toward the day when we have cleared away what divides us and can come together honestly. You see, I believe that basically all people are born united. We don't come into this world hating or fearing each other. Racism and anti-semitism and the other forms of oppression are something we learn. And that means we can unlearn them. What these African principles teach me is that *Umoja*, this place of unity, is very real."

She looked around the circle. Kisha had propped her head on her elbows, Maritza sat next to her, crosslegged, and I had my knees pulled up. We were all taking in every word. "I really take pride in knowing each of you," she said. "Oooh, this is quite a group." Kisha and Ned smiled.

Outside the streetlights went on. I noticed how dark the room was and remembered it was the first day of winter, the shortest day of the year. I liked being together in the large, dim room.

Zack shifted forward. "Vera, I've been thinking. What would you say it means to declare an outbreak of peace?"

"Zack, you and your questions. Let me think." Vera took a deep breath. "For me, I guess, it is a decision inside a person. It means they decide to do everything they can to break the chain of violence and oppression that people have learned and repeated." She rested her eyes and then opened them. "Declaring an outbreak of peace is saying we want to return to *Umoja*, to who we really are."

Coreena rocked forward and put her face in her hands. Vera glanced at her with a warm look in her eyes and added, "At Kwanzaa we also celebrate *Kuujichagalia*, the second principle. It means defining who we are, being totally true to ourselves. Unity cannot exist without it. *Kuujichagalia* means loving who we are."

I thought about Terry trying to sort out what she really liked to do from what her father assumed she liked to do.

"Sometimes," said Vera, "we need seasons, maybe even lifetimes, apart from one another so we can know who we are and not who others want us to be." I knew she was thinking of Coreena, and maybe of herself.

We were quiet together. It was like the stillness of late

winter when you are so tired of the endless snow and the first faint smells of spring start to return. I rested in that silence. I wanted to say to Coreena, "Tell us. We want to hear you." But I thought she'd feel betrayed that I'd overheard.

Coreena and Vera exchanged glances. Coreena's look was a question; Vera's look said, "Yes, I'm with you."

"I want to read you something," said Coreena, finally.

Vera looked as if she saw all the life deep inside of Coreena bursting through.

Coreena read to us strongly, like she had sung as Deborah Gannett. She read every word I'd heard her read to Vera, and when she got to the end of her words, she put the paper aside and kept speaking. "What would you do if you stood on a basketball court and people yelled ugly things at you? Usually racist things. And players made little remarks so nobody else could hear? Would you stop playing and lose all that you have worked for? This is what it's like for me right now. And *nobody* has done anything to help me. Not my coach. Not the other players. Not even Pam. Do they think that it's okay?" said Coreena. "Is it supposed to be just part of the game? Is it supposed to be just my problem and not theirs? As if I've created the problem by joining the team! What would you do if every time you went out on that court you had no idea what was going to hit you?"

Coreena let her words stand in the silence. I looked over at Zack. We were both crying, not wanting to stop, not wanting anyone to notice. Wanting to keep listening. Vera had followed every word with her whole body, moving slightly. Now, she sat still and let her gaze speak.

"I've decided," said Coreena, "that this problem is not mine. I didn't create it. I'm just the target. And I can't change it alone."

CHAPTER TWENTY-TWO

Tolltorgan

Zack had a haircut. "Are you nervous?" I asked him. He was supposed to see Mr. Cameron in the afternoon.

"I'm an ice cube," he said. That seemed an odd description of being afraid. I took a closer look at him. His face looked tight, and he seemed more business-like than usual. I hadn't heard a single joke from him the whole morning.

I lifted another handful of hangers out of a bag. We were lining them up straight on the coat racks in the balcony. It was a chance to talk alone. "Because of seeing Mr. Cameron?" I asked.

"That, and last night."

"What happened last night?"

"Langston and I drove to the basketball game. It was in Bolton. And we sat on the Bolton side."

"You did?"

"Yeah. They were losing and Coreena was racking up more points than any other player. You know how she is. She starts driving, and she just keeps dropping them in. She was definitely the high scorer."

"Did anyone from Bolton give her a hard time?"

"At first, there was just the usual razzing that happens at games. But then this one guy around my age starts yelling at her, and I didn't like what he was saying at all."

"What did you do?"

"I yelled for him to cut it out, but that didn't do any good."

"So you couldn't stop him?"

"Well, it turned out he was drunk, and we didn't know whether to mess with him. I didn't know what to do. Then Langston said we should go over and ask the guy's friends if they could get him to be quiet."

"Did that work?"

"They agreed with us that he was out of line, but they didn't do anything about it."

"At least you tried."

"I was really mad. I just felt helpless. Langston and I talked about it a lot on the way home. We're going to try to go to more games this season and get other kids to come. Langston said we should ask Coach Armstrong if he could mention the problem to the other coaches at a district meeting. That would help with comments other players make. And maybe the coach could get the officials at the game to do something about the guys in the stands."

"That's good."

We had all the hangers on the racks. Zack seemed pretty down. "Right now, when I see them tacking up pages from my notebook," he said, "I feel like a phony. I just collected those things. I don't claim I'm an expert at living them yet."

I could see Riley waving his arms at Zack. "Clemmons! Come here. I can't read your note. Come explain what this chicken scratch says."

As he left, I thought, he's really hard on himself. I'd never seen him this nervous before. "You can't be perfect," I wanted to say. "You can't make it all right in just one day."

At Yukiko's house, he'd said that he was afraid he would fail us when he went to see Mr. Cameron. It wasn't a matter of failing us! At least he was going to try! But inside me, something burned, too—something that reminded me a little of what I suspected Zack felt.

The main room of the town hall looked a shambles. School was out for the holidays, and a lot of people had come. Miss Leamon and Ms. Ochs were helping us. Their specialty was answering the question that came up over and over again, "What should I do next?"

Langston sat in the middle of a collapsed mobile with a pile of origami cranes waiting to be hung. They looked limp and lifeless now. Some people were helping him attach them with thread.

Later in the day, Derek's family would drive bulletin boards over from the elementary school. Ms. Ochs had suggested we put masking tape on the floor to mark where each bulletin board should go, and Miss Leamon had helped stack numbered drawings by each missing bulletin board. The floor was patterned with brown tape now, and piles of drawings were everywhere. It looked like a disaster area, but it was really organized chaos.

I took my newest drawing out of my backpack. It was the riskiest drawing I'd ever done. I looked around the room to find the right person to show it to. That burning feeling was inside me. Miss Leamon was sitting on the stage, drinking coffee from a paper cup. "Can I show you something?" I asked.

"Sure, climb up," she said, motioning next to her. She was wearing a yellow turtleneck and a pair of corduroy pants, no paint smock today.

"Let's talk over by the Heritage Display," I said. I didn't want to be interrupted.

"Do you think I should put this in the display?" I asked. My drawing showed a present-day Mohawk man looking at a white frontiersman with a gun over his shoulder. Everyone from Frontier High would know the Mohawk man was looking at our school emblem. In one corner, I had drawn a girl who looked like Treena taking down a poster from one of our pep rallies. The poster showed an Indian with a hatchet in his head.

"You've got a nice way of drawing people," Miss Leamon said.

I held my breath. This time, I didn't want her to pay attention to the way I did the sketching. "But, does the drawing make sense?" I asked her.

That word, "frontier," had been burning inside me. I could no longer hear it with a hopeful ring to it of new horizons opening. I thought of the history that I only dimly knew, of the killing of thousands and thousands of people who had lived on this land.

"You're criticizing the school emblem, is that right?"

I was trying to yell and scream in the drawing. Couldn't she hear me? I was trying to say that when our sports teams pretended to be pioneers standing up to "bloodthirsty" Indians, we weren't being fair to what really happened in history.

"So you think the emblem is glorifying the killing of Indians?" Miss Leamon asked. "That it's demeaning to them?"

"For all of us!" I wanted to yell.

Ms. Ochs ducked her head into the cubicle of bulletin boards where we were sitting. "So here you are, Marcy," she said. "I'm going over to Gus's to pick up a snack. Do you want anything?"

"Cassie's showing me an interesting new drawing," said Miss Leamon. I wish she'd asked me before mentioning it. "She wants to find a place for it in the display."

"No. I want to know if I should even put it in."

Ms. Ochs took a look. "Oh, this has got to go in. I've thought about this 'Down with the Indians' fixation I see at pep rallies. I'm glad to see you talking about it in this drawing."

"Well, I feel a little embarrassed," said Miss Leamon. "I've been at the school twenty years, and it's never crossed my mind before that there's anything wrong with that emblem, but now I see what you mean."

"I should have brought it up myself," said Ms. Ochs. "I gave myself the excuse that I was too new on the faculty."

"I'm kind of afraid to put my name on it," I said. "People might really hate me for drawing this."

"Well, we could put a petition right next to your drawing for people to sign," said Ms. Ochs. "Then you won't be raising this problem all by yourself. I'll write it, if you like. We could say that we think parts of the pep rallies are racist, that the picture on the school emblem should be changed, and that we want to talk about these things with the School Spirit Club."

I walked with Ms. Ochs to Gus's. I didn't need to buy anything, I just wanted a break. When we got back, I was ready to paste my new drawing to some colored paper and get it ready for the display. Then I saw Sam coming through the door. I wanted to push him back out again. He wasn't supposed to be here until it was all fixed up. I was sure he'd say something like, "You guys think you're going to open this mess to the public?"

"Zack around?" he asked.

"Somewhere. Why?"

"I've got that suit to lend him." So Zack wasn't going to wear his jeans jacket. Sam looked around the room. "You've got a lot of kids here today."

Sam seemed curious. Maybe he was feeling left out.

Zack tried on the suit, and it fit fine. It was probably a little more formal than Zack would have picked, but it would be just right for Mr. Cameron. Sam stuck around and visited with the kids he knew.

A "Sweet Honey in the Rock" tape was playing, as usual. When one side of the tape was done, the nearest person would turn it over or put on another tape of theirs. I had memorized several sections. The words to the song, "Seven Principles" stuck in my head the most. I'd hear clear and strong, *"Umoja,"* followed in harmony by, "Unity that brings us together." Unity, I thought, but don't fake it. Be united without having to give away who you are. Find the place where you don't have to pretend.

Sam picked up the tape cover, and read out loud, "B'lieve I'll Run On...See What the End's Gonna Be." He looked at me. "The end? That's hopeful," he said sarcastically. "Is that what you think?"

"That's not what the song says," I explained. "It's trying to get people moving to do something about it."

"Why try?" he said. He looked at four people moving a heavy bulletin board without casters. "They look like a bunch of ants. It's ridiculous. We're all going to end up squashed like an ant hill. Who cares?"

"You," I almost said. I was seeing it for the first time. He did care. Underneath that apathy and sarcasm, it did matter to him what happened.

"Well, thanks for the suit," said Zack to Sam. "See you around. I've got to go shovel debris."

"I think I'll stick around a little," said Sam.

Suddenly I heard Derek shouting over the music. "Don't put that in the display," he yelled.

"Of course I'm going to. I did it." said Ned.

"I don't want my father seeing some picture called, 'Dismantling the Last Nuclear Weapon' and thinking I agree with that stuff, because I don't. That's never going to happen. Why did you draw something like that?"

"Look, I have a right to put into this display anything I want. That was our agreement."

"Yeah, well, dismantling is a fantasy. I'm not going to lend my family's truck to help get a bulletin board so you can hang this thing up. I thought we all agreed this wouldn't be a bunch of hippy dippy fantasy trips."

"Hi, guys," said Zack. He sat cross-legged in front of them.

"I discovered an archconservative in our midst," said Ned.

"Wait. Don't start slugging," said Zack.

"Well, I discovered some kind of commie spy," said Derek. He was half laughing but trying not to.

"And that's called escalation," said Zack.

"Seriously, Zack, I don't want to put some of this stuff up," said Derek.

"This stuff being a drawing I happened to spend a lot of time on and even researched facts about in one of April's magazines," said Ned. "I don't think it's fair that just because he happens to be the one fixing up the display, he thinks he can act like some kind of censor and yank it out." Ned crossed his arms and glared at Derek. "It's undemocratic."

"Oh, God, that's ridiculous," said Derek. "You're calling me undemocratic? Ned, be real. We can't unlearn how to make nuclear weapons! If you take one away, somebody will build another one."

"Yes we can," said Ned. "You know Treena's picture of kids taking a class trip to a nuclear weapons museum. That's what I think is going to happen. Kids will learn that we can't use weapons anymore because they've gotten too dangerous."

"If we dismantle all the weapons, we'll be too vulnerable," Derek argued.

I imagined Zack flipping through notebook pages in his mind. What would he do? Get them to take a break? That's what I would have tried.

"What would be the worst thing that could happen if we left Ned's drawing in?" Zack asked Derek.

"I'd puke every time I saw it."

Zack gave him a look that said, "You can do better than that."

"Well," said Derek, looking away and then back at Zack, "the problem is that somebody could look at this display and judge the whole thing by Ned's drawing."

"Somebody like your father," said Ned.

"Not just him. Someone who knew more about nuclear technology and arms control than you do. They might dislike this drawing so much, they'd walk out and wouldn't give the rest of the stuff a chance."

"Got any solutions?" asked Zack.

"You're asking me?" said Derek.

"Yeah. You know the problem best so you get first crack at solving it."

Derek smirked. "I'll make sure all the pictures I don't agree with get hung in the basement so hardly anyone will see them." Derek gave Zack a look of frustration. "I don't know, Zack. You tell me. Hang Ned's drawing outside?"

Ned gave a big sigh of disgust.

"What is it you want the people who come to this thing to know?" asked Zack.

"That they should look at everything here," said Ned.

"Yeah," said Derek. "And that there's lots of different viewpoints. I want them to know we didn't all agree with each other, so they may like some drawings more than others. Maybe we could write something on a sign."

"That's a good idea," said Zack. "That might solve it."

"You mean kind of like in the movies where they say any resemblances to people living or dead are just a coincidence?" said Ned.

"No, not like that. That sounds stupid. I don't want them to think we're afraid to say what we mean," said Derek. "Why don't we list the rules we made in the Tigers. I want them to know that everybody could put in anything they wanted to. That we didn't have any judges or anything."

"You want to write it?" said Zack.

"No, you write it, Zack."

Zack shook his head. "I got someplace to go. You guys do it together."

"Me work with some hippy-thinking weirdo who buttons up his top button?" said Derek smiling.

"Yeah, I'll help," said Ned.

"Ready to roll, Zack?" asked Jill. Her hair looked freshly washed, and she was tossing car keys from one hand to the other.

Zack got up, "Ready as I'll ever be." He turned to Derek and Ned. "Carry on you guys," and they mumbled something in return. Then he disappeared into a tiny room near the front of the town hall to change into Sam's suit.

Just as Zack was trying to slip out the door without comment from anyone around, Ned saw him. "From Clark Kent to Superman, huh." Ned's jokes were definitely getting better. Riley was a good influence on him.

As we got into the car Jill had borrowed, we heard a voice call to us. April was leaning against a tree smoking. "Go for it, Zack." April was clued in. She and Louisa had been hunting up things for Zack to show Mr. Cameron. She caught his nervousness. April raised her hand in a fist. "Don't forget, we rule!"

In the car, I noticed that Zack smelled of after-shave lotion. I was glad he'd asked Jill and me to come along. Tolltorgan's grounds were beautifully landscaped. We went through the revolving door into the lobby and waited nervously for the elevator. Just being inside the building with its marble walls and six-foot-tall plants made me feel out of place. I noticed Mr. Cameron's name on the bronze plaque that listed the officers of the company. "He's a bigger deal than I thought," I said.

When we stepped out of the elevator on the fifth floor, Zack motioned us over to a nearby couch. "I've got to sit down for a minute. Monster butterflies are attacking the lining of my stomach."

"You've got your picture?" I asked him. He told me he'd been looking at a photo of his dad, not exactly practicing with it the way Vera had suggested, but thinking about him. He took out the photo of his family. He was sitting between his parents. I could see he had inherited his grin from his father.

"Not bad looking," said Jill. "Distinguished."

"Because of the graying temples? Naw, he's just a slob at heart." Zack smiled. "But I've been working on it. Trying to understand him better. It's like I'm sick of being so angry at him, but when I stop being angry I just get so sad." He looked down at his shoes and wiped a mud stain off on the cuff of his pants. "So I said to myself, 'Pretend that having a good talk with Mr. Cameron will help change things with Dad, too.' That seemed to help a little." He let his arms relax and shrugged his shoulders. "It's like the whole human family is trying to get a divorce, and we're in there fighting for them to make up."

"Did you get the papers from Lee Ames?" Jill asked. "Louisa wanted me to make sure you had them."

Zack lifted up a folder.

"What do they say? What did they find out?" I asked.

"About economic conversion? There's not a lot going on yet, but the university peace studies office had an article about two companies, Acurex and Varian, that used to make almost all of their money helping with nuclear weapons production and have now made a complete switch. Lee says now they're making more money than they did before because they don't have to worry about losing a contract with the Defense Department."

"Mr. Cameron would like that."

"So Lee copied that one for us. And there's an article about China from the Institute for Defense and Disarmament Studies in Boston. It says that in 1980, many weapons factories in China began converting to making peacetime products. Lee thought maybe he could find out about a computer firm in China that used to be like Tolltorgan. Maybe the Chinese computer company could be a model for them. But you know what? I'm tempted to leave all this stuff here and not take it into his office. It might seem too overwhelming, like we're pushing too much at him."

"No, bring it along, just in case," Jill urged. "I promised Louisa I'd make sure you would."

"What page in your notebook would help you now?" I asked.

"The page about Martin Luther King," Zack answered immediately. "It's a section called 'How to see everyone as your brother or sister.'"

"I'm proud of you, Zack," said Jill. She had the courage to say that out loud. I was so proud I couldn't stop grinning.

"Cassie, don't expect me to come back as part owner of Tolltorgan or anything," he smiled.

I wanted to hug him, but I didn't.

When Zack disappeared into Mr. Cameron's outer office, Jill and I waited there in the hallway on the couch. We didn't want Mr. Cameron to see us if he walked out of his office into the reception area. We could hear the voice of the receptionist letting Mr. Cameron know Mr. Clemmons had arrived.

"Now Mr. Cameron's offering him a chair," I said.

"A plush one, a yard wide," Jill joked.

"Now he's offering him a cigar," I said.

"No, he's asking Zack if he minds if he smokes his pipe."

"Okay, and Zack just waves his hand, very cool, to show he doesn't mind at all."

"Zack's letting him know he has meetings with busy executives all the time so it's no big thing."

"Now Zack is running out of the room scared to death," I added.

Jill laughed. "It's going to be fine, Cassie. Let's do something while we're waiting here."

I took out some half-crumpled origami paper. I'd gotten into the habit of always carrying some with me. Terry had just shown me how to make an origami frog. Jill and I folded some frogs and cranes.

About a half hour had passed, when we heard the door of Mr. Cameron's office open. I heard Mr. Cameron exclaim in a loud and friendly tone, "I certainly appreciate your invitation, and I'll look over the papers you've given me."

"It was wonderful to talk to you, sir," said Zack. He had just the right tone in his voice, polite without being fake and sugary.

"I have to say I admire your honesty, and I appreciate..." I couldn't hear much of the rest, except that Mr.

Cameron ended with, "I hope we'll get a chance to talk again someday. Goodbye."

Zack took a moment to pick up his coat. He opened the door of the reception area and walked into the hall. He looked a little dazed. Then he caught sight of us. He waved his arms in a silent cheer of hurrah.

We got into the elevator and waited until the door shut before we all began to yell. When the elevator opened at the ground floor, we were still yelling, and some people in the lobby turned to look at us.

"You've got to tell us every word you said," Jill exclaimed.

"I wish I could have been a fly on the wall," I added.

We dragged him into the coffee shop in the building and made him tell us every detail of what had happened.

Zack said he'd been relieved to find he liked Mr. Cameron. He said when he walked into his office, it helped to see all the pictures of Terry and the rest of the family and that there was a comfortable feeling in the room. But when Mr. Cameron realized this Mr. Clemmons from Frontier High wasn't a member of the Computer Club, but rather of the Tigers Club that was putting on the "Arts for Justice and Peace Display," he stiffened up.

"I wanted to put him at ease again," Zack explained to us. "So I got right down to it. I told him, 'I'm not here to criticize you or badger you with a lot of questions about your work. I know there are lots of sides to every issue.'"

"That was a good beginning," said Jill.

"Yeah. I told him I was there to give him the chance to meet someone from the Tigers face to face in case he had any questions for us."

"Did he ask any?" I said.

"He said that he appreciated that I'd come or some words like that. He was pretty formal. And he leaned way back in his chair—he has one of those leather swivel kind—and puffed on his pipe. He also looked at his watch and made it really clear that it was a busy day for him,

285

being right before Christmas and everything. I wondered if he was going to just shake my hand, lead me to the door, and call it quits right there."

"So what did you do?"

"I figured I might not have much more time, and I wanted to get some of the main stuff covered. I said, 'There's something I would like you to know about us. At the town debates, we're not going to bring up Tolltorgan and the issues Mr. Ames raised in the newspaper. Out of respect for you, we'd like to have the discussion happen in a different way.'"

"Then what did he say?" asked Jill.

"He only nodded and puffed on his pipe some more."

"Oh." I felt frustrated just hearing about it.

"So I brought out the next idea. I said we had thought of starting a town committee that he and other people from Tolltorgan and Mr. Ames and anybody else could be on.'"

"How did that go over?"

"He looked like he wouldn't touch that committee with a ten-foot pole." Zack paused and took the grilled-cheese sandwich a waitress was handing him.

"Go ahead and eat," Jill said. "We won't die waiting."

I faked a faint.

"So, let me try to remember what he said next." Zack's mouth was full of sandwich. "It was something like, 'That's the problem I have with your group. I was raised to believe that when someone is in charge, you've got to let them be in charge. I'm one of the people in charge of our company and the products we make, and Mr. Ames from the university has to recognize that it's going to stay that way. Our government is in charge of making peace and keeping us strong, and I think we all have to let them do that.'"

I put my cup of hot chocolate down and listened intently.

"That part was okay because at least he was talking. He was being really clear about his point of view. But then

286

he added, 'It's like in a family. The children have to obey their elders.'" Zack rolled his eyes. "I thought I was going to lose it when he said that. Those are the exact words I hear from my dad all the time—obey your elders. He's always telling me not to question him so much." He stuffed the last bit of sandwich in his mouth. "So when Mr. Cameron said that, I wanted to do the same thing I do with my dad, tune him out, way out."

"Is that what you did?" I asked.

"Yup, that's exactly what I did at first. I wanted to plug up my ears. Then I caught myself and tried to make myself listen. I mean, I'd promised all of you I would. The best thing I could think of was to ask him a question. Anything. It might sound weird, but I asked, 'Mr. Cameron, who is one of your heroes in American history?' I think that question really surprised him."

"'Thomas Jefferson. He had the mind of a true inventor,' was what Mr. Cameron said."

"That gave us something in common," said Zack. "I told him Jefferson is one of my heroes, too. I've read three books on him, and I have pages in my notebook on famous Americans. That interested him. It turns out we both have visited Monticello. He said that his favorite invention there was the dumb waiter Jefferson had built to carry wine up from the cellar. I said I liked the revolving door with shelves. Then I took a chance again and said, 'I'm in this peace group because I want to be like Jefferson I want to be one of the new patriots.'"

"'As one patriot to another then,' Mr. Cameron said, 'I want to tell you frankly that I'm really not in favor of your outbreak of peace declaration.'"

"'Well,' I said, 'I want to do what Jefferson would have done. I want to invite you to speak at the town hall. Every viewpoint has to be heard. That's what our country is about.' And he accepted the invitation."

"He did!" I said. It hit home how strange that was going to be. In a month, I'd be watching Mr. Cameron speak out against an outbreak of peace in front of the whole town.

"Then what?" asked Jill.

"Then I relaxed. I was so relieved. We'd finally gotten somewhere. Then I remembered the folder in my lap on economic conversion. Yeah, Jill, I nearly forgot it. 'Here's a report you might be interested in,' I told him, 'from a modern-day Sam Adams.' He laughed and took it. Then we stood up, and he walked with me to the door."

"We heard his voice when he said goodbye to you," I added. "He sounded really friendly."

"Yeah, and what surprised me was when he shook my hand. It wasn't 'so long, good riddance.' He gripped my hand and looked me right in the eye."

A waitress came over and took our dishes, but I hardly noticed. I reached into my pack for the cranes we had folded and handed some to Jill under the table. She looked at me like she had no idea what I was doing. Then she caught on.

Right there in the Tolltorgan coffee shop, we showered Zack with paper cranes. Cranes fell into his lap, into Jill's half-finished ice cream, and onto the floor. Someone at the next table gave us a funny look, but the waitress smiled.

And Zack just grinned.

CHAPTER TWENTY-THREE

New Year's Day

Ten, nine, eight,...the ball was dropping at Times Square as Terry and my family watched on the television. Five, four, three, two, one—HAPPY NEW YEAR!

Dad and Jill showered us with confetti as we tooted on paper horns and twirled noisemakers. Terry and I blew our paper horns at each other and jumped up and down.

"Tomorrow's the big day," I shouted. "I mean today."

"Twelve hours until the art display. Congratulations!" said Dad, and he threw another handful of confetti.

"January is going to be quite a month for Larkspur," said my mother. "First comes the art display and then in two weeks, there's the vote on the outbreak of peace."

"I hope everyone gets so inspired by the art display that the vote's a landslide," said Jill.

"You are really convinced it's going to be a big deal, aren't you," said Sam.

"Sam!" said my mother.

"What are you talking about?" asked Jill.

"I don't want them to be too disappointed if it's a small turn-out for the display. It's just Larkspur, you know. You can't expect much here."

Terry put her hands over my ears. "Don't listen to him," she said. "I know it's going to be wonderful."

"How many people do you guess?" asked Jill excitedly. "Two hundred?"

"Over the whole day? Probably at least that," said my mother.

"Okay, I'll bet you. I'll bet the most you get is one hundred, one hundred fifty tops," said Sam. "I'll bet you, Cassie. What do you want to bet?"

"I bet you're wrong, and if I win you have to buy me," I stopped to think a moment what I really wanted, "you have to buy me a box of pastels just like Louisa has."

"Pastels? Are they expensive? Well, when I win you'll have to buy me a new mitt. Okay?"

"You're on. And we can count how many people are there by their coats. Some kids are running a coat check, and they'll be handing out numbers. They're ready for two hundred. If they use up all their numbers, then we'll know I've won."

"You girls should try to get some sleep," my mother warned. In answer, I did a cartwheel. "I'm serious, Cassie, tomorrow's going to be an exhausting day."

"Not for me. For Terry maybe. She's got to do the origami demonstration."

"For both of you. And you're probably tired, Terry, from riding on the train for four hours from your aunt's house." Terry shrugged her shoulders. "Well, I'm convinced. A half hour more, and the two of you should have pajamas on and be in bed." We groaned.

"You're coming to the origami demonstration tomorrow, aren't you Cassie?" Terry asked, as I brushed my teeth.

"Sure, I will! I know it by heart. I've watched enough rehearsals. If you forget what happens next, just turn to me and I'll yell 'No, fold the paper inside out not upside down, or whatever.' Actually, I have no idea how you keep track of it all."

"I don't have to worry with Yukiko right there to help me if I start to mess up. Want to know a secret? I was going to surprise you, but..."

"No, tell me now, tell me now," I pretended to threaten her with a tube of toothpaste.

"Okay, okay. The *secret* is...," she tried to drag it out, but I held up that toothpaste. "Yukiko is letting me wear one of the beautiful silk blouses she made."

"You're so lucky."

"And it's black with gold flowers, and I love it."

"Oh Terry, you're going to look so beautiful."

"Okay, girls. Time for bed."

I let Terry have my bed and went to sleep on our guest cot. I was sure it would take me a long time to fall asleep, I was so excited from getting everything ready at the town hall. But all I did was curl up on my left side and pull the blankets up around me, and I fell into a warm swirl of sleep.

The next morning when the five of us drove downtown, I couldn't believe what I saw: there were cars parked everywhere. It was so crowded, we had to park in a friend's driveway and walk three blocks. Gus had taken advantage of the situation and had a sign in the lot next to his store that read, "Park here—50 cents."

"He'll probably set up a hot dog stand next," joked Sam.

"What do you say, do you give already? Looks like I've won the bet."

"Are you serious?" said Sam. "Ten cars in Larkspur looks like a lot. I'm waiting for the statistics."

As we entered, I waved at Ned taking the coats. He had his hands full. There was a long line just to get in the door. Stevie and Rodney were in their glory. They got to race up and down stairs to store the coats in the balcony.

"Why do you think there's such a big crowd?" asked my father.

"Dad!"

"No, I expected it to be crowded, but not this crowded."

"Maybe the newspaper stories and Riley's radio

announcements," Mom suggested. "And the school band playing."

"But this can't be just people from Larkspur," Dad continued. "I mean, I don't know half of these people."

"They must have come from the other towns nearby that get *The West County Daily*. Or they're relatives of the kids involved."

"I saw a couple of Vermont license plates," said Jill.

When Sam handed his coat to Ned and got back a ticket with a hastily scrawled 213, he finally conceded that I'd won the bet.

At the door, we selected a gift, a door prize as Riley had called it on the radio spots. There were sachets with rosemary, bumpy gourds in bushel baskets, sprigs of bittersweet tied with ribbons, and dried cornflower arrangements, all donated by Treena's parents and other farmers. The local bank had contributed playing cards that had their name, Country Bank, on the back of every card. Claude's family had given boxes of keychains left over from a promotion of their business. And there was one of Yukiko's huge pots, filled with paper cranes. My mother and I selected cranes.

Once you went into the main room, you felt like you were at a country fair. Kisha and Shari handed out programs providing a map of all the booths and displays in the building and listing the names of everyone who had worked on the project. I loved seeing Terry's name there along with everybody else's. A big banner hung from the rafters said "Happy New Year" in colors spread out like a rainbow. Cascading from the ceiling were garlands of paper cranes—one thousand of them.

Vicky Goldstein sat behind a booth decorated with pictures of the story of Sadako. She folded extra paper cranes to add to the door prizes while Terry joined Yukiko in arranging chairs for their origami demonstration.

"I'll see you later," I called to Terry and headed for the food booth. It was in the front-left-hand corner of the room, opposite the origami display. Both booths were expected to draw large crowds. I ran into Maritza there staring at the apple pie.

"I would have guessed I'd meet you at the food, Cassie," she teased.

"You have a worse sweet tooth than me," I told her. "Look at that cotton candy. I dare you not to eat some." It was maple syrup cotton candy. Treena's family had not only donated the syrup, but they had managed to borrow a cotton candy machine.

"I can't stand it, any longer," Maritza said finally, after watching Treena twirl the paper cones. "Treena," she called. "Could you teach Cassie and me how to twirl that cotton candy?"

"Sure, I'll let you help." We ran behind the counter and grabbed paper cones. "You try to catch the sugar as it first comes out of the machine," Treena explained. "Once you've got some of the cotton candy on the cone, the rest will attach itself."

"Kind of like lint coming out of a dryer," I said.

"But don't let any of the customers hear you say that," said Treena's mother laughing. Maritza and I got the hang of twirling the paper cones. The booth was so busy, we had less time to eat bits of the cotton candy ourselves than I'd expected.

When we were so full we never wanted to see cotton candy ever again, we persuaded two of Maritza's cousins to take our places at the machine.

"Where are you going to go now, Cassie?"

"I guess I'll take a stroll down the midway," I replied.

"You're going to be at the origami demonstration at three o'clock aren't you?" Maritza asked.

"Of course, why do you ask?"

"Oh, no reason." Maritza answered in a way that made me suspicious. "See you later," she called.

"Cassie, we've been looking all over for you." It was my parents. "We want you to be our special guide to the displays."

"Sure," I said excitedly. "Come over here first." I pulled

293

them over to a booth where Langston was sitting.

"Hello, Langston. It's nice to see you someplace other than in the midst of a blizzard," said my father.

"Now, what's this booth all about?" my mother asked. Langston pointed to the sign: "Draw the biggest change you've ever made in your life!"

"You can draw or write your answer," he explained, "and then, if you want, you can post it over there." He pointed to a bulletin board that was already filled with drawings.

"Look, Dottie Thatcher said the biggest change for her was giving up smoking. Well, good for her," said my Dad.

"Will you two do one?" I begged. I couldn't wait to see what they'd answer. They sat down on the chairs Langston provided and went to work. Several other people came by and Langston got busy in conversation, so I strolled over to the next booth while I waited for my parents.

It was Louisa's. The sign on the front announced, "We bet you're a peacemaker! Sit down for a five-minute interview, and we guarantee we can prove it to you." I watched as a girl dragged her younger brother over to Louisa.

"I dare you to find out if he's a peacemaker."

"Let go of me," he complained.

"Do you want to have an interview?" Louisa asked him.

"I don't know." His sister was leaning on the table.

"Do you want your sister to listen to it?"

"I don't know."

"Well, why don't we talk in private for five minutes," she said to the boy, "and why don't you come back in five minutes to hear the result," she said to his sister.

I read the display at Louisa's booth while they talked together. I wanted to hear the results, too. A bulletin board called "The Good News Times" showed newspaper clippings from Zack's notebook and others we'd collected. Another bulletin board held the results of the peacemaker interviews. One slip of paper read, "I'm a peacemaker because I volunteer each week at the nursing home," and another slip said, "I'm a peacemaker because I pick up litter around Larkspur Lake each spring with my scout troop."

"We've got a long list," Louisa said to the boy's sister as she returned. I leaned over to eavesdrop. "Would you like to say it yourself?" she asked him.

"No, you do it," he told Louisa.

"Okay. Marvin here is a peacemaker because he takes out the trash every week, and he helps your grandmother bake bread every Saturday, and he was asked to be a crossing guard at school, and he helped plant tulip bulbs this fall so your front yard will look beautiful in the springtime, and he gave you a Christmas present this year that he made himself."

"Pretty good," said his sister. "Will you do me next?"

I went back to my parents. They were both finished with their drawings and were comparing them.

"You know us," said my mother. "We couldn't just give one answer. We both gave two. And it turns out we both listed the same thing first. We drew you and Jill and Sam. Having you kids was definitely one of the biggest changes."

"And the most wonderful," added my father.

"Aw, cut the mushy stuff," I said.

"It gets mushier. For my second answer, I drew you and me standing up together at the selectmen's meeting," Mom said.

"And I drew this display," said Dad. "Cassie, you've helped begin an outbreak of peace as far as I'm concerned, no matter how the vote goes. I'm so proud of you." And then he kissed me in public.

I wriggled out of the hug, but I was pleased. "And you haven't even gotten to the artwork yet. Wait till you see it."

We'd placed the art and creative writing in four locations. The heritage section was set up on the stage, and the areas along the stairs and into the basement showed visions of Larkspur in the future. Then there was a maze of bulletin boards in the center of the room with pictures we'd set up like a story. Finally, there was a display near the booths that featured conflicting points of view. We had filled the hall.

"So how many drawings of yours are there in the whole display?" Dad asked.

"Twenty-four, plus the mask and the *wycinanka*."

"Cassie! I had no idea. Remember when you wouldn't show your drawings to anyone in the family?"

"Don't remind me."

"Let's see what Zack's doing," said Dad. "He said I'd find him next to the origami display."

We went over to the table where I expected him to be. The sign announced, "Peace Means Complicating Your Thinking." Six bulletin boards showed drawings and essays carefully grouped into topics. Zack had made sure, with Derek's help, that many sides were represented for each of the issues.

Neither Zack nor Derek were sitting there. Zack had a lot of different things to check on, and I guessed that Derek was probably over at the origami booth, flirting with Terry.

"Why don't we begin here? This section seems to have the smallest crowd right now," said Dad.

We started with a bulletin board on the topic, "What about the Soviets?" There was a picture from Zack's notebook of American and Soviet teenagers playing music together. The label said, "Peace comes by building relationships with all people, even our enemies."

Next to it was a picture of a satellite reading a license plate on a Soviet truck. It said, "You can't trust people in all circumstances. Peace means having good methods of verifying our treaties."

Another picture was captioned, "This could happen if we give up too many of our nuclear weapons." It showed the shopping mall after a Soviet take-over of America. The stores had become classrooms where people were forced to speak only in Russian.

There was another picture in contrast to it. It said, "This could happen if we work to break down the barriers between people." An office building in Crowningburg had been turned into an International Fellowship Center with training offered in twenty different languages and courses like, "Recovering Lost Family History," and "Unlearning Racism."

There were pictures of responses to all the controversies that had come up in our group. Should boys be drafted? Should we stop testing and building nuclear weapons? What kind of defense system makes sense if we don't use nuclear weapons? How do you help end unemployment, hunger, and lack of medical care?

Ned had made several things in this section. He enjoyed adding lots of details to his drawings. One of his pictures about hunger explained what it would mean to have a Food Bank for Larkspur. Ned drew food coming from lots of different places, like from local farmers who couldn't sell all of the squash they'd grown, and then going out to the senior center and to other places where it was needed.

"What if someone submitted something to you that you didn't agree with?" asked my mother. "Did you still include it?"

I pointed to a letter we'd gotten from a boy in eleventh grade who criticized the skit we'd done in the school cafeteria when the air force recruiters had come with their helicopter. We put it under the heading, "America Stands for the Right to Free Speech."

Dad read Ned and Derek's sign explaining the Tigers' commitment to airing all points of view. "You kids are so idealistic," he said. When I flashed him a look, he added, "No, I don't mean that as a put-down. I like it."

My parents and I walked next to the heritage section that filled the stage. While Dad started looking at the heritage squares, Mom and I were drawn immediately to the display at the far corner of the stage. There we saw two bulletin boards filled with Vera's photographs and a table with Yukiko's sculptures about the internment camps.

The sculptures were the opposite of Yukiko's large, graceful pots. She had made four pieces, each about a foot long, with intricate figures carved into them. The first three were rust-colored brown.

One was a long race-track building that sprawled like a centipede. The windows were filled with the faces of the people crowded inside.

One was a watchtower with eyes carved all over it.

One was a bulldozer driven by a half-human figure. He looked like one of the toy robots her sons played with.

The fourth sculpture was a beautiful, spirited horse. It was jade green. Her whole family rode on it, galloping away.

Behind the sculptures, a bulletin board covered with burlap showed a dozen of Vera's pictures of the Manzanar Internment Camp and the Santa Anita Assembly Center. They showed horse stalls and dusty ground.

I slipped my arm around my mother. "Did you know about these camps before?"

"Yes, a little." She was intensely quiet.

We read together what Yukiko had written.

My Family's Story

As I write this, I think of the lines I saw once in a poem:

*The world grows stronger
as each story is told.*

It is in this spirit that I share this with all of you.

My father's parents farmed sugar beets in the Vaca Valley in California. My mother's father was one of the tuna fishermen in San Diego who helped improve the American tuna industry by introducing the flexible bamboo poles common in Japan. Unlike the nets usually used, these poles caught the fish without damaging them. My grandmother was fond of pointing out that *issei* (first-generation Japanese

Americans) fishermen had given this gift of knowledge.

My parents were able to open a shop in Los Angeles a few years after their marriage. In December 1941, following Japan's bombing of Pearl Harbor, rocks were thrown through the window of the store. Four months after Pearl Harbor, they were given six days to pack the few belongings they were allowed and forced to leave their store and apartment. My grandmother told me that the night before their evacuation they slept on the floor because all of their furniture was gone.

Like the other 115,000 Japanese Americans, they were sent to one of the ten remote internment camps established in 1942. Looking back, former Senator Sam Ervin called this action "the single most blatant violation of the Constitution in our history." At the time, although many individuals did find avenues of protest, the war fervor made it impossible to stand up against mass evacuation in any large-scale way.

For my family, the task of packing up became a severing of all their links to Japan. My father burned letters from his uncle in Kyoto, Japan. My mother buried our family dishes and a wall scroll in a trunk. My grandmother gave her kimono to a neighbor who later burned it rather than take the risk of saving it for her.

In April, they were sent to the Santa Anita Assembly Center, a race track. There they spent six months before being sent by train to the Manzanar Internment Camp.

When I was born, the hospital at the camp was no more than a big shed. My parents were worried because the temperatures there were so extreme. It got up to one hundred degrees during the day but became very cold at night. After a hard first month, it became clear I would survive.

My father, John Yutsumi, was inducted later that winter and joined the American 442nd Regiment, a front-line combat team of Japanese Americans. He received a Distinguished Service Cross for his fighting in France

Today my parents live in San Francisco. When I was first born, they called me Jean, but when I was twenty-one, at my request, we had a family renaming ceremony in which I took back my Japanese name and became Yukiko.

Shortly after this, I sewed the kimono shown in the photograph. I made it to replace my grandmother's kimono which would have been handed down to me. I sewed into it my pride in my legacy, the strength of my family, and the forging of my identity as a Japanese American artist.

We looked at three photos of Yukiko next to the photos of the camps. In one, she held up a kimono that was black with gold chrysanthemums. In another, she was wearing a tweed suit at a gallery in New York where her pottery was displayed. In the third, she was working in blue jeans in her back yard, carving a tall wooden sculpture.

I was so absorbed that I was surprised when my dad came up to us. His mood was so different than ours. "Florence, after today, I bet you'll be back with the old petitions, right?"

Mom was quiet. "I don't know. Something else." She had a faraway gaze. She went back to the sculptures again, while Dad led me over to see how the petition about the school emblem was filling up.

Afterwards, we walked to the bulletin boards that were arranged like a maze in the middle of the room. We had to wait several minutes because the crowd ahead of us was going through in single file. They were taking time to look at each picture, talking a lot, and pointing.

The line moved on, and we walked to the beginning.

Two nuclear nightmares.   Dos pesadillas nucleares.

PLEASE! NO!
TAKE ANYBODY
DONT take my cat!
DONT take Him
He didnt do
ANYTHING
DONT TAKE him
please DONT.
NO
TAKE ME
TAKE ANYbody TAKE ANYBODY
He didnt Know!
AND HEs afRAID

A Feeling

In autumn the wind blows
dead leaves
down the dusty sidewalk,
a sad hearted girl

lifts her eyes
to the cloud darkened sky.
She has a feeling.

In winter the wind blows
ice crystals, stinging faces

a lonely man squints at the

threatening sky.
He has a feeling.

Distant from either
a ferocious wind
levels buildings
Fire consumes
the bodies of the innocent.

In later months
the girl and the man
sicken and die.
So ends Mother Earth.

Is this where we will go?
Tell them you love them now
for tomorrow
who knows what will be.

by Heather Swenson, age 15

Una Corazonada

En otoño el viento sopla
hojas muertas
por la sucia acera,
una niña de corazón
    entristecido
alza la vista
hacia el cielo oscuro y nublado.
Ella tiene una corazonada.

En invierno el viento sopla
partículas de hielo, quemando
    caras
un hombre desolado mira
    furtivo
al cielo amenazante.
El tiene una corazonada.

Distante a ambos
un viento feróz
derrumba edificios.
Fuego consume
cuerpos de inocentes.

Meses mas tarde
la niña y el hombre
se enferman y mueren.
Así termina la Madre Tierra.

¿Hacia esto nos dirigimos?
Diles que los amas ahora,
pues quien sabe
que ha de ser de mañana.

Translation by Debra Sicilia

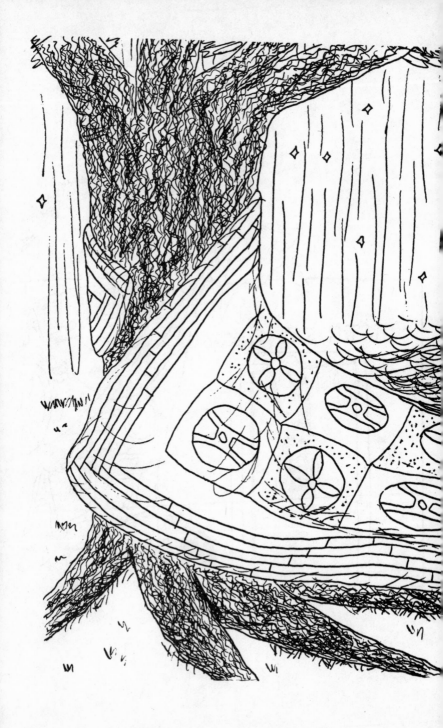

La Paz

La paz es la canción
del coquí
sentado en mi jardín.

Las paz es en viejo árbol
con raíces
bajando hacia el agua.

La paz es una colcha
   de muchos parchos
unida con las oraciones
   del mundo
que se hacen realidad.

La paz es el océano
fiero y fuerte
curando el mundo.

by Maritza Silva, age 13

Peace

Peace is the song
of the coqui
singing in my garden.

Peace is an old tree
with roots
going down to the water.

Peace is a quilt

sewn of all the prayers
   in the world
coming true.

Peace is the ocean
wild and strong
healing the world.

Essay

If people don't change the way we treat each other, we—I mean all the people and the animals on earth—will die. It makes me think about the dinosaurs because they couldn't change when they needed to.

There were also animals in history that did make big adaptations, like when reptiles evolved into amphibians. What did it feel like to leave the water for the first time and take gulps of air?

I think that's what it's like to leave behind our ways of threatening each other and to learn to build trust with people we're afraid of. It may seem impossible but we've got to find a better way than bombs and weapons. It's no harder than climbing out of the water and breathing air when you're used to swimming in water.

Personally, I'd rather change than die.

Wouldn't you?

by Jill Kaczenski, age 17

Essay

Help! I'm not so sure I'd rather change.
    Changing could mean:
        giving up my macho image,
        crying in public,
        admitting I'm not invisible,
        falling flat on my face occasionally,
        waking up early Saturday morning,
        learning to speak in new languages when I can't even
            spell in English,
        no longer waiting for other people to solve it,
        turning the other cheek.

by Riley McMurray, age 16

Nuevo—Fábrica de Sopas
(antes fábrica de misiles MX)

*Los trabajadores no se despiden—se emplean
*No se pierde dinero en reconstrucción
*No más bombas
*Sopas a bajo costo para los que tengan hambre

¡Sopas si, guerras no!

Nuclear Weapons Museum.   **Museo de Armas Nucleares.**

Marcha por la paz cancelado debido a la falta de guerras.

I looked over at both my parents laughing. "I want it to be that way for you children right now," Dad said. I hugged them. I didn't care if we held up the line.

"Is there a lot more?" asked my mother.

"One more section in the basement. Oh, I forgot! I'm supposed to help Zack at two o'clock. Is it time yet?"

"You've got ten minutes. What will you be doing?"

"We've set up a discussion room so that people can ask questions if they want. We're all taking different shifts. I'm supposed to get Riley and bring him down with me."

"Oh, the famous Riley," said my father. "I've been wanting to meet him." My parents walked with me over to his table. It was right at the exit near the food booth so no one could miss it.

"Make Your New Year's Resolutions Here," read the banner.

As we approached, I heard Mr. Goldstein, the selectman, say to Riley, "Ah, committees. You're a man after my own heart." He winked at my father, "Nothing better than serving on a committee, right? Now what are the choices here?"

Riley pointed to his sign. It read:

Join one of our four committees,
or make up a new committee of your own.

INTERFAITH COMMITTEE:
We will plan a commemoration of the bombings of Hiroshima and Nagasaki. Our focus will be on remembrance, on rededication to peace, and on forgiveness.

CONFLICT RESOULTION COMMITTEE:
Help develop and collect curriculum materials for all grades.

UNLEARNING ANTI-HUMAN VALUES COMMITTEE:
We will begin to address racism, sexism, classism, anti-Semitism, ageism, heterosexism, and ableism, by getting training in how these oppressions function and interlock and how to interrupt them.

U.S.–SOVIET FRIENDSHIP COMMITTEE:
We will set up a series of slide shows and speakers
and talk about a possible youth exchange program.

Vote January 15 to declare an
OUTBREAK OF PEACE!

"Wouldn't you say these Tigers are really on the ball?"
said Dad to Mr. Goldstein. "I get the impression there's
nothing they can't tackle."

"Well, Reverend Ames and Mr. Lewis and Ms. Ochs
helped think these up, not us," I said, but they didn't
seem to hear.

Mom did. "Who's running the committee on Anti-
Human Values? Is it Byron Lewis?"

"Yeah, he said he'd get it going. He wants to bring in
trainers from Equity Institute."

"That's the one I'm interested in then," said Mom.

Dad and Mr. Goldstein were wrapped up in
conversation. "Should we put those Tigers in charge of
the town," asked Mr. Goldstein with a grin, "and let the
rest of us sit back for a while and breathe easy?"

"Don't stop there," said my father. "Let's put them in
charge of the federal government. I think they'd clean up
the federal deficit in one four-year term." It was the
typical kind of joke my father liked to make while I
cringed.

"Why be modest? We could do it in a year," answered
Riley. "We'll make Cassie here the ambassador to the
United Nations."

"Don't say that, Riley. It only encourages my father's
dumb jokes. I came to get you. Aren't we supposed to go
down and help Zack?"

"Oh, yeah. I forgot. Well, let me take just one more
customer." I said goodbye to my parents and arranged to
meet them at the origami demonstration in an hour.

"Hello," Riley said to an unusual-looking older man.
The man had on a silver sweater that might have come
from somewhere in Europe like Switzerland, and the
color echoed the silver of his hair. "Take a look at our

display, and if you can think of any new committees, we'd love to hear about them," Riley said in his exuberant manner. You wouldn't know he'd probably repeated those same words a hundred times already.

"I read about this in the newspaper," the man replied, "and I have been giving it some thought."

"Good." Riley blinked. "What's your idea?"

"How about a committee that studies the facts of the arms race and finds ways to present the information to the rest of the town?" His voice was low and rich with an accent that reminded me of German or French.

"Sounds good," said Riley. "You're the first person who's given a suggestion all day. Let me take your name, and we can help set up the first meeting."

A woman was waving to him from a distance. "Rudolph," she called. "It's almost two. Let's go downstairs for the discussion."

He waved back. "I'll just sign here first." Then he assured Riley, "I'll be back to discuss this with you later."

He moved on to join her, but the impression of him remained, the way the wind leaves a silver shimmer on a pond in the winter. He looked both elegant and powerful in an unassuming way.

"Who is he?" I asked Riley. Riley leaned over to read his name.

"Dr. Rudolph Aurelia."

"The mystery man!"

"Sure, Dr. Aurelia," said Mr. Goldstein. "He's a physicist. He and his wife live a very secluded life. She stops by Gus's from time to time, but I don't see him much. I think he's a writer now."

I couldn't believe it. I had finally seen the very man whose house scared me so much.

Terry came up to me wearing a necklace of paper cranes that looked like a necklace of bright flowers. "I found you, Cassie. Guess whose artwork I've been admiring?"

"I don't know. Sneakers' famous paw prints?"

"Yours, dummy. I love standing by your drawings,

Cassie. I listen to people comment on them, and I think to myself, I remember when she'd only show her drawings to me."

I didn't know what to say. I looked at Terry, and then I looked at the ceiling.

"Want me to pinch you?"

"No, I want you to come downstairs with me when I sit in on the discussion. Give me courage if I have to say anything. You know how shy I get in front of groups."

We walked down to the basement. The stairs were lined with drawings of Larkspur in the Twenty-first Century.

We couldn't even find a seat in the small discussion room. "Good. I'll disappear into the woodwork," I said.

"There she is." Jill pointed us out. "That's my sister Cassie, Dr. Aurelia. She did the drawing you spoke about." All heads turned in our direction.

"Ah, Cassie. I was just saying how much this art display has meant to me. I arrived here discouraged about the world, and I am leaving feeling quite differently. Your drawing of hope says it all for me."

I had guessed immediately which drawing he liked. It was the one I'd worked the longest on. It had taken me three months to finish it right. I'd drawn a girl with her hands raised, rising up like a flower in early spring in the meadow. She had chestnut brown skin and her arms and hands were shaped like Yukiko's. Her eyes looked like Terry's, her smile was most like Maritza's, and she had a glow around her like Vera. She was a lantern of hope.

Just as I was thinking, I wish Sam could hear that, I saw him out of the corner of my eye. He didn't see me looking at him. His mouth was hanging open.

"What a day! I don't know if I can endure the landslide," I told Terry.

"Landslide?"

"Of compliments. I don't think I'm going to survive."

"You better get used to it." She smiled at me nervously. "I've got to go. I'm too excited." She went back upstairs to get ready for the origami demonstration.

I stayed and listened to the discussion. I didn't have to say anything because Zack or Jill or Riley answered most of the questions.

A woman asked about one of the pictures Treena had done that was in the section on visions of the future. "Now that was one drawing I just didn't understand. It was of a toy store, I think, and a girl was reaching for a doll off one of the shelves, but there were spider webs on some of the other toys."

"Oh, spider webs on the G.I. Joe's," said Jill. "I can help explain that one. What Treena meant was that in the future, she'd like to see kids just ignoring toys about war, not buying them or anything."

"Are you saying that kids should never be allowed to play with guns?" asked a man with a moustache. "I've got a three-year-old, and the problem is starting to come up."

"All kids play with guns. You can't stop that," said someone else.

"Well, I played with guns when I was little," said Jill. "Most of my friends did. We saw the guns on T.V. and everything. But we didn't have all these weird new guns and monsters with their own Saturday morning cartoon shows. I guess what I dislike the most is having kids get the impression that war is something fun."

A lot of people expressed their viewpoints on toys for children, and the discussion kept me so interested that when I looked at the clock, it was five to three.

When I got upstairs, the chairs arranged by the booth were almost full. I slipped into a place in the back row. I saw my parents in the front, and I waved to Coreena and Vera a few seats away from me. Yukiko's oldest son pushed a button on a tape recorder, and the music signaled the start of the program.

Terry and Yukiko came out wearing silk blouses over black turtlenecks. The blouses were made of the same material as the kimono Yukiko had sewn. They were black with gold chrysanthemum designs. They looked breathtaking. I remembered that Yukiko had said if

Sadako were still alive, they would be the same age.

Yukiko showed the audience a sheet of pink paper. She began to fold a series of triangles that got more and more complicated. After many folds, she held the paper on its side and blew gently into a small opening. The paper inflated into a round ball with two paper handles. She placed it on the table. "A sugar bowl," she explained.

I clapped loudly. I hoped somehow Terry would notice me, but she didn't seem to notice anything. I know her so well, I could tell how nervous she was just by how straight she was standing.

It was her turn. "Here's an animal for the children," she said. "See if you can guess what it will be." As she folded a green piece of paper, Yukiko's youngest son began to hop around, and someone called out, "A frog!" When Terry completed the tiniest folds, that's what emerged.

Then Yukiko and Terry worked to stack six intricately folded sheets of paper one on top of another to make a pagoda. The crowd clapped loudly.

"Now we want to share with you what is for us the most special part of origami: creating the peace crane." I knew what was next. I'd watched it twice in rehearsal. Terry would fold the crane while Yukiko told the story of Sadako. Yukiko's oldest son changed the tape to the delicate music of a single bamboo flute.

I wasn't prepared for what I saw. Maritza joined them, dressed in a blue leotard and a blue skirt. She began to dance the story of Sadako.

First she was Sadako's mother holding the young girl in her arms to try to protect her from the bomb's blast. Then she was the bomb itself tearing the sky with fire. Then stillness, and she became Sadako at twelve-years-old lying, dying, in her hospital bed.

I was so focused on Maritza's powerful movements that at first I didn't notice Terry. She had left Yukiko's side and was walking toward Maritza with one hand held open. She was entering the play. Terry became Chizuko bringing Sadako her first paper crane.

The two girls moved in slow motion. Terry circled around Maritza. She held outstretched in her arms the invisible paper crane. They raised their palms toward each other and reached out. The moment that their hands touched, Maritza burst into flight and became the crane.

She danced slowly at first, and then as Yukiko described the folding of crane after crane, she got stronger and stronger, until we could feel that her spirit would live on past any illness. Maritza fell back into Terry's arms at the moment of Sadako's death and I gasped.

Sadako lay nested there, until we heard that the children all over Japan were working to create her statue. Then she began to move and grow stronger and stronger, until at the end of the dance, she was soaring upward exactly like the girl in my drawing of hope.

When the music finished, there was a silence—and then applause growing louder and louder. Some people stayed in their seats, as if wanting the moment to linger. Some wiped away tears. Families stood up, children rushed off. I pushed through the crowd, but the chairs were scattered and blocked my way.

When I finally reached the front, a circle of people were around the three performers, congratulating them. Vera was off to the side, waiting to speak to Yukiko. Out of the corner of her eye, Terry saw me trying to reach them. She tapped Maritza on the shoulder, and the two of them broke away from the circle to meet me as I leaped forward to hug them both.

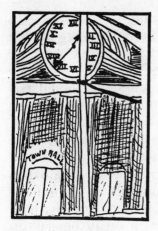

CHAPTER TWENTY-FOUR

The Risks of Peace

"The snow hasn't hurt the turn-out for this town meeting," said a local cable T.V. reporter bundled up in earmuffs and a scarf and speaking into her microphone. She moved aside to allow two townspeople in wheelchairs to go up the ramp Louisa and April had made sure was placed there. "I'm standing outside the Larkspur Town Hall to bring you the outcome of this unique vote." The crowd around her created a path. "Here's the group of young people who started this whole campaign."

We had decided to enter the hall together. It was Terry's idea; she wanted to be with me and the others. We'd told everyone to meet at the Congregational Church and walk the two short blocks to the town hall. We hadn't intended it to look like a parade, but when you get sixty people together on the main street of Larkspur, it can't help but look like one.

We filed into the hall in silence. I don't know who began it, but when we came in the door, people turned to look at us and stopped their conversations. One by one, folks began to stand up, clapping. They gave us a standing ovation.

Mr. Sweeney called the room to order. "I have to warn you that we're saving the outbreak of peace vote for last today."

A voice that sounded like Riley's groaned.

"You don't begin a meal with dessert," continued Mr. Sweeney. "You start with the bread and butter, so that's where we're beginning today, with our school budget."

The town treasurer, Ned's mother, stood up and made a report.

"What could be more of a bread-and-butter issue than peace," a familiar voice whispered. I turned around.

"Oh, hi, Dr. Aurelia." He surprised me. It was hard to get used to this mysterious figure being an actual flesh-and-blood person who'd want to talk to me.

"Don't you agree?" he asked.

"Yeah, I guess peace really does include the whole menu," I replied.

He smiled. I hadn't gotten a close look at him before. He was shorter than I remembered, and a little bent over. I guessed his age to be sixty or seventy. His face was freckled and sand-colored against the silver of his hair. "I want to get a message to one of the girls in your group," he said. "I read a paper of hers on the stage at the art display."

I had the impression that he'd studied everything in our display more closely than even my parents had. "Who was it?"

"She said she was going to Howard University. There's a man in the physics department there I used to teach with."

"Oh, Coreena's the person you're talking about." I looked around to see if I could point her out, but it was too crowded to find her.

"When you see her, tell her I know an outstanding teacher I want to recommend, even if physics hasn't been her interest before."

"No, she's good at physics. She might really like to know about him."

He seemed to want to keep talking to me. "And which of the new committees will you be joining?" he asked.

I'd already picked one out. "Community Pride." I saw his quizzical expression. "You know the recreation building at Larkspur Lake?" He nodded. "Well, lots of people have been saying how ugly it looks, and I want to enter the contest to paint a mural on the walls so it will look better. That is, if the vote wins."

"It certainly looks as if it's going to."

It was another half hour before our vote came up. When all the other business was out of the way, the room became quieter. Lots of people had been whispering like we had, and they stopped now to listen. Parents scooped up their toddlers and sat them on their laps.

"Here we go," said Mr. Sweeney, rubbing his hands together. "Now let me outline again what this vote is about. This is a non-binding referendum. What we're voting on here is a recommendation. It's something that's never been tried in any other city or town in America, as far as we know. So we need to give it our most careful consideration. A 'yes' vote for an outbreak of peace would mean that everyone here, everyone who's old enough to be in school that is, would select at least one thing to do for peace in our town, our country, or our world within the next year. And we would celebrate this on July Fourth this summer. That's what 'yes' would mean, but there's lots of sides to this issue. We're going to start out with speakers 'for' and then speakers 'against' the vote. Who's here to speak in favor of an outbreak of peace?"

Langston and Treena stood up.

Our group had spent a long time discussing who would be our spokespeople at the meeting. Zack insisted that he wasn't the right person. "I want the town to understand that all of us are doing this together," he explained. "If I stand out too much, they might not get the message."

They turned to me. "Cassie, you should do it. After all, it was your idea to declare an outbreak of peace."

"No!" I'd told them. "I'd rather be stuck in a blizzard

for a week than stand up in front of the whole town. You'd have to drag me up there."

Eventually, Langston and Treena volunteered. Seeing them standing together at the podium, organizing the papers of their speech and getting ready, I was wild with excitement. Terry was sitting next to me. She reached out and squeezed my hand.

Langston didn't have to look down at his prepared speech. He had it memorized, and he looked straight out at the audience. "It is an honor to stand here on Martin Luther King, Jr.'s birthday to ask all of you in Larkspur to consider the ways of peace for which he stood all of his life. There was a time when Treena and I could not have stood here together. There was a time when we might not have been friends because the color of my skin is black and the color of her skin is white."

Treena leaned forward toward the microphone. "Because my father and mother are farmers and Langston's mother teaches at the university, there was a time when our families might not have been friends."

Langston's voice was sure and strong. "Now is the time for us to come together and understand that a safe world means caring for the needs of all people. Now is the time to begin to question the weapons we have built up—not only the weapons that are made of metal, but the weapons that live inside our hearts. Our differences are not a cause for fear. They are a source of our strength. We must begin to understand where our true security lies. Our security lies in laying aside these weapons and turning to our trust and caring for one another."

The way he spoke reminded me of the way Yukiko worked with clay on the wheel. He took time with each word and sent it ringing out, full of meaning. Would people listening to him understand all that was behind those words, or would they see us only as people younger than them? Yukiko said you had to turn the clay over and over before you could really sense it. Would they know that the things he spoke of were things we had discovered not easily but over weeks and weeks of hanging in there working with each other?

Treena continued, "People have asked us, 'What do you mean by peace?' We are not here to decide this for you. We want each of you to define and discover for yourself what peace means to you. We believe that everyone has his or her own special contribution to make. No one is too young; no one is too old. We need what everyone has to give. We have a family we must save, the family of Earth."

As Langston spoke again, his face changed from solemn to lively, like a waterfall. "If you want some help getting started, we have some ideas for you. Just because you're choosing your own action for peace doesn't mean that you have to work by yourself. Riley and Louisa are going to describe groups and events you could join if you like."

Riley and Louisa carried a six-foot-high thermometer drawn on thick cardboard and a large chart up to the front of the room.

"The magic word is committees," said Riley, and Mr. Goldstein gave a hearty laugh. Riley held up a chart. "Here's a list of the eight committees that are ready to start now. And, of course, anyone here can suggest other groups not mentioned." His list included four more committees than the ones described at his New Year's Resolution table at the art display. The new ones were:

> COMMUNITY PRIDE:
> Our first job will be to hold a contest for a mural to be painted on the cinder blocks of the bath house at the lake.
> CONFLICT MEDIATION:
> We will set up a conflict resolution center here in town.
> FACTS ABOUT THE ARMS RACE:
> We will create a display giving all sides of the issues at the July Fourth celebration.

PEACEFUL ECONOMICS:

> We will figure out ways to support local farmers and other local businesses. Also, we will help companies whose work is part of the arms race to research economic conversion possibilities.

"Our goal is to have one hundred percent participation by July Fourth," said Riley. "This means you! Everyone. And here's how we'll measure it." He held up the thermometer. There were tiny numbers written along the edge. It was almost as tall as Riley.

Louisa added, "This thermometer goes up to 2349, the exact number of people eligible to participate. When we've colored in the whole thermometer, we'll know we've made it."

Louisa and Riley sat down, and Treena and Langston finished the presentation. Treena began. "July Fourth is one of the most important days of the year to many Americans because it represents our birthday of independence. But for others, July Fourth reminds us of the gap between the ideals our country stands for and the injustices that are actually part of life in America."

"This is why we say that the American Revolution is not over," said Langston. "Our fight for freedom must continue. Now we are fighting to be free to survive in a healthy, safe world. We are fighting to be free of violence, war, hunger, prejudice, and oppression."

"We don't want America to lead the world in armaments," said Treena, "but to set an example of the strength we can have when we settle our conflicts through negotiations instead of threats."

"When we ask you to join us in declaring an outbreak of peace, we are asking you to live with us the ideals of democracy," said Langston. "Vote 'yes' today so that each of us, and all the generations after us, may live in peace."

As they finished, their families stood up and clapped with pride. Vera hugged Treena's parents. Treena's father clapped Langston on the back when they returned to their seats.

People hooted and hollered, and the whole audience applauded, but I noticed that from some areas of the room, it wasn't as loud and strong as that first standing ovation.

"Do you get the impression that some people are having second thoughts?" I asked Terry.

"I know what you mean. If they vote for it, it means that everybody here will actually have to do something for peace. Maybe they don't want to be so involved."

As I scanned the crowd, I saw Arnold the Tiger out of the corner of my eye. Riley and April were holding him. I wondered how they'd gotten him off the wall in the church. Maybe they planned to parade with him if the vote passed. I pointed to them, and Terry chuckled, despite her growing nervousness.

Mr. Sweeney stepped back to the podium. "We've heard from the affirmative side of the issue. Now we've arranged for two speakers on the negative side. Would Mrs. Shipley and Mr. Cameron please step forward."

Terry grabbed my arm. "Will you go with me if I want to leave?"

"I don't know," I said, being honest. "I want to hear everything."

"But if I really, really have to leave?"

"I'll try, Terry."

Mrs. Shipley walked up to the microphone. She had on a silky, flower-print dress and a string of pearls. "I will be brief and to the point," she began. "I believe that our weapons are the cornerstone of the strength of our country. They represent the safety of freedom around the globe. Without our weapons, the Russians are free to walk into our country tomorrow." She paused to take a drink of water from a glass on the podium.

I listened to the point she was making, but it didn't make sense to me. Treena said we had thirty thousand nuclear weapons. We didn't need that many no matter what we thought the Russians would do. When I thought of Hiroshima, it seemed that one nuclear bomb alone was enough—but if it were up to me, I wouldn't have any.

And what about the Russians? Dad said they have enough problems trying to take care of their own huge country. They were hardly about to take on ours, too, no matter what was said on T.V.

Mrs. Shipley turned over a note card in her hand. "These young people say that if Larkspur should declare this outbreak of peace, I am free to interpret peace in my own way. This is all well and good, but it has a dangerous ring to me. Americans must stand united, looking to the guidance of our leaders for the meaning of peace. After all, we know what America stands for."

I wasn't sure anymore that America stood for one thing or that even the word democracy meant the same thing to every person in the room. I saw Langston paging through a school book, maybe looking for a passage to read from later.

Mrs. Shipley cleared her throat. "We elect the officials of our government to do a certain job, and that is to keep America strong and safe. I think it is a mistake for any town to interfere in the work of the government. We must leave these duties in the government's hands and mind our own business which is the business of running this town. Thank you." The audience clapped. Gus, who was up near the front, clapped particularly long, although his wife gave him a dirty look.

I got a queasy feeling in my stomach as Mr. Cameron stood up and walked over to the podium. I knew he was a good speaker, and I was afraid he'd win over the crowd.

"I can't stand this. I can't watch," said Terry. "I want to get out of here."

"No, wait," I told her. "You won't know what he said if you leave." I held onto her.

"I don't need to know," she said, and she stood up. When she noticed many people looking at her, she sat down again. "Okay, I'll stay. I don't want everyone seeing me walk out. But this could be terrible." She gripped my hand.

"Thank you, Mr. Moderator, and thank you Mrs. Shipley," Mr. Cameron began. "First of all, I want to thank these young people for their fine, well-organized presentation. I respect what they're doing today. I also think that this outbreak of peace as it's been described is a risk. I want the people of Larkspur to understand the extent of this risk." He paused and I let out my breath.

The risks of peace. I felt I had already tasted how risky it could be.

How many chances had I already taken? It had been a risk to show my drawings to Zack, and going to the group alone had been scary. I had risked my friendship with Terry by daring to let her know what I really thought, and now we were closer than ever. I had new friends. And two dozen pictures of mine had been on display in front of the whole town, pictures that shared exactly what I thought. There might be more risks up ahead, but I wanted to try them.

Listening to Mr. Cameron was a risk in a way, that is, really listening to what he was saying without closing my mind and expecting to disagree. I tried to turn my attention to him.

"In America, I am free to work and to raise my family as I choose. I'm concerned that these committees could be a threat to this freedom. We're a town with a lot of different viewpoints, and I believe that if we start examining them, we'll end up destroying the peace, not creating it.

"Now, if we were living in another part of the world, I could understand why we might focus on declaring peace in our town. But we are in Larkspur, U.S.A. We're in a town with a long, proud heritage and community spirit. We have the kind of town people in other countries are longing to live in. We already have peace here."

"In conclusion, an outbreak of peace is not needed in

our town. Our community is strong right now. We don't need to be strengthened. Such a change is risky and unwise. I recommend that each of you reconsider your support and vote 'no' to retain the strong and peaceful town we already have."

"He's quite a speaker," I said. "I bet he'll win some people over." She nodded. "But he didn't attack the group, Terry; that was good."

"It's a lucky thing he met with Zack first. You should hear what he says at the dinner table. It could have been a lot worse."

The mood in the hall had altered. I could feel it in the applause Mr. Cameron got. What would happen next? Could we lose the vote?

"Next, we want to open the floor to comments from anyone here," said Mr. Sweeney. People seemed reluctant to talk first. Mr. Sweeney looked around the room. "We've heard some good points raised on both sides of the question. Who would like to speak to them?"

Four people raised their hands, and Mr. Sweeney motioned for them to come up to the front and speak into the microphone so that everyone could hear them.

A woman with a plaid dress spoke first. I recognized her. She used to babysit for me when I was in nursery school. Mrs. Nesbitt shook her head. "I came here undecided. I saw the display, and there was a lot of good art work, but I was impressed by what Mr. Cameron said. I like the town just the way it is. Besides, most of us with families are too busy to do anything more than we're already doing. There's always someone sick, or something else that needs attending to. But something about the art display really got me worried. Frankly, I don't understand why so many of the children did pictures about nuclear bombs. This focus on peace will just make things worse. I don't believe that bombs are a healthy thing for children to be thinking about. That's all I have to say."

The man who spoke next went even further. "I'd like to speak as an adult in this community to the other adults here. This has all been very enchanting, but I want to come out of the clouds and back down to earth." He pressed his finger against his palm to emphasize his point. "With all due respect, I don't want a bunch of children deciding what to do. You kids may be afraid of nuclear war, but frankly, I don't think about it, and none of the adults I know ever speak about it either." A friend of his in the audience yelled his agreement. "This whole idea of new town committees really sounds like a mistake. The town's running really smoothly as far as I can tell. I'm strongly against changing it."

Then Mr. Armstrong, the basketball coach, got up. I already guessed what he would say. One more negative speaker. Three strikes, and we'd be out. He stepped up on the stage. "I was at the art display, too," he began, "but I had a different reaction. I saw the drawings about nuclear nightmares, and I went home and asked my girls —they're ten and twelve—if they ever thought about things like that. They said 'sure.' 'But how come you never told me?' I asked. 'Because you never asked.' Now that really got me thinking. Here I am spending all this time getting the kids to run laps and stay healthy, and for what? Well, I saw the whole display, every picture. And I think they're talking about a whole lot more than nuclear war. You may like Larkspur the way it is, but I like their ideas of the ways it could be even better."

I watched Coach Armstrong sit down by his daughters. Probably the conversations he had had with Zack and Langston had made a good impression on him.

The debate was like a yo-yo. One minute, the vote was losing, the next minute, it was winning.

A slightly balding man in a neat brown suit was next. I knew Mr. Barker even from the back of his head. "I felt very favorably about the art display, too," he said. "It gave me a different impression of these young people than their skit in the cafeteria did, that's for certain. I think everyone in town has heard about that skit by now, so I believe I can refer to it here." The murmur in the crowd said he was right. "I'm not saying it was a disgrace or a spectacle as some people have. It had an amusing quality to it, but it didn't fully model for me what the American Revolution stands for, and that was what it was supposed to be achieving." He cleared his throat. "It is too easy to merely overthrow what one does not wish. It is another matter entirely to build up that which one truly wants." His voice was taking on a quality I recognized from math class.

I watched Mrs. Fairchild go to the edge of the stage and pass a piece of paper to Mr. Sweeney. "Now Mr. Barker is going to turn around and grab Mrs. Fairchild's note," Terry whispered to me.

"And read it out loud," I added. "Just hearing him up there makes me want to write notes myself."

"I guess I'd like what he's saying if I could understand it," she said.

"People think of mathematicians as dwelling in the realm of the certain, the factual. But we also have a penchant for definitions and discovery. The section of the art display that spoke to this aspect for me was the sign, 'Peace means complicating your thinking.' If that can be our watchword today, I think we'll have a basis for some commonality from which we can create this July Fourth celebration that has been suggested. I want to urge us not to form a mental picture of merely overthrowing nuclear weapons. I want us to think of complexity, of building up new ways of communicating, of creating systems of national security that do not hinge on man's tooth and fang nature, but rather on our ability to reason."

Mrs. Fairchild looked like she was about to speak next, when Mr. Barker searched the audience. "I really need an answer here from one of the young people. Which is the emblem for the peace you're talking about? Your skit or your art display?"

Treena and Langston looked at each other, but April stood up first. She was a lot different from when I'd first met her. She didn't crouch her shoulders and shuffle up to the stage. Her arms swung as she walked.

She leaned her elbows on the podium and pulled her long black hair behind her ears. "Hey, I'll take the heat. I liked our skit a lot. I know it surprised a lot of people, but we had to do it that way because nobody was listening to us. It's different now. More people than I ever expected have been talking to me about the art display. Everyone I talked to said that they found at least one idea in it they want to try here in Larkspur. That really made me happy.

"Besides, it's not just us kids behind this. There's teachers and my dad and my stepmother and lots of other adults. We spent months working on it. I don't want what we said at the display to be lost and forgotten. That's why we're here today."

April shifted from one foot to the other. "Mr. Barker, I don't know if you remember this, but I got a D minus my first quarter in your class." People in the audience laughed and she looked at them and shrugged her shoulders. "But by the end of the year, I had a solid B! That's what I mean. You gotta keep trying." She paused to think of a way to finish. "So, I hope you'll all vote 'yes' so we can try to change things together."

I could see Mrs. Fairchild's distaste for April as she passed her on the way up to the stage. Mrs. Fairchild tried to control her voice as she began to speak, but the wait had made her impatient. "My people, my forebears, have been living in this town for six generations. Six generations. We've seen a lot of history, and we're in a special position to know what makes this town great."

Even though I could already tell that she was against the proposal, I forced myself to remember what Vera had said, that each person needed to tell their story, needed to tell how things looked through their eyes.

Mrs. Fairchild relaxed more as she spoke. "When I sit there on the stage at the July Fourth celebration and represent the oldest family in town, I get a thrill of pride. Our town has been like the beacon of the statue of liberty.

We've made room for newcomers. Ours is a friendly town. We have differences, but we don't let them get in our way. We know how to let each other be."

I was growing angry at the undercurrent beneath her words.

"What is best for Larkspur?" asked Mrs. Fairchild. "I agree with Mr. Cameron. We should appreciate Larkspur just the way it is today. If we declare this outbreak, as I sit up there on the stage, I will feel as if I've let down not only this town but also my ancestors. I stand here today asking you to cherish the values we have treasured for generations."

Byron Lewis leapt to his feet. "Values aren't something you just make once and then fold your hands and you're done with it."

"Mr. Lewis, I'll have to ask you to come up here and be recognized formally if you want to speak."

Vera was sitting next to him, and she said something to him as he stood up. I could imagine my mother saying to Dad about Mrs. Fairchild, "Don't let her get to you so much."

"Okay," said Byron Lewis as he stood at the podium, "When I hear you say that everything is fine the way it is, I'm at a loss for words. You must read the local paper. We have thirty-three people homeless just in our county alone. What about them? And there are elders right here in Larkspur who aren't getting enough money from social security and only eat one meal a day. These kids have thought of a way for us to come together and address these things." He shook his head. "We've got a government that's cutting back spending for the poor and buying new weapons instead. Who's going to help out if not our community right here at home? We can't just stand still and bow our heads and pray and hope everything will work out. We've got to live what we believe in. When I think about why we're here today, I think we're trying to declare an outbreak of caring."

Several people cheered. "Now we're back on track," I

thought. "Things in the world aren't right yet. Everyone knows that, and now we can admit it to each other and start to do something about it."

I started feeling itchy from sitting so long. I didn't see how adults could stand such long meetings. I scrunched my shoulders up to give them a stretch and looked around. Gus was trying to stand up and speak and his wife was trying to pull him back.

Gus made it to the podium. "I'm going to save you a whole lot of trouble debating this thing. The way I understand it, you're trying to get one hundred percent, and as long as I'm here, you won't. I can't. I'm too busy. I'm saying a big 'no,' and that's not going to change.

"I've got nothing against these kids. I know them, most of them, and I like them a lot. That's not the issue. And I agree with Mr. Lewis here that there's a lot about this old world of ours that's not fair, but I just plain can't do one more thing."

"Gus," Mr. Goldstein called to him from the stage. "You understand this is a non-binding issue, don't you? That means you wouldn't be required to take part."

"We might not be bound to do it, but we still got to decide what we think of it, and the picture I'm getting, looking around the room at my neighbors—and I know them pretty well—is that we're already up to our ears taking care of our own matters. Things are bad, but what can we do? This outbreak of peace stuff won't mean anything if nobody signs up for it. So, I'm saying it to you real plain. Why have it?"

A lot of hands went up at once, and without hearing what they had to say, I guessed that most of the people waiting to speak agreed with Gus.

"These kids are trying to lead us down the Soviet path," a tall, thin man called out.

"Keep things as they are," yelled another.

I felt a chill go up my spine. We'd lost. We'd pushed and pushed, and we could go no further. Was Mr. Cameron right? Was it just too big a risk for our town?

335

Was it just too hard for all of us to sit down and listen to one another?

I felt bone tired. Now it would be as if the Tigers and our peace display had never existed. Everything would go back to the way it had been.

I craned my head to see who could speak out for us. Maybe Langston would read from the Constitution and let everybody know that we were speaking for democracy. Maybe Treena would get up and say the kinds of things she said in our meetings when she got mad and determined. Or Zack. Zack could save us. But none of them raised a hand.

CHAPTER TWENTY-FIVE

The Vote

Mr Sweeney looked at his watch. "I hate to cut off debate, but I guess that's it," said Mr. Sweeney. "Time to put it to a vote."

"No need," said Mr. Fairchild who was sitting on the stage with Mr. Sweeney and Mr. Goldstein. "We've already gotten our answer. It's a meaningless proposal. The way this thing is formulated, it says everybody would do something. We've already heard a number of people say that they don't want to take part. No matter how many people vote for it, it can't be carried out. Why vote?"

"I guess that makes sense," said Mr. Sweeney. He looked over at the row of Tigers sitting in the front. "Sorry kids. You gave it a good try."

I sat frozen. Did this mean the meeting was over? Were we just supposed to file out and go home and cry in our beer, as my dad would say. Nobody knew quite what to do. A couple of people got up and stretched. Parents ran after their kids.

"Wait a minute, here. With all due respect to my colleagues, I, too, have something to add." It was Mr. Goldstein "I agree that a vote can't be held at this point,

337

but a democracy means more than just voting. It means dialogue and participation. We've opened up a lot of topics today. Can we go home and just let them be swept back underneath the rug? We've come here today not just to say yes or no to an issue but so that people in our community can understand each other better—and even more so that we can understand our place in the world. I think we should call a recess for half an hour and then return and see if we can create some kind of compromise." He looked at Mr. Sweeney, who nodded.

"Wait a minute," said Mr. Fairchild. "I thought this was all settled."

"Take a break and then come back," yelled a loud voice from the audience. It was my dad.

"Okay, see you in half an hour sharp," said Mr. Sweeney over the growing noise in the room.

Gus called out that his store would be open. I saw Sam and his friends run outside, probably for a snowball fight. That sounded pretty good to me, too. Ms. Ochs yelled that she had her guitar and would play music downstairs for whoever wanted to come. She said it would be music from the civil rights movement to celebrate Martin Luther King Day. Everyone was talking at once. Riley made a bee-line for Coach Armstrong. Terry wanted to join the singing, but I knew I had to go outside.

"I find this all very disturbing," I heard Dr. Aurelia say behind me.

I wasn't sure which part he found disturbing, but I felt like a coiled spring about to pop. One moment it seemed we were on the edge of something great and unheard of, something that no town had ever tried before. The next moment, it had shrunk away. I wanted to scream, "This is our last chance." I wanted to shake Zack and say, "Fix this!"

I went out and looked up the street at the route we'd walked today. The snow had stopped, leaving little, white caterpillar trails on the branches. My breath made frosty puffs as I walked up to the church and back down again.

By the time I'd turned around and seen the crowd of people in front of the town hall, an idea had come to me.

"There's one way to compromise," I said to myself. "It would be better than losing everything." I took a pencil from my pack and wrote some notes on the back of an old math quiz. I walked a few more steps and had another thought. I jotted it down.

When I went back inside, Terry and Maritza were walking up from the singing. I told them my idea, and they both said it sounded fine. As Mr. Sweeney called everybody back to to their seats, I ran up to find Zack and tell him.

He squished his face to one side and thought. "That would be okay with me," he said.

Mr. Sweeney banged his gavel to try to bring everyone to order.

"Will you go up and tell them?" I asked Zack as the tide of people pushed me away.

"Vera's speaking next. I'll ask her."

Vera climbed up the three steps to the little stage, and I turned back to my seat.

"Here, here. Let's have some peace and quiet," said Mr. Sweeney. "Let peace reign here and now." He got a few chuckles.

The tall, thin man kept on talking to Riley with angry gestures. "Whose side are you on?" he demanded. He was speaking so loudly, I could hear him from where I was. "This isn't the time to be questioning America. The Soviets want to take over the globe. Look, I've worked all my life against them. I wrote letters years ago against the United Nations when it was starting, and now you can bet I'm supporting the freedom fighters in Nicaragua. Maybe you'll see it like I do when you're older. We've got to stop this communist menace, or it will stop us."

I admired the way Riley was standing there listening cheerfully instead of reflecting back the man's angry scowl. He shook his fist at Riley. "I'm not having a bunch of kids like you who are being duped by the communists bring this stuff to our town. Don't you understand the meaning of democracy?"

Mr. Sweeney banged his gavel again. "Everyone sit down, please." Riley took his seat, but the man paced the aisle.

"Now, during the break, one person indicated that she had something to say. We'll start with her. Vera Taylor, come right up."

Vera took a deep breath. Her face was at once serious and playful, a look she and Langston both shared. "If we throw out this proposal," she began in her clear, comforting voice, "we will lose the most important opportunity that has ever come to our town. We can't let it go; it's a gift."

"I want to speak about our country," she said, looking at the tall man who was still red in the face. He sat down to hear her. "I think these young people are suggesting something crucial for America. They are asking for a deeper democracy. I know we've heard that word a lot this afternoon, and I've decided that democracy means to me caring for the whole...," she searched for the words she wanted. "I guess the whole ball of wax! Our government is meant to be for the people, and that means all the people. It means not leaving anyone's needs out.

"In the old democracy," she continued, "each person was free to act as they please, even if it polluted the air or threatened the conditions for life which we pass on to our children. These young people are asking us to help build a new democracy where we can learn to work not as separate, independent people free to do anything we want but as people aware of the others around us.

"They want us to ask hard questions and have hot debates. But above all, they don't want us to let our fears decide for us. They don't want us to go back home again, shut our doors, and be silent once more."

It was as if she were blowing gently on the embers of a campfire to help it ignite. The spark of hope wasn't lost

"I have something to add," said a very agitated voice.

Dr. Aurelia was edging over to the front of the room. "I didn't come here today planning to speak, but I feel now that I must."

"Do come up here," said Vera, and Mr. Sweeney nodded that he could be next.

Dr. Aurelia bent the microphone down. He was hunched over like a little gnome. "We have a serious matter before us today, and so I will speak to you seriously —and personally. I know all too well what it means to be silent and to stay behind locked doors. I have kept to myself, and I have tried to hide." Terry and I looked at each other. What secret could a man like Dr. Aurelia possibly be hiding? He seemed like one of the most intelligent people we'd ever met.

"I..." He stopped and scanned the audience. "Zack, would you come up here, please?" Zack looked startled. He stood up and loped his usual walk up to the podium. He was wearing his familiar blue jean jacket. Dr. Aurelia put his hand on Zack's shoulder.

"Here is one of the greatest peacemakers I've ever met." Zack looked at the floor. "I've asked him to come up so that he can give me courage as I tell you the secret I have already told him." Zack put his hand behind Dr. Aurelia, and they stood there arm in arm.

"You know that I'm a physicist. What you don't know is that I am one of the physicists who helped to create the nuclear bombs that were detonated over Hiroshima and Nagasaki, Japan in 1945." I wondered where the other Tigers were sitting and how they were taking the news.

"I was not just one of the hundreds of scientists who created a tiny part of the bomb and could shrug their shoulders and pretend they didn't know where that part was going." He looked directly at Mr. Cameron as he spoke. Mr. Cameron received his message. "I was one of the chief scientists I helped kill thousands of people in Japan."

His voice dropped low and he looked down, away from the audience. "I moved here to Larkspur after I retired from teaching, but I have not made friends. I find I think about it more than ever before." His whole face changed as if once again he were back in the isolation of his memories. "It is unforgiveable."

Zack leaned over and whispered something to him.

Dr. Aurelia met his glance and continued speaking. "Then I heard about the committees for peace. I saw what these young people could do at the art display. They weren't just talking pretty words. They meant business.

"I suggested that I be part of a committee on the facts of the arms race and sought out Zack. My mind started churning out all kinds of ideas of what we could do. My mind was there. But my heart," he thumped his chest, "my heart was still sore."

"And that is why I say Zack is such a brilliant peacemaker. He was excited about my ideas for the Arms Race Committee, but he suggested that I be on another committee as well: the committee preparing a commemoration for the day we bombed Hiroshima. Zack said that the ceremony would include something about forgiveness and he wanted me to be there. That has meant so much to me."

He paused and took a deep breath. "The work that these young people are doing, that so many of you are doing, calls me out of my house. I want to work with you, I…" He blinked his eyes and looked out at the audience, halting as if the immensity of all he had revealed were suddenly striking him. "I don't know what else to say. I'll let someone else have a turn."

"I'd like to speak next," said my mother, who had quietly gone up to stand next to Dr. Aurelia. He looked startled and tried to retreat, but she grabbed his hand. "I thought I'd come over and say this to you afterward, but my heart has been pounding, so I guess I have to speak now. I've heard every word you said. Now please hear me."

Dr. Aurelia dropped her hand and stiffened. He looked

342

awkward and afraid. I thought, don't give up. Don't go back in your shell.

Mom looked at him gently. "It is not just your own guilt. We've all taken part in things or allowed things to happen that we regret and feel ashamed of. But we have to go on from here. We have to live and work with each other regardless of what has happened."

My mother took his hand again. "We must forgive what has been done in the past—and I don't say that lightly." I felt so proud of her and the look in her eyes. "I don't want you to go back and hide in your house. I want to be working with you."

Tears choked me. I leaned over and said to Terry, "We'll find a way to talk more with your father." I didn't know if it would make sense to her why I was saying that.

"Yes," she answered.

"Cassie!" A voice from the podium was calling. "Cassie!" It was Zack. Why was he doing this? I shook my head, but he continued. "Cassie, will you come up here?"

"There is one person whose heart and mind have been behind this from the very start. I don't think she herself realizes what a difference she has made. Not just that she thought up this outbreak of peace, but in how much she cares," Zack said.

"You have to go up there," Terry whispered.

"Of course I'm not going up there," I replied. "He'll stop calling my name soon."

But Zack insisted. "Now she's come up with a compromise that I'd like her to tell you about herself."

I looked at Terry with a feeling of panic. "I'll walk with you," she told me.

"What about your father?"

"You've got to go up there," Terry said. "And I'll help you do it." She got me to stand, but I was still reluctant. She led me through the seats and up the long aisle to the podium. Everything was a blur.

Zack placed me in front of the microphone. I couldn't

focus my eyes on anything in front of me. I felt as if I were inside a cloud.

"Yea, Cassie!" yelled a voice that must have been Maritza.

"The Awesome Threesome are with you," yelled Riley.

Zack and Terry sat next to each other on the floor in front of the first row. I decided to speak just to them. I took out of my pocket the crumpled piece of paper where I'd written my notes.

"It's just a simple idea," I began. "I started to think about what is the most important part of an outbreak of peace." I looked only at Zack and Terry. I felt as if I were falling into their faces, as if I could talk on and on.

"I know it's not going to work to try to get everybody in town to sign up. But I don't think that's the important thing any more. Right now, when you care about the world, you can feel kind of alone. It seems like war and violence and cruelty are what people expect, and anyone who speaks about peace and justice is just called a dreamer. An outbreak of peace means we're reversing that. We're not accepting war as something normal. It doesn't mean we have the answers about how to make that switch, but it means we're going to do everything we can to try."

I looked at my notes. There were three words: "actions," "committees," and "thermometer."

"I think we should still have people sign up for peace actions if they feel like it," I continued. "Then we can each figure out what matters to us and how we want to help. And lots of people might not choose a peace action themselves, but they'd be glad that other people were doing one. It doesn't mean that you have to do something publicly. Everything is helpful."

I didn't want to embarrass my mother, but I thought of her as an example. "Like my mother thinks she's been too busy to do anything for peace since she and my dad opened their shop, just because she hasn't been collecting petitions like she used to. But she's done lots of other things. She's printed posters for us and let me know that she really believes in me. I'm not putting down letters and petitions and stuff, because somebody's got to do that. Everybody has their own way, and now April's father has taken up where my mom left off."

I didn't want to forget the thermometer. "I guess you can't really measure what you do for peace, but I think we should keep the thermometer that Louisa and Riley made and record how many people sign up. It will be neat to look at it and watch the number climb."

For a second, I wondered how I could be saying so much? But I concentrated on the last thing I wanted to say. I didn't need the paper to remind me.

"I get really excited when I think about what it would be like if the whole town could stand together on July Fourth and say we want to declare an outbreak of peace. Because I think we all do. We all want to leave war and violence behind. That's what I think we should vote on: saying together on July Fourth that we're beginning the switch over from violence to peace in the world. Even if it takes a thousand years. If we're all standing there together, we'll know that we all really do care and that we can make a difference. Do you know what I mean?"

I stopped for a moment. Terry and Zack nodded their heads. They were pulling for me.

"Tell them why you work for peace," Zack said.

What could I say? I couldn't tell them about my grandmother's death. And that was only part of it. I'd never tried to put it into words before. I'd finished saying everything that was written on my paper. I was about to blank out, there in front of all those people.

Then I felt my grandmother with me, and I heard her voice saying, "Don't give up. Keep on going."

"But how can I?" I wanted to say.

The answer came back: "All the faces out there. They are all your friends." I looked at Terry. She had one hand open in a gesture that said, "Hang on, I'm with you." I noticed that Maritza and Langston and Jill had moved up

345

to sit with Terry and Zack. They all seemed to be reaching out to me with their eyes and faces.

"I want to grow up," I began. "I want to have children, too, maybe grandchildren. And someday I want to take them to the meadow behind my house." The five of them welcomed every word.

"It's not just for me," I continued. "I want my friends and my family to live long, happy lives. Everybody here. I want us to know that there'll be people living after us, enjoying the same things we enjoy: the mountains, the lake, snowball fights, fresh corn in the summer. And right now, none of us can say for sure that life's going to go on. That's so terrible."

I paused. I don't know where I got my next idea. Maybe it was something Mr. Barker would have said in math class. He always had us imagine some impossible problem and then showed us how to get out of it. "Just imagine if everyone in Larkspur had to climb some incredibly steep mountain to survive, what would we do? We'd probably help each other out. People would take turns carrying the babies and giving people who needed it a lift. We'd pull each other up. We'd be encouraging. That's what I want us to do now. If we work together—those of us who can and want to—then miracles can happen. I want us to know, no matter what happens, that we tried our very hardest."

I stopped. All I remember was loud applause like drums or thunder.

I sat down between Terry and Maritza and rested with their arms on my shoulders. Up on stage, Mr. Sweeney said in his own words the compromise I'd suggested. More people talked. There were a couple of questions, and Mr. Goldstein answered them.

Then Mr. Sweeney put it to a vote.

I saw many hands waving like tall grass all around me. And then I heard him say the words, "The town of Larkspur has just declared an outbreak of peace."

Sam came out of nowhere to lift me up on his shoulders.

346

Riley and April carried Arnold the Tiger, and the aisles filled with people clapping.

"I'm so proud of you, Cassie," Sam kept saying. Zack lifted Terry on his shoulders, and we stretched our arms out to each other.

Pinky came up and tugged on Terry's sleeve. "How do I join? I want to be the first drop of red paint in the thermometer."

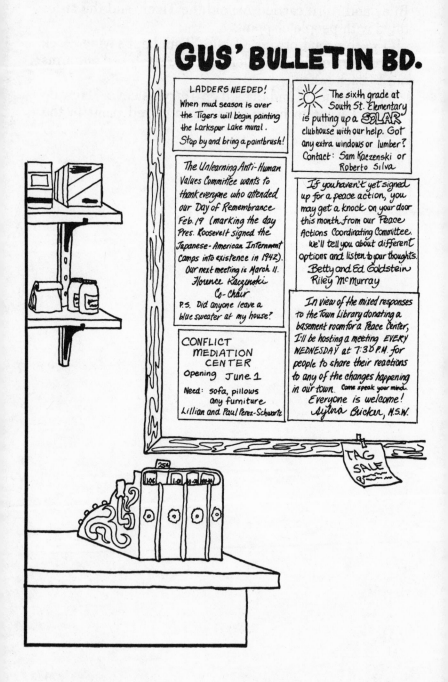

CHAPTER TWENTY-SIX

Duża Rośnij

I floated in happiness like a bird soaring over the meadow. Everytime someone stopped me in the hall at school to say they liked my speech or told me how glad they were that the vote won, my happiness grew and I floated higher.

The Saturday morning after the vote, I woke up to a heavy snowfall. I wrapped myself up in my rose-colored down jacket and matching hat and gloves and went for a walk to the meadow. The snow had stopped, and the sun was very bright, with hardly any wind.

Dry ends of old cornstalks stuck up above the snow drifts in the cornfield. Ice covered all the weeds and bushes and sparkled in the sun.

I had visited Miss Leamon in the art room recently, and she had asked me, "How do you feel now?"

I knew why she had asked. The thermometer that marked the number of peace actions was climbing, even if it wasn't climbing fast. And kids who'd never said much to me before wanted to talk to me now.

I had just said, "Great." How could I describe it? It wasn't like fireworks. It was more a feeling that lingered,

349

like being full after a huge, delicious dinner. I felt full and content.

When I walked into the meadow, the hills in the distance looked like white envelopes. The swamp was all frozen. Usually, I like to throw a rock to hear the ice crack and splinter and see little pieces skitter across the surface, but this day I wanted to let it be.

I came to the part of the field that's shaped like a bowl. The ice crystals coating the tree branches looked like jeweled spiders' webs.

I enjoyed having no place I had to go and nothing I had to do. I walked lightly on the powdery snow and noticed frozen, red berries. When I looked closer, I saw a snowshoe rabbit crouched in a tangle of branches. I stayed very still and watched until it ran off.

A cardinal flew from one bush to another, and up above me, jet trails crisscrossed like smoke from a giant's pipe. I wanted to write a message in the sky.

When I got to the willow, I reached my arms up high to hold onto a thick branch. I rocked forward on my toes and stretched. I could hear *Babcia* saying, "*Duża rośnij.* There's no mistaking it; you're big now. You've grown to your full height."

When I got back home, I spent the whole afternoon rearranging one wall of my room. I took down an old poster and put up a piece of corkboard. Then I selected photos and clippings of our group to put there.

Now when I wake up in the morning the sun comes in the window and lights up the photographs of my friends.

There's a newspaper photo of Langston propping up the thermometer on the lawn in front of Gus's store, and a photo of Treena painting the first dots on the thermometer.

There's a page torn out of the school newspaper with Riley holding up the box where kids could register their peace actions. He said it was his shining moment to stroll into the school office with it, wait for someone to assume he was there for a detention, and instead plunk the box into place on the counter.

And Sam's present to me is on my desk. It's a wooden box with pastels inside in neat, rainbow rows.

Right above it in a frame is my favorite photo. Vera took it of Maritza, Terry, and me, and she wrote a note with it that I taped to its border: "Here's the new Awesome Threesome."

The photo shows the three of us standing in the snow in front of the recreation center at Larkspur Puddle. We are planning what our mural will look like painted on that wall. We're going to paint **a** row of people, some famous and some unknown, to stand for all the people in the world. And they'll be holding hands like the chain of hands I saw in my dream.

CHAPTER TWENTY-SEVEN

Webs

The June sky was robin's egg blue as Zack and I walked through the wet grass to decorate the trees in the meadow with streamers. It was our last chance to have a huge party together now that lots of people in the Tigers had graduated.

Soon, dozens of people were walking along the secret path I had walked so many times. They came over the rise and into the bowl-shaped part of the meadow where Dad and Mr. Silva were setting up tables with food.

Maritza, Terry, and I handed out pieces of yarn, and Mom paired up people to hold each piece for the spider web that Vera had insisted be part of the celebration. We had all sorts of colors: purple, blue, lime-green, and soft, hand-died shades like cranberry and goldenrod.

We couldn't give the pieces out fast enough. More and more people arrived, and they crowded around the box. Yukiko waved and said she had a surprise for us. Mr. Barker nodded, and Ms. Ochs stopped to ask how our work on the mural was coming along now that school was out.

I was especially glad to see Coreena because I thought

she had already left for the summer. Vera had gotten her a job in Washington D.C. doing tech work for a theater company. But Coreena told us she stayed an extra weekend to be here for the party. We made her promise that she'd add some paint to the mural before she left.

Vera showed us how to crisscross our pieces of yarn, and people began weaving the web. I watched the circle grow as each pair laced their yarn through the central web and then stood opposite each other and pulled their ends tight.

As more and more people joined and the yarn got interlaced, they became one wheel of color. It reminded me of the game of knots, only here everybody was far apart, nearly two hundred of them, stretched out across the whole bowl of the meadow.

When most everybody had a piece, Zack handed me a strand of turquoise yarn, and we wove it into the others and stood on either side of the circle. Zack stood next to Jill, and I waved to them across the sea of faces. They yanked on the string and waved back.

Terry finished lacing her yarn through the central web and came to stand next to me. "I guess my parents aren't coming after all," she said.

"Well, it was worth a try, but we didn't really expect them," I said. We had sent invitations to all of our families, and since Terry considered herself a full-fledged member of the Tigers now, we hadn't left her parents out.

Maritza was on the other side of Terry. "Didn't you say that Dr. Aurelia was trying to get them to come today?"

"Yeah," said Terry. "He visited this week. They've been working together on a computer game for July Fourth. Daddy says Dr. Aurelia's one of the most brilliant people he's ever met. He's really in awe of him, so I thought he'd be convinced."

"What's the game about?"

"It's a quiz about something; I'm not sure what. There's so much whispering around the house lately. I walk into the den and my parents are in the middle of a big argument, I mean debate. That's the way my mother wants me to look at it. 'We don't have fights in this house,' she always says."

I searched for my parents. They were standing up the slope with the other hosts for the party: Vera, Yukiko, and Dr. Aurelia.

Having the party here was Dr. Aurelia's idea. I'd found out that he often came to the meadow during the day when I was at school and that he loved being in the meadow as much as I did. I'd met him here one day when school had gotten out early. He'd been the one who had planted the daffodils and tulips and crocuses that bloomed every spring.

Now a row of orange lilies bobbed behind the five of them as they got ready to talk. The flowers looked like attentive faces turning toward them.

My eyes went back to Jill across the circle from me. She had turned to Zack and was giving him a kiss. That was nothing new. I'd go into the kitchen and they'd have their arms around each other, or I'd see them kissing in the hall.

When they had first started going out together, it had bothered me a lot. I remember the afternoon when Zack got off the bus at my stop and walked home with me to talk about it. He told me that I'd always be important to him. He said a friendship like ours could never be lost.

After he told me, I went straight over to Yukiko's for my weekly pottery lesson. I took a large lump of clay and smacked it down hard. I wanted to pound something. While I kneaded the clay against the board, I thought about the year and figured out that it must have been Jill that Zack had had a crush on all along.

If they had started going out together before this, like in the fall, I would have slunk away from the Tigers and never come back. Back then, Zack had to be my friend first. Now that had changed. I didn't know why or how, but it had, and I guess he could tell. Maybe Zack had

been waiting not just for Jill to lose interest in Eddie but for it to be ok with me.

Both he and Jill made an effort to make sure I didn't feel left. Sometimes just Zack and I would do things, like putting up the streamers for the party.

I'd even made a special bowl at Yukiko's that day. When Yukiko had noticed my sadness, she had said, "Let's see what the clay can do for you now," and she had taught me how to make a willow bowl.

I raised a bowl on the wheel and let it dry leather hard. Then I decorated it with willow leaves from my favorite tree. I pressed them along the sides, and when they burned off in the first firing, their imprint was left behind. Now the bowl sat on my bureau. It reminded me that I no longer needed someone else liking me to believe in myself.

The celebration was beginning. Vera spoke first. She had a wide-brimmed sun hat on. "This web of yarn stands for the web we have created here in Larkspur. We have crisscrossed our lives and started a web that now goes beyond our town. On July Fourth, hundreds of people will come together at our fairgrounds for a celebration of interdependence."

"Thousands," yelled Riley.

"Maybe thousands," said Vera with a smile. "But what we want to do today is to thank all of you who made this possible. As many of you know, the peace thermometer is at 1407 right now. That means about sixty percent of the town has declared an action for peace." Cheers and whistles rang out to the hills.

On July Fourth, Langston would read the Declaration of Interdependence that he and others had written, and we'd set off helium balloons high in the sky. The baseball team was planning to stay up all night in the gym to blow them up.

Kyle's mother would describe her work to make Larkspur a hunger free zone. Pinky and the elementary school stage band would perform as "The Pink Panthers of Peace." There'd be more songs and speeches, and a group of Soviet scholars from Boston would say a few words.

One of the Soviets would be staying with us overnight. Mrs. Shipley had been asked by April's father to host another couple, and she had agreed. I really respected her for that.

Mr. Goldstein stepped forward to speak. He kept hold of his strand of yarn as he opened up a letter. The sun was getting hot. Maritza's younger sisters tugged so hard on their piece of yarn that it broke, and Mrs. Silva had to knot the broken ends together.

"I'm happy to report that there are two towns in Vermont following in our footsteps," Mr. Goldstein said. "They'll be declaring an outbreak of peace in early August at the anniversary of the bombings of Hiroshima and Nagasaki. I've been writing letters back and forth to the people there and offering any help we can give. But they didn't have you Tigers to start them off."

He smiled as he looked around the circle. "Here we are in this meadow, all ages. It feels to me like a large group, but compared to all the people in the world, we're just a drop in the ocean. Even though no one knows we're here, we're making a difference, and I bet there are other circles of people right now just like ours, maybe on hilltops in Vermont, that are coming together to celebrate peace."

"And in Kawasaki, Japan," Yukiko added, "I have a friend who works in the Peace Information Center. I've been sending him clippings of our peace events. Nearly a thousand towns in Japan have voted to be nuclear free zones, and Kawasaki was one of the first. They have a ceremony each year that is like our outbreak of peace, and now Kawasaki wants to celebrate with us. They have asked me to create a sculpture for their peace park, and in turn, one of their artists will send a display for the Larkspur town square."

Our town square! I shouted and clapped with the rest

of the crowd. It mattered to people in Japan what we were doing here in Larkspur! We were reaching across the ocean.

"We've started something in Larkspur that will go on from here like ripples upon ripples," said Yukiko. She asked us to place our yarn on the grass and hold hands, and you could tell that people wanted to.

Vera waited until the circle was still. I could hear birds calling and the wind in the trees. She recited a poem by one of her favorite poets, Langston Hughes. "Hold fast to dreams," she said. The words traveled around the circle. I let my eyes jump from face to face. There was Treena with her sisters, Kisha and her friends, Coreena, Yukiko's sons, and Sam. The yarn on the ground between us made a bright, uneven design.

It was Dr. Aurelia's turn to speak. "Here is a dream I hold onto," he said, "that we will always have beautiful places like this to come to. For I believe that peace is born not in houses of government but in the wild green spots on earth. When I come here, I find again the voice of peace that lives inside me."

Hold fast to dreams. I imagined the spider looking at me from her web. I remembered the dream I had spun with her of finding a way I could help to bring peace. And now it was coming true.

I stood with Terry on one side of me and Langston on the other. Their hands were warm. I felt as if they could speak through their hands. Terry's seemed to say, "Remember when we were just kids together?" And Langston said, "I feel like I've known you for a long time, for a lot longer than the nine months it's been!"

I looked around the circle again, and each person seemed to have their own music. Riley was a marching band, Maritza, pirouettes of flute music, and Yukiko, wind chimes. The strands of music wove together.

Across from us, the circle shifted to make room for a few latecomers. I looked over and saw Dottie, and to my surprise, Gus. Zack let go of Riley's hand to make room for them, and Dottie pulled her hat firmly on her head and reached over for Riley's.

Gus stood off to the side, watching. He had on a plaid shirt that looked a little warm for the June sun, more suited to the cool inside his store. He put his hands in his pockets and scanned our faces.

Dad nodded to Gus and motioned for him to join us in the circle. Zack opened the place next to him again. Then cautiously, as if he were putting a toe into cold water, Gus took Zack's hand.

The sun was beating down harder now. Something about Gus's gesture sent a ripple through me. I felt that I was in the circle of hands I had dreamed of, the circle we were painting, that necklace of light I saw when I fought the tide of fears in my nightmare.

I felt scores of invisible people with us, each of us reaching beyond our fears. There might be peace circles right now all over the world, maybe a thousand circles like a thousand paper cranes. Or a hundred thousand.

We didn't have to wait for the ceremony with the whole town. That moment with all of us together I knew.

We had declared an outbreak of peace.

Scenes from the Book

"Pinky & the Pink Panthers of Peace" *by Fiona Kaul-Connolly*

"Mailbox" *by Molly McGarrigle*

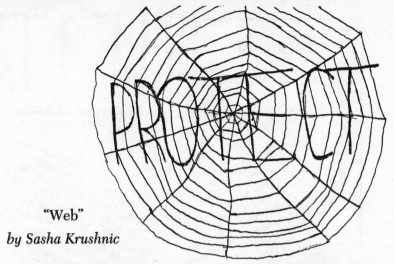

"Web"
by Sasha Krushnic

"Vera" by Bethany Schneider

Footnotes to Zack's Notebook

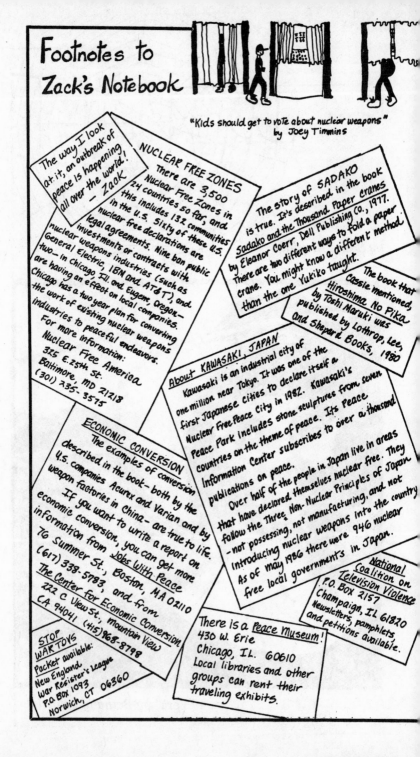

"Kids should get to vote about nuclear weapons"
by Joey Timmins

The way I look at it, an outbreak of peace is happening all over the world!
— Zack

NUCLEAR FREE ZONES

There are 3,500 Nuclear Free Zones in 24 countries so far, and this includes 132 communities in the U.S. Sixty of these U.S. nuclear free declarations are legal agreements. Nine ban public investments or contracts with nuclear weapons industries (such as General Electric, IBM and AT&T), and two — in Chicago, Ill. and Eugene, Oregon — are having an effect on local companies. Chicago has a two year plan for converting the work of existing nuclear weapons industries to peaceful endeavors.
For more information:
Nuclear Free America
315 E.25th St.
Baltimore, MD 21218
(301) 235-3575

The story of SADAKO is true. It's described in the book Sadako and the Thousand Paper Cranes by Eleanor Coerr, Dell Publishing Co., 1977. There are two different ways to fold a paper crane. You might know a different method than the one Yukiko taught.

The book that Cassie mentioned, Hiroshima No Pika by Toshi Maruki was published by Lothrop, Lee, and Shepard Books, 1980

About KAWASAKI, JAPAN

Kawasaki is an industrial city of one million near Tokyo. It was one of the first Japanese cities to declare itself a Nuclear Free Peace City in 1982. Kawasaki's Peace Park includes stone sculptures from seven countries on the theme of peace. Its Peace Information Center subscribes to over a thousand publications on peace.
Over half of the people in Japan live in areas that have declared themselves nuclear free. They follow the Three Non-Nuclear Principles of Japan — not possessing, not manufacturing, and not introducing nuclear weapons into the country. As of May 1986 there were 946 nuclear free local governments in Japan.

ECONOMIC CONVERSION

The examples of conversion described in the book — both by the U.S. companies Acurex and Varian and by weapon factories in China — are true to life.
If you want to write a report on economic conversion, you can get more information from Jobs With Peace, 76 Summer St., Boston, MA 02110 (617) 338-5783, and from The Center for Economic Conversion, 222 C View St., Mountain View, CA 94041 (415)968-8798.

STOP WAR TOYS
Packet available:
New England War Resister's League
P.O. Box 1093
Norwich, CT 06360

National Coalition on Television Violence
P.O. Box 2157
Champaign, IL 61820
Newsletters, pamphlets, and petitions available.

There is a Peace Museum!
430 W. Erie
Chicago, IL. 60610
Local libraries and other groups can rent their traveling exhibits.

We found out about anti-racist and anti-sexist children's books from: **The Council on Interracial Books for Children**

1841 Broadway, N.Y, N.Y. 10023

They put out a Bulletin (*16 yr./8 issues) and have resources for teachers.

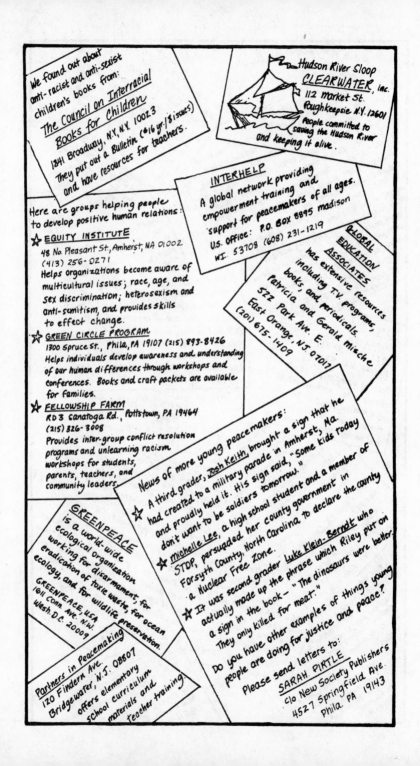

Hudson River Sloop CLEARWATER, inc.
112 Market St.
Poughkeepsie, N.Y. 12601

People committed to saving the Hudson River and keeping it alive.

INTERHELP

A global network providing empowerment training and support for peacemakers of all ages.

U.S. Office: P.O. Box 8895 Madison WI 53708 (608) 231-1219

GLOBAL EDUCATION ASSOCIATES

has extensive resources including T.V. programs, books, and periodicals.

Patricia and Gerald Mische
552 Park Ave. E.
East Orange, N.J. 07017
(201) 675-1409

Here are groups helping people to develop positive human relations:

☆ **EQUITY INSTITUTE**
48 No. Pleasant St., Amherst, MA 01002
(413) 256-0271
Helps organizations become aware of multicultural issues; race, age, and sex discrimination; heterosexism and anti-semitism, and provides skills to effect change.

☆ **GREEN CIRCLE PROGRAM**
1300 Spruce St., Phila, PA 19107 (215) 893-8426
Helps individuals develop awareness and understanding of our human differences through workshops and conferences. Books and craft packets are available for families.

☆ **FELLOWSHIP FARM**
RD 3 Canatoga Rd., Pottstown, PA 19464
(215) 326-3008
Provides inter-group conflict resolution programs and unlearning racism workshops for students, parents, teachers, and community leaders.

News of more young peacemakers:

☆ A third grader, Josh Keith, brought a sign that he had created to a military parade in Amherst, Ma. and proudly held it. His sign said, "Some kids today don't want to be soldiers tomorrow."

☆ Michelle Lee, a high school student and a member of STOP, persuaded her county government in Forsyth County, North Carolina to declare the county a Nuclear Free Zone.

☆ It was second grader Luke Klein-Berndt who actually made up the phrase which Riley put on a sign in the book — "The dinosaurs were better. They only killed for meat."

Do you have other examples of things young people are doing for justice and peace?

Please send letters to:
SARAH PIRTLE
c/o New Society Publishers
4527 Springfield Ave.
Phila. PA 19143

GREENPEACE
is a world-wide ecological organization working for disarmament, for eradication of toxic waste, for ocean ecology, and for wildlife preservation.

GREENPEACE, USA
1611 Conn. Ave. N.W.
Wash. D.C. 20009

Partners in Peacemaking
120 Findern Ave.
Bridgewater, N.J. 08807
offers elementary school curriculum materials and teacher training.

News of things young people are doing

CHILDREN OF WAR

Young people from war torn areas of the world toured and spoke in the U.S. In 1984 and 1986. They included young people from Cambodia, Guatemala, South Africa, Palestine, Israel, Lebanon, and 12 other countries. In 1986 there were also 18 young people from the U.S., either representing particular communities — Navajo, Black, Puerto Rican, farm crisis — or youth peace and justice concerns.

Their stories and their presence made a huge impact in the 27 cities they visited. At the end of each four-day stay in a city, they held a city-wide youth peace conference. This has planted seeds for an ongoing network of young leaders for peace throughout the world.   Contact:

Children of War / Religious Task Force
85 South Oxford St. Brooklyn, NY 11217
(718) 858-6882

These active groups can answer questions if you're starting a youth group in your area:

* Youth Task Force of the Boston Mobilization for Survival, 11 Garden St. Cambridge MA 02138 (617) 354-0008

* Young Peacemakers and Teen Peacemakers 801 Box 171, W. Edmeston NY 13485 (315) 861-2335

* Children of War Network 85 So. Oxford St. Brooklyn NY 11217

The Children's Art Exchange links

U.S. and Soviet youth through art and curricular activities. Their K-8 "child to child" art collection is on tour around the country through the Smithsonian. Contact: Box 503 Middlebury, Vt. 05753 for their newsletter and program listing.

National Forum

Milton Academy students coordinate national campaigns for television coverage of key concerns. Their first petition drive worked for a national televised forum on nuclear weapons. They reached a thousand U.S. high schools.   Milton Academy
170 Centre St, Milton, MA 02186

Peace Child Foundation

3977 Chain Bridge Rd,
Fairfax, Va. 22030

Casts of young people all over the world have participated in this musical based on Bernard Benson's book. Records, scripts, and musical scores can be purchased.

Some of the many CAMP opportunities:

ROWE CAMP and Conference Center
ROWE, MA 01367
Summer camps for 8-18 years.

EARTH AND WILDERNESS CAMPS
Plymouth, Vt. 05056
Camps for 9-17 years.

MEADOWLARK CAMP FOR PEACE
Box 152, Monterey, MA 01245
Camps for 9-12 year olds. To awaken cooperation and respect for diversity.

War plays:
* Janet Hubbard Brown wrote "The Heart of the Mountain" a children's political musical. Parents and Teachers for Social Responsibility Box 517, Moretown, Vt. 05660

* Maya Gillingham directed "Changing the Silence" and wrote it with other high school students in 1983 at Northfield Mt. Hermon School, MA.

International Children's Crusade for Peace: Charity Grant
Box 123 Iowa City, Iowa 52244

It's Our World, Too began in Maine in 1982 when 11 year old Paul Gravelle was told only adults could sign a Nuclear Freeze petition. He responded, "It's our world, too," and he and a friend wrote a children's petition. Now, after more and more others joined their group, they have presented petitions to the Governor of Maine and have thousands of signatures.

This organization, which is by kids and for kids 5 to 18 years old, links with young people all over the U.S. They do music and public speaking and send out 4 free newsletters a year.

It's Our World, Too
Box 326
Winterport,
Maine 04496

Tree planting!
Children of the Green Earth

has a booklet which helps young people plant and take care of trees.

Write: Box 95219
Seattle WA 98145

Children's Campaign for Nuclear Disarmament

collects letters to national leaders

C.C.N.D.
14 Everit St.
New Haven, CT
06511

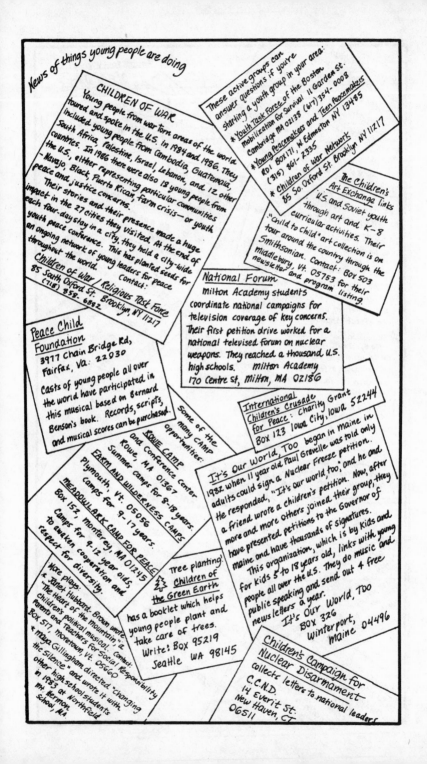

Do you have <u>artwork</u> you'd like to share?

☆ <u>CONNECT</u> sets up exhibits in the Soviet Union and also arranges for U.S. schools to display art by Soviet young people.
CONNECT: Paula De Cosse
4835 Pennsylvania Ave. S.
Minneapolis, Minn. 55409

☆ <u>PAINTBRUSH DIPLOMACY PROJECT</u> links students, teachers, and classrooms around the world through artwork and letters. This project has been growing for 14 years, and has held an exhibit at the United Nations.
Char and Rudy Pribuss
11 Pinecrest Terrace, San Mateo CA 94402

International Arts for Peace sponsors youth arts collaboration trips to the USSR and has a video "Children Are the Future."
P.O. Box 1063 Brookline MA 02146

Looking for a <u>newsletter</u> about peace?

☆ MILWAUKEE PEACE EDUCATION RESOURCE CENTER, Jacqueline Haessly, 2437 N. Grant Blvd., Milwaukee, Wisc. 53210 has a newsletter by, for, and with 7-14 year olds called "<u>Peacemaking</u>" for children." It's $10 for 5 issues/year with a bulk rate for classrooms. The center has a wealth of other materials including <u>Peacemaking</u>: Family Activities for Justice and Peace, and <u>Gentle Gifts</u>: A Children's catalog of Gift Giving Ideas. Both are $5!

☆ <u>LASER</u> is for 9-15 year olds. It started in 1982 and has 10 issues/year for $12. There were so many great ideas in the back issues that they've been gathered into two books: <u>Peace Porridge One</u> — what kids are doing and can do, $12 and <u>Peace Porridge Two</u>: Russia, To Begin With, $11.
Write: Teddy Milne, 15 Walnut St, Northampton MA 01060.

☆ SAMANTHA SMITH FOUNDATION has a newsletter for 10-15 year olds. $6 for 5 issues. Write: BOX 60, Manchester, Maine, 04351.

Want to meet other citizens of the world?

☆ <u>THE EXPERIMENT IN INTERNATIONAL LIVING</u> arranges summer abroad programs (14 yrs and up) and opportunities for your family to host students from other countries in your home. Write Box 676, Kipling Rd, Brattleboro, Vermont, 05301.

☆ <u>VOLUNTEERS FOR PEACE</u> offers international workcamps. There are some opportunities for 13-17 year olds; most are for young adults 18 yrs. and up. For more information: Belmont, Vt, 05730.

☆ <u>US-SOVIET YOUTH QUEST</u>. Write the Fellowship of Reconciliation, Box 271, Nyack, N.Y. 10960

☆ <u>US-USSR YOUTH EXCHANGE PROGRAM</u>: Find out about mountaineering, learning about computers, and creating friendship gardens with Soviet young people. EARTHSTEWARDS Network, Box 10697 Bainbridge Island, WA 98110

☆ <u>CHILDREN'S INTERNATIONAL SUMMER VILLAGES</u> brings young people together from many countries. The 11-18 year olds who participate are selected by their local chapters. U.S.A. National Office: 206 N. Main St, Casstown, OH, 45312

INSTITUTE FOR PEACE AND JUSTICE has led peace studies programs for schools, parents, and houses of worship for over 16 years.
Contact: 4144 Lindell, St. Louis MO 63108. Resources include curricula, and a slide show about Nicaraguan children for ages 8-15 called "Amigos Los Niños." See also their book <u>Parenting for Peace and Justice</u> by Kathleen and James McGinnis.

Do you have a design that could be used for a quilt? Contact the <u>BOISE PEACE QUILT PROJECT</u>
P.O. Box 6469, Boise, Idaho, 83707.

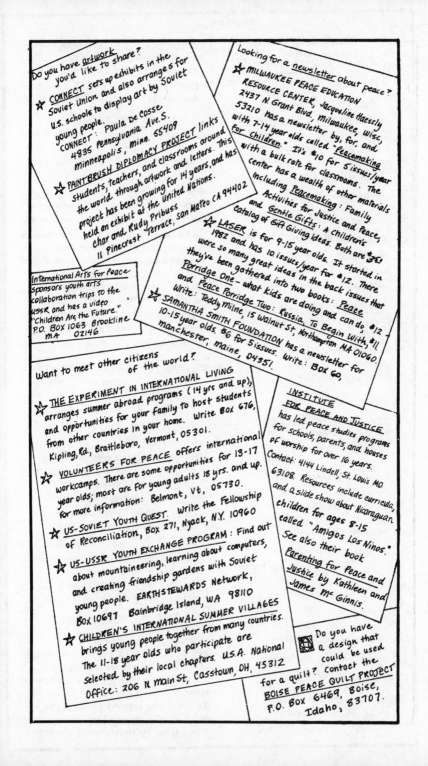

☆ From New Society Publishers

OUR FUTURE AT STAKE

A Teenager's Guide to Stopping the Nuclear Arms Race

by Melinda Moore and Laurie Olsen,
Citizen's Policy Center, Nuclear Action for
Youth Project: paperback #7⁹⁵

BAREFOOT GEN: A CARTOON STORY

OF HIROSHIMA by Keiji Nakazawa
For teenagers and adults: $9⁹⁵

WATERMELONS NOT WAR!

A support book for parenting in
the Nuclear Age

by Kate Cloud, Ellie Deegan, Alice Evans,
Hayat Iman and Barbara Signer $9⁹⁵

A MANUAL ON NONVIOLENCE AND
CHILDREN Compiled and edited

by Stephanie Judson $9⁹⁵

• To order send check or money order
plus #1⁵⁰ postage, 40¢ additional books
to: NEW SOCIETY PUBLISHERS

☆ Other books to note:

• And Justice for All: An oral history
of the Japanese American Detention
Camps (Random House, N.Y. 1984)
    John Tateishi has collected the
    stories of thirty people.

• Journey to Topaz by Toshiko Uchida
(Creative Arts, 1985) describes for young
people a Japanese-American family during
World War II including life in a detention camp.

Books about young people:

• Journey to the Soviet Union (Little,
    Brown + Co., 1985), about
    Samantha Smith.

• Trevor's Place: The story of the
Boy who brings hope to the homeless.
(Harper and Row, 1985)

An outstanding book for teachers

• Creative Conflict Resolution:
More than 200 Activities For
Keeping Peace in the Classroom K-6
    by William Kreidler
    (Scott, Foresman, 1984)

☆ A GENTLE WIND: Songs and stories
on tape for children, including
recordings by Sarah Pirtle.
BOX 3103, Albany, NY 12203
Free catalog of over 30 recordings on tape.

☆ EDUCATORS FOR SOCIAL
    RESPONSIBILITY (ESR)
    23 Garden St.
    Cambridge, MA 02138
    (617) 492-1764

ESR is a national organization of educators
which helps students think clearly and
independently about public issues so they
will be able to make informed and responsible
choices. ESR offers outstanding, well-
balanced resources including the high school
curriculum, Decisionmaking in a Nuclear
Age, and over 7 other curriculums. A
packet of materials about Military
Recruiting in the High Schools and
videotapes including "A Day at School
in Moscow" are also available.

☆ CHILDREN'S CREATIVE RESPONSE
    TO CONFLICT PROGRAM (CCRC)
    An affiliate of the
    Fellowship of Reconciliation
    BOX 271 Nyack, N.Y. 10960
    (914) 358-4601

Workshop facilitators offer inspiring
programs for teachers and students
all over North America.

The Friendly Classroom for a Small
Planet: Creative Approaches to Living
and Problem Solving — Their basic
workbook: $7⁹⁵ plus $1²⁰ postage.

"Sharing Space"— the CCRC newsletter
$3/yr for three issues.

"Children's Songs for a Friendly
Planet"— songbook, $6⁷⁵ plus $1 postage.

☆ ARK COMMUNICATIONS INSTITUTE
    250 Lafayette Circle
    Lafayette CA 94549
offers PEACE TREK by Diane + Joel Schatz.
It's a detailed picture showing the
present transforming into a multi-ethnic,
ecologically sound, harmonious world.
It comes as a poster, a jigsaw puzzle,
and a family coloring book which is
very useful for social studies classes.

Multicultural Glossary

Foods, holidays, and expressions which are not fully explained in the text are described here.

Babcia—Polish; grandmother.

Buen provecho—Latino; enjoy your meal.

Duża Rośnij—Polish; expression meaning "grow big"—"You're going to grow so big for being so good."

Gołąbki—Polish; cabbage rolls stuffed with meat and rice.

Góralka—Polish; mountaineer, from the word *góral* which describes a person who is a native of the Carpathian Mountains in the south of Poland. *Góralka* is the form of the word used when addressing a girl or woman.

Hola—Latino; hi.

Kwanzaa—East African; *Kwanzaa* is an Afro-American holiday that began in 1966 and is patterned after traditional East African harvest festivals. Kwanzaa begins on December twenty-sixth and lasts until January first. Each of the seven nights celebrates one of the seven basic values of the African community.

The principles are: *Umoja*, or unity, *Kuujichagalia*, self-determination, *Ujima*, collective work and responsibility, *Ujamaa*, cooperative economics, *Nia*, purpose, *Kuumba*, creativity, and *Imani*, faith. Families light a candle on the *kinara*, the seven-place candleholder, and talk about the principle for the day.

Kwanzaa decorations are left up to individual tastes using the color scheme of red, black, and green. Black stands for the faces of Black people and their beauty. Red is for the struggle and the blood of the ancestors. Green symbolizes youth and renewed life. Frequently, a woven straw mat is used to represent tradition as the foundation for everything else. *Kwanzaa* means "first" in Swahili, and stands for the "first fruits."

Mira—Latino; hey or look.

Pierogi—Polish; dough is folded like envelopes and stuffed with meat, vegetables or fruit, then boiled and fried.

Pierniki—Polish; little honey cakes served especially at Christmas.

Pisanki—Polish; Easter eggs decorated with fancy designs using a stylus that draws lines in wax.

Shekere—Nigerian; an instrument made by hollowing out a calabash gourd—like a pumpkin but with a long neck—and then stringing it with beads or shells.

Wycinanki—Polish; traditional cut-paper designs once done with sheep shears and now with smaller scissors Some show ornate flowers and birds, some relate to the seasons, and some represent work or ceremonies.

Behind the Scenes
by Louise Godchaux

I'm drawing for peace, in a church in Northampton, Mass. It is early afternoon. I'm drawing because it is a small part of a large part of a larger part of the Earthly effort for peace.

It was a warm day in April of 1984 when I first carried my entire collection of ink pens and drawing pencils to the center of Amherst to meet my good friends, Amanda Cohen, author of the above nugget of eloquence, and Heather Swenson, at the big, gray, stone church which was to be the birthplace of . . . well, of many things, but most of all *An Outbreak of Peace*.

That day at the church was the first time I met Sarah Pirtle. From the very first meeting, I knew Amanda and Heather had let me in for much more than I'd expected. Sarah's undying enthusiasm and compelling energy made it hard to imagine not being involved. She said that we were working on an experiment—making drawings expressing our hopes and fears for the future—and that maybe a book would come from it.

My two friends and I were the oldest participants. We were juniors in high school at the time, and facing an otherwise boring spring break. The other people involved were mostly fourth, fifth, and sixth graders.

Near the middle of the week, Heather drew a picture of two girls standing on a basketball court labeled "ground zero." She said one represented her youngest sister, Jill, who was deeply afraid of the possibility of nuclear war. We suggested that Heather invite her sister to the group. The next day Jill showed up. In fact, each day more and more new kids arrived.

When the week ended, we felt like a family breaking up, though we tried to soften the sorrow with a party and a chocolate cake (all natural, of course). There were two groups then, one in Amherst and one in Northampton. The other group had decided to release helium balloons with peace messages tied to the strings. We never imagined that that simple week of drawing pictures about peace would become a far-reaching, three-year project.

We didn't meet again until winter. During the summer, Sarah's son Ryan was born, and the project lay dormant for a while. Ryan's birth was complicated—he was two pounds, four ounces—and the first weeks of his life were precarious. When we were certain that he would survive, we took it as a strong omen that our work and our vision would also survive, and that our dream for the future would become a reality.

At the end of the summer, I received a letter from Sarah saying that copies of a number of the drawings we had done had been accepted in an exhibition, "A Vision of America at Peace," and that they'd be displayed at the Democratic and Republican National Party Conventions and later at the Pioneer Palace in Moscow.

I immediately called Amanda. I had scarcely said hello

370

when she blurted, "I got the letter from Sarah! Isn't it great?!"

After that, the pace of the project picked up considerably. At first, the groups from the two towns had been linked only through Sarah, but when we finally met again, we blended into one. The most committed kids from both became a core group, and amid songs and games and general pandemonium, we created the character of Cassie and conceived the possibility of a book.

Sarah says the seed for this book was Amanda's note (the one at the top of this essay). She found it hidden in a pile of our drawings. There was no name on it. Sarah felt that the voice speaking in the note could be the main character of the book. She brought the note to us and asked for our help. We decided her age and what she looked like. Fiona Kaul-Connolly suggested the name Cassandra, Cassie for short, and we liked it.

Our pile of drawings grew while the text of the book went through many changes. At first, it was a series of letters from Cassie to Zandi, a make-believe being who lived on a peaceful planet named Z. But it shifted. More of us and our experiences together began shaping the book.

Heather brought in some of her private poetry about fears of nuclear war. One of them is in the art display in Chapter Twenty-three. Sometimes as we drew, we talked about our own fears. A fifth grader, Lori Nolan, wrote about an experience with her neighbor:

> I wish the world would just stop on war. I have a neighbor who watched television and heard about nukes and war. She's seven, and now she has terrible nightmares. She said she never wants to see what

war is like. She started to cry. I wasn't sure what to do. She ran back in her house. I went home.

We brought our friend Alex—a computer whiz—to the group, and his jokes helped create the character of Riley. Sarah says that the friendship of the three of us helped inspire both the Awesome Threesome and one of the book's themes: that building a peaceful world depends on people supporting each other.

Sarah also drew upon some of her experiences as peace education coordinator at Traprock Peace Center. For instance, a high-school junior once asked the center to help put on an alternative assembly after an army helicopter landed on her school's football field. Sarah helped organize a panel of speakers and got involved in the Veterans Education Project. The recruiter's martial arts demonstration in Chapter Twelve, "The Second Revolution," portrays an assembly she watched at another high school in our area where two girls actually walked out.

A core group of us read through each of the early drafts of the book, offering our suggestions. The meetings continued even through difficult periods and transitions in other areas of our lives, like our graduation from high school and our first year in college. Then came the day that Sarah announced that New Society Publishers, the same people that brought you *Watermelons, Not War!* had agreed to publish *An Outbreak of Peace*.

We hardly knew what had hit us. We suddenly became paid illustrators producing a serious work of literature. There were standards and deadlines to meet. Our project had become a genuine professional venture

From the very beginning, the special magic of our project lay in seeing merit in everyone's ideas and talents and

finding them a place in the project. We agreed that everyone who had worked on the book would have at least one drawing included, if not in the main text, then in the back of the book. In addition, those drawings not used in the book were shown in an art display held in Northampton in September of 1986 and then as part of a traveling exhibit. Thus, happily, we made sure that no one in our loyal group was left out.

I think back on the name of Cassie. The Cassandra in the Greek myth was a princess of the city of Troy and a prophetess gifted with knowledge of the future. When Troy went to war with Greece, Cassandra predicted there would be bloodshed and destruction and that Troy would fall tragically. She begged her brother the king to abandon his military campaign, but he did not listen. No one believed her warning. Similarly, the Cassie in our story sees the world she loves heading for a fall, and cries out, in words, pictures, and actions, against the danger. Unlike the Greek prophetess, our Cassie is heard—because she speaks words that we have always known, in the depth of our hearts, to be true.

The Illustrators

Artists from Northampton, Amherst, Greenfield, and other towns in western Massachusetts, ranging in age from seven to nineteen, created the drawings for *An Outbreak of Peace*.

Self-portraits
Group drawing of twenty-six members (opposite page)

Amanda Cohen
CHAPTER SIX: "Louisa"
CHAPTER SEVEN: "Surprise Cake"
CHAPTER EIGHT: "Amphibians"
CHAPTER NINE: "Bouquet"
CHAPTER TWELVE: "Flag"
CHAPTER THIRTEEN: "Maritza with Drum"
CHAPTER FOURTEEN: "Polish Easter Egg"
CHAPTER FIFTEEN: "African Instruments"
CHAPTER SIXTEEN: "Palette"
CHAPTER EIGHTEEN: "Apple Cart"
CHAPTER TWENTY: "Raising a Bowl"
CHAPTER TWENTY-ONE: "Menorah"
CHAPTER TWENTY-THREE: "Happy New Year"
THE ART DISPLAY: "Peace Like the Ocean," "Economic Conversion," "A Nuclear Weapons Museum," and "Peace March Cancelled"
CHAPTER TWENTY-FOUR: "Town Hall"
CHAPTER TWENTY-FIVE: "Sunset"
CHAPTER TWENTY-SEVEN: "Web"

Tanya Demarais
BEHIND THE SCENES: "Throw Food Not Bombs"
THE ILLUSTRATORS: "Mouse"

Britt Dionne
CHAPTER ONE: "Larkspur Puddle"
BEHIND THE SCENES: "Chain of Hands"

Adam Fisk
THE ILLUSTRATORS: "Horse"

Noah Fisk
THE ART DISPLAY: "Dismantling with Care"
THE ILLUSTRATORS: "Rabbit"

Louise Godchaux
TABLE OF CONTENTS: "Peace Lives in the Dark Waiting to Be Born"
CHAPTER ONE: "Cassie"
CHAPTER FOUR: "Girl from the Children's Campaign for Nuclear
    Disarmament" and "Zack's Friends"
CHAPTER SIX: "Treena and Arnold the Tiger"
CHAPTER TEN: "Origami Crane" and "Coreena, Pam, and Langston"
CHAPTER THIRTEEN: "Drum"
CHAPTER FIFTEEN: "Langston"
CHAPTER SIXTEEN: "Louisa"
CHAPTER SEVENTEEN: "Snowball"
CHAPTER EIGHTEEN: "Bluie"
CHAPTER TWENTY-ONE: "Coreena"
CHAPTER TWENTY-TWO: "Zack"
THE ART DISPLAY: "Welcome" (with Judy Miller), "Not Here" (with
    Alex St. John), and "An Outbreak of Peace"
CHAPTER TWENTY-FOUR: "Treena and Langston"
CHAPTER TWENTY-SIX: "Gus' Bulletin Board" (with Sarah Pirtle) and
    "Cassie's Pastels"

Fiona Kaul-Connolly
BEHIND THE SCENES: "Pink Panthers for Peace"
THE ILLUSTRATORS: "Chipmunk" and "Lion"

Sabine Kaul-Connolly
THE ILLUSTRATORS: "Cat"

Elena Kaulenas
CHAPTERS TWO AND TWENTY-SIX: "Bird"
CHAPTER SEVENTEEN: "Nightmare"
CHAPTER NINETEEN: "Violets"
THE ART DISPLAY: "Nuclear Nightmare—Not My Cat!"
MULTICULTURAL GLOSSARY: "Lithuanian Design"
THANK YOU: "Bouquet"
SARAH PIRTLE'S BIOGRAPHY: "Two Hands Hold the Earth"

Misha Krushnic
THE ILLUSTRATORS: "Robin" and "Unicorn"

Sasha Krushnic
SCENES FROM THE BOOK: "Web"
THE ILLUSTRATORS: "Kangaroo"

Thank You

I wish I could bring into one photograph all of those who have been important to the making of *An Outbreak of Peace*. This book would not be here without the collaboration, support and honest commentary of many, many people.

The artists, to whom this book is dedicated, have been its cornerstone. Their influence comes through in numerous ways, both seen and unseen. Many pictures which could not be included inspired characters and situations in the story. Even more than this, their dedication, humor, and friendships were crucial to the book. It has been a total delight to get to know them better and better over the last three years. This book is really *our* book.

I want to thank:

Louise Godchaux
Heather Swenson
Bethany Schneider
Fiona Kaul-Connolly
Britt Dionne
Noah Fisk
Sasha Krushnic
Joey Timmins
Rachel Page
Lori Nolan
Alex St. John
Justin Cutler

Amanda Cohen
Elena Kaulenas
Judy Miller
Sabine Kaul-Connolly
Tanya Demarais
Misha Krushnic
Molly McGarrigle
Adam Fisk
Zoe Leven
Heather Stone
Joni Schriver
Noah Montena

I have three "snapshots" to share. The first is of Louise Godchaux, Heather Swenson, Elena Kaulenas, and Amanda Cohen sitting at my house at the end of the summer. We had been meeting regularly for two months to create more artwork, and now college was about to begin for them. This meant we had to have a party. Amanda agreed to make her specialty, weird-colored cookies, and to my two-year-old son Ryan's delight, they arranged for a surprise visit by a clown. I surprised them by fixing Baked Alaska. A party for the book wouldn't have been complete without it.

Another snapshot is of a warm summer day in Heather's kitchen with this same foursome. Amanda was rehearsing a comedy routine while the others gave her encouragement—clapping, yelling, telling her to go for it. She had been chosen as one of three finalists in a national comedy contest called "The Big Break" which was to culminate in a performance at Caroline's in New York City. I kept thinking that the support they've consistently shown for each other is what the book is all about.

The final snapshot is of our own art display where all the hundreds of drawings and paintings completed over the last three years were mounted and honored. Judy Miller, Bethany Schneider, Fiona and Sabine Kaul-Connolly, and Britt Dionne were sitting at our "We Bet You're a Peacemaker" booth, watching the crowd circulate through the display. Daria Fisk and her sons Noah and Adam were there, and Daria, who in real life is the solar architect who inspired the interview in Zack's notebook, was able to see her idea sketched out by her son Noah. I liked watching the group receive so much praise from the crowd.

Other participants in our school-vacation group sessions whose work was in the display include Bart Simon, Casey Rothschild, Carrie Steele, Jacob Leos-Urbel, Christina Robertson, Aaron Steele, Jill Swenson,

Gabe Simon, Peter Simon, Maggie Bittel, Jeffrey Osterman, Ebony Anderson, Emily Davis, Lynne Rogerson, Ginny Rogerson, Elizabeth McPhee, Matthew Mitchell, Tyrone Bergin, and Alex and Omar Felgentreter.

I want to thank Kathy Swayze for her assistance and her encouragement. She helped set up the art display and led meetings of our Arts For Peace group. Also, Debi Andrew and Cathi DePorte assisted at the very first, week-long session of the group.

This book was also enriched by the many people who took time to read the manuscript and respond to it. *An Outbreak of Peace* could not have grown and developed without them. Thanks to the readers:

Laurie Loisel	Debra Sicilia
Pat Schneider	Kevin McVeigh
Andrea Ayvazian	Deborah Lubar
Shelley Berman	Susan Jones
Maya Gillingham	Ann Egan-Robertson
Margie Kolchin	Lucy Pirtle
Maggie McVeigh	Jane McVeigh-Schultz
Louise Godchaux	Judy Miller
Mary Jo Cally	Gloria Ayvazian
Bette Shulman	Paul Wiley
Kathy Swayze	David Chambliss
Debi Andrew	Bethany Schneider
Marcia Yudkin	Carole Johnson
Joan Lester	Ruth Pelham
Sue Woodfork	Karen Shelley
Sondra Radosh	Staś Radosh
Jennifer Blomgren	Jessie Nelsen
Julie Robinson	Lee Middleton
Matt Virkstis	Elizabeth Murtha
Carla Fantini	Krissy King
Peter Richards	Joe Towle
Fiona Kaul-Connolly	Britt Dionne
Tanya Demarais	Mark Nevin

Susan Jones's fourth grade class, Lincoln School, Brookline, Massachusetts

Ann Egan-Robertson's eighth grade class, Dummerston, Vermont

The A.F.S.C. Peace and Justice Summer Project, Oakland, California

Thanks to those people who helped me check the accuracy of sections of the book: Debra Sicilia, Staś and Sondra Radosh, Genevieve Tusinski, Helen Pokladok, Paul Wiley, and Maya Gillingham. Thanks also to Debra Sicilia for her translations and helpful insights.

Two readers, Pat Schneider and Laurie Loisel, devoted long periods of time to the manuscript and were invaluable in their ability to see to the heart of the book. During the final stages, the positive voices of Pat Schneider's Amherst Writers Workshop kept echoing in my ears.

Thanks also to Tom Leamon for his helpful consultation on the art work, and to the Western Massachusetts Society of Children's Book Writers critique group run by Jane Yolen.

I feel particularly blessed to be able to work with members of New Society Publishers—David Albert, T.L. Hill, Ellen Sawislak, and Barbara Hirshkowitz. My respect for them keeps multiplying. I am grateful for the way they carried the spirit of the book through every stage of its production.

I also want to thank three groups which have provided nurturing environments for me. When I was Cassie's age, I attended Rowe Camp and Conference Center in the Berkshires. This was the place where I first met people concerned about peace and justice. I've kept coming back to Rowe over the last twenty years and am so thankful for Rowe's place in my life.

The second group is the Traprock Peace Center in Deerfield, Massachusetts. As a staff member coordinating peace education, I had many experiences that were synthesized into this story. Even more than this, the community spirit at Traprock has deeply affected my vision of what is possible. This is where I learned how to celebrate victories and about how much can be accomplished when people band together.

Most of all, this book could not have been written without the Interhelp network, a web of people spanning eleven countries. There are many layers of gifts from these friends. They gave me firm encouragement to believe in and speak from my own unique voice. They taught me that we don't have to work in isolation but can actively support one another. And by helping me look squarely at my fears, they helped me find a grounded sense of hope for the future. They have been the window toward an ever deepening sense of what peace and justice mean. It is because of the people I've met and worked with in Interhelp that this project was collaborative from the outset.

Thanks also to the steady sources of inspiration in my life:

I give special thanks to Bette Shulman, who believed in and stood behind this work since the very beginning when it was just a flickering intuition. She helped to chart its direction, and her vision has provided a clear beacon for me. Thank you, Bette! You have been a midwife to this book.

Andrea Ayvazian, Deborah Lubar, Karen Shelley, and Jody Lester helped me begin this project in 1984. When I see the commitments they live by and when I experience their delight in living, I'm renewed and inspired.

Shelley Berman and Susan Jones provided encouragement right from the chrysalis stage.

Finally, I cannot say enough to thank my family members, Kevin McVeigh and Ryan Pirtle McVeigh. Their love is thoroughly woven into these pages. They taught me that we can begin to declare an outbreak of peace right at home.

Sarah Pirtle

Sarah Pirtle writes songs and poetry as well as books. "Two Hands Hold the Earth," her recording of eighteen original songs, was named one of the best children's recordings of 1985 by the American Library Association. Her latest recording is called, "The Wind Is Telling Secrets." Both are released by Gentle Wind.

Sarah offers workshops in "Music to Build Friendship," developing multicultural awareness and cooperation skills. She provides training in conflict resolution and is on the professional development staff of Greater Boston Educators for Social Responsibility.

Sarah's work as a peace educator also includes leading empowerment workshops for adults and for teens. She was chief editor of the nationally acclaimed flip-chart series on the arms race, "Facing the Facts," from Traprock Peace Center and Peace Development Fund.

Sarah toured with the feminist poetry troupe, Big Mama, for seven years in Ohio, and then moved to western Massachusetts, where she directed an integrated arts program about whales for the Living Poem Theater. She has a masters degree in education from the University of Massachusetts, and has been an elementary classroom teacher and consultant.

She lives in Greenfield, Massachusetts with her husband, Kevin McVeigh, and their son, Ryan.

Afterword
by Shelley Berman
and Susan Jones

We have just read *An Outbreak of Peace*, and what an "outbreak of hope" it gives us! Cassie and Zack and the rest of the Tigers seem to step right out of the pages of the book to take on a life of their own in our vision for the future. Their voices seem at once refreshingly inspired and surprisingly familiar. They eloquently express our own feelings about the state of the world and about what the world needs most.

There are many young people like Cassie and Zack. As educators, we've worked over the past few years with many students who have expressed similar feelings of fear and concern and hope. Unlike Cassie and Zack, however, many young people today find themselves feeling paralyzed and silent, perhaps out of embarrassment and perhaps just for lack of a place to share their feelings. We hope this book will help us all break that silence.

These feelings aren't new to this generation. We can easily remember scenes from our own childhood: how ridiculous and futile it felt to hide under a desk during the air raid drills in school; how the sound of an unseen airplane could bring on an utterly irrational fantasy of bombs; how unspoken fears came out in our dreams or in our writing; and how there was a taboo against raising the subject of nuclear weapons and nuclear war. These were not things to talk about, not with adults, not even with other kids.

We know now that our feelings were neither abnormal nor unhealthy. Even though there are still people today who want to believe that adolescents are ignorant or unconcerned about nuclear weapons (and there may be many young people who don't think about the subject), we know that there are also a lot of kids who *are* aware of the dangers of nuclear war, who are frightened about the future, and who wish there were something they could do both to deal with their own feelings and to act to make the world a safer place.

We hope that *An Outbreak of Peace* will show these young people that they aren't alone with their feelings. The good news is that feelings of fear and hopelessness can be the first step—just as they are for Cassie—toward connecting with other people and taking action. People all over the world are participating in "an outbreak of peace" *right now*. It's something anyone can do at any age, at any time, in any place, and in all sorts of ways both large and small.

Students at Cambridge (Massachusetts) Rindge and Latin High School, for example, saw an interview with Soviet children on the topic of peace and nuclear war and decided to make a videotape of themselves to send to the Soviet students.

A group of high school students from the town of Harvard (Massachusetts) asked their school to offer a course on nuclear issues. When the school system refused their request, they contacted Educators for Social Responsibility and found someone to teach a class after school. Twenty students met for fifteen weeks on their own time to study the variety of viewpoints on the arms race.

Half a dozen middle school students in the Boston (Massachusetts) area worked with WBZ-TV to make their own documentary about their questions on the nuclear arms race. Their twenty-minute film became the heart of an award-winning, hour-long documentary, *A Message to Our Parents*, which WBZ-TV produced on how these young people went about finding answers to their questions.

Students from Newton (Massachusetts) collected ten thousand signatures from young people across the country and carried them to Washington where they lobbied their congressional representatives about ending the arms race.

Even at the elementary level, things can be done to work for peace and justice. An entire elementary school in Brookline (Massachusetts) organized to learn about hunger in Africa and to raise money. They were able to raise enough to buy a camel for the relief effort in Ethiopia.

Teachers all across the country are listening to the students' concerns and helping them learn about the reasons for war and the many ways to work for peace. Recently, in fact, the Massachusetts Association of School Superintendents issued a statement that recognizes the importance of nuclear and peace education and encourages teachers to explore this area.

These are just a handful of examples we've seen happen right here around us in the Boston area. The more it goes on, the more other people in other places will be able to find the hope and the inspiration to join in the "outbreak of peace" in their own ways—including new ways not yet even dreamed of! The energy and fresh outlook of young people offer so much to the world. We hope everyone who reads this book will feel encouraged to add their efforts to the "outbreak of peace."

—Shelley Berman and Susan Jones
Educators for Social Responsibility

Back cover: *back row, left to right*—Amanda Cohen, Louise Godchaux, Heather Swenson; *front row, left to right*—Judith Miller, Sarah Pirtle, Bethany Schneider.

More Resources from New Society Publishers

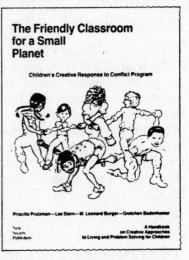

The Friendly Classroom for a Small Planet: A Handbook on Creative Approaches to Living and Problem Solving for Children

by the Children's Creative Response to Conflict Program

The Friendly Classroom for a Small Planet is a handy resource book for teachers, parents, and all those who work with children. With materials tested over a period of more than ten years, it contains exercises and plans that help develop a community in which children are capable and desirous of open communication; enable children to gain insight into human feelings, capabilities, and strengths; encourage children to share their own feelings and become aware of their own strengths; and help each child develop self-confidence about his or her ability to think creatively about problems and preventing and solving conflicts.

112 pages. Illustrated. Resource lists. Bibliography. Index.
Paperback $9.95
Hardcover $29.95

To order directly from the publisher, add $1.50 to the price of the first book, 50¢ each additional. Send check or money order to New Society Publishers, P.O. Box 582, Santa Cruz, CA 95061.

More Resources from New Society Publishers

The Power of the People: Active Nonviolence in the United States

Edited by Robert Cooney & Helen Michalowski

The Power of the People is a pictorial encyclopedia of the struggles of U.S. women and men working for peace and justice through nonviolent action. With sections ranging from the roots of American nonviolence and the original peace churches through the Civil Rights movement, women's peace encampments, and today's ecological struggles, and with dozens of capsule biographies and hundreds of photographs and illustrations, *The Power of the People* invites us to reclaim our history, placing our current struggles in the context of a noble and empowering tradition.

"This volume incorporates the highest standards of research for a work intended for a popular audience."
—*Choice*, American Library Association

272 pages. Illustrations. 400 photographs. Bibliography. Index.
Paperback $18.95
Hardcover $39.95

To order directly from the publisher, add $1.50 to the price of the first book, 50¢ each additional. Send check or money order to New Society Publishers, P.O. Box 582, Santa Cruz, CA 95061.

More Resources from New Society Publishers

A Manual on Nonviolence and Children

Includes "For the Fun of It! Selected Cooperative Games for Children and Adults"

Compiled and edited by Stephanie Judson
Foreword by Paula J. Paul, Educators for Social Responsibility

"Stephanie Judson's excellent manual has helped many parents and teachers with whom we have worked. An essential part of learning nonviolent ways of resolving conflicts is the creation of a trusting, affirming, and cooperative environment in the home and classroom. This manual has a wealth of suggestions for creating such an environment. We highly recommend it."
—Jim & Kathy McGinnis,
Parenting for Peace & Justice Program,
St. Louis, MO

Recommended by *School Library Journal* and *The Horn Book*.

160 pages. Large format. Illustrated.
Paper $12.95
Cloth $24.95

To order directly from the publisher, add $1.50 to the price of the first book, 50¢ each additional. Send check or money order to New Society Publishers, P.O. Box 582, Santa Cruz, CA 95061.